praise for let there be linda

Think of the most bizarre, broken collection of characters you can possibly dream up, then intertwine them into a story that moves at break-neck speed through the most impossibly insane sequence of nutty twists and turns your mind can fathom. Got it? Okay, now take all of that and intensify it by a factor of ten. Now you're approaching the level of pure absurdity that Rich Leder has masterfully created in his novel *Let There Be Linda*.

— Sherman M—5-Star Amazon Review

A Tarantinoesque comedy that is so deliciously wicked and so totally on the left of nutsville that it'll have readers with a warped sense of humor chuckling with abandoned glee. An addictively delicious romp!

— Marta C—5-Star Amazon Review

With the world inundated with chaotic events, out pops Rich Leder – most assuredly one of the most significant comedic writers of today! Highly Recommended.

— Grady Harp—Hall of Fame Top 100 Amazon Reviewer

praise for let there be linda

Let There Be Linda is like a comedic car chase: breakneck speed, and you never know what's coming around the corner. By the end, Leder is juggling a number of different characters, plot points, and moods, and he does it so expertly well. You'll laugh, you'll cringe, and your heart will pound all at once. This is a hugely entertaining book from one of the more inventive crime writers to come along in a while.

— Self-Publishing Review

Strange, bloody, a little violent, and impossible to explain in a way that does it justice. You just have to read the silly thing. It's one of the most unpredictable novels I've read in ages. Just the right mix of black comedy and criminal activity and family. If this is what all of Leder's books are like, I need to read more of them.

— The Irresponsible Reader

A caper of epic proportions with so many twists and turns it's impossible to get bored – or to see the next bit coming.

— Rankin Reviews

praise for let there be linda

A freefall down Niagra Falls in nothing but your swim trunks. If you survive, the rapids are going to shred your funny bone!

— Tome Tender

Stands alone as one of the most bizarre, dark, and surprisingly human comedies to ever grace the Amazon store. If you like fast-paced stories, crazy antics, unforgettably strange characters, and dark humor, *Let There be Linda* should definitely be on your reading list!

— Cheap Reads

If you like dark humor and you like to laugh out loud, then *Let There Be Linda*! Rich Leder has created yet another fabulously bizarre cast of characters and placed them in a surreal adventure that grabs your attention from beginning to end. The book has so many twists, turns, and surprises it keeps you on edge, both horrified and hysterical, from page one. I highly recommend a leap into the wild world of *Let There Be Linda*!

— Lauren L—5-Star Amazon Review

praise for let there be linda

Let There Be Linda is an instant favorite of mine. Leder weaves an intricate story full of colorful characters, and the twists and turns will send readers on a rollercoaster of emotions. You know when a book just blows your mind? The moment when you a finish and you gasp out loud? This book does exactly that. It will get you hook, line, and sinker. It's a breath of fresh air in a genre that feels so familiar. Dare I say *Linda* maybe the best dark comic thriller of the year! If you're a fan of Rich Leder's other works, you will not be disappointed in *Let There Be Linda*. If you haven't read anything by him, what are you waiting for?

— The Book Girl

Fans of Python and Tarantino will *love* this dark comedy horror thriller!

— Writopia

Big laughs from the first page to the last. Each eccentric character defines a new brand of crazy. When they join forces it's a bizarre, terrifying, and hilarious concoction!

— Alexandra F—5-Star Amazon Review

let there be linda

rich leder

LAUGH
RIOT
PRESS

tuesday

1

how does someone become paul the pervert?

THE CLIMAX OF THE PERFORMANCE, so to speak, was an enormous dildo that the clown had hidden in his pants. He'd rigged it with a squirt bottle that held hand lotion, and he pushed the dildo through the slit at the fly and masturbated it while singing the birthday song with pornographic pleasure until he shot the lotion out of the dildo all over Danny's office floor—*Happy birthday, dear Danny; happy birthday to you.*

The clown called himself "Paul the Pervert."

He wore a rat-shit clown costume he'd found deep in a dumpster on Van Nuys Boulevard. It was stained with grease and filth and what looked like blood, as if the last clown to wear it had been murdered mid-performance. Danny thought he might murder Paul the Pervert too.

The rat-shit clown costume colors were faded, the edges were frayed, and the sleeves were torn. Rather than wear big funny shoes on his feet, Paul the Pervert wore beat-up Docksiders supinated beyond recognition. His creepy makeup—black eyes, red bloody nose, blue skin that made him look like a stone-cold corpse—would terrify a two-year-old birthday boy or even a twenty-two-year-old. His teeth were painted as well—blacked out with silver highlights so they looked like barbed wire. He wore a rainbow wig he took off a Mardi Gras hooker. He smoked a cigar that smelled like bad body odor. Or maybe it was Paul the Pervert's bad body odor. It was hard to tell.

Danny Miller sat behind his secondhand desk and tossed Paul the Pervert a box of tissues. The desk had pineapples carved into the walnut trim. A hula dancer lamp provided amber light. Plantation shutters on the windows allowed the brutal LA sun to shoot between the wooden slats and make horizontal lines of light and shadow on the opposite wall. Danny gestured for the clown to clean up the mess and said, "Nice touch, my name in the song." Then he shuffled papers as if somewhere between the headshots and printouts and Post-its and casting reports and back issues of *Variety* was the gig the clown would be perfect for.

"A moment of magic," the clown said.

"In this town, magic means money," Danny said. "But where does it come from? The magic, I mean. How does someone become Paul the Pervert?"

The Miller Talent Agency was two rooms on the second floor of a dilapidated two-story strip mall on Reseda Boulevard in the distant northern reaches of the San Fernando Valley, so far from Hollywood, Danny thought when he'd rented it, that it might as well have been Key West. The front room, the reception room, was much smaller than the big back room, which was Danny's private office. With the Key West concept in mind, Danny had decorated the place with thrift store wicker and bamboo furniture in shades of brown. The cushions were floral prints, blues and reds and greens. There was a rug with palm trees and parrots—and now several shots of hand lotion. There was a sitting area on the other side of the office with a rattan sofa and armchairs and a bamboo coffee table showcasing industry magazines. There was an honest-to-God Tiki bar with swivel stools in one corner. In another corner, Danny had set up an audition area, including a used digital camera on a tripod with one ancient

Fresnel and a blue-screen backdrop. Danny's feng shui was out of the tropics, very *Casablanca*.

"I was minding my own business, working for LA Water and Power, a guy on the line, and I got electrocuted on Fairfax," Paul said. "They told me I was in a coma for two days. I didn't give a shit because when I came out of it, like right when I opened my eyes and got back in the world, I had the idea of being a pervert clown. It was like a movie running in my head—Paul the Pervert, Paul the Pervert, Paul the Pervert, running like that the minute I woke up. I went to some other talent agents, but they turned me down. I was going to give up, then I saw your ad in the paper—*Last Chance to Dance*."

"And that, Paul, is the silver lining to your story," Danny said. "Before we make it official, let me ask you a question. Did LA Water and Power cover your medical expenses, honor your pension, give you a severance? How are you paying for your life now that you've got it back and you're Paul the Pervert instead of a guy on the line?"

"I got a settlement," the clown said. "It's in the bank."

"Good for you," Danny said.

The clown cleaned the lotion off the rug and looked for somewhere to deposit the tissues. Danny forced a smile and held out his hand. He had signed worse talent, but none more repulsive. Paul gave him the tissues, and Danny discarded them.

"I have an idea," Danny said. "It's big, and it's bold, and it's got your name written all over it. Call me crazy, but you're perfect for porn."

"This isn't my dick," the clown said. "It's a dildo. Nobody wants my dick in a porno. Ever since I got electrocuted, it does weird things I can't control."

Danny didn't want to touch that with the far end of a flagpole. "Not as an actor, Paul, as a clown at porn parties."

"Porn parties?"

"Porn people have parties all the time—premieres, anniversaries, weddings, birthdays, cast parties, wrap parties, just general orgy parties."

Danny watched the gears burning in Paul's brain—there was a large vein in the clown's freakish forehead that pulsed abnormally, as if sending out a warning in Morse code: *crazy man at work, crazy man at work*—and wondered if the effect wasn't similar to the moment when Paul had been electrocuted.

"You could get me those jobs?" the clown said.

"It'll take two, three months to get your name circulating, but I'm thinking you'll be the richest clown in the Kingdom of Clowns when it's all said and done," Danny said.

He had meant to say *Los Angeles*, but it had come out of his mouth as *Kingdom of Clowns*. He wrote it down. He had coined a new phrase for LA, and there was money to be made. He didn't know how yet, but he would figure it out. He had figured out Paul the Pervert; he could figure out anything he put his mind to. He could find an angle, make a wedge, and work his way in.

"Where do I sign?" Paul the Pervert said.

Danny slid the contract across the desk and held out a pen for Paul. "It's a ninety-day deal. It says I represent you exclusively in all media. Either one of us can terminate the agreement after ninety days, or we can agree to renew. I'm thinking renewal is in our future. There's a clause on page three that outlines my commissions and fees and expenses—contract, administration, headshot photography, audition video, postage, phone calls, travel, meals, meetings, and whatnot, but you get that money back out of my commissions until you're paid in full. It's a standard, non-signatory agreement that allows me to dig deep and get you working."

"I pay you?" the clown said, forehead pulsing.

"You invest in your career," Danny said. It was almost true if he put it like that.

"Spend money to make money," the clown said, and he signed the contract.

Danny countersigned, checked his calendar, and said,

"Exactly. That's a hundred for today, contract fee. We'll meet tomorrow at four and shoot your headshots and audition video, the fee for that's two fifty. Cash is best for me."

The clown fetched his wallet from the depths of his rat-shit clown costume and counted out five twenty-dollar bills. He put them on Danny's desk and said, "Big damn day for Paul the Pervert. Want to celebrate?"

"After your first gig," Danny said, putting the twenties in his pocket and thinking *When hell freezes over*. He decided against shaking the clown's hand and walked him to the door. The clown exited Danny's office and crossed the reception room, supinating past a young woman sitting quietly in one of the wicker waiting chairs.

The clown paused before expelling himself into the debilitating Valley heat, where he would be sucked into the rushing tide of normal human people not expecting to see a Paul the Pervert at the post office, say, or the grocery store or, God forbid, the community pool, and turned back to Danny. "I'm not a bad guy when you get to know me," he said.

"Neither am I," Danny said. And then the clown was gone into the ether.

Danny turned to the woman in the chair. She wasn't pretty—that was the first thing he took in. It was always the first thing he took in because he knew it was always the first thing *everyone* took in. He knew it was often the *only* thing people took in. He knew—*personally*—that in the Kingdom of Clowns, looks mattered first and most.

He was six feet tall and one hundred sixty-five pounds, thin and trim and wiry. He lifted weights and rode his bike back and forth across the Valley to stay young and fit and handsome. He wasn't a regular smoker or drinker or drug user, though he wouldn't turn those things down if they crossed his path in the course of business or pleasure—as they often did. He had a hip, scruffy beard and a full head of stylishly long brown hair that he kept behind his ears. People told him he looked a little like Brad

Pitt. He agreed with that assessment and liked the sound of it. *"I resemble that remark,"* he'd say when someone mentioned it.

He liked the sound of it so much that he made sure to catch a glimpse of himself in the bamboo-framed mirror he'd hung on the reception area wall—ostensibly to make the space feel larger but actually so he could see himself walk across the room. He liked that mirror a lot, but then again, he'd never met a mirror he didn't like. He had been a runway model in his twenties, which is how he'd gotten into the talent game in the first place, and he still looked damn fine at the age of thirty-seven. He looked better than he actually was, in fact, which, he told himself, meant he *was* better than he actually was, which was how he had to think about things these days because he was back living with his mother because it had been a bad couple, three years, and the money he made he needed to pay the rent on his office and place the occasional wager on a horse. Once he signed some real talent, he would get his own place again, maybe a small house just south of the Boulevard in Studio City, maybe a nice apartment on Dickens Street in Sherman Oaks. Anyway, he looked like a leading man—just ask him, he'd tell you.

He never held it against talent if they were unattractive, but it made his job less Sisyphean if they were as easy on the eyes as he was, and though she wasn't exactly unattractive, she wasn't a looker either. She was as plain as a gum wrapper, as vanilla as a young nun.

"I'm Danny Miller," he said, taking the chair next to her, "President of Miller Talent Agency." There was a bamboo reception desk, a wicker loveseat, the two chairs, the big mirror, and a fan that made a dying animal noise. There was no receptionist.

She was sitting, but Danny thought she might be five foot five or so. She had straight-as-string brown hair that was pulled back in a tight ponytail. Her skin was smooth and clear and white, as if she never went out into the Southern California sunshine. She wore zero makeup. No gloss, no eye shadow, no blush. She wore thick black glasses. She was thin, he thought, but he couldn't really tell what was happening under her blousy blue shirt and gray Catholic-school skirt. She wore knee socks and sensible shoes. She had brown eyes that made him think of coffee. She was younger than him, late twenties. She wasn't wearing a wedding ring. She was unadorned in every regard. It was as if she were trying not to be here—or anywhere—trying to be unnoticed by any and all. There was no guessing what kind of talent she thought she had.

"I'm Jenny Stone," she said in soft voice void of confidence, a voice that in and of itself was trying to be unnoticed.

"What do you do, Jenny Stone?" Danny said, putting his hand out.

She shook his hand and said, "I bring dead people back to life."

2

happy first day of summer

MIKE MILLER STARED at the numbers on his computer and drifted back in time. Back then, he was studying to be an accountant, taking the exams and gaining accreditation, and the numbers were exciting to him. They represented blazing profit potential, the hidden secrets of cost efficiencies, the hopes and dreams and lives of the people who built things and bought things and saved things and sold things and made the world turn. The numbers stretched into infinity, and Mike coaxed from them their mysteries of success. *The Numbers of Life*, he called them.

But with the economic meltdown and the ensuing slog of recovery, particularly in the building sector, they had become *The Numbers of Ruin*.

"You listening, Mike?" Judd Martin said. He was fifty-five years old and was pacing the floor in Mike's office, expressing extreme displeasure at how those particular numbers on Mike's screen were ruining him.

"You don't like the numbers," Mike said.

"I can't finish the third building," Judd said, angry enough that spittle had pooled in the corners of his mouth. He was a big loud man with a red-ruddy complexion and was the general size, shape, and color of one of his brick office buildings. He carried construction dirt in on his work boots and left it on Mike's floor.

"Because you drew down the loan on the third building to finish the second building," Mike said, "because you drew down the loan on the second building to finish the first building because you didn't tell the bank your true construction costs up front, so you didn't borrow enough money to complete the project in the first place."

"If I told them what it cost, they wouldn't have given me the loan."

"Then you could have and should have redesigned your plans to lower your costs or raised your rental projections. Instead, you lowballed the bank to get the money."

"Your numbers are killing me," Judd said. He had sold his soul and built three office buildings in Studio City and was about to lose them—and everything else.

"They're not my numbers. They're your numbers. I'm your accountant."

"You're an asshole with bullshit numbers."

As Judd paced, the numbers on Mike's computer went away, and his screensaver appeared. It included the time and date, eleven thirty-five in the morning, June 21, with a note that said *Happy First Day of Summer*, the market reports—stocks and bonds and various interest and mortgage rates—the business world headlines, and the weather.

The weather got his attention because every local and national weather forecaster, The Weather Channel, the National Weather Service, and the *Old Farmer's Almanac*, had predicted the hottest summer of the century for Los Angeles, with temperatures averaging well over one hundred degrees for the next three months. Today, Tuesday, the first day of summer, it was one hundred five before noon. There was no humidity, sure, but as Mike's mother often said, "There's no humidity in an oven either, but if it's a hundred degrees in there, I'm not going in. Hot is hot."

Exactly, Mike thought. On one side of the table were thousands of climate scientists around the world, with no common language other than the science of weather, who had looked at the facts and agreed that global warming was real and the result of mankind's mad march. On the other side of the table were five guys who denied it. Whether or not you accepted the science, you couldn't ignore the numbers at the table.

"Hot is hot," Mike said.

"What?" Judd said.

"We both know that's not true," Mike said.

"We both know you're going to do something about it," Judd said. He was an asshole and a bully.

"What do we both know I'm going to do?" Mike said.

"Change the numbers so the bank will float me through the summer," Judd said.

Mike turned away from his computer screen and caught his reflection in the window. He was forty years old, but he looked ten years older than that. His hair had thinned, and sitting in a chair behind a desk in front of a computer, day after day for thousands of days, had made him pale and pasty and doughy. Mirrors were murder on Mike these days. He was five eight and one hundred eighty-five soft and squishy pounds. Had he really let himself go like this? He had. He was twenty-five pounds overweight and without definition—physically, emotionally, and spiritually.

His marriage was twenty-five pounds overweight too. He thought he still loved Marcy and also thought she still loved him, but the two of them together had let their marriage get as pasty and doughy as Mike. Stale and pale is what they were.

This was the summer they were going to change all that.

He had said just those words to Marcy, and they had agreed and conspired to send the girls to the grandparents (Marcy's parents) in Paramus, New Jersey, for eight weeks, the entire summer, so they could work on themselves and their marriage. Mike was going to get back in shape, like when he put himself through UCLA, studying nights while working days for Paul Bunyan Tree Service, clearing lots and removing stumps, pruning healthy trees and cutting down dead ones, all with a badass chainsaw he'd bought from the company when grad school started, partly so he could do tree work later in life but mostly to remember these good old days, when he was tan and happy and in the best physical and mental condition of his life.

His daughters were headed to Paramus, and this was his summer of rejuvenation. When Marcy got back in a week—she was flying the girls there and staying for a visit—they would renew and rekindle their romance while he did pushups and sit-ups, jogged loops around the neighborhood, gave up cheeseburgers and milkshakes and fries, dropped twenty-five pounds, and redefined his body, his marriage, and his life.

"The bank will not float you for the summer."

"They will, if you make the rental income from buildings one and two look like it covers my nut."

"Building one is less than forty percent leased. Building two is less than twenty percent leased."

"I can produce leases to fill both buildings."

"But you can't produce the tenants to fill those leases."

"How would you know? You're an accountant; you never go to the buildings."

After UCLA, when he'd passed the exams and attached the letters CPA to his name, he took a job as a junior accountant at Wasserman and Waddell, a Santa Monica accounting firm that focused on construction companies and mortuaries, a pairing, Mike learned, that had more in common than first met the eye.

This was his fifteenth year at Wasserman and Waddell, and he was a senior accountant up for partnership. The firm traditionally added partners in the summer, and Stan Wasserman himself had told Mike that, all things being equal, this was Mike's summer. Partnership would mean more money, which he needed just like everyone else in the world, but more importantly it would mean that all his effort and loyalty had been duly noted and appreciated and rewarded, an ego stroke he had earned (and needed) after a decade and a half of managing mortuary accounts and real estate developers who might as well be dead.

He had told Marcy what Stan had said about this being Mike's summer and had seen a spark in her eyes, the first such spark in a long time. Partnership was an important piece of the puzzle as far as repurposing his marriage, and Mike decided right there to record the pending Moment of Partnership on his iPhone as a gift to his wife.

"I've built my career on hard work, accuracy, honesty, and proficiency," Mike said. "I'm not changing the rental income numbers so you can scam the bank on Wasserman and Waddell stationary."

Judd moved to the credenza across the room. Mike had covered it with framed photographs of his family. Judd lifted one, a shot of them all on the Santa Monica Pier, and said, "If you change the numbers so the bank floats me two mil, I will make a two hundred thousand dollar cash donation to the Miller Family fund, and no one will know."

That's a lot of money, Mike thought, definitely enough to overlook his hard work-accuracy-honesty-proficiency credo. His girls, Bethany and Julia, were fifteen and thirteen. College was on the horizon—two tuitions at the same time. Plus, his house needed a new roof and landscaping. And the girls would want cars. Two hundred thousand dollars was close to the exact amount of money Mike needed. Tantalizingly close. Hypnotically close. He could change the numbers. That's how close.

No one will know, Judd had said. That was true. Mike was a master with the numbers. He could massage them in such a way that the two hundred thousand was invisible. He could magically input the rental income from the new leases, and the bank would fund the construction shortfall. Bankers never went to the buildings either. And if anyone ever did find out the leases were fraudulent, then that would be on Judd. Meanwhile, the signed leases would be locked in Mike's file cabinet. *No one will know.*

The problem for Judd was that he had chosen to lift a photograph that included Mike's mother, Linda.

She was seventy-two and still working as the bookkeeper at El Caballero Country Club. She had raised Mike and his brother without any help from their father, who had left town early on to live a nefarious life in New Orleans. She had taught Mike everything he knew about hard work, accuracy, honesty, and proficiency. Her DNA was strong in him. She was a saint. That's how he thought of her. What would she think about Judd's two-hundred-thousand-dollar offer to cheat the books? He asked her in his head and included the part about no one ever knowing. Her answer was: *"You'll know, Michael. You'll always know."* Saint Linda.

At that exact moment, Mike's assistant, Bonnie, opened the door and stuck her face in the room. She looked like her dog had just died.

"Your mother's in Northridge Hospital, Mike. She had a heart attack. You need to go now. I'll reschedule your meetings. I'm so sorry." And then phones were ringing in the background or somewhere, and Bonnie went to answer them or something.

Mike stood and then couldn't move. He could feel the shock numbing his legs. He knew he had to come out from behind his desk, but he couldn't do it.

"Hospitals cost money, Mike," Judd said.

Mike moved around his desk and took the photograph of his family and his mother from Judd's hand. "I'm not changing the numbers," he said, and he left his office, not at all conscious of the fact that he was taking the photo with him, though he was gripping it with both hands as if his mother's life depended on it.

3
nuclear loathing

HARVEY MINERAL DID NOT like women. He didn't like men either. And he couldn't tolerate children. He despised pets too, especially dogs. Originally from London, he was a San Fernando Valley dwarf and the owner of Pacoima Pawn and Loan, located in an L-shaped stucco strip mall on Glenoaks Boulevard near the corner of Van Nuys Boulevard in Pacoima, a working-class San Fernando Valley town of one hundred thousand predominantly Hispanic Los Angelenos, including a dozen Latino gangs.

He had a violent British mean streak and bad feelings for everyone except Omar Creech, the six-foot-six-inch, two hundred eighty-pound brute he loved like a son. For everyone other than Omar, Harvey had impatience and anger and hostility and malice. For people who owed him money, Harvey had all that and more. For Dr. and Mrs. Donald Greenburg of Encino, he had nuclear loathing.

"Mrs. Greenburg, you and your husband owe me eighty-five thousand dollars in principal plus thirty-five-percent interest, and your loan is past due," Harvey said, his beautiful British accent softening the ever-present contempt in his voice. "Your

14

jewelry is worth three thousand to me, not even an interest payment."

Harvey charged interest in the thirty-five percent range, it was true, but he knew her jewelry was worth twelve grand straight up and that he could easily sell it for fifteen. He also knew she wasn't done begging, which is why he was still speaking to her.

"Screw you and your interest, Harvey. I need to walk out of here with fifteen thousand dollars," she said, taking the jade earrings out of her ears and putting them in the pile. "My husband paid ten thousand for those in Tokyo."

Carol Greenburg was a fifty-five-year-old junky. Her drugs were plastic surgery and vodka, and she was addicted to both. Since she had been borrowing money and pawning her possessions with Pacoima Pawn and Loan, she had undergone the following procedures for which she'd paid cash: liposuction, tummy tuck, body contour, breast augmentation, breast reduction, breast augmentation (again), breast lift, face lift (five times), chin reconstruction, nose reconstruction (three times), eyelid reconstruction, forehead lift (four times), buttock augmentation, chemical peels (seven times), lip enhancement, cheek augmentation, upper arm lift, laser skin rejuvenation, Radiance-Botox-Hylaform (dozens and dozens of times), and hair implants. She looked like a plasticized human Halloween doll-woman fabricated by German scientists during World War II to scare the Allies into surrender.

Harvey lifted a jade earring, examined it with the jeweler's loupe he wore around his neck, and said, "I'll give you three for the tennis bracelets, seven for the earrings, and loan you five, making your principal loan amount ninety thousand past-due dollars. Tell your plastic surgeon to send me a letter of thanks." He lowered the loupe and scooped the jewelry, worth twenty-five grand to him, into an envelope.

"Listen carefully, dwarf," Carol said. "The money is not for plastic surgery. I've never had plastic surgery in my life. Everything you see is real. The money is for the orphanage in Woodland Hills. I committed to funding their immediate need for cash, and I'm short of funds because I bought a commercial kitchen for a homeless shelter in Sun Valley, and..."

As she droned on about her charitable cash contributions, Harvey considered the Gabrielino Indians, who'd settled this land long before the first white pioneers arrived in 1769 and named it "Pacoima," which meant "Rushing Water" in Gabrielino-ese, and signified the rushing water (of course) from nearby canyons in the Santa Susan Mountains to the west and Santa Monica Mountains to the south. *Had the Gabrielinos known Carol Greenburg,* Harvey thought, *they would have named it Pukecoima after the rushing vomit from nearby Greenburg's mouth, stretched preternaturally from her left ear in the east to her right ear in the west.*

"...and my husband has one of the largest dental practices in the Valley; he's good for the money," she said with a finishing flourish. "So give me fifteen thousand dollars in large bills, and make it snappy. I have an appointment in Beverly Hills."

Harvey gestured across the store to Omar, who was polishing a solid silver tea set that had been pawned not five minutes before Carol Greenburg's arrival. Omar nodded and followed the counter around the store to where Harvey and Carol were waiting.

Pacoima Pawn and Loan occupied a large double unit that took up most of the short end of the L-shaped strip mall. Its neighbors included a *panaderia,* a *taqueria,* a *groceria,* a *zapateria* and a *peluqueria.* Only Harvey's sign was written in English.

The inside of the store featured a grand and gleaming U-shaped glass counter that stretched along one side of the store from front to back, made a ninety-degree right turn, spanned the entire width, then made another sharp right and ran all the way back to the front of the building. The case was filled to bursting with gold and silver and platinum rings and bracelets and necklaces and earrings and teeth (gold, of course) and watches and cell phones and digital cameras and lenses and CD players and DVD players and radios and laptops and tablets and coins and stamps and baseball cards and gloves and bats and fishing gear and knives and swords and brass knuckles and handguns galore.

Behind the glass counter were shelves displaying golf clubs and bicycles and flat-screen digital TVs and drills and sanders and air compressors and generators and fishing gear and enough shotguns and hunting rifles (all of them locked in gun racks) to arm a militia. At the rear of the store, surrounded on both sides by the shelves, were double doors that led to Harvey's huge private office. There were security cameras in the ceiling. There were rollback bars on the front windows.

Also behind the counter, following it exactly around the pawnshop, was a two-foot-tall ramp, built for Harvey, who was three feet, ten inches tall when standing on the floor but was a five-foot-ten-inch dapper dwarf when standing on the ramp behind his counter doing business. He was dapper indeed, favoring fine tailored suits, high-end jewelry, expensive haircuts, and manicures at a Japanese nail emporium in Studio City, where the girls who serviced him were as delicate as porcelain and just as easily broken.

Omar was massive and muscled, with coal-black eyes, a long black ponytail, pockmarked skin, and enormous hands and facial features that suggested a touch of Marfan's. He wore a shoulder holster under his sport jacket for his fully automatic Glock (as if anyone would anger the giant enough to make him pull his Glock). The truth was Omar didn't have to be angry to perform insane violence. He simply needed direction from Harvey. Whatever Harvey asked him to do, he did without hesitation.

The giant was devoted to the dwarf, who had raised him like a son since Omar was twelve and nearly beaten to death by a gang in the alley behind Harvey's store. Harvey heard the commotion and came to Omar the Orphan's rescue with a shotgun, which he'd used to obliterate the kneecap of the gang leader. Harvey nursed Omar back to health, clothed him, fed him, educated him, and loved him. They were inseparable.

"Omar, please bring me one hundred and fifty hundred dollar bills from the safe for Mrs. Greenburg," Harvey said, knowing the dentist drove an expensive luxury sedan. He wanted to add *and remove her right arm with your teeth*, but he knew that would come later, and later was fine. *In the meantime*, he thought as she exited the store with his money, *I'll dream about crushing her legs with my Range Rover.*

4

she wasn't here or there or anywhere

JENNY STONE SAT on the rattan sofa in Danny's private office. Danny was behind the Tiki bar. He had suggested they have something cool to drink since it was impossibly hot outside. But really he was stalling for time. He suggested a drink because Jenny had said she could bring dead people back to life, and he had never heard anyone say that before, and he had no idea what to do about it.

He didn't believe her. *Of course* he didn't believe her. No one could bring dead people back to life. It was impossible to bring dead people back to life. So why did she say it? Why in the world would she say she could bring dead people back to life when there was no way she could do something like that? Dead people were dead, and that was the end of it, the very fact of it: *death is the end.* She was conning him, and he needed time to figure out how and why. He needed time to find her angle.

"Nobody can bring dead people back to life," he said.

She'd asked for lemonade, but he didn't have any. He had Sprite, which had both lemons and limes on the can. She said that was fine, and he poured it over ice for her and then poured one for himself.

"I can, Mr. Miller," she said. "I can breathe life into all living things that die."

"No, you can't," he said.

"Yes, I can."

"No, you can't. And call me Danny."

"My mother said I should use my talent to make money, and I don't know how to go about that. She made me come see you, Danny. That's why I'm here."

"Your mother sent you to a talent agent so you could make money bringing dead people back to life?"

"Plants, pets, people, yes."

"Why me? Did you see my ad?"

"No. I'm a checker at Ralphs on Woodman in Van Nuys. You come to my register sometimes. I overheard you talking to a woman behind you in line about representing her. She said she was a dancer, and you said she should come and audition for you, that you were a talent agent, and you gave her your card. Then you left with your bags, and she gave your card to me. I told my mother about you, showed her your card, and she made me come here. She's in the car outside. I'm sorry. I didn't mean to waste your time."

She got up to leave. Danny stopped her. "Wait, your mother's in the car, for Chrissake. The least I can do is find out why she drove you here."

He moved from behind the Tiki bar to one of the chairs opposite the sofa. He handed her the drink, and they sipped Sprite and sat across the bamboo coffee table from each other. On the table, along with the industry magazines, there was a potted plant, a fern—a gift from his mother that had died a miserable, desiccated death. He couldn't even remember forgetting to water it, that's how brown and dead it was. Jenny looked at the dead plant and made a sad little face that emitted a sad little sigh.

She's a little mouse afraid of her shadow, Danny thought. At least with Paul the Pervert, there was something to him, something disgusting, granted, but something. There was nothing to Jenny Stone. She was sitting right across from him, and it was like she wasn't here. She wasn't here or there or anywhere.

Still, if her mother had been gung ho enough to drive Jenny to a talent agent, then she might be willing to fund her daughter's career for ninety days. And if Jenny's mother was willing to fund Jenny's ninety-day career, then he would sign the little mouse anyway, despite her not even being here.

"Can you sing?" Danny said.

"Tone deaf."

"Dance?"

"Bad rhythm."

"Play an instrument? If you can do show tunes, I can get you work at retirement homes."

"Not musical."

"Juggle?"

"Terrible juggler."

"Card tricks?"

"No card tricks."

"Can you draw? We'll call you Jenny the Caricaturist and set you up at flea markets and craft fairs."

"I can't draw."

"There must be something you do."

"I breathe life into death."

She leaned forward and cupped the dead fern in her hands, put her face close to the plant, and gently blew on it. Then her lips turned ever so slightly up at the corners, and she released the fern, which fell back into its utterly dead posture.

Aaaand we're done here, Danny said to himself. If she was conning him, he couldn't see it. Rather, he now thought she wasn't conning him, and that was a problem too. He could deal with an invisible, no-talent, plain Jane for ninety days if there were a few bucks in it for him. He did it all the time. He'd just signed Paul the Pervert for five twenties, for shit's sake. He could deal with bizarre. But what he couldn't do was deal with crazy. The clown was sick and fried (literally) and repugnant, but he wasn't crazy like Jenny, who might start talking to his hula lamp any minute.

He stood and said, "I don't know what to do with you, Jenny Stone, so let me think about it and get back to you if I come up with anything."

She straightened her skirt, stood across the coffee table from Danny, and said, "I told my mother this was a bad idea."

"It's a tough business," he said, gesturing her toward the door.

She started that way and said, "I told my mother no one should make money breathing life into death."

"Probably not," he said. "Maybe Jesus, but that's about it."

It was a joke, but she didn't laugh. He wasn't surprised. Sense of humor was just another thing she couldn't do, another talent she didn't have. He walked her across the reception room and opened the door. The San Fernando heat blasted through the doorway. The dying animal fan groaned with agony. *Maybe it will die completely, and she can breathe on it and bring it back to life,* he thought.

"Thank you for your time," she said, and she managed an embarrassed smile and followed Paul the Pervert into the broiling chaos that was LA.

He watched her go and leaned through the doorway. "Ralphs on Woodman?"

"Yes," she said, and like a little mouse wearing a Catholic school skirt and black glasses and sensible shoes, she scurried away.

Danny went back into the office, stopped in front of the bamboo mirror, and his cell phone rang. He watched his reflection answer the call and thought he looked like a big-time talent agent. He *would* be a big-time talent agent if he could meet some talent other than the pervert clown and the breather of life and the fire-breathing fat guy and the paraplegic magician and the redheaded kid who eats nails and the—"Miller Talent."

"Dan, it's Mike."

He could feel the arctic wind in his brother's voice and was happy to blow it back at him. "Not a good time, Mike. Business is booming. Try me in three years."

"Don't tempt me."

"Make it five years."

"It's not a personal call."

"No shit?"

"I know it's hard, but try not to be a douchebag for the next two minutes."

"What do you want?"

"Mom had a heart attack. She's in Northridge Hospital, on Roscoe between Reseda and Lindley. She's very weak. You should come here as soon as you can."

"I know where the hospital is. What does 'soon as you can' mean?"

"It means now...if you can break away from your booming business."

He'd hated his brother's sarcasm even before he knew what sarcasm meant. Maybe he was five when he realized he hated it. He still hated it. "Kiss my ass."

"Room 304."

They clicked off the call without saying goodbye to each other, and Danny took a step closer to the mirror. For the first time all day, all week, he had nothing to say to himself. It was bad news that his mother was in the hospital. But it was also bad news that he had to see his brother.

For a moment, it was a toss up as to which news was worse, but then he admitted his mother's heart attack was truly bad news and seeing his brother was just bad news. He even felt something, a moment of genuine emotion—sadness, maybe, a bit of regret and remorse—then pulled himself away from his reflection, hurried into his office, walked to his pineapple desk, retrieved his keys and his sunglasses, and exited again in a hurry, missing completely the fact that the fern, the dehydrated-dry-and-shriveled-brown dead fern, was now vibrant and green and alive.

5
omar holds the dog

SIDE BY SIDE, Harvey Mineral and Omar Creech leaned against the liquid platinum Lexus LS 600h L of Dr. Donald Greenburg. The luxury sedan was parked in the long, narrow lot belonging to Valley Beverage on Ventura Boulevard near the corner of Kester. The lot was on the south side of the Boulevard and was surrounded by buildings. The sun was high in the cloudless sky and wicked hot. It was one hundred five degrees in the shade, which meant it had to be one twenty in this narrow box of concrete and cars. Heat waves wafted off the hoods of the automobiles like steam. The macadam was broiling.

"I'm unhappy, Omar," Harvey said. "Dr. Greenburg is making me wait in the sun, and my skin is on fire."

Parked in the spot next to the Lexus was Harvey's black Range Rover with tinted windows and a license plate that read: *Mineral*. Omar opened the Range Rover rear door, removed an extendable umbrella from a storage pocket, shut the door, opened the umbrella, and held it over Harvey to block the sun.

"If I had a dozen like you, I could rule Los Angeles," Harvey said.

"Here he comes," Omar said.

Dr. Donald Greenburg was a thin man in all regards. His

nose, his lips, his face, his arms and legs and ass and hair were all thin, as if he hadn't been given a full share of these things at birth. He drank Tanqueray and tonic at lunch on stressful days, and they all were stressful days now. And then, of course, there was the cocaine. He held a brown bag in one hand and the leash of his little poodle in the other. The dog was like a furry pillow or perhaps a purse, white and white and white and white.

As Greenburg crossed the lot to his Lexus, Harvey could see the dentist was rattled by the scene awaiting him, and he knew it wasn't so much that a giant with a long black ponytail and pock-marked skin was holding an umbrella over a well-dressed dwarf; it was that the giant was Omar and the dwarf was Harvey.

Greenburg spoke first. "Harvey, I know—"

"I'd prefer to have this discussion in the air-conditioned comfort of your car," Harvey said, cutting him short. "You drive, I navigate, Omar holds the dog."

"I'd like to do that, but I have to get back to the office. I have patients," Greenburg said.

"And I have no patience," Harvey said, perversely pleased by his wordplay. "Get in the car, Doctor, or Omar will put you in the car."

"What's your dog's name?" Omar said, retracting the umbrella and taking a size-seventeen footstep toward Greenburg that made the doctor shrink back.

"Chachi, after the character on *Happy Days*," Greenburg said. "He's a spunky little guy. He's my wife's dog, but we're best buddies."

Omar bent down and lifted the tiny poodle with one massive hand. "Come on, Chachi," he said. "We're going for a drive."

They situated themselves in the car the way Harvey had described it—Greenburg behind the wheel, Harvey riding shot-gun, Omar seated behind Harvey with Chachi on his lap—and immediately Greenburg started complaining.

He whined about how hard his life was; he whimpered about

how slow his dental practice had become; he groaned about how the government was killing his cash flow; he bellyached about how the Valley was draining his life force dry; he grumbled and griped about how he was in over his head and just needed a little time to find his footing and straighten it all out.

Greenburg complained, the engine ran, and the air conditioning cooled the car. It was a beautiful sedan, more modern art than automobile, with a soft, semi-aniline leather and rich wood interior, streamlined modern technology within easy reach, and audio-visual capabilities usually reserved for Hollywood screening rooms.

Harvey admired the car while he looked at his fingernails, wishing he were in the middle of a manicure with that eighteen-year-old Japanese geisha, while really wishing he was tying her with leather straps to his bedposts and hurting her in his special way.

But he caught himself in the middle of that thought, heard Greenburg's sniveling voice bewailing the state of the union, and slapped the dentist across the face as hard as he could. *Whack.*

"Ow, Jesus, shit, Harvey, what the hell are you—" Greenburg said.

"Today, your wife borrowed an additional five thousand dollars, so do you owe me ninety thousand dollars, yes or no?" Harvey said.

Greenburg's cheek turned bright red, and he said, "I was going to call you but—"

Whack. Harvey hit him again, bouncing the dentist's skull off the headrest.

"Ow, fuck, that hurts, Harvey," Greenburg said.

"Do you owe me ninety thousand dollars, yes or no?" Harvey said.

"Stop hitting me, and I'll—"

Whack. "Do you owe me ninety thousand dollars, yes or no?"

Greenburg leaned toward Harvey as if he might physically stop the dwarf from cracking him in the face again but saw

Omar in the back seat, holding the dog but drilling the dentist with his bottomless-pit eyes, and he froze. Omar never said a word, just kept petting the poodle.

Harvey lifted his hand to strike again, and Greenburg flinched. "Yes, I owe you ninety thousand dollars."

"Omar," Harvey said. "Progress."

"Progress, Chachi," Omar said. The poodle couldn't have been happier. He was melting in Omar's lap, the sweetest little spunky poodle anyone had ever seen.

"Drive the car, Doctor," Harvey said. "Take the 101 to Calabasas."

Greenburg pulled out of the Valley Beverage parking lot, went east on Ventura, north on Van Nuys, and took the entrance ramp onto the 101 North. As always, there were thousands of cars traveling through the Valley, but today, instead of crawling along in bumper-to-bumper traffic, they were flying down the freeway at eighty miles per hour.

"You paid your dealer with the money I loaned you, your wife sent her plastic surgeon's son to college with the money I loaned her, and your collective due date with me has expired," Harvey said.

Greenburg concentrated on maintaining his speed. He was in the middle lane, and there were cars doing eighty all around him. "I need more time," the dentist said. His cheek was angry, swelling around his right eye.

"There is no more time. Do you have my money?"

"Harvey—"

"Do you have my money?"

"No."

"Throw the dog out the window, Omar."

"What? No, no," Greenburg said.

Omar opened the back window.

"No, Harvey, no, stop. Omar, stop, don't..."

The hot Valley wind blasted into the Lexus, and Omar threw

Chachi out the window into the zooming Ventura Freeway traffic.

To the other cars, the poodle was nothing but a white blur that required no braking or even horn honking; Chachi was a small white bump in the road. There was a moment of distant, echo-y yelping, but then, almost immediately, there was nothing but a steady relentless roar. Omar closed the window. The dog was no doubt dead, a bloody poodle mess, but that was behind them now, literally and figuratively.

"Jesus Christ, Jesus Christ," Greenburg said. He was shocked, hyperventilating.

Harvey watched the dentist wheeze and gasp and imagined that Greenburg's profound physical anguish was a result of the idea exploding in Greenburg's brain that there were people on this Earth who would throw a living dog, *his* living dog, his best buddy, out the window of a speeding car into the path of other speeding cars.

"Chachi, oh my God, oh my fucking God. Chachi," Greenburg said, panting.

"Breathe, Donald. Eyes on the road. Hands on the wheel," Harvey said, thinking, *Oh, Doctor, there are people on this Earth who will do far worse than that.*

"You killed Chachi," Greenburg said, squeezing the words out.

"Yes, Chachi is dead, but you are alive, and that is a fact to be strongly considered. You are alive, Doctor. As is your wife."

"If you touch my wife..." Greenburg said in what he intended to be a brave and threatening tone that came off as scared shitless.

"I liked your dog," Omar said casually from the back seat. "I could like your wife too."

Greenburg was silent.

"What you're going to do, Dr. Greenburg, is pawn the Lexus to me," Harvey said.

"I'm not pawning my Lexus," Greenburg said.

"I'll sell it to you or to the first person who'll pay ninety thousand," Harvey said.

"It's a hundred-twenty-thousand-dollar car," Greenburg said.

"Depreciates the minute you drive it off the lot," Omar said. "That's why I lease."

"I'm not giving you my Lexus," Greenburg said.

"What floor is your practice on, Doctor?" Harvey said.

"Twenty-second," Greenburg said.

"Omar, when we get to the Doctor's building, accompany him to his office and throw him out the window," Harvey said.

They made a U-turn at Parkway Calabasas and took Ventura Boulevard back to Valley Beverage. No one spoke. When they returned to the narrow parking lot, a spot two cars down from the Range Rover was open.

Greenburg parked the luxury sedan, Harvey presented the dentist with a written agreement that contracted the Lexus to Pacoima Pawn and Loan, Greenburg signed it, and all three men got out of the car.

Harvey climbed up and into the Ranger Rover, which was custom outfitted so that he could drive it like a normal-sized person, and Omar slid behind the wheel of the Lexus. The dwarf and the giant drove away to Pacoima, leaving the dentist without a ride in the Valley Beverage lot, holding his bottle of gin and thinking about his dog.

6
dying heartbeat

HOSPITALS MADE MIKE MILLER NAUSEOUS. Even at home, the sights and sounds and smells of illness made him queasy. When his daughters had sore throats and stomachaches and earaches and fevers, Marcy did the lion's share of nursing them back to health because Mike got anxious around the accouterment of care—the medicines, the chicken soup, the saltines, the ginger ale, and the unbuttered toast. He couldn't eat graham crackers because that's what his girls ate when they were vomiting up everything else. The bottom line was he didn't like being around sick people.

And being around dead people was even worse, which was unfortunate because he was a mortuary accountant. Meetings at mortuaries when dead bodies were on display were tough for Mike. He'd lost his lunch in mortuary restrooms more times than he cared to recall.

His mother's room in Northridge Hospital had a smell he could hardly keep down. It was the aroma of medicine mixed with antibacterial cleaning solutions mixed with old age mixed with institutional food mixed with death. He had to concentrate to keep his stomach in his stomach.

The room was pale blue with white trim. The floor was tiled, white with blue speckles. It was a single room, and his mother was in the mechanical bed. There were trays and screens on metal arms that stretched from the wall out over the bed and rotated and moved and bent and adjusted to whatever position the patient was in.

Linda was flat on her back with just a slight elevation to her head and shoulders, not that she would know it. There were tubes in her arms connected to bags of clear fluid and wires attached to her body running to medical monitoring machines that beeped and buzzed and flashed and printed out numbers and lines of code that were indecipherable to laymen but told doctors and nurses the story of his mother's heart attack. There was an oxygen mask over her nose and mouth. Her skin had no color, no pink at all. Instead, it was picking up the blue of the walls, making her look dead, though she wasn't. Her eyes were closed. Her hair was brushed to the side. Her heart was ever so slightly beating, a dying heartbeat, intermittent and faint. She was conscious but drifting in and out of the world.

There was a white bedside dresser with a potted plant on top and two white-framed prints of serene landscapes on the wall just above it. A blue reclining armchair sat in one corner, in case a family member wanted to spend the night. There was a wide window with a sheer blue curtain that had been pulled completely across the glass so that light could bathe the room with midday glow. Non-stop air conditioning made the room— the entire hospital, for that matter—uncomfortably cold.

Dr. Thieman, the cardiologist, was standing with Mike at the end of the bed, talking about the flow of oxygen-rich blood, about how heart attacks were the leading killer of both men and women in the United States, about atherosclerosis, which was the building up of plaque in the arteries over many years.

"Heart failure is a condition in which the heart can't pump enough blood to meet the body's needs," Dr. Thieman was saying, but Mike wasn't especially hearing him.

Instead, Mike was looking at his mother, Saint Linda, and

thinking about the day his father left for New Orleans. He was ten years old. His brother was seven. They lived in Canoga Park, near the intersection of Saticoy and Farralone, in a small yellow house with a scrubby lawn in the front and an above ground pool in the fenced-in backyard. It was a rental house, one in a long line of Valley rental houses they'd lived in when the boys were young. Mike remembered thinking they were never settled, were always moving, running out of one house in the dead of night and into another.

On the day their dad ditched them, Linda was playing catch with the boys in the front yard, teaching them to throw strikes. She had a good arm. She was petite and pretty with a good figure, brown hair and green eyes that sparkled in the late afternoon sun. She was soft spoken and loving but firm and serious about raising her sons right. She was forty-two at the time. Her husband, Jeff, was a little older.

Mike knew his father should have been the one out there instead of his mother, that it was Jeff's job to play ball with his boys like he had seen other fathers do, and he was already suspicious that his used-car-salesman dad was a loser.

Beyond his suspicion, Mike didn't like his father. He couldn't remember ever liking his father. His father was mean to him and to his mother, though not to Danny. Mike knew it when he was very young and didn't like it. His father was a flimflam man. He didn't know what that meant, *flimflam man*, when he was ten, but he heard his grandmother, Linda's mother, call Jeff that to his face one day and never forgot it.

Danny had a connection with Jeff. They looked alike, for one thing—the hair, the shape of the face, the lean and lanky build. But it was more than that. Jeff and Danny seemed to get each other in a way that Linda and Mike did not get Jeff. Mike was on the outside with his mother, who he looked like and acted like and thought like and idolized.

On this particular late afternoon at the small yellow house in Canoga Park, Mike and Danny were throwing strikes when the front door opened and Jeff stepped out carrying a single suitcase and smoking a cigarette, looking like James Dean or Johnny Cash, dressed in all black and looking like a badass. He stood on the front step for a moment, dropped the cigarette, rubbed it out, and walked to the Camaro parked in the one-car driveway. He opened the car door, turned to Linda and the boys, and said, "Going for a drive."

He drove to New Orleans. They never saw him again.

Linda said right away that he was gone for good. And instead of falling apart, she went to night school at Pierce College while working full-time, got her two-year accounting degree, and landed a job in the office at the swank El Caballero Country Club in Tarzana. In five years, she was the head book-keeper, a job she had held for twenty-three years while raising her boys as a single mom in the San Fernando Valley, putting dinner on the table night after night, doing the laundry, helping with homework, teaching them, by example, with love and patience and kindness, how to work hard, be accurate, honest, and proficient, and to throw strikes. Saint Linda.

She promised never to move her sons again and lived in the small yellow rental house in Canoga Park—with Danny—to this day, the day of her heart attack.

"If the clot becomes large enough," Dr. Thieman was saying, "it can completely block blood flow through a coronary artery, which is what happened to your mother."

"Will she live?" Mike said.

"She's strong," Dr. Thieman said. "I don't know if she's strong enough."

At that moment, Danny walked into the room. The physical contrast between him and Mike, as always, was sharp. Mike looked dumpy in a blue suit with wing tips. Danny was slick in hip jeans, a smooth satin shirt, and sweet Nikes.

"This is my brother, Danny. This is Dr. Thieman," Mike said.

"Nice to meet you," Danny said. "Thanks for taking care of my mother."

Danny shook Thieman's hand and nodded, acknowledging Dan's gratitude, which sounded real and perfunctory at the same time. The brothers had not seen each other in six months, since Christmas at the small yellow house, but they did not greet each other at all. No handshake, no hug, no hello. Mike wondered if Thieman sensed the awkwardness between the brothers and decided the doctor could have sensed it if he were in another wing of the hospital.

"We're watching her around the clock," Dr. Thieman said. "If you need anything, ask the nurse to find me."

The machines attached to Linda whirred and buzzed. The air conditioning was an umbrella of white noise. Mike realized the back of his neck was cold, though it could have been his brother who made him feel that way and not the frigid hospital.

"I'll have another chair brought in," Thieman said. "I'm assuming you're both going to stay.

Mike nodded immediately and looked at his brother. Danny hesitated, and Mike could see in his eyes that his brother wasn't planning on staying; he was going to fade like he always faded. He was unreliable as a human being, selfish and irresponsible. It infuriated Mike. It had always infuriated him.

"Yes, get him a chair," Mike said.

The brothers gave each other a look that was even colder than the hospital.

"Sure," Danny said to Thieman.

The cardiologist nodded at both Mike and Danny and left the room.

"Incredible," Mike said, meaning not Linda but Danny.

"Maybe she wakes up in an hour and lives twenty-five more years," Danny said.

"Maybe she doesn't wake up at all," Mike said, and the thought ran through him like a nightmare.

Danny didn't take that conversation any further. He moved to the bed, looked down at his mother and said, "So, what happened?"

"She had a heart attack," Mike said, moving to the other side of the bed.

Danny made a noise that said, *what an asshole.* "At work, at the house?"

"She was at her desk at the club, and then she was on the floor, and then she was in an ambulance, and then she was here," Mike said.

"She looks small and old," Danny said. "She looks blue."

"She's dying," Mike said.

"Marcy on her way?" Danny said.

"Flying the kids to New Jersey. I couldn't get her. Left a voicemail for her to call me but didn't say why. Girls are staying with Marcy's parents all summer. Marcy comes back in a week."

"Wish I was in New Jersey," Danny said, "or somewhere else. I'll take the remote."

Mike handed it to his brother and thought, *I wish you were somewhere else too.*

7

great stuff

LAPD DETECTIVE GARY SCHULER was a comedian. No kidding. He was a stand-up comic. He spent off-duty evenings polishing his routines at open mic nights at comedy clubs around Los Angeles, including Sal's, Ha Ha, Flappers, Echoes Under Sunset, Improv, Dangerfield's, and a dozen more. He was a comic at any club, café, or coffee shop that would give him a stage, twenty minutes, and a microphone on a night he wasn't working. His goal was to retire from the police force one day soon, get on the late night talk show circuit, go on a cross-country tour, and see his name in bright lights. A role on a network sitcom wouldn't be bad either. His own sitcom would be even better.

He was forty-eight years old and had worked out of the Devonshire Community Police Station on Etiwanda Avenue before moving to an empty office at an LAPD towing lot, where he investigated the weirdest crimes in the Valley. Detectives from all seven Valley Bureau Patrol Divisions as well as the Traffic Division called Gary whenever the crime in question was too bizarre for them. He liked these cases, Gary said, because they provided him with material for his act—in the sense that these cases *were* his act.

Gary would take the stage—*"Ladies and gentlemen, give it up for 'Detective' Gary Shuler"*—and tell the audience about a crazy crime he was investigating that he thought was hysterical. (Like many of his LAPD colleagues, the comedy club folks didn't believe Gary was an actual detective either.) The problem was that Gary had been working these wacko crimes for too long, and his sense of humor had become as twisted as the cases themselves, and he was alone in thinking they were funny. He often laughed his way though the set—and was often the only one laughing.

So when the Traffic Division got a call about a white poodle being tossed out the back window of a speeding Lexus in heavy freeway traffic, their first thought was Gary Schuler. Gary's first thought was *Excuse me, waiter, I'll have the poodle paillard*, a thought that made him chuckle. He wrote the joke down in his pocket pad with a note that read: *this is the one I've been waiting for.*

The dog had been scooped up with a shovel, deposited in a black garbage bag, and delivered to Gary's tow-lot office. Gary opened the bag and examined the dead dog. Remarkably, it was not a flattened, bloody mess. Instead, it had been hit by a car going eighty and shot like a cannonball forty feet in the air to the side of the freeway. Its neck and back and bones were all broken, but this was no poodle pancake. The tag was still around its neck. It said *Chachi* on the front. An address was engraved on the back.

The woman who'd contacted the police was driving the other way on the 101 and didn't get the Lexus license number. No one else on the freeway even bothered calling it in. Either they thought *Tarantino must be shooting a movie* or they thought *I don't like poodles anyway*. The result was the same: the only place for Gary to start his investigation was Dr. Donald Greenburg's house on Escalon Drive in Encino.

Gary parked his jet-black, two-door, 1965 Chevy Impala SS on the street, grabbed the garbage bag from the trunk, and started up the walk toward the front door. It was a hilly Encino neighborhood of large LA ranch homes landscaped to within an inch of their lives—lush, manicured, edged, and mown and blown by Mexicans driving red pickups towing flatbed carts jammed with lawn care gear and pesticides. The houses were close together, but the landscaping ensured total privacy from the neighbors. It was the ideal place to be wealthy and weird. *Great stuff for the act*, he thought.

Gary held the garbage bag in one hand and rang the doorbell with the other. No one answered, but there was a luxury Mercedes coupe in the driveway next to an Enterprise rental car, so he rang again. He was about to ring a third time when Dr. Greenburg opened the door.

It was just after five on the first day of summer, so the sun was still in the sky, though leaning toward the horizon. The temperature had dropped all the way to one hundred three. Gary could feel the air conditioning blasting out of the Greenburg ranch. A portico shaded the entrance patio, so he didn't have to squint to see that Greenburg had white powder all over his nostrils. The dentist was wearing a hip Hawaiian shirt and board shorts. He looked incongruously cool, a fifty-six-year-old, hawk-like human wearing palm trees. His eyes were red and wired. *Hilarious*, Gary thought.

"Dr. Donald Greenburg?" Gary said, showing Greenburg the badge clipped to his belt.

"Yes," Greenburg said, eyes darting back and forth between the garbage bag and the badge.

"Detective Gary Shuler. I'm guessing your wife was baking sugar cookies and you couldn't believe how good they smelled."

Greenburg cocked his head to the side like a dog that has no fucking idea what you're saying, then suddenly straightened up and wiped his nose. "Yes. I mean good, or, you know, I mean—"

"I'm afraid I have bad news for you today, Dr. Greenburg."

Again, the cocked head. "Bad news?"

"Very bad. And I think you might already know what it is."

"I do?"

"May I come in? It's a hundred degrees, and I can only imagine what's germinating inside this bag."

Greenburg swallowed, rubbed his nose, and licked his teeth with his tongue. He couldn't stop staring at the garbage bag.

"Today would be good, Dr. Greenburg," Gary said.

Greenburg moved aside, and Gary went into the house. It was an open floor plan. To the left was the kitchen, to the right was a hallway to the bedrooms, and straight ahead was the large living room/dining room combo. The interior design channeled Dr. Seuss—walls and floors and rugs and lamps and curtains and cabinets and tables and chairs and great big fat sofas with cushions stuffed to bursting and all of it in shocking bright blues and reds and greens and yellows. Gary expected the Cat in the Hat to run around a corner, followed by Thing 1 and Thing 2.

The entire back wall of the house was French doors (each one painted a different eye-popping color) that opened onto the pool, where Carol was doing yoga in a multi-colored polka dot leotard that made her look a hell of lot like the leopard from *Put Me In The Zoo*, if that hopeful Seuss cat had undergone an unimaginable amount of plastic surgery. Gary stopped to take in the house and the yoga woman. He was speechless but thinking, *Conan, here I come.*

"My wife is the decorator. Obviously," Greenburg said. "My office is down the hall."

Gary followed Greenburg a few doors down the hallway and into the dentist's home office, possibly the only room in the house that didn't look like the Lorax lived in it. There were floor-to-ceiling bookshelves, a flat-screen television, a leather sofa, a desk and credenza, a leather lounge chair, a few floor lamps, and a coffee table upon which was a small mirror with a tall pile of cocaine and several heavy lines laid out.

Gary looked at the coke and then looked at Greenburg and thought the dentist had been so distracted by the black garbage bag that he'd forgotten he was in the middle of snorting half of Columbia before his doorbell rang.

Greenburg looked at Gary and then at the cocaine and then at Gary. "I'm having a terrible day," he said.

"I can see that," Gary said.

"Are you going to call the police?"

"I am the police."

"Right. Detective Schuler. Are you going to arrest me now?"

Gary wasn't interested in the cocaine. He was sympathetic to addictions of all kinds. For years, he couldn't quit Oreos no matter how hard he tried. "Studies show lab rats get more addicted to Oreos than cocaine," he said, "so, no. Now I'm going to show you what's in the bag."

Gary opened the bag and held it so that Greenburg could see its contents. The dentist's face fell three full inches (while it was falling, his tongue took the time to lick his teeth), his shoulders sagged, and the light in his coked-out eyes went dim.

"I thought you'd want to say good-bye, bury him in the yard or something, instead of him being incinerated at the dump," Gary said.

Greenburg nodded and was quiet and then said, "My wife thinks the maid left the door open and the dog ran away."

"Doesn't sound good for the maid."

"We fired her."

Gary closed the bag, tied the top in a knot, handed it to Greenburg, and made notes in his pocket pad, investigating the case and writing his new act at the same time.

"The call came in from a Camry going south on the 101, a woman named Christine Bender," Gary said. "Ms. Bender said she saw your dog get tossed out the back window of a silver Lexus heading north."

"Did she get the license?"

"She was going too fast. She saw the Lexus and the dog fly out the window and that's it."

"So you don't know whose car it is."

"No. But I know more than you think. Your address is on the back of Chachi's name tag, so I looked you up before I rang your bell. I know your date of birth and Social Security Number. I know you're a dentist. I know your office is in the City National Bank building at the corner of Sepulveda and Ventura. I know you're married to Carol Wilson Greenburg and that she does yoga and maybe some plastic surgery?"

He'd dialed down his detective tone one click for the improvised yoga and plastic surgery comment because Greenburg looked like he was going to pass out and he needed the dentist to stay with him a few minutes more. He wanted Greenburg to understand the seriousness of the moment but to also know that Gary appreciated the craziness of it all as well, that they were both just a couple of addicts on different sides of the fence.

Greenburg nodded, and the left corner of his mouth even tried to smile but couldn't manage it. "She'll deny it with her last breath," he said without humor.

"And I know you own a silver Lexus LS 600h L, license plate RNB1807, though I didn't see it parked in the driveway. I'm guessing the rental car is in that spot. Enterprise. We'll pick you up. So where's your car, Dr. Greenburg?"

"Somebody stole it," Greenburg said without conviction.

"And whoever stole it threw your dog out the window?"

"Seems like that's what happened."

"From the back seat doing eighty?"

"Could have been two of them. I don't know. It was stolen."

"How come you didn't report it?"

"Maybe I didn't know it was stolen until you told me."

"Then why did you rent a car?"

Greenburg's coke-infused brain circuits were overloading. He couldn't think it through, and now his legs were wobbly. He sat in the leather lounge chair and put the black bag on his lap. He started to pet it but then stopped and gripped the armrests.

"Where's your car, Dr. Greenburg?"

"Chachi's dead."

"It wasn't stolen was it?"

"I pawned it in Pacoima."

"You pawned your Lexus?"

"Poor Chachi," Greenburg said, and right in front of the detective, as if he'd completely forgotten Gary was there, he leaned forward and snorted two lines.

Gary watched Greenburg suck in the powder, rock his head back, and vanish into a cocaine-fueled bliss zone, and he thought about the Oreo four-pack in his pocket.

8
suffering to serenity

IT WAS one thirty-five in the morning, and Danny couldn't sleep. For one thing, his mother's hospital room was a freaking meat locker; for another thing, the reclining chairs were uncomfortable to the point that Danny thought they were engineered to keep family members awake so if something happened to their ailing relative overnight, they wouldn't miss it; for still another thing, Mike snored and snorted like a hog, something he had done since they'd shared a bedroom as kids; and for another thing, the hospital didn't carry TVG, the Television Games Network, so there was no way for him to watch the horses, and he had missed his race.

He liked to bet on the races, liked to learn about the horses and the jockeys and the owners and the trainers, liked to study the bloodlines and watch the interviews and the race analysis and the handicapping tips, liked to make educated hunches before sliding his money through the window, virtual or otherwise. It wasn't an obsession or an addiction, Danny told himself —and anyone else who inquired—it was a hobby, like golf. He liked to go to the track when he could, Hollywood Park near the airport or Santa Anita by Pasadena, and watch the horses run, buy a few drinks, win a couple bucks. Maybe he lost sometimes, but he won more than he lost when he added it all up, which he never did.

This morning, he had gone all in on a superfecta in the sixth at Santa Anita, the most educated hunch he had ever made, and then his mother had a heart attack, and he couldn't watch the race, and then his phone died, and then he didn't have his charger, and then Mike wouldn't let him borrow his phone because he didn't have his charger either and was waiting for Marcy to call, but she sometimes forgot to check her phone, and so she could call at any time, and now he was just going to wait until tomorrow to find out how his horses ran, though he'd never felt better about a bet in his life, and now it *was* tomorrow, and he couldn't sleep.

His asshole brother would never bet a nickel on anything. He didn't see the sport in it, couldn't feel the adrenalin rush as the odds unfolded in real time while horses ran around the track. Danny imagined that Mike was born without adrenalin or had drained the pool dry after fifteen years of stultifying marriage to Marcy.

Spending the day here in the meat locker with him, waiting for their mother to die, had been miserable, the longest dose of Mike he'd had in years. The ego, condescension, and chronological rank Mike threw at him like rocks off an overpass took Danny back to when he and his brother were boys and their father left for New Orleans.

Right up to that afternoon, as best he could recall, they were normal brothers—with normal defined as fighting, laughing, running, pretending to be heroes and monsters and cowboys and soldiers, riding bikes, chasing ice cream trucks around whatever neighborhood they were living in, watching cartoons, playing baseball, being kids in a family that moved around a lot. They were like an Army family, their father told them, and Danny and Mike were like Army brats.

The day after Jeff drove to New Orleans, Linda had sat the boys down at the kitchen table. She was signing up for classes at

Pierce College and knew she would be home less than she had been, less than she wanted to be, less than they needed her to be.

"Michael," she had said, *"you're the oldest. You've got to take care of Daniel while I work and go to school. Make sure he washes his face and eats his dinner and brushes his teeth and does his homework and goes to bed early."*

Mike's messed up sense of moral superiority started that very minute, Danny thought, *and then kept on going every minute of our lives after that, including right up to these last miserable sixty seconds.*

"Michael." It was Linda, conscious and calling out in a weak and dying voice. She had taken the oxygen mask off her mouth with her hand but beyond that could not move. Her eyes were open.

Danny got out of the recliner, crossed to Mike, and shook his arm. "Mike."

Mike snorted and came to life. "What?"

"Mom's awake. She said your name."

"What?"

"Mom said your name."

Mike looked at his mother and saw that her eyes were open.

"Michael," Linda said again.

"Mom, you're awake," Mike said, climbing out of the chair and hurrying to the bed.

Linda nodded weakly, and even that took tremendous effort. "Is Daniel here?"

"I'm here," Danny said, moving to the opposite side of the bed from Mike.

Linda shifted her eyes that way and saw Danny standing over her, then turned her eyes back to Mike. "He looks thin. Is he eating?"

"I don't know," Mike said.

"Make him eat," Linda said.

"I'm standing right here, Mom," Danny said. "I'm eating like a horse. It's my metabolism. I'm the thin one; remember? Mike's the fat one."

"I'm not fat," Mike said.

"You look fat," Danny said.

"I'm losing weight this summer," Mike said.

"I was walking into the light," Linda said.

"What light, Mom?" Mike said.

"The white light," Linda said, "and I saw my brother, Brian, and he told me something very bad was going to happen, so I came back to tell you so you could promise me something."

"Uncle Brian's dead, Mom. He died ten years ago," Mike said.

"That's why he was in the white light," Danny said in a voice that implied: *what an idiot*.

"She's delusional, Danny," Mike said with no small amount of professorial condescension. "It happens when there's not enough oxygen in the brain. If you read anything about heart attacks, you'd know that."

"White light or low oxygen, he still said something bad was going to happen," Danny said.

"Something very bad," Linda said.

"What is it, Mom?" Mike said. "What did Uncle Brian say was going to happen?"

"He couldn't tell me," Linda said. "He was sworn to secrecy. He said that's the problem with the white light—everything's a secret."

"A bad secret," Danny said.

"Very bad," Linda said. "That's why I came back. I told Brian to save me a seat on the bus."

"They have busses in the white light?" Mike said.

"It's a figure of speech," Danny said, and this time it wasn't just the tone of his voice. "Jesus, you're an idiot."

"I'm comforting her," Mike said, doubling down on the condescension. "If you read anything about hospice, if you read even one thing, you would know that making the patient feel comfortable eases the transition from suffering to serenity."

"I read," Danny said.

"The superfecta at Santa Anita is not reading," Mike said.

"Picking the first four in order is like reading ten tax returns," Danny said.

"You don't know anything about accounting," Mike said.

"You know less about horses," Danny said.

"I want you to promise me something, Michael," Linda said.

"Mom, you should rest, save your strength," Mike said.

"Soon I'll be resting a very long time," Linda said.

"On the white light bus, Mom?" Danny said.

"You're a douchebag," Mike said to his brother.

"I'm comforting her," Danny said.

"I want you to promise me that no matter what happens, you'll take care of Daniel," Linda said.

"I can take care of myself," Danny said.

"No, you can't," Linda said. "You're my son, and I love you with my last breath, but you're a flimflam man and a mooch, like your father, except there's a good and kind soul somewhere inside you waiting to come out, and your father had the soul of a jackass."

"I'm not a flimflam man. I'm a talent agent," Danny said.

"She rests her case," Mike said.

"Promise me, Michael," Linda said.

"He won't listen to me," Mike said.

"I'm not listening to him," Danny said.

"He hasn't listened to me since he was seven years old," Mike said.

"I'm never listening to him," Danny said.

"Promise me," Linda said.

"I have a life," Danny said.

"I have a life too, Mom," Mike said. "I don't want to take care of him."

"I don't want anyone to take care of me," Danny said, "especially him."

"Stop this nonsense," Linda said. Her voice was barely audible now, and the brothers had to lean over and put their faces close to her mouth so they could hear her. And what they heard was that she was as serious as a, well, heart attack. They knew that particular tone of voice no matter how soft and weak it was. It was the tone of voice that made them seven and ten years old in an instant. "Give me your hand, Michael."

Mustering what little strength she had left, she lifted her hand and gestured for Mike's hand. He gave it to her, and she guided it to her chest, to her heart, and put it there. Mike became very still, and Danny watched the emotion of the moment overwhelm his brother. Something powerful and solemn, something spiritual and profound was happening to Mike and, son of a bitch, to him too.

"Swear to me, Michael. Swear to me that when the very bad thing happens to Daniel or to you or to you both, that you will watch over him and take care of him, whatever that means, whatever is necessary. Swear to me that when the very bad thing happens, anything you *can* do you *will* do. He is my son and your brother and you must swear this to me on my dying heart, on my deathbed. Swear it now and forever."

Danny watched his brother hold his breath. He could almost see the hurricane of thoughts blasting through Mike's head, could almost hear the war raging in his brain. He didn't want to do it; he couldn't imagine doing it; he wasn't going to do it.

After an eternity that took two seconds, Mike dropped his head forward in defeat, the war lost, his hand still on Linda's heart, and said, "Jesus, Mom. Okay, I swear."

"Swear what? Say it, Michael," Linda said.

"I swear to you that no matter what very bad thing happens to Danny or to me or to us both, I will watch over and take care of my brother," Mike said, "whatever that means, whatever is necessary. Anything I can do, I will do."

"Good. I love you both with all my soul," Linda said.

And then she died.

wednesday

9

how much do you know about judd martin?

IT HAD BEEN a hellacious day and night for Mike Miller, and the replay was running on a loop in his head. It was noon, and he was seated alone in the Wasserman and Waddell conference room, waiting for Stan Wasserman and Ira Waddell to give him the good news of his promotion to partner. But all he could think about was that though it seemed like ages ago, it was only yesterday that Judd Martin had bullied and bribed him to falsify the rental numbers so that the bank would give Martin the money to finish his office buildings. Mike had said no, and while he was standing his ground, his mother had a heart attack, and he'd spent the rest of the day in her hospital room with his brother, watching her drift in and out of consciousness until the early hours of the morning, at which time she woke up and made him swear an oath upon her dying heart that he would take care of Danny no matter what the hell happened to either of them, since her own dead brother had told her, in the white light of Heaven's bus stop, that something bad was coming down the pike. And then she'd died.

He had grieved by her bedside until four thirty in the morning. It was a deep and terrible loss for him. *Whatever anyone's mother meant to anyone,* he'd thought while he wept, *my mother meant more than that to me.* She'd been his *saint*, for God's sake. She'd taught him everything about everything. He was an accountant because of her skill and determination as a country club bookkeeper. He was a loving and patient parent because of her example. What he did, how he lived, what he knew and thought and believed was all a result of her love and strength and guidance. And now she was gone. His grief poured out of him, but he did not share it with his brother.

Danny had stood by the window, looking out at the Northridge night. If he cried at all, he did so quietly, not that Mike would have noticed through his own sobbing. They did not console each other. They were separate planets in different orbits.

It was Mike who had made the arrangements with the hospital and the mortuary, which made sense since he knew many mortuary managers by name. He had chosen George Edwards Mortuary in Mission Hills because George had kept a consistent profit margin, a clean ledger, for the fifteen years Mike had been doing his tax returns. It was George himself, not some outside bookkeeper, who had placed a steady hand on the mortuary monetary tiller. It stood to reason that he would be an unwavering emotional guide in the difficult days ahead.

At four thirty in the morning, as they were leaving, Mike thought maybe their mother's death had created an opening for him and Danny to connect.

"Now what do we do?" Danny had said.

"We try to pull together," Mike had said. "We try to give each other support when we need it."

Danny had looked at his brother like Mike was from Mars. "You're an idiot. I mean, what do we do right now? Do we get breakfast on Ventura somewhere? Do we go home and sleep for a few hours? What do we do right now?"

Mike had nodded. The emotions of the night had momentarily clouded his judgment. "I know it's hard for you, Dan," he'd said, "but if you can manage not to be a douchebag for the next few days, while we eulogize and bury mom, that would be swell."

And then the door swung open and Stan Wasserman entered the conference room. "Mike, thanks for waiting. Sorry we're late. Last minute crisis on the Cushing account."

He was fifty-seven years old, tall and marathon-runner thin, the poster boy for both midlife fitness and male pattern baldness. His sleep-away-camp buddy and partner Ira Waddell, a five-foot-eight-inch block of triathlete granite, followed him into the room and shut the door behind them. The partners sat across the conference table from Mike.

The room was decorated with framed photographs of iconic Los Angeles landmarks. A credenza that housed a bar was at one end of the room; a large, flat-screen monitor wirelessly connected to a computer and used for client presentations filled the wall at the other end. The table was cherry. The chairs were red leather.

If I had a dollar for every meeting I've attended in this room was the first thought Mike had while Stan and Ira got settled. But that thought, and the emotional turbulence of the past twenty-four hours, was washed away with the excitement Mike felt at finally being tapped for partnership. He wished Linda had lived just a little longer so he could share this moment with her. She would have been so proud of him. He was proud of himself. He had earned this promotion. He could feel himself smiling.

"Mike," Ira said, "we have to let you go."

"Excuse me?" Mike said.

"We're firing you," Stan said. "Bonnie's packing your office right now."

Mike had the feeling that someone had pulled his shirt up over his head and was spinning him around and around the conference room. He could feel nausea rising up from his knees.

"You can't fire me, Stan. You're promoting me to partner," Mike said.

"We're not promoting you. We're expelling you from the

firm," Ira said. He had muscles on his muscles, and Mike knew that he disapproved of employees who were overweight and out of shape. *That can't be it*, Mike thought, *there's no way they would fire me because I'm twenty-five, okay, thirty pounds heavier than I should be.*

"I'm a good accountant," Mike said, "maybe your best accountant. You know I am. I'm accurate and honest and hard-working and loyal. Fifteen years."

"No argument there," Stan said. "You were a partner until an hour ago."

"And then Judd Martin happened," Ira said.

"The bank called in his loans this morning at nine o'clock sharp, all his loans," Stan said. "By eleven, he had lost everything—his buildings, his company, his house, his cars, everything. He was mortgaged to his ears, couldn't cover a dime of it. The bank came down like a ton of bricks, made an example out of him. He has nothing."

"Look, I feel bad for Judd, not really, but I had nothing to do with his fall from grace," Mike said. "What could possibly be the connection between my partnership, my employment, and Judd Martin's crash landing?"

Stan and Ira looked at each other. They had been friends since the age of eight and communicated without words. In that moment, Mike imagined, they had a silent conversation and decided to tell him more than they had originally intended.

"How much do you know about Judd Martin?" Ira said.

"I've had his account for a year. I know his numbers, that's all," Mike said.

"Judd Martin is mentally ill and emotionally unstable," Stan said. "Severely imbalanced."

"Dangerously volatile," Ira said.

"He's been arrested for assault and battery five times," Stan said. "He's a serial stalker, and it always ends with extreme violence perpetrated on the person he's stalking."

"He went to prison in Nevada," Ira said.

"And Colorado," Stan said.

"Psychiatric ward both times," Ira said. "Walking time bomb."

"He called this morning to say he was homeless and penniless and pissed off at Wasserman and Waddell," Stan said. "He said he was coming after us."

"We assured him that the firm had nothing to do with his bankruptcy," Ira said.

"We told him you were completely responsible," Stan said, "and that you acted alone."

"You told him what?" Mike said.

"We had to for the sake and safety of the firm," Ira said.

"A violent stalker would be bad for business," Stan said.

"It's not personal," Ira said. "It has nothing to do with your job performance or body mass index or anything of that nature."

"We had to point his anger and aggression in another direction," Stan said.

"Yes," Ira said, "another direction."

"So you pointed him at me?" Mike said incredulously.

"We did," Stan said. "That's true."

There was no possibility that Mike could corral the thoughts in his brain. If his thoughts were numbers, there would be no way to catalogue them, to codify them, to compose them in columns and tabulate them. *The Numbers of Life* had become *The Numbers of Ruin* had become *The Numbers of Chaos*. He thought of his wife and children, his house and his cars, his insurance and his yearly nut. He had minimal savings, enough to last more than a month, maybe less than that.

"I have to get another job," Mike said out loud instead of in his head, where panic was winning the day.

"In some other industry," Ira said. "Accounting is no longer viable for you."

"Excuse me?" Mike said, but he slurred the words as if he were drunk.

"Lawyers from the bank got involved, depositions and so on," Stan said.

"They wanted to know why Judd Martin had a two-million-dollar shortfall in his construction funds account," Ira said.

"The word *embezzlement* was bandied about," Stan said, "and you were the accountant of record."

Mike's eyes went wide with terror. "He lied to the firm, to me, to the banks."

"No one accused you formally," Ira said. "You're not going to be charged. But that word is attached to your name now, like a scar on your face."

"But you'll fix that. You'll write me a letter of recommendation," Mike said.

"We can't, and we won't," Stan said. "We have to enforce an unmitigated break from you in all regards. We can't be associated with you in any positive, productive way. You went rogue on us; that's the public position of the firm."

"You're a rogue accountant," Ira said, "unemployable in your field."

It was too much crazy-bad information for Mike to take in at once. He could feel his heart pounding like thunder in his head. "Jesus Christ, Stan..." he said, his voice fading to nothing.

"It could be worse," Stan said, rubbing his hands together in an awful way that signified *that's that* and looking at Ira.

"If Judd Martin finds him," Ira said, "it will be."

10
one-two-three-five-by-a-nose

IT WAS one hundred seven burning degrees at high noon, and Danny lugged the last load of his stuff up the strip mall steps and into his office and thought, *Fuck Mrs. Alemi and all six of her sons.*

He'd left the hospital at four thirty in the morning, stopped for breakfast on Ventura Boulevard, checked the race report, and then, wanting to shower and change his clothes, driven to the small yellow house in Canoga Park, where he found his mother's landlord, Mrs. Alemi, and all six of her sons loading the contents of the house onto a flatbed truck parked in the narrow driveway.

He hurried to the handsome eighty-year-old woman, whose roots were in Persia, before the Shah fell, and said, "What are you doing in my house, Mrs. Alemi?"

She wore a black pantsuit and a colorful scarf wrapped around her shoulders. Her hair was gray and elegantly styled. Her nails were manicured. Her teeth were white and straight. Her eyes were clear and sharp. She was nobody's fool, and no one knew that better than her six sons. "This is not your house, Mr. Miller." Her accent was deep and strong and melodic. "This is my house. And with my blessing, it was your mother's house on a month-to-month lease for thirty years. And now she has died, God rest her soul, and that lease is ended, and you are out. Your brother called me this morning. I am packing your mother's things and putting them in storage at my expense. You can pick them up when you find a home of your own."

"What about my things, my bed and dressers, my couch and TV, all the stuff in my bedroom?" Danny said.

They stared at each other, the heat melting them, the six sons carrying furniture and boxes out of the house. For thirty years, Danny knew, she had never raised his mother's rent, never levied a late fee, never sent a stern letter when Linda was struggling with school and work and two young boys and would occasionally miss a due date. He knew—because she had told him—that she respected his mother's work ethic, which was much like her own. He also knew—because she had also told him—that she did not respect him, that his move back into the small yellow house and his three-year stay had made him, she said in not so many words, a flimflam man and a mooch.

Mrs. Alemi agreed that for three hundred dollars cash in advance she and her six sons would drive Danny's possessions to the dilapidated strip mall on Reseda Boulevard in the distant northern reaches of the Valley and deposit them in his two-room office. So Danny threw his clothes in garbage bags along with his personal items and a few towels and blankets and pillows and, followed by the flatbed, drove his worn out 1998 Pathfinder to his office, now his home-office since this is where he would be living.

One hour later, the office was a wreck. His bed and dressers and night tables and lamps and flat-screen TV and bags and bags of clothes were unceremoniously dumped wherever the hell Mrs. Alemi's six sons had felt like dumping them. It looked like a cluttered thrift store, The Salvation Army, maybe, or Goodwill. His *Casablanca* feng shui was feng fucked. The vibe here was horrible. He would never sign a soul in this place, and he would lose the talent he had. Even Paul the Pervert would desert him now.

He sat on his rattan sofa and looked around his private office. Besides the fact that it looked as if a tidal wave had rolled through, something struck him as wrong, as odd, as offbeat and out of tune, but he couldn't put his finger on it.

"Love what you've done with the place," Harvey said, coming through Danny's office door. "*Secondhand Shithole*, I think they call it. Where did we see that, Omar?"

The giant followed the dwarf into the room. "HGTV."

Danny made a face accompanied by a sound that said: *oh crap.*

"I don't think Danny's happy to see us," Harvey said to Omar.

"I don't think he should be," Omar said.

They walked to what used to be the sitting area but was now the gerrymandered bedroom-living room quadrant. Omar moved a garbage bag of clothes off the other end of the rattan sofa from where Danny was seated, and Harvey climbed up, stood at his end, and sang, "Oh, Danny boy, the pipes, the pipes are calling, From glen to glen, and down the mountain side, The summer's gone, and all the flowers are dying, 'Tis you, 'tis you must go and I must bide."

Danny was blown away. Harvey was an inconceivably remarkable tenor. The startling and stunning voice that emanated from his miniature body was bold and glorious, radiant and passionate. Had he not been a sadistic loan shark, he could have been a client and toured with Placido, Jose, and Luciano—Three Tenors and a Dwarf.

"But come ye back when summer's in the meadow, Or when the valley's hushed and white with snow, 'Tis I'll be here in sunshine or in shadow, Oh, Danny boy, oh Danny boy, I love you so."

"Impressive," Danny said. "I had no idea you could sing like that."

"Never judge a book by its cover," Omar said, sitting in a rattan armchair.

"Unless that book is about a talent agent who owes you twenty-five thousand dollars he bet at the track," Harvey said.

"Exception to the rule," Omar said. "Noted."

"How did your horses do?" Harvey said, smiling. "Did they finish one-two-three-four?"

Danny knew Harvey knew the answer to that question but so enjoyed the pain and suffering the question caused that he couldn't keep himself from asking it. Danny hung his head and massaged his brow with his thumb and index finger. "One-two-three-five-by-a-nose," Danny said.

"Only the nose knows, Where the nose goes, When the door close," Omar said. "Muhammed Ali."

"This was the bet that was going to pay off all your other bets," Harvey said.

"My mother died last night," Danny said. "I was at Northridge Hospital until four thirty. My asshole accountant brother called her landlord first thing in the morning, and she threw me out. It's been a bad day, Harvey. Can we do this later in the week?"

Harvey walked down the sofa to Danny and said, "You owe me twenty-five thousand dollars. Do you have my money?"

"I had to give the landlord three hundred cash to move me here," Danny said. "I got seven hundred in the bank and thirty bucks in my wallet."

Whack. Harvey clocked Danny on the side of the head.

"Ow...shit, Harvey," Danny said.

"Do you have my money?" Harvey said.

"Things are looking up," Danny said. "I just signed a pervert clown; he's going to be huge on the porn party circuit and—"

Whack. Harvey hit him again. "Do you have my money?"

Danny stood up, red in the face, as if he was going to do something about being punched in the head by a dwarf, but Omar stood up at the same second, reached across the bamboo coffee table, and grabbed Danny by the throat with one massive hand and by the belt with the other hand and lifted Danny up into the air, high over the coffee table, above his head like he was a barbell.

Out of reflex, Danny put his hands on Omar's hand on his throat, which was applying enough pressure to make it difficult to breathe.

"Do you have my money," Harvey said.

"No," Danny said, wheezing.

"Omar, progress," Harvey said.

"Discontent is the first necessity of progress," Omar said, looking up into Danny's bulging eyes. "Thomas Edison."

Harvey nodded at Omar with approval, looked around the office, and shook his head with disappointment. "Pitiful. Even all together, it's worth nothing."

"Can't breathe," Danny barely said.

"I can see that. How much is your rent?" Harvey said.

"A thousand," Danny said with a rasp.

"That is the amount you're going to pay me for the next three years, thirty-six consecutive payments of one thousand dollars. Then your loan will be paid in full and off my books."

"That's nine thousand in interest," Danny said.

"He's conscious of the numbers," Harvey said to Omar.

"He's about to be unconscious of the numbers," Omar said.

Danny knew Omar was right; he was about to black out. He could sense the sun setting, even though it was the middle of the day. And he could hear Harvey singing the last verses of "Danny Boy."

"And if you come, and all the flowers are dying, If I am dead, as dead I well may be, I pray you'll find the place where I am lying, And kneel and say an *Ave* there for me,"

I'm going now, Danny thought, but something happened split seconds before he lost consciousness, something he knew was important in spite of the singing dwarf and the giant choking the air out of him. It was the thing that was wrong with the room, the odd thing, the offbeat and out-of-tune thing.

"And I shall hear, though soft you tread above me, And all my grave will warm and sweeter be, And then you'll kneel and whisper that you love me, And I shall sleep in peace until you come to me."

It was the fern on the bamboo coffee table, the dehydrated-dry-and-shriveled-brown dead fern that Jenny Stone had taken in her hands and breathed on. He was looking straight down right at it. *Alive*, he said in his head, *it's alive*. And then everything went black.

11

his friends said she was crazy

IT WAS WEDNESDAY NOON. Donald the Dentist only worked a half-day (one to five), which was a good thing because he had been up all night doing cocaine in his office after Detective Shuler had handed over the garbage bag holding his dead dog. He couldn't bear going to bed and listening to Carol cry herself to sleep.

He had finally dozed off somewhere around six and was awakened by the sound of music—literally; *The Sound of Music* was blasting in the living room—Julie Andrews, Christopher Plummer, and all the various Von Trapps singing "So Long, Farewell" as they slipped into the night and across the border.

He rubbed his index finger through the white dust on the mirror on the coffee table, ran the finger across his gums, got out of the armchair, picked up the garbage bag that held Chachi's carcass, and walked out of his office. He went down the hall, intending to grab a shovel from the garage so he could dig a hole in the backyard behind the trees beyond the pool and bury the bag, but he arrived at the large living room just in time to see his wife kick the chair away from her feet—the chair she was standing on, so she could hang herself with the rope she had looped over the rafters that spanned the room beneath the twenty-foot, tongue-in-groove, cathedral ceiling painted Dr. Seuss red.

Donald didn't even have time to blink in disbelief. He dropped the garbage bag, ran into the living room, grabbed Carol around the legs, and lifted her up so that there was slack in the rope, so she wouldn't break her neck or asphyxiate herself or both.

"Jesus, Carol," he said, holding her up for dear life—hers.

"I can't live without my beautiful boy," she said.

"Yes, you can," he said.

"I loved him so much, and now I've lost him and have nothing to live for."

"You have me."

"Too much water under the bridge. Let go, Donald. Let go..."

For a moment, it occurred to him that he *should* let go, that they would both be better off if they were out of each other's lives (even if that meant one of them was hanged to death, gallows like, from the living room rafters). She had not loved him for many years, and he had not loved her, but they were snarled together in the Web of Life and could not be disentangled. *Let go*, he told himself, *let go of her legs and walk away; you can do it*. But he could not do it because he remembered.

They had been undergrads at SUNY Plattsburgh in might-as-well-be-Canada upstate New York. He was from Albany; she was from Oswego. They fell in love, or he did, at freshman orientation. She was eccentric and peculiar, whimsical and weird; he was serious and studious, earnest and eager to please. He was attracted to her mercurial energy like a kid to candy and couldn't explain why. His friends told him she was crazy. He knew it was true but didn't care. "I'm stuck to her," he said to them, kidding at the time, "and she's stuck to me."

"I can't let go," he said.

"Chachi is dead, Donald. Eaten by a coyote somewhere in the wild, wild woods."

After four years in Plattsburgh that felt like four decades in

Antarctica, they had dreamed dreams of a life in the sun. He was accepted into the UCLA School of Dentistry, and they drove across the country to start their new life in LA. They rented a two-room apartment in Laurel Canyon and lived on ramen noodles, Corn Flakes, and Campbell's Soup. He carved teeth out of wax. She became an interior designer. Her muse was Dr. Seuss. His muse was her frenetic aura, which gave him the high-wire sense that his life could turn down any goddamn street in the world—the adrenalin of her was a rush. They married in Santa Monica and honeymooned in Barbados, where, when they were playing in the blue Caribbean, he accidentally smacked her in the face with a forearm and broke her nose. They returned from the island, she had a surgeon make her a new one, got addicted to Percocet, and then did her nose again for the drug. His friends said she was crazy. He knew it was true but couldn't quit her. She was in his blood.

"There are no wild woods in the Valley," he said.

"Then he's dead in the aqueduct, drowned like a little white angel. Let me go, Donald. He needs me now more than ever. Let me go to him in heaven."

He bought a small practice in the Valley and worked hard and long to make it go. She never got pregnant and turned to her Dr. Seuss reading group for support. The bigger his business grew, the further away she seemed to get, and the deeper she slipped into her addictions. As hard as it was to live with her— the terrible cycle of surgery and pain pills and vodka and Dr. Seuss, over and over, ad infinitum—it was even more painful to think of living alone. And alone he would be because he'd discovered gin and cocaine, and no one worth living with would live with a cokehead, alcoholic dentist wasting away to skin and bone because his appetite for life had died with his wife. His friends said she was crazy. *You have no idea,* he'd thought, but he couldn't stand to see her in so much pain. In the end, she was still the girl he fell for in Plattsburgh, the girl who excited him so.

"Maybe he's not dead, Carol. Maybe he's out there alone, waiting for you to find him."

"I'll never find him."

"Yes, you will. I'll help you."

"What will we do?"

"We'll make flyers and posters and tape them up all across the Valley. We'll put his picture on milk cartons and on TV. We'll start a Facebook page and a Twitter account. We'll rally your reading group and scour the neighborhood."

Years ago, he couldn't remember how many now, he had stopped paying for her plastic surgery. She'd found Harvey Mineral and borrowed and pawned them into trouble. His practice suffered, and his income declined, and he drank and blew coke, and then he'd borrowed from Harvey too. As she transformed into a plasticized remnant of a human woman and he became a stick of a broken-down dentist, his friends said she was crazy. *"Fuck you,"* he'd told them. *"Fuck all of you."*

He held onto her legs, lifting her up, and she looked down at him, her eyes clouded with pain and suffering and Percocet and vodka.

"Do you think he's alive, Donald? Do you really think Chachi's alive?"

He glanced over at the garbage bag on the floor and then met her eyes. "Yes. I'm sure he is. Chachi is alive, and we're going to find him."

"Get the chair," she said. "I'll call the girls."

He pulled the chair over with his leg and let her down slowly until her feet landed on the seat. Then he pulled another chair right beside her, climbed up on it, and lifted the rope off her neck and over her head. While they were very close, she looked at him and said, "If we don't find him, I'll kill myself and leave you here alone. You'll have no one, not me, not Chachi, no one."

She knows me so well, he thought, *she knows me too well. We are the sad and sorry definition of co-dependent.* Yes, he was addicted to cocaine and Tanqueray, but he was mostly addicted to her. She was the best and worst and strongest drug he had ever taken. He could quit coke and gin if he wanted to (he *didn't* want to), but he couldn't quit her if his life depended on it—or, especially, if hers did. "We'll find him," he said.

When she left to call the Seuss women and put together a scouting party, he picked up the bag and walked out of the room. Just like he didn't have the heart to tell his wife the truth about Chachi, he also didn't have the stomach to bury his best buddy in the backyard. So he put the bag in the garage freezer, where he knew she'd never find it.

12
laugh a minute

AS GARY PULLED the Impala into the Pacoima Pawn and Loan parking lot, he ate his eighth Oreo of the day, finishing off his second four-pack, and thought about his parents, Jack and Sharon Shuler, who had as much to do with his addiction as Nabisco, which had started making the habit-forming, cream-filled, double-chocolate-cookie drug in 1912.

Gary grew up in Chula Vista, California, a sun-splashed San Diego city of two hundred fifty thousand scenically set between the coastal mountain foothills and the San Diego Bay. His parents were public school teachers—Jack taught middle school chemistry, and Sharon taught third grade. They had a tidy house on a tidy street and all signs pointed to a tidy life, until Gary got to elementary school, where his path as an Oreo-addicted comedian cop was set in motion.

On the first day of first grade, all the kids had to stand and say their names out loud for the rest of the class. Gary stood and said, "Gary Shuler," and a smart-ass kid said, *"Gary Shuler Vista,"* and the name stuck like Gorilla Glue.

Everyone in the city of Chula Vista, the city of San Diego, and the greater San Diego metropolitan area called him Gary Shuler Vista and only Gary Shuler Vista. Every kid, every teacher, every coach, every friend, every friend's family, even his own sisters, even his own parents called him Gary Shuler Vista—never Gary, never Shuler, never Gary Shuler, always Gary Shuler Vista.

"Now batting for Eastlake," the high school announcer would say over the loudspeaker, *"number five, Gary Shuler Vista, number five."* When his friends would greet him in the halls during the day, they would say, *"Hey, Gary Shuler Vista, what's up, man?"* When he graduated and was called to receive his diploma, he was announced as Gary Shuler Vista. When his San Diego City College girlfriend, who became both his first wife and his first ex-wife, Maryanne McCarthy, would have sex with him in her family's darkened basement TV room after criminal justice class, she would say, *"I love you, Gary Shuler Vista, I love you so much."*

Early on, when he was six, seven, and eight years old, when he was hurt and confused because he was the one and only child who was addressed by his full name plus a name that wasn't his name, his parents had pacified him with tall cold glasses of milk and stacks of Oreo cookies. The cookies became physically, emotionally, and intellectually synonymous with safety and comfort. He ate them constantly throughout his life. He couldn't stop eating them. At the same time that they were feeding him Oreos, his parents also recognized there was nothing they could do to stem the Gary Shuler Vista tide, so they taught their son to ride those waves with laughter, to be in on the joke instead of being the joke.

Oreos and comedy became the subconscious pillars upon which his life was built. He became the class clown in every class and carried an Oreo four-pack everywhere he went. He was popular and smart and a good athlete. But he was also a bit offline, not your normal everyday kid. He saw the world at odd angles. He was an odd angle himself. *"He's a good guy, Gary Shuler Vista,"* people would say, *"but he's a strange bird."*

He went to college, studied criminal justice, and landed a position with the LAPD. He had inherited his father's scientific mind and his mother's comedic timing, so he was a natural at police work. He was promoted to detective and made a name for himself by solving weird crimes. He was drawn to them. He thought they were hysterical.

He married Maryanne—*Do you, Gary Shuler Vista, take Maryanne McCarthy to be your lawfully wedded wife?*—but the marriage didn't last. She'd wanted some semblance of normalcy. *"I want us to play tennis, Gary Shuler Vista,"* she'd said to him, but it was too late for tennis. Someone had sawed six inches off all the chairs at an LA comedy club, like that episode in *Cheers*, and Gary took the case and found stand-up comedy and knew it was his destiny. *"I love you, Gary Shuler Vista,"* Maryanne had said as she was leaving him, *"but you're even weirder than the crimes you solve."*

Am I weirder than the crimes I solve? As he sat in his unmarked Impala parked across the lot from Pacoima Pawn and Loan looking at the Lexus (parked next to the black Range Rover) that had been speeding down the 101 when the cokehead dentist's poodle was tossed out the rear window into traffic, he considered the possibility. It'd be funny if it were true, he decided. He could put it in his act.

He turned off the car and opened the Impala door and was mauled by the one-hundred-seven-degree heat. It was astonishing how overpowering the San Fernando Valley weather had become. It was as if the air were on fire. The entire city of Los Angeles seemed to be burning. Everyone was on edge. Laid-back Los Angelenos weren't meant to live in Amazonian temperatures. It felt like hell. Or Phoenix.

Greenburg had been no help. After saying he had pawned the Lexus in Pacoima, he had coked out and clammed up, afraid to say anything more. When Gary had asked him what, exactly, he was afraid of, the dentist sucked up a long line and said, *"Dying."*

Gary opened the door, walked into the pawnshop, and let the scene wash over him. It was so brightly lit that it took a moment for his eyes to adjust, and the air conditioning was set so low that he thought his skin might crack like glass that goes from too hot to too cold too fast. To his right, a Hispanic pawnshop clerk behind the counter was negotiating with a black woman who was holding a Civil War sword to her breasts as if she would never let it go no matter how much money he offered her. She could hide the clerk in her cleavage.

He turned to his left and saw a giant human dressed in black slacks and a black silk T-shirt hurtling toward him like a mountain landslide. The giant had a long black ponytail and the remains of terrible teenage skin. His hands and feet were enormous. His ears and nose and teeth were larger than life. He had diamonds in each earlobe. There was a gap between his two front teeth. His eyes were the color of charcoal. Gary considered reaching for his gun, which he kept in a belt holster above his backside, hidden by his sport jacket, but he didn't have time. The giant was here, and he was laughing for some reason.

"I know you," the giant said.

"You do?" Gary said.

"You're the cop comedian. Hey, look who's here," he said to the counter clerk and the black woman with the sword. "Detective Gary something, the laugh-a-minute guy. That's who you are, right, Detective Gary something?"

Like most everyone else on the comedy club circuit, when Omar said the word *Detective*, he put it in air quotes. No one believed Gary was an actual cop. The truth, Gary realized in that moment, was that it was getting harder for him to believe it too.

"Shuler," Gary said. "Detective Gary Shuler. Who are you?"

"Omar Creech," Omar said, putting his massive hand out. "We saw you at Flappers in Burbank. You told that story about the dumbest bank robber in the world, the moron with the plastic gun and the blonde wig and the fake boobs who clipped four banks in one day and wrote the robbery notes on the back of his personal checks, then went home and made a YouTube about the stick ups, fanning the cash in front of the camera."

Gary shook Omar's hand and, like a switch, flipped from cop

to comedian. "I knock on the guy's door, and he lets me in, and I arrest him and show him the video, and he says, 'Not me.' So I point to his video camera on the couch, and he says, 'Not my camera.' So I point to the stolen cash next to the camera, and he says, 'Not my money.' So I point to the fake tits next to the cash next to the camera, and he says, 'Those are my girlfriend's tits; I was just using them.' So I said, 'Using them for what?' And he says, 'Disguise for the bank jobs.' It's a laugh a minute out there."

Omar cracked up. Something about Gary's delivery was hilarious to him. The clerk and the sword woman looked at Omar and Gary with confusion, the humor lost on them. "What are you doing here, Detective?" Omar said. Again, he used the air quotes.

"Working on a new routine," Gary said. "This one starts with a silver Lexus LS 600h L that someone pawned in Pacoima. I mean, come on, there's a silver Lexus LS 600h L parked right out front. What are the chances?"

Omar cracked up again and said, "I got to take you to Harvey. He won't believe it's you."

Still laughing, he grabbed Gary by the elbow and led him across the store. Gary couldn't have shaken loose if he'd wanted to, and he did want to. They went through a gateway cut into the counter and walked to double oak doors set in the rear wall. Omar knocked once, opened the doors, and led the comedian cop into the twilight zone.

13
omar, feed the fish

HARVEY MINERAL'S private office was nearly the width of the store, about fifty feet, and close to thirty feet long. To Gary's left was Harvey's large desk area with four fancy leather chairs in front of it. Behind the desk was a long row of low file cabinets. A full kitchen dominated the far left corner. Straight ahead in the middle of the space was a living room area with two leather sofas and two recliners facing the far wall, where an entertainment unit included a seventy-inch flat-screen television and enough add-on electronics to make Best Buy green with envy. *Holy moly,* Gary thought, *it's the Pawn Palace,* and he made a mental note to add the Pawn Palace to his act.

To the right was a three-thousand-gallon freshwater aquarium that made Gary's eyes pop. It was at least twelve feet long by six feet wide by five feet tall. It was softly lit and had a jungle of plants inside. There were more than one hundred fish in the water, all the same kind, all eight to ten inches long, all with red bellies. *Uh oh,* he thought.

But what he noticed most of all was the well-dressed dwarf standing on the three-foot raised platform that encircled the tank, holding a live mouse by the tail over the edge above the water, just now ready to drop it into the drink.

"Harvey, you can't believe it. Look who's here," Omar said, still laughing.

Harvey turned from the fish tank, saw Gary, and started to laugh like Omar. "It's a laugh a minute out there," he said, dropping the mouse into a box of mice by his feet.

"He's working on a new routine," Omar said, holding Gary's elbow and guiding him to the fish tank. "It starts with a silver Lexus LS 600h L that someone pawned in Pacoima. He saw the one parked outside the shop. Isn't that hilarious?"

"Hysterical," Harvey said. "Detective Gary something, am I right? He put *Detective* in air quotes.

"Shuler. Detective Gary Shuler," Gary said.

The dwarf and the giant, both of them laughing, looked at each other, made air quotes, and said at the same time, "*Detective.*"

Harvey wore gray Armani slacks and a blue Armani sweater. He had little black cowboy boots and a gold Rolex. He was immaculate. "How does your routine go after the Lexus?" Harvey said. "I can't wait to hear it."

"It's a work-in-progress," Gary said, "but it goes like this: a cokehead dentist goes for a ride in the Lexus on the 101, and his white poodle flies out the back window into speeding traffic, like it suddenly thought it was a bird...a little white poodle-bird. You can't make this stuff up."

Harvey and Omar both laughed out loud. Everything about Gary and his routine was funny as hell to them.

"You can't make this stuff up," Omar said.

"Poodle-bird...you're killing me, *Detective*," Harvey said— with air quotes.

"So the poodle-bird, because it has no wings, is smashed forty feet in the air to the side of the freeway. A woman speeding by in the other direction sees the airborne pooch and calls 9-1-1. Highway patrol collects the canine and gives it to me, *Detective* Gary Shuler." He put air quotes around Detective, and Harvey and Omar roared.

"Here's where it gets good," Gary said. "The dog tag has the owner's name and address, and I go see him, dead dog in a bag, and he's a cokehead dentist, and he tells me, between the lines, pardon the poodle pun, that it's his dead dog."

Harvey and Omar could hardly catch their breath, they were laughing so hard.

"Between the lines," Omar said.

"Poodle pun," Harvey said.

"He says he pawned the car in Pacoima, so I go looking for it because you know why?"

"Because it's a laugh a minute out there?" Harvey said, about ready to crack a rib.

"Yes," Gary said, "and because it's against about a dozen laws, including the laws of humanity, decency, and civility, to throw a dog out a speeding car window into freeway traffic and also because I'm trying to keep the routine going because if I had this routine and an agent, I could get on Jimmy Kimmel."

"We know an agent. Let's get this guy on Jimmy Kimmel," Omar said to Harvey.

"Let's feed him to the fish first," Harvey said.

Still laughing, Omar grabbed Gary's arms from behind, pinning them to Gary's sides, and stepped up on the platform next to Harvey, lifting the detective as if he were made of paper mâché and forcing him down on his knees so that he was facing and flush up against the tank, the surface of the water just below his chest, not far from his face.

"This is a shoal of two hundred red-bellied piranha," Harvey said. He turned Gary's head so that it faced him, and they were eye-to-eye. "They're dangerous to all creatures, including man, when they're hungry, which they are because I haven't fed them because I like them to be famished when I do feed them; the carnage is spectacular."

Gary looked into Harvey's eyes and thought, *What a goddamned handsome dwarf!* "It's against the law to own piranha in California. I'm a detective; I should know. I'd put air quotes around detective, but I can't feel my arms."

"Can't feel my arms, that's hysterical," Omar said, cracking up but crushing Gary's arms like a vise, not letting him move one inch.

"I don't precisely own them," Harvey said, laughing. "They were pawned to me by an Asian man from Calabasas. They're the collateral property of Pacoima Pawn and Loan. You can't arrest me for piranha I don't precisely own."

"If Omar lets go of my arms, I could arrest the Asian guy," Gary said. "Where is he?"

"Fish food," Omar said.

"Eaten by his own piranha," Harvey said. "Spectacular carnage."

"Laugh a minute," Gary said, and Harvey and Omar kept laughing.

"Let's give Detective Gary Shuler an up-close-and-personal look at our carnivorous friends," Harvey said. "I imagine he's never seen teeth like this."

Almost without effort, despite Gary's resistance, Omar bent him forward so that his face was two inches above the water line. The shoal swam into the jungle, skittish, hungry, and momentarily fearful.

"I want to help you with your flying-poodle routine, Detective, but I don't think I can," Harvey said. "Certainly, you noticed the Lexus was without license plates, so there's no way you can be sure it's the car in your story."

"You could open the door. I could check the serial number, collect some flying-poodle DNA, maybe lift some fingerprints," Gary said. "That would be funny."

"Not as funny as this—Omar, feed the fish," Harvey said, laughing.

"Deep breath, Detective," Omar said, also laughing, and he pushed Gary down until the front of his face broke the surface.

Gary managed half a breath and held it. He opened his eyes

and with watery vision saw red-bellied piranha swimming madly around the tank. He saw rows of razor-sharp teeth. He saw the shoal, two hundred strong, considering him, taking some kind of communal and telepathic vote as to whether or not they should eat his fucking face off.

And then the shoal moved toward him with bad intent. Its teeth were hideous and terrifying and also, in a sick and twisted way, hilarious. Omar pulled Gary's head out of the water one spilt second before there was blood in the tank.

Gary spit and gasped and blinked the water out of his eyes. "You're right," he said. "Much funnier than fingerprints." He meant it too. Almost having his face shredded by a pawned shoal of piranha would definitely be part of his new act. *Letterman will love it*, he thought.

"'Much funnier than fingerprints,' I'm going to laugh about that for days," Omar said, cracking up again.

"So your search continues, Detective. Your Lexus is somewhere, but it's not here. Are we agreed? Before you answer, I should tell you that Omar knows worse ways to remove your face."

"Blow torch, steak knife, vacuum cleaner," Omar said, "just to start the conversation."

Gary thought it was possible that these were the two craziest maniacs in the San Fernando Valley. He was a LAPD detective, for Pete's sake, and they had just threatened him with death-by-piranha to quit his case. He couldn't do that, of course, but he also didn't want to be eaten by bloodthirsty fish—or lose his face by any of Omar's techniques. *How*, he thought, *can I stay close to them, nail them for the poodle toss, and keep writing my new act all at the same time?*

"Agreed," Gary said.

Omar stood him up, stepped them both down off the platform, and released Gary's arms. Harvey handed the detective a handkerchief.

While Gary dried his face, he became conscious of the fact

that his cop intuition was in conflict with his comic instincts. He knew these guys were guilty. He could walk to his car, call in a phalanx of officers, tear Pacoima Pawn and Loan to pieces, and nail the dwarf and the giant for the murder of Chachi, the possession of face-eating piranha, and probably a dozen other crimes. But how would that help his comedy career, his new routine? He weighed the options on his personal scales of justice and discovered, not surprisingly, that comedy was king.

Harvey stood on the platform. Gary gave him back the wet handkerchief. "You said you knew an agent."

14

that's why my life is worse than yours

THE PROBLEMS WERE many and manifest, and Danny ran through them in his head. One: Mrs. Alemi had reclaimed the small yellow house, so all his personal possessions were now in his office. Two: he didn't have an office because he couldn't pay Harvey a thousand bucks a month *and* pay the rent, so the office had to go. Three: he had to move everything currently in his office to wherever it was he was going to move them. Four: he had nowhere to move them. Five: even if he had somewhere to move them, he would need a truck. Six: he didn't have a truck. Seven: the only person he knew who had a truck was Paul the Pervert.

He called his clown client and arranged for Paul to meet him at the office and help him haul his things somewhere still to be determined. He had to get everything out of the office to avoid paying any more rent; that was priority one. Actually, that was priority two. Priority one was that Danny had an early afternoon appointment with his dentist to clean and whiten his teeth. He would ponder his next landing while his gums were bloodied, his plaque was excavated, and his enamel was invigorated, and then he would meet Paul, load the truck, and drive into his ethereal future with a sparkling smile.

When his teeth were gleaming, the hygienist stepped out of the room, and the dentist slid onto the stool beside the dental chair.

"How are you, Dan?" Dr. Greenburg said.

"I've been better, Doc," Danny said.

"I know what you mean," Greenburg said.

"My life's lousy right now," Danny said.

"Mine's worse," Greenburg said.

"Want to bet?" Danny said, only half-kidding.

"Twenty bucks," Greenburg said, also kidding by half.

"You're on," Danny said.

"You go first," Greenburg said, moving to the sink to wash his hands.

"My fourth horse lost by a nose, and then my mother died," Danny said. It occurred to him as he told Greenburg the story of his bad bet and his mother dying and the snowball effect of losing his house and his office and having nowhere to go and how it almost didn't matter because even if he had somewhere to go, the only way to get there was his pervert clown client...it occurred to him as he told the dentist his sad sack story that there might be some people in the world who thought he was shallow for equating a lost horse race with the death of his mother. He wondered if Greenburg was one of those people.

I'm not emotionally shallow, Danny thought. He'd had a moment in Linda's hospital room, right after Mike had sworn his oath and their mother had died, while he was standing at the window and looking out into the night, where his eyes became damp with tears. It happened while his brother was weeping a bedside ocean. Like Mike, he had felt a wave of sadness in the pit of his stomach and continued to feel it as it climbed past his chest and into his throat. Like Mike, he expected the wave to wash through him like a tsunami, but only the last bit of salt-water foam came to his eyes.

That didn't make him an *unfeeling freak,* which is what Mike had said he was as they'd left the hospital. He had deep feelings too. It was just that by the time they reached the surface he had reconciled them; that's all. He was a quick study as far as his feelings went. He knew what he felt, and he felt it fast and was done with it and was ready for the next race, the next bet, the next client, and the next deal. His fourth horse had lost by a nose, and his mother had died, and a bad-luck chain of events had happened to him that sucked rocks to the point that his life was twenty bucks lousier than Greenburg's. He had felt what he felt and that was as far as those feelings went. The point was that he had feelings too.

He looked over to the sink to see the dentist's reaction. His first thought was, *Two tens or a twenty, whatever's easier for you, Doc.* His second thought was, *What the fuck?* Greenburg was frozen at the sink, the water running and running, his face focused somewhere far away. Danny waited a full two minutes for Greenburg to turn off the water and say something, but Greenburg didn't move a muscle.

"You okay, Dr. Greenburg?"

Nothing. Greenburg had left the building.

"Doc, you okay?"

Danny thought about getting out of the chair. Maybe the dentist was in the middle of some kind of standing stroke, if there was such a thing. Or maybe he had fallen asleep on his feet, like a cow. "Dr. Greenburg?"

Greenburg turned off the water. He didn't move his mouth at all, yet words came out. "My dog, Chachi, was murdered." He turned his head to face Danny. His eyes were clouded with pain and desperation.

"I'm sorry to hear that. Are you sure it was murder? Dogs don't usually—"

"He was murdered, and my wife can't live if he's dead. I caught her hanging herself at high noon today."

"Jesus, Doc. Your wife committed suicide today?"

"No. I caught her, literally."

"Is she okay?"

"She's looking for Chachi."

"But you said he was murdered."

"I lied to her. I told her he was alive and lost and that she and her Dr. Seuss reading group friends would find him. I told her we would find him. Now, if we don't find him, she's going to keep killing herself until I'm not there to stop her."

Danny decided to let the "Dr. Seuss reading group friends" part of the story go for now. "But you won't find him. He's dead."

Greenburg moved from the sink to the stool beside the dental chair, sat down, and put on latex gloves. "That's why my life is worse than yours." He grabbed a mirror and a miniature medieval torture blade off the tool tray and moved his hands into position. Danny opened his mouth, and the dentist checked the hygienist's handiwork. "I'd pay any amount of money to bring him back."

Danny closed his eyes for five seconds and then opened them and turned his head so that Greenburg had to take his tools out of Danny's mouth. "You're saying if someone could bring your dead dog back to life, if that sort of voodoo were possible, that you would pay that person?"

"Any amount."

"Twenty thousand dollars?"

"Yes."

"Thirty thousand?"

"Where do I sign?"

"Fifty?"

"If they could bring back my dog."

"Seventy-five thousand dollars?"

"I'd sell my soul to give Chachi life."

Danny looked into Greenburg's eyes. They were unfocused and red from stress and exhaustion, but he decided that the dentist had spoken the truth and at the same time made a mental note—while sitting up and getting out of the chair—not to let Greenburg put the sharp tools back in his mouth until the next appointment.

note—while sitting up and getting out of the chair—not to let Greenburg put the sharp tools back in his mouth until the next appointment.

84

15
it's a lovely casket

THE GEORGE EDWARDS MORTUARY in Mission Hills was a massive, one-story, free-standing structure on Chatsworth near Sepulveda that looked a lot like an Olive Garden restaurant —and might as well have been one because when you were here, most likely you were family. The exterior walls were white-washed brick, and a somber dark-green awning at the roofline encircled the entire building. Italian statuary of robed religious men flanked the front entrance. Marble fountains gurgled watery white noise to block out the sounds of traffic and put full focus on the recently deceased. A tall hedge acted as a fence to give privacy to those who had lost a loved one. A covered carport ran the length of the east side of the building. A hearse was parked there, waiting for the next parade of mourners to follow it to the cemetery.

Inside was a stately maze of large and small public and private rooms that were hushed and solemn like a library or a court of law. The floors were covered with thick burgundy carpeting. Each room was softly lit and furnished with dignified leather sofas and side chairs, oak tables with brass lamps, and framed pastoral paintings of, well, pastures that left little doubt as to the business at hand—embalming, arranging, and conducting funerals.

Mike stood with George Edwards in the display center, where a dozen caskets were showcased like Porsches in a dealership showroom, including pin spots on tracks, plush upholstered walls, custom oak shelving, and decorative informational plaques.

"I don't know, George," Mike said. "They all seem masculine to me, very handsome, very strong. I can't picture my mother in any of them."

"I understand," George said.

It was what he always said. They were the two most important words in the funeral business, and he had been saying them, no matter the mortuary discussion, for thirty years. He was sixty-two, about six feet tall and trim, with impeccable ramrod posture. His full head of swept-back hair and manicured beard were gray. He wore wire-rimmed glasses. His suit was tailored. His shoes were shined. He wore a gold watch and a wedding band but no other jewelry. He was kind and courtly and formal, with a ceremonious air and a deep soothing voice that had calmed countless bereaved families.

"I want her to look as beautiful as she was," Mike said.

"She will. There was minimal putrefaction. I'll do the cosmetology myself. She'll be beautiful and peaceful, I promise."

"Thanks, George. You agree that a business suit is best?"

"I do. Your mother was a professional woman to the last moment. I think she'd be pleased to be interred in feminine yet classic business clothing."

Mike nodded. It was Wednesday afternoon. He had said good-bye to Bonnie, his assistant, left Wasserman and Waddell with a box of his personal office possessions, and driven mindlessly around the Valley for...he didn't know how long, trying unsuccessfully to make sense of his unexpected dismissal. Somewhere in Sylmar, he had called Marcy, his wife, who was visiting her parents in Paramus with their daughters, and given her the bad news, which she took badly. Then he had stopped for lunch at a taco joint (he couldn't remember where, he was so distracted) and fallen asleep in the car in the taco joint parking lot like a homeless man. He awoke soaked with sweat after an unsettling dream and had driven to the Mission Hills mortuary to finalize the funeral arrangements with George. His mother was in the reposing room, waiting for hair, makeup, and wardrobe. The funeral was scheduled for Saturday.

"There's a casket in the viewing room I'd like you to see," George said. "I don't have it on the display floor, but I can have one delivered before Saturday. It has soft rounded edges and a matte maple finish with a Rosetan interior. Thirty-three hundred. I think it would be perfect for Linda."

They walked through the maze of carpeted hallways, turned a corner, and went through double doors into the huge viewing room. There were sofas and chairs and tables and lamps lining the perimeter walls, leaving a large center area that could accommodate one hundred folding chairs or more. At the far end, bathed in a gentle spotlight, plush curtains on either side, was an open casket.

As they crossed the long room, Mike heard George talking to him about the casket. He heard the mortician mention something about non-corrosive linings and something else about seals and gauges and something further about weights. But none of what George was saying sunk in because there was a dead woman in the casket.

Being around sick people was uncomfortable for Mike—he could hardly tolerate it. But being around dead people was another level of discomfort altogether. After he was done weeping in the hospital, he had been so edgy and anxious around Linda's lifeless body that he couldn't stay focused during the conversation of transporting her to the mortuary, couldn't concentrate on the hospital paperwork. He had done it, of course, because he was the adult in the room, but he had been woozy and nauseous and weak-kneed until he'd left the hospital and went to Wasserman and Waddell, where he had been fired for no good reason.

They arrived at the casket. The dead woman's eyes were closed. She was very old. Her cheeks were blushed. She was wearing lipstick. Her hair was done. It looked like she was sleeping. But she wasn't.

"This is Mrs. Peterson. She was ninety-five. Your mother will look at least this good." George said. "It's a lovely casket."

"Mr. Edwards," said a calm and quiet mortuary woman in dark business attire. She had opened a viewing room side door and was leaning in around it. "I'm sorry to interrupt, but Heather Thomson is on line two. She's emotional and would like to speak with you."

George nodded at the mortuary woman, and she shut the door and vanished. "Can you excuse me for five minutes? I'm sorry, but Ms. Thomson is in distress."

"Of course," Mike said, and George walked to the same side door and exited.

As soon as he was gone, Judd Martin stepped out from behind the curtains, pointed to Mrs. Peterson, and said to Mike, "One day soon, this is you."

Mike was blown back as if shot with a cannon ball. He had already been out of sorts simply by standing so close to a dead body, and now his heart was racing, and his eyes were blinking, and his head was pounding, and his palms were sweating. "Jesus Christ, Judd. What the hell are you doing here?"

"Following you."

"Following me?"

Even as Mike was asking the question, his brain was accessing the morning meeting at Wasserman and Waddell, where Stan and Ira had said that Judd was mentally ill, emotionally unstable, severely imbalanced, and dangerously volatile. He had been arrested for assault and battery five times and gone to psychiatric prison in Nevada and Colorado. What had Stan said? *"He's a serial stalker, and it always ends with extreme violence perpe-*

trated on whoever he's stalking." Right, that was it. The partners had blamed Judd's bankruptcy on Mike so Judd wouldn't stalk the firm, so that his anger and aggression would be pointed in Mike's direction, so if he stalked anyone, it would be Mike. And now he *was* stalking Mike. What the fuck? *What the fucking fuck?*

Judd stepped into the light, away from the curtains, and walked toward the casket, toward Mike. "You killed me. I'm a dead man. I'm a zombie."

He had the look of a zombie, Mike thought, backing away from him. He was a massive, barrel-chested man, and his red-ruddy complexion was on fire. His red-gray hair was wild, untamed. His eyes were crazed, the eyes of a man who hadn't slept in weeks or months or ever. He hadn't shaved, and he was filthy, as if he had rolled in the dirt at one of his bankrupt construction sites. He wore ragged blue jeans, heavy work boots, and a camo hunting vest with no shirt. He was a mad mess. "It wasn't me," Mike said.

"You took two mil from my account, and the banks called in the loans, and I lost everything. You're a rogue accountant. That's the word on the street."

"That's not the word on the street. There's no word on the street. There is no street. I didn't take two cents out of your account. What are you talking about?"

Mike backpedalled across the viewing room, which right now felt as big as a football field. Judd followed him, facing him, a few strides away. Mike wanted to make a run for it but knew he wasn't fast enough or far enough away to get out of the room before Judd could grab him.

"I'm talking about putting you in that coffin," Judd said, and he pulled a hunting knife from a leather sheath that was strapped to his leg. It was a huge, nasty Bowie knife, more than a foot long with a nine-inch blade, one side serrated, and a burl wood handle.

Mike's eyes went wide when he saw the knife. *Jesus Christ,* he thought, *where the hell is George? Heather Thomson, whoever she is, definitely isn't in more distress than me.* He realized all at once how much he had to lose here. He thought of his daughters, and his knees buckled. "Whoa, whoa, come on, calm down, Judd," he said, trying to smile and maybe change the tone of the moment. "You can't kill me in a funeral home, right? There's too much irony in that."

The humor was wasted on Judd. "I can kill you any goddamn place I want, any goddamn time I want. There are no rules."

And then Judd took two big strides, grabbed Mike by his shoulder, getting a handful of Mike's suit jacket, and walked him back across the viewing room to Mrs. Peterson's casket, holding the knife to Mike's carotid artery. The blade was cold, and Mike wondered if that was where the expression *cold steel* came from.

"Please, Judd," Mike said, the words fighting past the lump in his throat. "For God's sake, my mother died last night."

"Swell. You can join her. Get in the casket," Judd said when they reached Mrs. Peterson.

"What?" Mike said.

"Get in the casket."

"It's occupied."

"It's not a fucking toilet. She's dead. Take her out and get in."

"I'm not taking her—"

He couldn't finish the sentence because he felt the knife pressing harder against his neck, and it scared him to silence. He didn't think he had pissed himself, *but there's still time for that*, he thought.

"Do it," Judd said.

Mike knew he had no choice. He reached in, grabbed Mrs. Peterson under the arms, and lifted and dragged her out of the casket, and put her on the floor. Waves of nausea rolled through him. He could puke any minute.

"Now you," Judd said.

Mike climbed up and slid into the casket. He was sweating profusely. He couldn't feel his hands.

Judd moved behind him, at the end of the casket, leaned down and put his mouth by Mike's ear, the Bowie still at Mike's throat.

"From now until the end, I'm in every shadow, watching you, measuring you. I'm a zombie, and it's the Day of the Dead."

Mike felt Judd move away, felt the blade lifted from his neck. He couldn't move. He wanted to, but he simply couldn't. He realized his eyes were closed. He wondered how long ago he had shut them.

"Unconventional choice, Mike," George said. "Very unorthodox. Thirty years in the funeral business, and this is a first for me. Trying it on for size when the deceased is already...well, anyway, what do you think?"

Mike opened his right eye. His left eye wouldn't obey the command. "It's a lovely casket."

16
your clear, durable, all-weather agent

PAUL THE PERVERT used an overburdened bungee cord to tie down the ragged blue tarp that inadequately covered the dangerously tall and shaky mountain of Danny's office and personal furniture that had been stacked helter-skelter in the bed of the clown's battered Ford pickup.

"You won't be able to see who's behind you," Danny said.

"Way I look at it, they got to see me," Paul said.

He wore the rat-shit clown costume, the creepy makeup—with black eyes, bloody nose, and barbed wire teeth—the rainbow wig, and the supinated Docksiders. A vile, half-chewed cigar hung from his mouth. He smelled like a decaying dumpster filled with rotting food. In other words, Danny thought, about status quo since yesterday's audition. He imagined that Paul had not slept, bathed, or changed his clothes since their meeting—or possibly since he had been electrocuted on Fairfax.

They pulled away from the dilapidated two-story strip mall and drove south on Reseda to Sherman Way, made a left, and went east to Woodman, where they turned into the Ralphs parking lot. Danny stopped the Pathfinder as far from the store as possible—no need to subject innocent bystanders to the pervert clown unless necessary—and the pickup parked beside him.

Danny's clothes, files, and camera gear were piled in the back seat. His hula dancer lamp was riding shotgun next to the dehydrated-dry-and-shriveled-brown dead fern that was now vibrant and green and alive—the fern Jenny Stone had breathed on. He lifted the fern, got out of the car, and walked to Paul's open window. "Wait here."

"I'll take roast beef on a roll," Paul said.

"No you won't," Danny said. "You'll eat later."

"Hope so," the clown said. "Ever since I got electrocuted, my bowels do weird things I can't control. It's worse when I'm hungry. You'll see."

Danny threw up a little in his throat, put on his shades, and walked across the lot to the grocery store. It was like crossing Egypt. The temperature was one hundred and five degrees but it felt like one fifty on the tarmac. Baking in the smog, the sea of cars was inhumanly hot. He could feel solar flares radiating off their chassis.

Inside, he was met by an arctic blast of air conditioning. There was a late afternoon crowd, and half a dozen registers were open. Checker number three, at the far end of the store, was Jenny Stone.

Danny walked down the row of registers, grabbed a random construction magazine from the rack, and got in line. Jenny didn't notice him until she had scanned his magazine and looked to see who was building an outdoor deck in this hellish weather.

"Hi, Jenny," Danny said. "I don't know if you remember me."

"Danny Miller. We met yesterday. I remember," she said, looking at her line. There was no one behind him. She held up the magazine. "Are you a talent agent and a carpenter?"

"Yes, I mean, no, no, I'm not a carpenter. Yes, talent agent. No, carpenter."

"Then why are you buying a build-your-own-outdoor-deck magazine?"

"I'm not. I mean, I am, but I'm—what I mean is I came to talk to you about this." He put the fern on the checkout ramp. "Are you scamming me?"

It took her a second to recognize the plant, and then she did. "No."

"You breathed on it, and it came back to life?"

"Yes."

There's something different about her today, Danny thought. *Not everything, but something, maybe one thing, that's night-and-day different from yesterday. What is it?* "Plants, pets, people. That's what you said. If they're dead, you can breathe life into them. You told me that in my office. I heard you say those words— plants, pets, people. I mean, look at this plant. Is this true, or are you playing me for a fool?"

"It's true." She checked her line. Still no one behind him, but down by the juice aisle, there was a woman with a full cart heading for her register.

In that same moment, Danny realized what had changed since they met in his office—she was wearing a bit of blush, a little lip gloss, and a pretty shade of eye shadow. She wasn't a little mouse today; she was a little mouse with makeup. She had worn none at all to her talent agent interview, but to check groceries she had put on mascara? It was curious to him, but he didn't have time to think it through right now. "Your mother said you should use your talent to make money."

"My mother was wrong."

"Your mother was right."

"You said entertainment was a tough business."

"I said I would think about it and get back to you if I came up with anything, and I came up with something."

He saw a glimmer, a faint spark of hope in her mascaraed eyes. "What?"

"The way we use your talent to make money is...we get

people to pay you...to breathe life into death. It's so simple, it's genius."

He watched her look down at the build-your-own-outdoor-deck magazine as if one of the feature articles, perhaps the one about the latest floor-abrasion technologies, would help her remove the abrasion from her life and leave a clear, durable, all-weather finish. *That's me*, he thought, catching a ghosted glimpse of his handsome self behind the price of the magazine on her checkout screen, *your clear, durable, all-weather agent.*

"How will we find them," Jenny said, "these people?"

"We don't have to find them. They're everywhere."

The full-cart woman was behind him. She was overweight, and everything about her was orange—her hair, nails, makeup, clothes, shoes, everything. She looked like a pumpkin. Danny looked in the Pumpkin's cart and saw can after can of cat food. He thought of Greenburg's misery and said to the Pumpkin, "Do you have a pet at home?"

"I have a cat," the Pumpkin said, perking up and looking for the hidden camera. "His name is Frodo. He looks like a Hobbit. Am I on TV?" She took out her smart phone and pulled up a picture of him. *Damn*, Danny thought, *he does look like a Hobbit.*

"We're all on TV," Danny said. "But this is much more important than being on television. This is a matter of life and death."

"Oh my," the Pumpkin said.

"If Frodo died, God forbid, would you pay to breathe life back into him?"

The Pumpkin looked at Danny and Jenny and at the picture of Frodo and went from shock at the question to sadness to grief —a vast emotional journey that took two seconds there and back. "That's a terrible thing to say to me. Why would you say that?"

"Because it's a matter of life and death," Danny said. "If Frodo was hit by a car and was dead in the street, would you pay to bring him back to life?"

"Yes," the Pumpkin said, tears coming to her eyes. "Poor Frodo..."

"If he fell off the roof and died?"

"Yes, yes..." the Pumpkin said, tears spilling over and running down her cheeks.

"If he was killed by a coyote?"

"Oh my God, yes, I would..."

"If he fell into Silver Lake and drowned."

"Please, please, stop, I would, I would..."

Shoppers at adjacent registers noticed the crying Pumpkin and watched the show. The Pumpkin saw them and held her phone out so they could see her poor dead cat. Jenny offered the Pumpkin a box of tissues. She grabbed two and dabbed her eyes.

"It's all right. Nothing happened," Danny said. "Frodo's fine. He's home and probably waiting for you by the front door. Now, here's the big question, for all the marbles, how much would you pay to bring him back? Final answer?"

The Pumpkin blew her nose and said, "Anything. Oh my, everything."

"You win," Danny said.

"So I am on TV?" the Pumpkin said, brightening again.

Danny nodded and pointed to the multiple Ralphs security cameras overhead and then turned his attention to Jenny, feeling emboldened. He removed a Miller Talent Agency contract from his pocket and put it on the conveyor belt. "I want to sign you, Jenny. I want to represent you. I want you to be my client."

"You do?"

"I do," he said, handing her the pen people used to sign credit card receipts and personal checks. "It's a ninety-day deal. It says I represent you exclusively in all national and global media. Page three has a clause that spells out my fees and expenses—contract, administration, headshot photography, audition video, postage, phone calls, travel, meals, meetings— you get paid back out of my commissions. It's standard, non-signatory stuff. What do you say?"

"It doesn't sound like entertainment."

"Not yet. First, we establish your talent in the entrepreneurial marketplace, and then the whole, wide, multi-media world will knock on your door—movies, books, television, all of it."

Jenny looked at the contract, looked at Danny, and looked at the Pumpkin, who held up her photo of Frodo. Then she took the pen and signed the contract.

Danny countersigned and said, "That's a hundred for today, contract fee. Cash is better than a check. I don't take cards."

While Jenny reached for her purse beside the register, the Pumpkin said, "Do you want to represent me too?"

"Absolutely not," Danny said, leaning in and speaking softly in her ear. "But with your financial support and his good looks, Frodo could be famous."

17

the deep end of the dark water

ON HIS WAY home from the George Edwards Mortuary, Mike called the police to report Judd Martin for forcing him into Mrs. Peterson's coffin and holding a knife to his neck. He told the desk sergeant that the bankrupt real estate developer and contractor was stalking him and claiming to be a zombie. "Stalked by a real estate zombie, got it," the sergeant said. "Hold on a minute, I'll file your complaint under 'No One Here Believes You.'"

Then Mike called Marcy at her parents' house in Paramus, a phone call that went worse than the conversation with the desk sergeant. Now, in addition to being one part furious and one part freaked out about her husband losing his job at Wasserman and Waddell, she was all parts positively not flying home so long as there was a crazy man with a knife stalking him. In fact, there was no way—*no way in hell*, she had said—that she and the girls were moving back to Woodland Hills *ever*, unless Mike could confirm that the crazy man with the knife was behind bars. Marcy had let Mike talk to his daughters only after making him swear he wouldn't mention anything about being fired or stalked. He had tried to sound upbeat, like things in the Valley were clicking along as always, but his life was falling apart, and he didn't think he had pulled it off. "Get some sleep, Dad," Bethany, his fifteen-year-old, had said. "You sound beat up."

He was beat-up. What a miserable couple of days it had been. He told himself he would start dieting tomorrow and stopped at the In-N-Out Burger on Ventura, near his house, and overate himself into a stupor—two Double Doubles, two fries, a root beer and a chocolate shake. Then, buzzed on fat, salt, and sugar, he drove home to pass out.

His house was across Ventura, north of the Boulevard, on Penfield near Hatteras. It was a 1960s California ranch, slab-on-grade, long and narrow with a sloping roofline and flower boxes beneath bay windows. An attached two-car garage was at the south end, the bedrooms were at the north end, and the public rooms were between them. It was a blue-gray house that had faded over the years to gray-blue. Mike and Marcy had bought it fifteen years ago, when Wasserman and Waddell first hired him.

Since moving in, they had redone the kitchen and bathrooms and closets, laid wood floors from end to end, replaced the windows, put in a pool and new air conditioning units, upgraded the plumbing, added a sunroom, and refurnished to their heart's content. This was going to be the year, with his partnership, that they were going to redo the roof, resurface the driveway, replant the landscaping, and repaint the place.

They were going to do this with Mike's raise and partner profit participation because there was no equity left in the house. Mike had maxed it out and refinanced at a lower rate enough times over the years that his mortgage payment was only somewhat higher than when they had originally purchased the property, but his mortgage amount was considerably higher. His equity was gone and gone with it was his safety net, his margin for economic error. Mike and Marcy had spent and spent and saved nothing. *I'm in the same boat as my clients,* he thought as he pulled into his driveway. *Where the hell did the money go? Why the hell didn't we save more? What the hell will happen to us?*

He also thought, *Who the hell's truck is that?*

Backed up to his garage in such a way that he couldn't get past it to park inside was a beat-to-shit Ford pickup. It was always Marcy's Honda hybrid that blocked his access—either it was too close to the middle of the garage for him to fit his five-year-old Acura sedan inside or it was left in front of the door (like the Ford). But her car was at the Park 'N Fly on West Century Boulevard, and so he had thought, on the way home from the In-N-Out, at the end of this miserable couple of days, maybe he could at least and finally find some solace by actually parking inside his garage instead of in the driveway. Maybe that small moment would have signified he had bottomed out and his luck had changed. Maybe it would have propelled him forward to find a job, lose some weight, and reassemble the pieces of his life. A man's fate had turned, he had seen on *Duck Dynasty*, on less than that. Now even that moment had been taken from him.

He parked facing the Ford, grill to grill, got out of his Acura, and walked around the side of his house to the backyard, looking for the owner of the pickup, completely missing Danny's Pathfinder parked in the shadows of the far side of the horseshoe driveway. It was possible that his wife had scheduled some kind of pool repair and not told him, but there was nobody working on his pumps or filters. Very often, the girls would be out here when he got home from work, swimming before dinner, making a racket and a half. But the house was dark and quiet.

Except it wasn't. The lights were on inside the garage, and he heard someone talking—or singing—in there. His brain began to burn. How could this be happening?

He moved to the back garage door and tried the handle, locked. He listened again. Yes, someone was in his garage. *Someone was singing in his garage.* He took out his keys, opened the door, stepped into the garage, and stopped breathing.

The two-car space was filled with Key Largo furniture. One side was an office; the other side was a bedroom. A Tiki bar with a hula dancer lamp (plugged into the electric garage door opener directly above it) was the room divider.

Some kind of disgusting clown was standing in front of a blue screen singing a foul-mouthed version of "Farmer in the Dell" while being filmed by Danny. The clown was holding a blow-up sex doll and was doing vile things to it. Neither his brother nor the clown exhibited the slightest bit of shame or embarrassment upon Mike's entrance. Indeed, Danny looked at Mike and gestured for him to remain silent until the clown was finished singing and doing whatever it was he was doing to the doll.

The scene was so surreally revolting, so shockingly nauseating, that Mike didn't at first feel his own rage. What he felt instead was that somewhere inside him a line of switches, like in the cockpit of a fighter jet, switches inside him that had never before been touched, were now being toggled on, one at time, all in a row down the line. As each switch clicked on, lights flashed and bells rang and he lost a little more of himself, got a little bit closer to the deep end of the dark water.

He stayed silent not because Danny had told him to but because he was processing the fact that his brother had somehow for some reason moved both his talent agency and his bedroom into the garage—and had brought this sub-human clown creature with him. And then the last switch switched, and the last light flashed, and the last bell rang, and he couldn't keep the screaming insanity inside him. "What the fuck, Danny?" he said, shouting at the top of his lungs. "What the fuck?"

"Cut, cut. Jesus, Mike. I told you to be quiet," Danny said. "Now we have to go again. That was a good one too, Paul."

"I like this doll," the clown said. "I'm calling her Jackie."

"You can't work here. You can't live here. Get the hell out of my garage," Mike said to his brother.

Danny moved to Paul and made some adjustments to the light. "I'm not leaving, Mike. This is where I am now."

Mike took an angry step toward Danny. "This is *not* where

you are now. What the hell does that mean, this is where you are now?" He was red in the face and breathing fast and heavy, not hyperventilating, but filling with adrenalin at a furious pace.

"It means you swore an oath on Mom's dying heart that when the very bad thing happened to me or to you or to both of us, that you would watch over me and take care of me, whatever that meant, whatever was necessary," Danny said. He walked back to the camera, refocused the lens. "You swore that when the very bad thing happened, anything you could do you would do. You swore it now and forever."

Mike blinked and blinked and blinked and blinked. He could feel his circuits and synapses snapping and sparking and overloading. He could physically feel himself losing his grip on reality.

"Well, guess what, Mike? The very bad thing happened. Mom died, I lost my race, I lost my house, and I lost my office," Danny said. "I have no money and nowhere to go, so this is where I am now, and I'm not leaving. Here we go, Paul. And...action."

Paul the Pervert sang the sick version of "Farmer in the Dell" and did unthinkable things to Jackie while Danny worked the camera.

Mike stood wide-eyed, watching them, looking around his garage, sweating bullets, breathing like an angry bull, and then found one final un-switched switch in his head. It toggled on, and he felt his mind go haywire.

Beside him, sitting on the built-in shelving, was the Makita chainsaw he had bought from Paul Bunyan all those years ago. Mike moved to the Makita, plugged it into a long extension cord, plugged the cord into an outlet, fired up the chainsaw, and walked toward his brother with bad intent.

The sound of the chainsaw churning echoed so loudly inside the garage that Danny had to scream at the top of his lungs to be heard. "What the fuck, Mike? Are you kidding me? What are you doing?"

Mike knew what he was doing; he was going to spill Danny's guts all over the garage. Danny backed away, and Mike walked after him, holding the Makita in front of him like a broadsword. And then Danny's back was up against the garage door, and Mike was in front of him, the chainsaw three feet from Danny's chest.

"Pull the plug, Paul. Pull the goddamn plug," Danny said, yelling across the garage at the clown.

"No way," Paul said, yelling back. "Do it, fat man."

"I'm not fat," Mike said, staring at Danny but screaming at the clown.

"You look like you ate a beach ball," Paul said.

"I'm losing weight tomorrow," Mike said.

"So what's the problem?" Paul said. "Tomorrow's tomorrow. Now is now. Cut the man in half."

"*What's the problem?*" Mike said. "The problem is my mother died—she was my saint, and now she's gone. The problem is I lost my job—instead of promoting me to partner, they fired me and killed my career. The problem is a real estate zombie with a hunting knife is stalking me. The problem is my wife and children are in Paramus, and they're not coming home until I straighten everything out, and I can't straighten everything out because I don't have any money. That's the goddamn fucking problem."

He moved the Makita two feet from his brother's body.

"I can help you, Mike," Danny said, panicking.

Mike kept the chainsaw roaring. "How?"

Danny told him about Greenburg and the dead dog and the amount of money the dentist would pay to bring the dog back to life and about Jenny breathing life into death. "I'll pay you. Seventy-five/twenty-five split."

Mike moved the chainsaw one foot from Danny.

"Sixty-forty, sixty-forty, sixty-forty," Danny said.

Mike moved the chainsaw six inches closer.

"Okay, okay, okay, fifty-fifty, fifty-fifty. We'll be partners. Jesus Christ."

Mike looked into his brother's eyes and saw a reflection of himself as a madman with a chainsaw and then looked deeper and saw the two of them wearing towels as capes and running around the small yellow house in Canoga Park saving the world from disaster, and he powered the Makita down and wept like a child.

"Your brother's a pussy," Paul said.

"I know," Danny said.

Mike looked at his brother and at the clown and at the chainsaw. There was too much emotion in play for him to process the proceedings, too much crazy shit hitting the fan all at once. And now here was his promotion to partner? Really? Linda had said something very bad was going to happen to them and something very bad *had* happened to them. He had sworn an oath on her dying heart—*whatever is necessary*. He had sworn it forever. "This is insane," he said.

"No," Danny said, pointing at the clown holding Jackie. "That's insane."

thursday

18

to audition the tick or not to audition the tick

DANNY WOKE up disoriented and soon wished he could have stayed that way. Instead, the clouds cleared and he remembered where he was and, worse, why he was here. The smell of motor oil, lawn tools, bicycles, and kerosene made the air heavy and hard to breathe—like the inside of a Jiffy Lube. Danny's dying-animal office fan struggled to blow a breeze over the bed, but it was no use because it was a hundred degrees in this un-air conditioned, two-car sweatbox.

It wasn't ideal, reaching rock bottom in Mike's garage, but thanks to *The Oath*, as he now called it, his new home office was free for as long as it had to be, and it had to be three years because he owed Harvey a grand a month for exactly that long. But three years, three days, or three hours, he would have to find a cheap window air conditioner and mount it in one of the soot-encased, cobweb-covered windows. If life wasn't sweet, it had to at least be temperature controlled.

And then he remembered how much money Greenburg was going to spend to bring his dead dog back to life: enough to pay off Harvey, get his office back, buy a new car, and bet on a few fast horses. All Danny had to do was convince the distraught dentist that breathing life into death was possible. He got out of bed, pulled on his pants, stepped over Mike's chain saw, found the remote on the Tiki bar, and punched the button.

The garage door groaned and then lifted. Paul's truck was gone—thank God—and Danny stepped outside. It was roasting hot, a hundred five at ten in the morning. He imagined that some San Fernando Valley housewife could hold a chicken in a pot, stand outside for a few hours, and then bring it inside and serve it for lunch.

Danny put his hands up to block the sun and saw a vintage Impala parked behind his Pathfinder and a man standing at the front door. The man was wearing a suit, holding the jacket, slung over his shoulder, with his right hand. He had a gun in a holster attached to his belt in the middle of his back. *Cop*, Danny thought. *Detective.*

The man looked at Danny, stopped knocking, and said, "Mike Miller?"

"Mike's not here," Danny said. "He went to a storage unit to get some clothes for our mother. She died yesterday, Wednesday, early in the morning. It is Thursday, right?"

"All day," the man said, coming down the driveway toward Danny and putting out his hand. "Detective Shuler. Sorry about your mother."

"Danny, Mike's brother," Danny said, shaking hands with Gary and nodding thanks for the condolences.

"Your mother kept her clothes in a storage unit?"

"No. That's just where they are now. Why are you looking for Mike?"

"He called in a complaint. Said he was being stalked by a real estate zombie."

"You're the zombie cop?"

"Zombies, vampires, anything voodoo. Know anything about that, somebody stalking your brother?"

Danny did not care for cops. Five years ago, he had signed a Shirley Temple look-alike who'd sang and danced and acted so miserably that it physically hurt to watch her work. But the girl's mother had money, and Danny liked money, so the girl became a client. After ninety days—and five grand in cold cash—the mother opted out of the deal and sued him for fraud and emotional damage. Danny had to sell his house to hire a lawyer to settle the case outside of criminal court. After that, he had moved in with his mother, and Mrs. Alemi had called him the Persian version of a flimflam man. Anyway, the detective who'd investigated him was a tick that had burrowed under his skin and given him a disease that hurt like hell. Danny definitely didn't want a cop hanging around looking for zombies and finding a talent agent who'd settled out of court instead.

"Nope," Danny said, turning and walking back to the garage. "I'll tell him you stopped by, Detective..."

"Shuler. Gary Shuler."

"Shuler. I'll tell him."

Instead of heading back to his Impala, Gary followed Danny to the garage. "You live in your brother's garage?" Gary said.

"My new home office, courtesy of Pacoima Pawn and Loan," Danny said, thinking, *Jesus, a tick. I knew it.*

"Pacoima Pawn and Loan?" Gary said.

They reached the front of the open garage and stood facing each other in the narrow piece of shade the house provided. In two hours, when the sun was overhead, there would be no shade at all anywhere in Los Angeles, and it would be a hundred nine.

"You've heard of it?" Danny said, and he took a closer look at Detective Tick. Five-ten, maybe one sixty, athletic build, about fifty or a little younger, curly hair the color of sand, clean shaven, nothing unusual about his appearance, just an average Joe. Except for the eyes. There was something skewed about his eyes, something odd that Danny couldn't put his finger on.

"Wait...Danny Miller?" Gary said.

"That's right," Danny said.

"Miller Talent Agency, that Danny Miller?"

Shit, Danny thought. "That's me."

Gary smiled. "Harvey and Omar told me about you. Harvey

said, 'Tell Danny Boy I said he should audition you and offer you a contract and get you on Kimmel.'"

Danny wasn't expecting anything remotely like that sentence. Suddenly Shuler wasn't a random tick detective. He had burrowed in with Harvey and Omar, and Danny wasn't sure how to play his hand. "What do you do, Detective?"

"I'm a stand-up comedian."

"You are not."

"I play the clubs."

"I've never heard of you."

"I'm up-and-coming."

"Good luck with that."

And then they stood there. Danny looked over Gary's shoulder at the Impala, conveying the vibe that it was time for Shuler to go and for Danny to return to his life in Mike's garage. But the vibe shot right over the detective's head.

"I can audition right now," Gary said.

"You can?" Danny said in a way that meant: *no, you can't.*

"Give me five minutes. I'm working on a new act that's off the hook. Five minutes, Danny. You're going to sign me up and get me on Kimmel."

To audition the tick or not to audition the tick, that was the question. *Which path would result in less personal pain?* Danny said to himself. He decided they were equally awful choices. "Can I put a shirt on first?"

They went into the garage, and Danny put on a T-shirt and sat on the corner of his pineapple desk. "Five minutes, Detective. Starting now."

Gary went from cop to comedian in less than half a second, which made Danny think that there wasn't any difference between the two.

"I'm *Detective* Gary Shuler, back again, hello, hello, happy to be here, happy to be anywhere. For those of you who don't know me, I'm the cop comedian with the crazy cases you can't believe, and when I say crazy, I mean it's a laugh a minute out there, but you know that, right? Of course you do. Anyway, now I got one that *I* can't believe, and you have to hear it. No, really, you have to. Captive audience. I'm a cop, right? What do you say, crime fans, want to hear a case even I can't believe?"

He paused, hand cupped to his ear as if listening to the laughter, waiting for it to die down, but he was in Mike's garage, and Danny wasn't laughing.

"Okay, then, strap in and hang on and here we go. I get a call one day from a woman who sees a little white poodle get tossed out the back window of a Lexus. I know, I know, not a big deal if the Lexus is sitting in the driveway. But this one was doing seventy-five on the freeway—the car, not the poodle, although the dog might have been doing seventy-five when he went out the window, I'm no good with physics. Anyway, I know what you're thinking: poodle puddle. Not this time. This time the poodle was punted to the side of the road, dead as a doorstop, and the ID tags send me to a broken-hearted dentist addicted to cocaine and gin who says he pawned his car in Pacoima..."

Danny used every ounce of willpower to hold himself in check when what he really wanted to do was jump up and down and scream: *What the fuck, Shuler? Are you kidding me with this shit?*

Gary talked about the Pawn Palace, the black woman with the Civil War sword who could hide a clerk in her cleavage, and the red-bellied piranha practically eating his face off. He laughed at most if not all of his own jokes and reminded Danny it was a laugh a minute out there every sixty seconds or so.

It wasn't a laugh a minute for Danny. This was no joke; this was a nightmare. Shuler's routine petered out after the piranha, although there was a mention of the real estate zombie that wasn't causally motivated—and so felt tacked on—followed by an improvised bit about coming to the house and auditioning for the agent who signed him in a sweltering garage, which was a ballsy assumption by the detective, so it seemed like Shuler didn't know about Jenny and the plan to charge Greenburg up the wazoo to bring Chachi back to life. But definitely the detective was on the case. *"I'm working on a new act,"* the tick had said. *Working on it,* that was the key thing about the new act. The question was whether Danny's play was to get rid of the tick or keep him close. In other words, which choice was the better bet to keep the improvised part improvised and stop the story in its tracks?

If Danny didn't sign Shuler, the rejection might piss the cop off enough that he would dig deeper into the Miller Talent Agency just to cause trouble. He would ask for the client roster and find Jenny. Or go back to Greenburg. Or back to Harvey and Omar. And all of that would be out of Danny's control. Not a good idea when the plan is to bring a dead dog back to life for big bucks. Better to keep the detective close, keep an eye on him as he works on his new act, stay one step ahead of the story, as it were.

Danny went around his desk, opened a drawer and pulled out a contract. "It's a ninety-day deal, Detective," he said. "Standard non-signatory stuff."

19
nature and science and religion and reason

INSTEAD OF SPENDING his lunch hour behind a closed door in his private office drinking a tall Tanqueray and tonic on ice and blowing a few lines of Columbian white powder while his nurses sterilized dental tools down the hall, Dr. Donald Greenburg sat across his desk from a patient named Dan Miller, a talent agent who said his client could breathe life into death. They were waiting for that client, a young woman named Jenny, whose mother was supposed to have dropped her off fifteen minutes ago. They were going to pitch her talent to him, and he was going to pay to have Chachi brought back to the world of the living.

Was he really that desperate? Oh, yes, he was. He had never been more desperate in his life.

Just yesterday, after he had caught Carol committing suicide in their living room and convinced her that Chachi was alive and they could and would find him, she had rallied her Seuss reading group, and they had spent the remainder of Wednesday painting Seuss-like signs to hang across the Valley. They called themselves *Seuss Search And Save*.

This morning, while he was leaving for the office, they were gathered in the driveway, sharing a motivational moment before going forth to post posters.

The excitement with which Carol was approaching her quest, flying high with focus and hope and Percocet and vodka, he knew, would be more than matched by the ensuing *Seuss Crash and Burn*—and subsequent re-suicide—when Chachi wasn't found.

"I went to UCLA dental school," Greenburg said to Danny.

"I see your diplomas," Danny said, gesturing at the framed papers on the wall behind the dentist. He wore a black V-neck T-shirt with jeans and black New Balance running shoes. His sunglasses were up on his head, pushing back his movie star hair.

Greenburg's private office was small, maybe ten by twelve, wood paneled, with one wall of bookshelves containing volumes of dental reading material, a maple desk with a matching credenza behind it, two tan leather chairs in front of the desk for visitors and a tan, two-seat leather sofa on the wall opposite the bookshelves. There was a computer on Greenburg's desk, along with a lamp, various and sundry office supplies, multiple patient folders, a phone, and a small fishbowl with two goldfish swimming endless-mindless-infinite laps around the perimeter, hoping, Greenburg imagined, that just once they would come upon a way out. During lunch, while he sipped gin and snorted coke, he often thought of himself as just another goldfish in the bowl. A wireless printer was on the credenza with multiple photographs of Chachi.

"I'm an educated man," Greenburg said.

"A wall of diplomas, I get it," Danny said.

"So if I'm an educated man with a wall of diplomas, why am I taking time out of my day to wait for a woman who you say can breathe life into death?"

"Because you want your dog back," Danny said, gesturing at the pictures of the poodle.

Greenburg didn't know Danny very well. He barely knew

him at all. Danny was a newer patient with only a few fillings and a couple crowns who liked his teeth to be especially white. He had told Greenburg that a bright smile was the key to new clients. *"Nobody signs with an agent who has yellow teeth,"* Danny had said to him not even a year ago. Maybe it was true. Or maybe Danny was vain. Maybe both. Greenburg had no idea. The truth was that the dentist didn't know any of his patients very well. Even the patients who had been with him for twenty years or more he hardly knew.

He could thank his wife for that. Like the sun, she had mesmerized him, blinded him, kept him in close orbit, and commanded all his energy. He had no friends and no hobbies and no life. Actually, he had Chachi. They both had Chachi. One day soon, he admitted to himself, he would have no one.

He was thinking about how deeply he missed his dog and how insane he was to think that there was a human person on Earth who could raise the dead when one of his nurses knocked on his office door. He told her to come in, and she opened the door and moved aside, and Jenny Stone stepped into the room. The nurse shut the door again, and the three of them were alone.

Danny stood up. To Greenburg, he seemed surprised somehow, thrown for a loop, as if Danny didn't quite recognize her, as if this was some other client, an actress, maybe, or a singer who had gotten her time and date and place wrong, not the Breather of Life.

"Dr. Greenburg," Danny said, "this is my client, Jenny. Jenny, this is my dentist, Dr. Greenburg."

Greenburg did not stand. Instead, he stared at Jenny and tried to decide if she looked like a person who could breathe life into death. She was twenty-eight or nine, five foot six, with the kind of figure that most men find attractive, curvy but thin. She had straight brown hair with golden highlights that was parted on the side and reached below her shoulders. She did not wear glasses, and her eyes were green. She wore a breezy red sundress and leather sandals. Her nails were painted red to match the sundress. She wore makeup and jewelry and was, to his eye, a pretty young woman. Years ago, before his life went off the rails, he would have dreamed about having sex with her. But now he was too far gone for dreams like that.

"My mother was running late," Jenny said. "Sorry about your dog."

"Not as sorry as I am," Greenburg said, gesturing at the chair beside Danny. "Have a seat."

Danny and Jenny both sat down, and Danny told Greenburg the story of the dehydrated-dry-and-shriveled-brown dead fern that Jenny breathed on and how it was now vibrant and green and alive. He showed Greenburg a photo of the plant on his phone. He left out the bit about Omar lifting him up like he was a grade school boy and choking him until he passed out.

Greenburg was unimpressed. The breathing-on-the-plant part is when he realized the whole thing was a con and wished Danny and the woman would leave his office so he could crack the Tanqueray in his credenza, pour a drink, do a line, and face the rest of the afternoon and the rest of his miserable life.

"So I'm supposed to give you cash and, in return, you're going to breathe on my dog and he's going to come back to life?" Greenburg said.

"Absolutely," Danny said.

"And I'm supposed to disregard the fact that such a thing is impossible and against the laws of nature and science and religion and reason?" Greenburg said.

"Yes," Danny said.

"And the proof is the picture of the plant?" Greenburg said.

"It was dead, and then it wasn't," Danny said.

Greenburg was sad and angry and disappointed and forlorn. Chachi was on ice in the garage freezer, and now he would have to bury him in the yard. The Seuss Search and Save posse would fade to failure, and his wife would hang herself one day while he was filling a cavity. This was the only future he could see.

"Either I'm blinded by grief, in which case you are a heartless asshole con man, or I'm a moron, in which case you are a mean-spirited, son-of-a-bitch con man," Greenburg said to Danny. "Probably I'm both, but either way I need to have my head examined for giving you ten minutes of my time."

"It's not a con," Danny said. "I saw it happen. Jenny can—"

"And you," Greenburg said to Jenny, "the fact that you allow yourself to be pimped like this makes you even more pathetic than I am. You should be ashamed of yourself for taking advantage of someone's sadness."

Jenny looked into her lap as if ashamed of herself for taking advantage of someone's sadness.

Greenburg turned his eyes back to Danny. "I would report you both to the police, but they would arrest me for stupidity."

"I'm telling you that—" Danny said.

"That what," Greenburg said, "you're the most unethical talent agent in the history of the entertainment business? I may be at the end of my wife's rope, but even from here I can see that. Now get out of my office, or I *will* call the police."

"Dr. Greenburg—"

"Get out," Greenburg said, "and find another dentist while you're at it."

The dentist stared at Danny, and Danny stared back.

"We're not leaving until you give us a chance," Danny said, sounding nearly as desperate as Greenburg.

Greenburg hit a button on his phone and said into the speaker, "Kathy, call building security, and then call the police. Tell them—"

Before Greenburg could finish his thought, Jenny stood up, put her hand into the fishbowl, grabbed one of the goldfish, and dropped it on the desk in front of the dentist.

"Jesus Christ," Greenburg said, pushing his chair back against the credenza. He looked at Danny, but the talent agent seemed as stunned as he was.

The poor little fish flapped violently on the desk, fighting for its life, and then suffocated and died. It was completely and utterly dead.

They all stared at the fish in silence, and then Greenburg looked up at Jenny and said, "Are you crazy? What the hell was that?"

Jenny said nothing. Greenburg turned to Danny. "She killed my goldfish. It's dead on my desk."

And then Jenny leaned over and put her face close to the fish and gently blew on it. She stood again, and her lips turned ever so slightly up at the corners.

Greenburg didn't know what to do. He started to speak, but Danny cut him off with a wave and said, "Wait."

There was silence for thirty seconds, and then the fish started to flap around the desk, slowly at first and then like a house on fire. Jenny took the fish in her hand and placed it back in the bowl. It commenced swimming circles, completely and perfectly alive. She made eye contact with Greenburg and then walked out of the office.

"Seventy-five thousand in cash," Danny said. "Any questions?"

20

the agony of all this defeat

IN ADDITION to owning sixty-four homes in the Valley, Mrs. Alemi owned three self-storage facilities. She chose the one in Chatsworth, on De Soto near Plummer, to deposit the contents of the small yellow house until Mike could make arrangements to move them elsewhere.

"I had a great deal of respect and admiration for your mother, Michael," Mrs. Alemi said as she unlocked the roll-up door to a double unit. "I'm sorry for your loss. Please do not feel hurried. Settling your mother's affairs will take time. Her possessions may stay here without expense until the end of the summer. Does that sound fair to you?"

It was one hundred seven degrees but it felt twenty degrees hotter in the middle of Mrs. Alemi's Valley Storage facility, which was constructed entirely of cement and held the heat like a Dutch oven.

"More than fair, Mrs. Alemi. Thank you," Mike said.

She stepped away from the door, and Mike moved in and lifted it up. Everything Saint Linda owned was inside this unit.

"No rush, Michael. I'll wait in the office," Mrs. Alemi said, and she walked away toward the large front building that held the office, a supply store where she sold boxes and tape and other appropriate supplies, and an apartment for the facility manager.

Mike nodded thanks, took a breath, walked into the unit, and turned on the light. It was hot as hell in this concrete box, but he was out of the sun, and that was a relief. He had forgotten what relief felt like. Thirty-six hours ago, his mother had died of a heart attack, and since that frozen moment in time, he had lost his job because of a real estate zombie who was stalking him under false pretenses, had lost his wife and daughters in Paramus, New Jersey, had lost his garage to his flimflam brother, and had lost his mind by agreeing to bring a dead dog back to life for a cash payment.

But those thoughts fell away as he looked around the unit. Mrs. Alemi had made sure her six sons were careful with Linda's things. Boxes were labeled—*LR* for living room, *K* for kitchen, *DR* for dining room—furniture was covered with plastic and duct taped for safe keeping, and things weren't stacked on other things. He moved deeper into the unit and looked for his mother's dresser or a wardrobe box labeled *MBR* for master bedroom that would hold his mother's clothes. He was searching for a business suit that she would literally wear to her grave.

It was a journey through time.

Here was the sofa Danny and Mike played on as kids. They would remove the cushions, set them on the floor in a big square, stand on top of the back of the sofa, jump down onto the springs, and shoot up into the air and land on the cushions. They called it their indoor diving pool and did flips and jackknifes and cannonballs, scoring each other like Olympic judges, taking breaks for Kraft cheese slices and Kool-Aid and cookies. Linda loved that sofa because her sons had loved it. She had reupholstered it several times and bought new cushions when the originals gave out, but she had never replaced it.

Here was the dinette set that fit in a corner of the kitchen. How many meals had they eaten at that table? It had to be ten thousand or more. This is where Linda made them macaroni and meatballs, enchiladas, tomato rice soup, scrambled eggs with crumbled bacon and jack cheese, Thanksgiving turkey, Christmas ham, birthday cake, and all of the comfort food he would never eat again.

Here was the desk where he did his homework, where his mother sat beside him and showed him how to figure fractions and percentages and quizzed him before spelling tests and history exams. This desk, *this desk*, was where his mother had taught him about hard work, accuracy, honesty, and proficiency.

He came upon a tall wardrobe box labeled *MBR* and opened it and found his mother's dresses and blouses and skirts and jackets and business suits. He chose a navy blue suit and a white blouse, held them to his face, smelled his mother, fell to his knees, and began to weep.

He'd thought he was done crying, thought his emotional landslide in the hospital had been the end of it, but grief wins over logic every time, and he had grief aplenty. Saint Linda had been dead a day and a half, and his soul hurt, physically hurt, at the thought of never seeing her again.

His life was suddenly a cesspool of pain and failure. He had spoken to Marcy just this morning, told her that in addition to losing his job and career, in addition to being stalked by a madman zombie, Danny had moved into the garage because he, Mike, had sworn an oath on Linda's dying heart. Marcy had been quiet for a minute and then said she would start looking at apartments and researching the Paramus public schools in case she and the girls never came back.

The agony of all this defeat poured out of him without inhibition, and then he heard Judd Martin say, "You're a pussy, fat man. A fat fucking pussy."

Mike opened his eyes, and Judd was standing immediately in front of him, pointing a Smith & Wesson Snubnose revolver directly at his face. How long had he been there? How could Mike have missed him? What the hell? *What the hell?*

"Stop stalking me, Judd," Mike said loudly and with power.

Here, in Mrs. Alemi's storage unit, amidst the memories of his life and his mother's possessions, he had reached the outermost limits of his sanity. "This is stupid, and I'm tired of it. Get the hell out of my face, you fucking freak."

He was on his knees, holding his mother's blue business suit and white blouse, and he was conscious of Judd raising the gun. Then he was aware of the gun moving toward him with speed and force. But it was so surreal—the whole damn business of his life these last two days—that this moment was just part of his racing river of madness, so he didn't react, didn't move a muscle.

There was an explosion of unbelievable pain when the gun hit him in the side of the head, and then there was nothing.

And then it hurt to open his eyes. It hurt to breathe, and his head was throbbing. What the hell had happened to him? Then he heard a voice that sounded far, far away. It was Judd Martin.

"I'm going to kill you, Mike. That's the thing you have to understand."

Oh my God, Mike thought between flashes of excruciating pain and throbbing in his skull, *now I remember*. And remembering made the pain worse, not better.

"I may kill you today, but I may wait a week or two because this is better than I thought it would be, and I thought it would be pretty fucking good to begin with."

Mike tried to run for his life, but he couldn't move his arms or legs. He tried to yell for help, but what came out was a muffled moan, unintelligible and animalistic. And he was sitting. He opened his eyes, and the reality of his current condition hit him like, well, a snubnose in the head.

He was duct taped to a dinette set chair, possibly the very chair he'd sat in while growing up in the small yellow house. He was wearing his boxers and his socks and nothing else. Judd had stripped off his clothes and duct taped him to a chair in the back of Mrs. Alemi's storage unit, behind the dressers, out of sight.

Judd had not changed one iota since making Mike climb into

the coffin at the mortuary yesterday—*Jesus, that was yesterday,* Mike thought—except to become even more zombie-like, dirtier, crazier, more wild-eyed, more tattered and unkempt. He was six feet away, very close by, sitting opposite Mike on a matching dinette set chair, sifting through the contents of Mike's wallet—Mike's clothes on the ground beside him.

"You call me a freak, but look at you, Mike. You're so fucking boring that you're the fucking freak. Look at your pathetic life. Who the fuck lives a life this fucking pathetic? Look at your wife and kids. Are you fucking kidding me? You think these people love you? They don't. They hate your fucking guts. You're boring, and you're a loser, and that's what everybody who knows you thinks, whether they say it to your face or not: you're a fat fucking freak loser.

I'm not fat, Mike said, shouting, but it got lost in the duct tape and sounded instead like begging for mercy.

"Anyway," Judd said, flipping the wallet aside, "the question on the table is what am I going to do to you today, and I think the answer is beat your ass. I think that would make me feel like a fucking champ."

He stood up, cracked his knuckles in a disturbing manner, took a step toward Mike, and a cell phone rang. Both Mike and Judd looked at Mike's pants. Judd picked them up, took the phone out of the back pocket, and answered it.

"Hello. Yeah, it's me. I got bad reception in the storage unit; doesn't sound like you either."

He covered the phone, pulled out his knife, looked at Mike, and said, "It's your brother. I'm going to put him on speaker. If you make any noise, I'll cut your cock off."

The thought of Judd cutting his cock off with the hunting knife shut Mike up in half a second. Judd put the call on speaker, moved closer to Mike, and held the phone so they could both hear whatever Danny had to say.

"We met with Greenburg, me and Jenny," Danny said. "She did it, Mike; she really did it. I saw it with my own eyes. Greenburg had a dead goldfish on his desk, and she breathed on it, and then it was swimming in the bowl. I thought he was going to pass out. I thought *I* was going to pass out. It was incredible. She walked out of the office, and I said seventy-five grand cash, and he said he was in. Tonight. He's in tonight, after work, at his house. His wife's got a search party going for the dog, and he's got to get this done before she gets back. We're on for tonight. You still there?"

"Still here," Judd said.

"Seventy-five grand cash," Danny said, and he clicked off the call.

Judd tossed the phone aside, picked Mike's shirt up off the floor, tied it around Mike's head like a blindfold and said, "Okay Mike, the only way to stop this beating is to tell me who Greenburg is and where he lives. I'd take the tape off your mouth, but I think you'd tell me before I got to beat you at all, and that's no good for me."

Mike clenched and clamped and waited to be hit. His body ached; he could feel his heart pounding, the blood rushing to his head. He thought he might die from the tension, and then he heard Mrs. Alemi say, "Michael, what is the meaning of this?"

21
a giant fuck you to his killer

THERE WERE three cars parked one beside the other in front of Pacoima Pawn and Loan: Harvey Mineral's black Range Rover, Donald Greenburg's silver Lexus, and Carol Greenburg's white Mercedes Coupe. Omar inspected the Mercedes while Harvey and Dr. Greenburg, nervous and twitchy and high on coke, stood by, sweating in the sun.

It was one hundred eight degrees at two o'clock in the afternoon on Thursday, and the Weather Channel woman said the heat index in the San Fernando Valley would reach one fifteen. There was an unseasonal Santa Ana, a *Devil Wind*, blowing down from the mountains with a vengeance. It was hot and inhuman air that felt like a blast furnace in the face and whipped the people of Los Angeles into a foul and burning frenzy, causing a quantifiable increase in suicides and homicides that turned the City of Angels into the City of Satan. Just the kind of day that made Harvey remember his mother.

She was Georganne Dunn, a beautiful dwarf from Manchester, who'd fled England after shooting a man in the head with both barrels of a stolen shotgun. That the now headless man was a known violent criminal would not have helped her defense in a court of law since that same court would defi-nitely have discovered she was illegally selling him drugs and guns in the back room of the working class bar of which she was the owner and proprietor. The fact that she had never paid any taxes and also had active interests in prostitution and grand theft auto would have been bad barrister moments for her as well.

She had won the bar in a card game from a man who'd stayed on as a bartender and fallen in love with her and impreg-nated her and whose throat she'd later slit while he slept after learning he had cheated on her with one of her barmaids and also with one of her prostitutes. Harvey smiled at the thought of his mum holding the knife in the middle of the night. She was not a woman to be trifled with.

After doing the calculus with the smoking shotgun still in her hand, Georganne had grabbed her young son and flown to America, where she and Harvey vanished amidst the sunburned hordes of Southern California. She changed their name from Dunn to Mineral and became the owner and proprietor of a failing pawnshop in Pacoima.

She was well read and wonderfully articulate and immacu-lately dressed—and cruel as Cromwell when it came to business. Under her cutthroat (literally) leadership, the pawnshop pros-pered. She traded prostitution for gambling and ran a high-stakes game in the back room. She continued to "steal cars" and "deal guns" but under the flimsy veil of pawn legality. She lived a cash-only life and gave the government nothing, which is what she gave everyone. She had no patience for people other than Harvey, who she doted on and spoiled and raised with all the love and poison in her hardened heart. She taught him every-thing she knew about life and business and people and pain and pawn and profit and cash money.

She died when he was twenty, and he inherited the business, and while it was profitable on the right side of the law, it became a cash cow on the wrong side. Harvey had no interest in poker, and he knew his mother would have been disappointed by that, but he also knew she'd have been so proud of his work as a loan shark.

"The real money, Mum," Harvey had said to her as she lay dying of cancer, "is in illicit loans."

"Make me proud then, boy," she had said with her last breath.

"2012 CL63 AMG, excellent condition," Omar said. "Like new."

"It's worth a hundred five thousand dollars," Greenburg said. "I looked it up."

Harvey knew exactly what the Mercedes was worth. He had looked up it as well. "The question isn't the value of your wife's car, it's why you're pawning it in the first place."

"I need seventy-five thousand in cash today," Greenburg said in his most condescending voice while licking his teeth with his tongue, "that's why."

"Too much," Harvey said.

"You'll sell it for ninety next week," Greenburg said. "That's fifteen for you, a twenty percent profit. If you don't want it, I'll go to another pawnshop. For Chrissake, do the math, Harvey."

Harvey had already done the math. He looked at Omar. "Do you like the car?"

"It's cherry," Omar said.

Harvey turned back to Greenburg and tasted bile. The dentist was a pitiful man living a pitiful life. He detested Greenburg and wanted to cause him physical pain, break his kneecaps or remove his testicles with scissors. But there was something about the dentist today that was unusual: his *attitude*. It was as if Greenburg thought *he* was the one holding the cards, as if he knew something Harvey didn't. Harvey *hated* that thought, hated knowing Greenburg was thinking it. What could this pathetic excuse for a human being possibly have over him? What information did the coked-out dentist have that Harvey didn't? Harvey had to know, and he had to know

now. "All right, I agree to your terms. Omar, take the doctor's keys, draw up the papers, and remove seventy-five thousand in cash from the safe. Now let's go inside before we burn to death."

They went into the store, and Omar walked to the office. Harvey went behind the counter and up onto the ramp so that he was eye to eye with Greenburg, who stood across the counter. On the opposite side of the shop, an elderly couple was painfully pawning their heirloom jewelry, and the big-breasted black woman was back again—three days in a row now—working the same Hispanic clerk to get her price for the Civil War sword.

Harvey looked at the dentist with disgust. Greenburg was lost in the one big thought Harvey was not privy to. *It's the most outrageous, important, and delirious thought that Greenburg has ever had,* Harvey imagined, and he was infuriated by not knowing what it was. "Is it experimental plastic surgery?"

"No."

"Three pounds of clean Columbian cocaine?"

"Stop asking."

"Back taxes?"

"I'm not telling you."

"Why do you need seventy-five thousand dollars in cash today, Doctor?"

"None of your business, Harvey. Just give me the money and fuck yourself."

Harvey smiled. *Greenburg,* he said to himself, *does not yet know this because he is lost in his preposterous thought, but he is soon going to share his secret while experiencing impossible pain, and then I will keep my money and his wife's car.*

Omar arrived at the counter with a sales contract and a large fat manila envelope. He put the contract and the envelope on the counter and took a pen from his pocket.

"Dr. Greenburg refuses to share his immediate need for my money," Harvey said to Omar, "and I have lost patience with his insistence for privacy."

"I could push this pen through his eyeball," Omar said. "That might open him up."

"I would enjoy that immensely," Harvey said.

Omar took Greenburg by the arm and began to lead him to the office. Harvey watched them go, savoring for a moment the joy of Greenburg's fear. But then the dentist did something out of character. Rather than collapse into silent terror from the anticipated agony waiting for him in Harvey's soundproofed office, Greenburg pulled against Omar, planted his feet, held onto the counter, looked at the other customers, and shouted at the top his voice.

"Somebody help me, please. I'm a dentist."

Omar turned to Harvey for guidance. Harvey looked at the clerks and customers and knew they were now witnesses and that a new geometry was in play. Should he have Omar drag Greenburg to the office? Should he instruct Omar to let go of the dentist's arm? Or should he tell Omar to throw Greenburg over his shoulder and carry him, kicking and screaming like a grade school girl, to the piranha tank and toss him in?

"Please, help me," Greenburg said, still shouting.

The elderly couple was frozen, clutching their jewelry as if each piece were a memory they couldn't possibly part with. The black woman was holding her sword like it was an infant child being put up for adoption. *Low risk*, Harvey decided. "We're conducting a transaction," Harvey said to the customers, "and simply collecting his information." And he gestured for Omar to get Greenburg into the office.

"Help me," Greenburg said as Omar lifted him off the ground. He looked at the clerks, but they knew their places. He appealed to the elderly couple, but they shook their heads in unison. So he looked at the black woman, and their eyes met.

"What's in it for me, skinny white man?" she said.

"Free dental care for the rest of your life," Greenburg said.

And then, wielding the Civil War sword like a samurai warrior, with astounding grace and speed for a woman with breasts the size of Catawba melons, she crossed the pawnshop and held the razor tip of the blade to Harvey's Adam's apple. It happened so quickly that Omar had no time to reach for his Glock and was still holding Greenburg in the air.

"Tell the ponytail to put the dentist down or you going to breathe through a new hole in the middle of your neck," the black woman said. She had a gold tooth in her smile that caught the light and bounced it into Harvey's eyes.

Harvey could feel the tip of the sword digging into his skin. Any increase in pressure and the sword would thrust through and open him up, and he would bleed out and die. "Release Dr. Greenburg, Omar. We'll collect his information another day."

The giant put Greenburg down and let him go, and the dentist walked to the black woman. "Donald Greenburg," he said, and he sniffed in hard, hoping for nostril residue.

"Ramona Clifton. What you think?" she said, showing off her smile.

"Beautiful," Greenburg said, and he leaned across the counter so that his face was close to Harvey's. "You want my information, you piece of shit? I wrote you a limerick on the way here. A talent agent named Miller, Had a client who was a real thriller, She came out of the fog, And breathed life in my dog, A giant fuck you to his killer. Ha. Figure it out from there, you sadistic son-of-a-bitch dwarf." Then he signed the contract on the counter, picked up the envelope, and waved it at Harvey and Omar. "You get the keys, I get the cash. A deal's a deal. Do you have a car, Ramona?"

"You got gas money?"

"Fill her up."

"Pedal to the metal."

Greenburg went out the door into the blazing sunshine, and Ramona backed out behind him, holding the sword with both hands, ready to slice somebody in half.

"I ain't *never* selling this sword," she said, and then she was gone.

The elderly couple took their jewelry and followed the dentist and the samurai into the heat. The clerks went back to work as if nothing had happened. Omar walked to the counter. Harvey was rubbing the spot on his throat where Ramona had placed her Civil War sword.

"Breathed life in my dog," Omar said.

"A talent agent named Miller," Harvey said.

22

she's not kidding with those weeds

JENNY STONE'S mother did not do as directed. She had driven her daughter to Greenburg's office and, instead of waiting, had left her stranded. So Danny had to take Jenny home to the flatlands of Northridge, near White Oak Boulevard and Hiawatha.

He had left the dentist's office in a state of amazement after witnessing the Breath of Life, yet his mind refused to accept what he had seen with his own eyes. The film in his head ran over and over, again and again, but the story stayed the same. The goldfish had died on the desk. It was dead. Jenny had pulled it from the bowl and dropped it in front of Greenburg, and it had suffered a violent, painful death. It was a fact. They had seen it happen. And then Jenny had breathed on the fish, and it came back to life. No matter how many times he replayed it, the fish came back to life. *Holy shit*, Danny thought, *Holy freaking shit*.

His mind was racing. He could hardly contain the mad rush of thoughts and ideas and feelings flying through him. He had witnessed a sight unseen since Christ himself—the dead had been risen. Yes, it was a goldfish in a bowl, but it was impossible and wonderful and miraculous and sensational and shocking and humbling and awe-inspiring. The world had changed, and he would never be the same in it. Everything would be different now that Jenny could raise the dead—his life, his view of the universe, his relationship with the nature of things worldly and otherworldly. The knowledge that the impossible was possible was too much for him to handle. What would he do now? What would he say? How could he translate *The Goldfish* into words and deeds? How could he live a life worthy of such a transcendental modulation?

I'm going to get so rich, he thought.

He knew that one day he would look back at the seventy-five grand from Greenburg as small change. Wealthy people would pay more than that. Hollywood royalty would pay through the teeth to bring back their dead pets. There were too many possibilities in play, too many angles to consider. After tonight, when Chachi was wagging his tail in Greenburg's living room—*living room*, ha, the perfect name—he would gather his thoughts. But he couldn't do that yet. It was too soon. He was as confused as he was excited as he was overwhelmed. There was no way to wrap his mind around *The Goldfish*. And there was no way to wrap his mind around Jenny Stone.

What the hell was going on with her? She was sitting beside him as if she hadn't just taken and then returned life to Greenburg's fish, as if her day had been ho-hum-plain-Jane checking groceries. And what was with her look? When she first came to his office, she was a little mouse with a Catholic school skirt and knee socks. Her hair was pulled back tight, and she wore zero makeup. She had tried to be nowhere, noticed by no one, and she had succeeded.

Then at Ralphs, when he signed her as a client while she was working, the Pumpkin in line behind him, Jenny was wearing makeup. He had forgotten about that until she walked into Greenburg's office.

He had been shocked by her appearance, so taken aback that he had physically stood up. Not because he was being polite but because he had to do something and standing was his only option. The highlights in her hair, the sundress, the makeup and the jewelry and the green eyes—she had worn thick glasses, but weren't her eyes brown like coffee? Anyway, now they were green. And they were pretty. *She* was pretty.

He glanced at her. They had not spoken during the trip to her house except for her telling him to turn here and turn there. He wondered about her life. Did she date? Had she ever been married? For all he knew, she was married now and not wearing her ring for, well, who the hell knew why she wouldn't wear her ring. No, he decided, she couldn't be married. Who would marry a woman that could raise the dead? Her relationships would never get past that little detail. Men would run for the hills the first time she blew on a dead fern or fish. It would be too much, too freaky for them. Her relationships would be doomed to fail. That was most likely her life story. And then thinking about failed relationships made him review the story of his own life.

There was no shortage of women. He looked like Brad Pitt. There were women whenever he wanted one. But they never went anywhere worth going. Most of the time they were dull, and he lost interest fast, or they didn't like that he was a talent agent or that he bet on the horses or that (for the last three years) he lived off his mother. One way or the other, the whole thing would fall in the shitter after a while.

So what? He'd liked to play the field. He liked his life, his women, and his horses fast and loose. Commitment was over-rated. (Look at his mother and his miserable asshole brother.) In their own way, relationships were like going to the track. Which horse would run? Which one would punk? Who would finish? Who would place? He had never been married. He had never even been close. If there were a woman out there who could hold his interest or whose interest he could hold, he hadn't found her yet.

He had decided to ask Jenny about the hair and the makeup and the sexy red sundress when she pointed through the windshield and said, "That's my house."

It was a sky-blue Craftsman cottage with a covered front porch enclosed by a wood railing and framed by brick columns that tapered toward the top. A brick walkway from the street led to wide steps that rose to the porch. It would have been a cute house if it weren't altogether skewed at odd angles. There were no straight lines. The shingled roof, the door, the windows, the railings, the brick columns, even the wide steps, were off kilter.

Jenny saw the confusion on Danny's face and said, "This was the epicenter of the Northridge Quake in ninety-four. The house was abandoned and empty for years after that. We bought it from the bank for pennies on the dollar and didn't fix it all the way."

Danny remembered the Northridge earthquake. He was a teenager at the time—four thirty-one in the morning on January 17. The small yellow house shook like the devil himself had hold of it. The very first violent jolt cut all the power in the Valley and beyond, crumbled freeway overpasses, leveled apartment complexes that crushed the cars parked below them, caused twenty-five billion dollars of damage, killed some, injured many, scared the skin off everyone else, and woke him and his mother and his brother and sent them screaming in the dark to get the hell outside. It had lasted twenty seconds that seemed like twenty minutes.

However, seeing Jenny's crooked house and remembering the Northridge Quake was not the reason for the confusion on Danny's face. Instead, it was the sight of Jenny's mother murdering the scrubby front lawn that made him recalculate his equations.

"And that's my mother," Jenny said without emotion as Danny pulled the Pathfinder to the curb and turned off the engine.

"What's she doing?" Danny said.

"Killing weeds," Jenny said. "Her name is Margaret. She goes by Maggie."

"She's not kidding with those weeds," Danny said, and he

and Jenny climbed out of the Pathfinder and started up the front walk.

Maggie was sixty-five years old with weathered skin that looked like leather. She was five foot eight, strong as an ox, and, Danny thought, swinging her serrated grass whip with its eleven-inch blade and hardwood handle like a wild woman with a golf club, looking to make trouble. She wore a denim shirt with the sleeves cut off, white Capri pants that came to her calves, blue Crocs, a wide-brimmed sun hat, and gardening gloves.

"Who's the Pretty Boy?" Maggie said, swinging her way across the lawn to where Danny and Jenny waited on the walkway.

"Danny Miller, Maggie Stone," Jenny said. "Mother, this is my agent, Danny."

"Agent?" Maggie said with a cocktail of derision, condescension, and scorn. "What kind of agent drives a piece of crap Pathfinder?" And she walked to the Pathfinder, kicked a tire, and answered her own question. "A piece of crap agent."

"Mother," Jenny said.

"What year is it, Pretty Boy?" Maggie said.

"Mother," Jenny said.

"1998," Danny said, wondering where in the world this woman was coming from. He was going with the flow because this was Jenny's mother, and Jenny was his golden goose, but he already had a bad feeling about Maggie Stone.

"How many miles?" Maggie said.

"Hundred fifty-six thousand," Danny said.

"Jap car, right?" Maggie said.

"Mother," Jenny said.

"Yes, Nissan," Danny said.

"They use metal or crepe paper?" Maggie said, and she kicked the door with her Croc hard enough to leave a dent.

"Mother," Jenny said.

"Hey," Danny said, and he took two steps toward Maggie, who swung the grass whip like a weapon. He stepped back, ducked in time, and felt the angry *whoosh* of air as the blade went by. In that moment, he had no doubt Maggie's intent was to decapitate him right here on the walkway.

Jenny stepped between Danny and Maggie and said without fear, "Go in the house, Mother."

"Just playing," Maggie said.

"Go in the house now," Jenny said.

Maggie waited ten seconds and then started up the walkway. "Make us some money, Pretty Boy, or you'll be *solly, Cholly.*" And then she cackled at her own joke and was up the steps and in the house.

"What the hell was that?" Danny said, turning to Jenny. It seemed to him that she was measuring her mother, gauging her, taking a temperature of some kind.

"Sorry, Charlie," Jenny said. "The StarKist commercial. She does it with a bad Chinese accent."

"She kicks my car, swings that thing at my head...why would she do that?" he said.

"It's a mystery," Jenny said, heading for the house. "See you at Greenburg's."

<h1 style="text-align:center">23</h1>

feculence most foul

JUDD MARTIN HAD DISAPPEARED into the shadows and sewers of the San Fernando Valley. Most cops would have written him off and closed the case, assuming they'd have taken it in the first place, which they wouldn't have—and didn't. A real estate zombie stalking his accountant? Give it to Gary Shuler.

It was a beautiful Thursday afternoon in Sunland-Tujunga. Sure, the temperature was pushing a brutal one hundred ten degrees, but Gary had signed with a talent agent this very morning, so his career was cruising right along. A spot on Conan was around the corner. All he had to do was finish writing his new act. And though on first glance the zombie was unrelated to the poodle, the accountant in question, the *stalkee*, had turned out to be the brother of his new talent agent, who was the patient of Greenburg, who was the owner of Chachi, who was tossed from the Lexus by Harvey and Omar, who'd recommended his agent. He had a hunch, Gary did, that these disparate factoids might find their way into his new routine as one long hilarious story, that they were a loose affiliation of threads to be tied together, and that he was the one to do the tying.

That's why he dug deeper when the normal LAPD shovels

didn't turn over the rock under which Judd Martin was hiding. Apartment complexes, construction offices, a list of banks, the post office, bars, coffee shops, food trucks, building sites, Home Depot, Lowes, gas stations, all of Martin's regular haunts—*a zombie with haunts*, he wrote that one down for his act—had not seen him for days and had no idea where he was.

He was gone; that's where he was. But Gary had inherited his father's scientific mind and knew that some investigations required another round of research, further experimentation, a reexamination of the data. Martin's family was out of state and out of touch; they had no idea where he might be lurking. He had few friends, actually no friends, so that was a dead end too. There were no credit card charges. There was no cell phone to trace. No vehicle in his name. He had not used an ATM anywhere in LA since he fell off the radar.

There was no flame to fan, not an ember or a spark. Judd Martin had wandered off into the woods; that's how cold the trail was. So how would *he* disappear, Gary asked himself, if he had no friends or family to help him? He would call in favors. And who would owe a contractor a favor? His subcontractors. So Gary got busy. Police work wasn't glamorous. It was ditch digging with a phone. You kept at it until you hit gold.

He called Martin's subs—electricians, framers, drywallers, painters, roofers, truckers, masons—until finally, on his last call, he found a plumber who stammered in fits and starts when Gary asked him about Judd Martin.

The plumber's name was Buddy Morris, and Judd had thrown him a job when Buddy's business was going under. The job was big enough to save Buddy's ass. It was a hell of a favor because there was another plumber who was supposed to get the gig. But Judd enjoyed having people in his debt and, like a Mafia Don, had told Buddy there would come a day when he would have to repay the favor. Buddy had given his word that he would. Anyway, that day had come, and the reparation was a vacant rental trailer Buddy owned in the Little Valley Trailer Park in Sunland-Tujunga.

Though it spilled into the northern edge of—and was considered to be part and parcel of—the San Fernando Valley, Sunland-Tujunga was actually nestled in the Tujunga Valley, bordered by the dramatic San Gabriel Mountains to the north and northwest and by the Verdugo Mountains to the south, which separated the little valley from Burbank and Glendale and all points southward. It was a valley within the Valley, known for being in the shadow of Mount Lukens, the highest peak in Los Angeles, and for having the cleanest air in the city—people came here to ride horses or just to breathe. But for Gary, Sunland-Tujunga was special because Pat Paulsen, his favorite comedian, once lived and laughed in this land.

Located on Sherman Grove near Foothill, the Little Valley Trailer Park was a run-down, low-rent place to park a mobile home, unattractive and worn out. The trailers were old and used up. There was cracked concrete everywhere. Struggling trees and shrubs were an afterthought.

Gary parked the Impala in a guest spot by the office, checked his pocket pad, found trailer seventeen on the map by the office door, and set off to find the real estate zombie who was stalking his agent's brother.

Between trailers sixteen and eighteen was a 1980s Airstream in poor condition, rusted and beaten and neglected, left to die in this Godforsaken place. Buddy Morris had bought it for cash as an investment property, had lived in it when he got divorced, then got remarried and moved out and couldn't find a tenant, and finally had repaid his debt to Judd Martin by letting him live here for free.

There was a beat-to-hell Ford pickup parked in front. Someone, perhaps the zombie, was home. Gary knocked. No one answered. He knocked again.

"I'm not here," said a voice from inside.

"Yes, you are," Gary said to the door.

"No, I'm not," said the voice.

"Yes, you are," Gary said. "Open the door. I want to talk to you about Mike Miller."

"Don't know the name," the voice said, "because I'm not here."

"I'm talking to you, and you're talking to me. We're having a conversation."

"We're not having a conversation."

"What do you call this?"

"A bad dream."

"This isn't a dream. It's two people talking to each other. That's the definition of a conversation. Even one person talking to one zombie is a conversation. Open the door, Judd. I'm a cop."

"You're a cop?"

"Detective Gary Shuler. Open the door."

"You going to arrest me?"

"How can I arrest you? You're not here."

A lock clicked, and Judd opened the Airstream door. Gary looked at him and had three immediate thoughts. One, *Holy shit, Judd Martin is a zombie.* Two, *Holy shit, Judd Martin is insane.* Three, *Holy shit, Judd Martin is dangerous.*

Martin was big and powerful and strong and looked to be completely out of control. His skin was ruddy-red-on-fire. His hair was madness. His eyes were bloodshot. His blue jeans and camo hunting vest and work boots were caked with dirt. He was unshaven for days. He wore no shirt. His hands and nails were black with filth. He teeth were crusted and yellowed. He was on the wrong side of human.

Gary reached back and took his gun out of its holster.

"You going to shoot me?" Judd said.

"I hope not," Gary said.

"Fair enough," Judd said, and he moved aside, and Gary climbed up into the trailer.

It was a wreck, like the inside of a rancid dumpster, filled with fast food wrappers, newspapers, cardboard boxes, empty beer cans and booze bottles, reeking litter boxes, and mold and muck and slime and sludge and feculence most foul.

"Love what you've done with the place," Gary said, wondering where he could sit and not catch a disease. He put on the latex gloves he had in his pocket and cleared a spot on a couch. Judd leaned against a cabinet across the living area. He was too physically large for the Airstream.

Immediately beside him, duct taped to the wall, was an enlarged image of Mike Miller seated behind a desk, wearing a suit and tie, hands folded, hair brushed back, tax returns to one side, accounting calculator to the other. It was Miller's Wasserman and Waddell staff photo, lifted from his online company bio and blown up as big as a Dave Matthews poster. Gary knew it was Mike Miller because under the picture were the words *Mike Miller, Senior Accountant*. Judd had stabbed a hunting knife in the middle of Mike's forehead—it stuck out of the wall at a jarring angle—and had written *Die Accountant Pig Fuck* and other happy-go-lucky phrases all across Mike's face and body.

"You got skills," Gary said, gesturing at the poster with his gun.

"I'm a zombie," Judd said.

"I'm a comedian."

"You said cop."

"Day job. Miller called the police and said you were stalking him. I caught the case. Coincidentally, his brother Danny's a talent agent, and I just signed a ninety-day representation deal this morning."

"He called when his brother was gagged and duct taped to a chair, so I told him *I* was Mike."

"You duct taped Mike Miller to a chair?"

"After I knocked him out and stripped him to his boxers, yeah."

"Why did you do that?"

"So I could beat his ass."

There was a fleeting moment where Gary thought, *This maniac might be the funniest man in America.* But then the moment was gone, and Gary pointed the gun at Judd Martin's chest, and this time he thought, *It might take three or four or five shots to bring this beast down.*

"Oh, well, then, yes, of course, makes perfect sense," Gary said. "So Danny thought you were his brother?"

"Seemed like it."

"What did he say?"

"Said he met with Greenburg, whoever the fuck that is, and someone named Jenny, whoever the fuck *that* is. Said Greenburg had a dead goldfish on his desk, and Jenny breathed on it, and then it was swimming in the bowl, whatever the fuck that means. Said Greenburg was going to pay seventy-five grand cash tonight for something about his wife's dog, whatever the fuck *that* means. Said Greenburg had to do it before his wife got back. If I knew where Greenburg lived, that'd be my money."

Instead of thinking about arresting the violently crazy Judd Martin for stalking, gagging, and duct taping Mike Miller, Gary thought, *Judd Martin is going to bring the two cases together; he's the missing link. He isn't a zombie; he's Bigfoot.*

Gary's cop radar clicked off, and his comedian radar clicked on, and he said, "Here's what I'm going to do, Judd. I'm going to make you my deputy. You stay close to Mike Miller and find out what's going on with this Greenburg guy and his dog. As long as you do that, I won't arrest you. But you can't kill Miller. No killing Miller."

"Can I hurt him bad?"

Gary knew he had crossed a line as precarious as the San Andreas. He saw the line and walked right over it. In his own way, he was as crazy as Judd Martin. But that's what artists did for their art; they crossed lines. He would cross back one day...or he wouldn't. It didn't matter. All that mattered now was his act. He had ninety days.

"You're a zombie cop," Gary said. "Use your judgment."

"Don't have any," Judd said.

24

ahab, ishmael, and the white whale

I WAS *the voice of reason*, Mike thought as he drifted in the middle of his backyard pool, suffering through the residual pain of the duct tape that had ripped clumps of hair and swaths of epidermis from his body when Mrs. Alemi had pulled it off. He'd told her a real estate zombie was stalking him under false pretenses and had followed him here and stripped him and duct taped him to the chair, and she had looked at him with a cocktail of doubt and concern and pity and recommended he speak to a professional about his grief, as if he had duct taped himself to the damn chair. After making sure he wasn't seriously injured, she had told him to wait for her and hurried off to reconfigure her security procedures and call the police (and maybe the psyche ward).

Instead, he'd gotten dressed, carried Linda's burial clothes to his car, and driven to the Fatburger in Granada Hills, where he'd inhaled two chili cheese dogs with bacon, an order of onion rings, an order of fat fries, a Maui-banana shake, and a Diet Coke. In the middle of the second dog, he'd realized he had become the voice of unreason.

I was the normal one, Mike thought as he floated on a Hello Kitty inflatable, a pink lounger that featured the kitty surfing somewhere swell. He was the one who got married and had a family and became an accountant and a grown-up. He was the one who followed Saint Linda's footsteps and built his career—*his life*—on hard work, accuracy, honesty, and proficiency. And yet he was the one who'd been fired, painted with the Embezzlement Brush, and banished from the Accounting Kingdom. And he was the one whose wife and children had flown to the planet Paramus at the far end of the universe, leaving him to face the ignominy of his reality with no family. And he was the one who had sworn *The Oath* on his mother's dying heart, which had led to his asshole brother moving into his garage, which had led to his firing up the chainsaw and nearly shredding his brother's guts all over the garage floor and walls and doors and himself and the perverted clown who smelled like a shithouse cesspool. Somewhere between his brother and the clown and the chainsaw, he realized he had become the abnormal one.

I was the moral compass, he thought as his body baked in the one hundred nine degree heat. As boys, he had told his brother it was wrong to blow up a neighbor's mailbox with a M80, wrong to leave a flaming bag of dog crap in front of a neighbor's door, wrong to climb through a neighbor's open window, take their car keys, and joyride the Valley. As men, he had told his brother it was wrong to run his talent agent business as a scam, a sham, and a con, wrong to bet everything on the horses, wrong to mooch off their mother. At work, he was the one who kept the firm on the up-and-up. If there were a question as to the legality of a deduction, Mike would make a stand because the fact that there was a question to begin with was also the answer: it was wrong. And in the name of Right versus Wrong, he had turned down Judd Martin's two-hundred-thousand-dollar bribe to cook the books. And yet he had agreed to bilk a dentist with his flimflam man brother by hysterically lying that they could bring the dentist's dead dog back to life. Somewhere between the dentist and the dog, he had become the amoral compass.

"Hey, Moby Dick, wake up," Omar said, tossing a river stone from the garden into the pool and splashing water on Mike.

Mike opened his eyes, shaded them from the sun, and saw two silhouettes by the side of the pool closest to the house, one giant and one miniature.

"We're looking for Danny Miller," Harvey said.

"Who the hell are you?" Mike said, annoyed at having his privacy compromised.

"Ahab and Ishmael," Harvey said.

"Who the hell are you, Moby Dick?" Omar said.

"I'm Mike, Danny's brother. This is my house," Mike said. "Stop calling me Moby Dick."

"Ahab, Ishmael, and the White Whale," Omar said.

"Are you saying I'm fat?" Mike said.

"Have you ever seen a skinny whale?" Harvey said.

"Where's your brother, Moby Dick?" Omar said.

"I don't know," Mike said, "and I wouldn't tell you if I did. And stop calling me that. I'm not fat."

"Perhaps a harpoon," Harvey said to Omar.

Omar nodded, lifted a handful of multi-colored river stones from the garden, and threw one at Mike, a fastball. The stone nailed Mike in the side with a thud.

"Are you crazy?" Mike said, and his heart rate rose. These were not nice people.

"Where's Danny?" Harvey said.

Omar fired another stone. This one hit Mike in the leg and stung like a bitch.

"Ow, shit, stop doing that," Mike said. "Who are you?"

How could it be possible, Mike wondered, that his life could spiral so utterly out of control in two days? He was tired of being put in coffins, duct taped to chairs, and pelted with river stones from his own garden. He considered paddling the Hello Kitty lounger to the side of the pool and making these two assholes, whoever they were, leave his property, but he knew Ishmael would crush him like a bug.

"Your brother is involved with a dentist whose dog died a dire death," Harvey said. "Both the dentist and your brother are business clients of mine, and my money is financing whatever idiocy these two morons have concocted concerning the dog."

A river stone zinged by close to Mike's head, and as he moved out of the way so as not get hit, he rolled off the raft into the pool. He came up for air and put his arms across the kitty so that he was treading water in the middle of the deep end, facing the dwarf and the giant. He debated telling them about the scheme to scam the dentist so they would leave, but he needed the money and decided to outlast them—as a teenager, he had passed the lifeguard test and could tread water for a very long time. "I don't know anything about a dead dog," he said. "My brother's a con man. I have nothing to do with him or his client or his dentist."

Omar whipped a handful of stones at the same time, a machine gun spray of projectiles that flew across the pool toward Mike's face. Mike ducked under water, stayed down until he thought it was safe, and came up gasping, clinging to the kitty.

"He knows about the client who came out of the fog," Harvey said to Omar, referencing the phrase in Greenburg's limerick.

"He's the dumbest whale in the water," Omar said, flinging stone after stone at Mike and his pink raft.

"Tell me about the client," Harvey said to Mike. "What does it mean *breathed life in my dog*?"

Mike could feel himself having a physical, emotional, and mental breakdown. He was alone in his pool, one hundred percent vulnerable, and these men were here on bad business, unafraid to threaten him in broad daylight. As he kicked his legs to maintain his position in the center of the pool, his eyes darted around the yard. There was no way to get out of the water and away from Ishmael and Ahab without getting caught and beaten or worse. "I don't know who she is," he said. "I don't know what *breathed life in my dog* means."

"If you refuse to cooperate, we will kill you in your pool," Harvey said.

"I told you; I don't know anything," Mike said.

"You knew without my telling you that your brother's client was a woman," Harvey said. "I suspect you know precisely what *breathed life in my dog* means. So I'm going to ask you one more time: What do your brother and Greenburg and the woman intend to do with the dog that requires me to fund the proceedings?"

"What's it going to be, Moby Dick?" Omar said, taking his Glock out and screwing a silencer on the end of the barrel.

Mike's eyes went wide. "For God's sake, please. I don't know," he said.

"Are all fat people this stupid?" Harvey said, shaking his head with incredulity.

"I'm not fat," Mike said.

"Shoot him," Harvey said.

And Omar pointed the silenced weapon at Mike and, *bang,* shot the raft. Mike screamed, and the pink lounger deflated, leaving him treading water without his kitty.

"Are you crazy? Are you fucking crazy?" Mike said. "It's the middle of the day."

Bang, bang. Omar fired two shots in the water in front of Mike.

"Okay, okay, okay, okay," Mike screamed, gulping and spitting water, struggling to keep his head up and move his arms and legs and not drown and still talk at the same time. "Her name is Jenny."

"Jenny, yes," Harvey said. "And?"

"And she can breathe life into the dead," Mike said. "Greenburg is going to pay to have his dog brought back to life. That's it. That's all I know."

"Am I wearing a sign that says: *Ahab is an idiot*? Or do you just think I'm an idiot?" Harvey said.

Mike didn't know what to say. *Bang, bang.* Omar fired two

more muffled shots into the pool. "Answer the question, Moby Dick," Omar said.

"You're not wearing a sign," Mike said.

"So you think I'm an idiot?" Harvey said.

"No, no, you're not an idiot," Mike said.

"Then why would you tell me a story about a woman who can breathe life into death when such a thing is impossible?" Harvey said.

"Because it's the truth if it's true," Mike said.

"Here's the truth if it's true, Moby Dick. I'm going to shoot you in the head if you don't tell us why they need the money," Omar said.

"Please, please," Mike said, "the dentist needs the money to pay Jenny to bring the dog back to life. She's going to breathe on the dog. That's all I know."

"Melville was right all along—the White Whale is a waste of time," Harvey said to Omar. "It should look like an accident."

"What?" Mike said. "What should look like an accident?" He could hear the terror in his voice, the abject fear, and it surprised him to hear himself afraid for his life. He wondered if other people were conscious of how they sounded in situations like this, and then he realized that most people never find themselves in situations like this.

Omar put his gun away and scanned the immediate area around the pool. His eyes stopped on the Bose Wave plugged into an exterior outlet with an extension cord.

"Not the Bose, not the Bose," Mike said. "I paid five hundred for it. The touch-top controls are completely invisible. It has dual independent alarms, Waveguide speaker technology. Don't kill me with the Bose..."

Omar lifted the Bose Wave off the little poolside table and threw it into the air over the water.

Mike's heart stopped beating and his life passed before his eyes, except the thing before his eyes was his Weber grill and backyard picnic table, and so his life with his grill and picnic table passed before his eyes—the burgers, the steaks, the pork chops and lamb chops, the hot dogs and sausages, the chicken, oh the chicken, and the potato salad, and the corn on the cob, how he would miss the sweet corn on the cob...

He could feel tears fill his eyes as the Bose fell fast to the water. He would be instantly electrocuted in his own pool only hours after being duct taped to a childhood chair in his boxers. Maybe it was better this way. Maybe in a past life he had been a bad person, and this was his karmic payback. No matter now. His life was over.

The Bose hit the water, and he tensed, waiting for the pain of the electric shock to rip through his body and fry his brain and burn his heart and kill him dead.

But as the Bose splashed down, the extension cord pulled out of the wall socket and nothing happened. Mike continued to tread water, blinking and blinking and blinking. Omar and Harvey stood poolside.

"I *am* Ahab," Harvey said.

"Do you have a longer cord, Moby Dick?" Omar said.

25

the bottom of bizarre

GREENBURG WAS WIRED. He'd started inhaling cocaine the minute he got home from work. Carol and her Seuss Search and Save posse were out and about in the Valley, pasting posters on power poles and brick walls and wide windows and bus stops and pet shops, and Greenburg needed a crutch to get him through what was coming.

One poster in particular made the dentist retch with embarrassment. Carol and the Seuss Women had dressed him in a yellow bathing suit, gelled his hair straight up, put a construction paper white collar around his neck, and painted a green star on his stomach so that he looked like an emaciated star-bellied Sneetch. He had resisted with what might he could muster, but he was weak-willed and soaked with gin and posed with drunkard's regret. The Seuss Women then photoshopped a picture of Chachi on his hind legs (begging for a treat) beside the dentist and hand-lettered the plea: *we've lost our lovable plain-belly Sneetch.* They put Chachi's name and the reward and contact information at the bottom. Greenburg's name wasn't on the poster, so at least there was that.

As the dentist pulled a fresh line from the pile of white powder, the doorbell rang. He looked at the fat envelope on his office sofa, the envelope with the seventy-five thousand dollars from Pacoima Pawn and Loan, and realized he was in so deep there was nothing left to do but drown.

He went to the front door and opened it. Dan Miller, his talent-agent patient, Jenny, Dan's client, the pretty young woman who'd murdered his goldfish and then brought it back to life, and another man he didn't know, overweight with blotchy skin that looked like it had been recently ripped off his body, stood under the portico.

"Who's he?" Greenburg said, gesturing at Mike.

"My brother. He handles the money," Danny said. "Do you have it?"

"I'm not paying you a penny until my dog is barking," Greenburg said.

"This is completely insane," Mike said.

"Shut up, Mike," Dan said.

"You shut up," Mike said.

"Where's the dog?" Jenny said, still in her sundress and sandals.

It was six thirty. Thursday's sun was sinking in the west, and the temperature had dropped to a broiling one hundred five. Greenburg stepped aside and let them in the house. He shut the front door and pointed through the living room to the pool and said, "Wait for me outside."

"Who's that?" Danny said, pointing at the black woman sitting by the pool, sipping a can of Coke and holding a Civil War sword.

"Ramona Clifton," Greenburg said.

"Why the sword?" Mike said.

"Why not?" Greenburg said, heading to the kitchen side of the house.

"Bring the money, Dr. Greenburg," Danny said, calling after him.

"When my dog's barking," Greenburg said, and he went through a swinging door into the kitchen.

From Pacoima Pawn and Loan, Ramona had driven the dentist to a gas station in her 1985 Cadillac Eldorado convertible, a white, two-door ocean liner with blood-red leather interior and retractable roof, where she'd filled up her tank on his dime and then taken him to his office. He'd put her in his chair and examined her mouth and decided between her left lateral incisor and canine that it might be prudent for him to have her attend the Chachi event at his home after work, in case Dan Miller double-crossed him or Harvey and Omar crashed the party.

She'd agreed to watch his back in exchange for new tires for the Eldorado. Greenburg didn't tell her exactly what was going to happen by the pool, just that there was cash money involved, and it would either be the most amazing thing she had ever seen or the biggest bust of all. As long as there were whitewalls in the deal, she'd told him, she and her sword were good to go.

Greenburg went through the kitchen into the garage and straight to the freezer. He opened the door and took out the garbage bag that held his dead dog, went back through the kitchen to the living room and then outside to where Danny, Mike, Jenny, and Ramona were waiting on the flagstone patio that surrounded the built-in pool.

He put the garbage bag on the ground, and they all looked at it for a full minute, as if they had forgotten what the hell they were doing here in the first place.

"He's in the bag?" Danny said.

"In the freezer since Tuesday," Greenburg said.

"A dogsicle," Mike said, though no one laughed because they now remembered what the hell they were doing here in the first place.

"That some weird shit right there, DG," Ramona said.

"Going to get weirder, RC," Greenburg said to her.

"Open it," Jenny said.

"Just like that, just open it?" Greenburg said.

"Open it, and put him on the ground," Jenny said.

Greenburg looked at her and then looked at everyone else

and then kneeled down, unknotted the bag, grabbed the closed end, and gently lifted the bag until Chachi slipped out onto the flagstone. The smell made everyone blanch and groan. Or maybe it was the sight of frozen death.

"That's a dead damn dog," Ramona said.

"Chachi," Greenburg said with emotion, and the dog's life raced across the screen in his head: Chachi running around the pool for thirty minutes straight while Greenburg swam laps and Carol did yoga; Chachi burying bones in the backyard after dinner; Chachi chasing birds he had no hope of catching; Chachi jumping in the pool and swimming with Greenburg and then climbing out and shaking the water on Carol while she rested on a lounge chair, recovering from augmentation mammoplasty. Good times.

"Froze all the way through," Ramona said, touching the dog with the tip of her sword. "Hard as a rock."

"Does it have to thaw?" Mike said.

"Can't cook no frozen steak," Ramona said.

"Swanson can," Mike said. "Steak, potatoes, green beans, apple crisp."

"Good point, dough boy," Ramona said. "They eat dog meat in China. Maybe Chowking got frozen dog dinners."

"Dog foo yung," Mike said.

"Kung Pao Pooch," Ramona said.

"This is a stupid conversation," Danny said.

"We're standing here looking at a frozen dead dog, waiting for Jenny to bring it back to life. That's what's stupid," Mike said.

And then they looked at Jenny and realized she was kneeling on the flagstone beside Chachi.

She looked at the dead dog and made a sad little sigh. Then she leaned forward, put her face close to Chachi's face, and gently blew on it. Then her lips turned ever so slightly up at the corners, and she stood.

They all looked at the dog and at Jenny and at the dog and at

Jenny and at the dog and at Jenny and at the dog, and nothing happened. One minute ticked by and then another and then another, and still the dog was dead on the flagstone.

"Donald, what is going on out there?" Carol said. She and the Seuss Search and Save posse had returned and were standing in the living room looking out through the wall of French doors at the circle of strangers standing poolside. "Who are these people, and where is my car, and why is that Cadillac parked in my spot?"

There were six of them in total, Carol and five other Seuss women, all of them plastic surgery abusers, all of them pulled and stretched and tucked and augmented beyond believability, all of them devoted to the fashion-forward style of Dr. Seuss.

Greenburg was used to them, and so he was able to keep his jaw in place. The others on the flagstone, circled around the dead dog, were mouths agape at the sight of this small tribe of excessively Botoxed and Juvedermed Seuss Women.

"Who is this African person, and why does she have a sword, and what are you hiding out there, Donald?" Carol said, starting across the living room toward the French doors and the pool.

Greenburg knew his wife was high on Percocet and vodka, and he also knew that the sight of Chachi, frozen and broken and dead as Dillinger, would crush her forever.

"I can explain..." Greenburg said, but he knew he couldn't explain a thing. What was happening here in his house was beyond explanation. If there was good news—and there wasn't —but if there was, it was that he had hit the bottom of bizarre. His life could not get any more inexplicable. Right here, right now, was the end of all explanation.

Bark, bark. Bark, bark.

Mike and Danny and Ramona and Greenburg looked down to see Chachi prancing on his paws, alive and well, wagging his tail like a puppy.

Bark, bark. Bark, bark.

Greenburg was blown out of his skin, as frozen as Chachi

was just seconds ago. He looked at Jenny with shock and astonishment and joy and fear and wonder, and she nodded as if she had simply found his lost wallet at the Studio City Starbucks and returned it to him with cash and credit cards intact.

Bark, bark. Bark, bark.

"You found him!" Carol said, screaming with excitement at the group by the pool and then turning to her girls. "They found my Chachi!"

The Seuss Search and Save posse started to jump and shout with crazy glee and relief, and the dog darted out of the circle and into Carol's arms. Chachi kissed Carol like crazy until she pulled away and said, "Don't just stand there, Donald. Give them their reward."

Greenburg looked at his wife holding his dog, wondered what kind of devil magic was happening here, and then decided he didn't give a shit. Chachi was alive, and Carol would not kill herself. He turned to say something to Danny, but Danny spoke first.

"Yes, Donald," Danny said. "Give us our reward."

friday

26

there goes the train

HARVEY HAD no patience for religion, which made his recurring nightmare all the more puzzling—and problematic—because it involved the sort of religiosity he abhorred. His nightmare was that he'd died a mysterious death and stood at the Gates of Heaven before St. Peter (who appeared in the nightmare as Peter O'Toole) and listened in horror as O'Toole reviewed the file of Harvey's life on Earth.

"It says here, Little Man, that you lived your life with illegality, brutality, depravity, and debauchery, all of which amounted to triviality, inconsequentiality, immateriality, and negligibility," O'Toole said in the dark dream. "It says here that you lived even smaller than you are...or were."

That's when Harvey would wake up in a sweat—when O'Toole would tell him, at the Gates of Heaven, that he had lived his life even smaller than he was. The idea that his life would amount to an anthill of beans was anathema to him, a loathsome fear he projected as sadism, which was better than internalizing the fear as insignificance.

He was reliving the nightmare on Friday morning, behind the wheel of his Range Rover, parked across the street from Greenburg's Encino house. Omar was in the front passenger seat, watching a busted underground sprinkler head shoot a spray of water straight up in the air, like whale blow from a big blue surfacing under Escalon Drive.

It was one hundred six degrees at eight thirty in the morning. The projected high for the day was one twelve. The smog index was *Don't Breathe.* Los Angeles was going mad in the heat. Violent crime was on the rise. *If the dentist doesn't come clean as to the whereabouts of my cash,* Harvey thought, *it will tick up a notch before nine.*

"The dentist and his new dog," Omar said, pointing at Greenburg's house.

"Carbon copy," Harvey said as Greenburg took Chachi across the covered front patio and down the driveway on an early morning jaunt through the neighborhood before heading to the office.

"Nobody spends seventy-five grand on a poodle," Omar said.

"Then where is my money?" Harvey said, and he climbed out of his Range Rover.

Omar followed him to Greenburg's driveway, and the dentist stopped in his tracks three feet from the dwarf and the giant, who stood in the street at the edge of Greenburg's property line.

"Let me guess," Harvey said, looking at Greenburg and his little white poodle with revulsion, "you named him Chachi."

"Spitting image," Omar said.

"We saw you parked across the street from inside the house," Greenburg said, gesturing behind him at Carol, who stood under the front door portico in a pink unitard and cartoon updo that made her look like Cindy Lou Who all grown up—if they'd had Percocet and plastic surgery in Whoville. "You have no business being here."

"I called the police," Carol said loud enough to be heard at the end of the driveway and holding up her cell phone. "They're on the way."

"Your identical twin brother and me were friends," Omar

said, kneeling down and sticking his hand across the property line toward the poodle. "And then I threw him out the window into traffic. I don't think we were friends after that."

"You're exactly wrong, Doctor," Harvey said. "I have a precise amount of business being here: seventy-five thousand dollars. I want to know where it is. I want—"

He was interrupted by a deep guttural growl that sounded as if it had emanated from the pit of hell. They all looked at each other and then looked down at the dog.

Chachi had bared his teeth and was snarling at Omar.

On its face, it was ridiculous. The poodle was the size of one of Omar's giant feet. But there was something about the growl, something fearless that was incompatible with the poodle.

"This is not a nice dog," Omar said.

"We know about Danny and Jenny," Harvey said.

"We're good at limericks," Omar said, still kneeling in front of the growling Chachi.

"Then you know this is the same dog you murdered in cold blood. You know she breathed new life into him," Greenburg said.

"If you believe that," Harvey said, "then you are a fool. And if you gave my money to Danny Miller because you believed that, then you are a moron and a fool and in breach of our contract, which means you owe me seventy-five thousand dollars."

"You got my wife's car," Greenburg said quietly so Carol wouldn't hear him, "and I got the cash. That's what the contract says."

Chachi strained against the leash, trying to get at Omar. Greenburg had to hold on like he meant it, like there was a pit bull instead of a poodle pulling on the other end.

"The fine print says otherwise," Harvey said, looking at the dentist and the dog and thinking that Greenburg was either the weakest man in Los Angeles or that whoever raised this clone dog had fed it full of steroids.

"Look at this fucking dog," Omar said.

Chachi snarled and growled and drilled the giant with laser eyes.

"What fine print?" Greenburg said, and he looked down at his dog with wonder. "Chachi, stop."

"If the money is used for reasons other than what we agreed upon, then the contract is breached, my money is paid back...and I keep the car," Harvey said.

"What do I get?" Greenburg said.

"You get to live," Harvey said.

"But your dog doesn't," Omar said.

Harvey did not remember Greenburg's poodle being vicious. He remembered the dog being docile, almost cat-like, *purring*, for God's sake, in Omar's lap, before being jettisoned out the window. Georganne had taught him to trust his internal radar, and it was telling him that there was something peculiar about the poodle. But more than that, it was telling him that he was missing the point of something much bigger than the dog, something so big it would make his life *consequential* and shut St. Peter O'Toole up once and for all. He had no idea what it was, but it had to do with the damn dog.

"I don't have it," Greenburg said. "Danny does."

"You're lying to me, Doctor," Harvey said. "You bought this poodle for two hundred dollars at PetSmart, and now you and the idiot agent are spending my money behind my back on some kind of fool's errand."

"I'm not lying. I paid Danny. I assume he paid Jenny," Greenburg said.

"To breathe life into your dog," Harvey said with sarcasm and frustration.

"It's no fool's errand, bringing dead dogs to life, and you're on the outside looking in," Greenburg said. "You're on the platform, but you missed the train."

Of all the quips and comebacks and wisecracks that Greenburg could have dreamed up at this particular moment, with

Harvey thinking about being small and insignificant, living a life that caused O'Toole to tell him he had figuratively missed the train, this was especially bad timing for the dentist.

Harvey felt the hatred rising from the bottom of his little feet. It was a living breathing entity, his hatred. It was hot and electric and burned inside him as it wormed its way up past his knees and into his chest. He could feel his face on fire and his eyes aflame with venom. (His feet weren't far from his knees, his knees weren't far from his chest, and his chest wasn't far from his face: the point being, it didn't take long for the hate to fill Harvey from head to toe.)

"I'm going to feed your new dog to my fish," Harvey said, "bring you his skeletal remains, and then we'll see if she can breathe life into a bag of bones."

"He's not my new dog," Greenburg said. "He's my old dog. He's Chachi."

The poodle's eyes were practically popping out of his head; he was straining and pulling so hard against the leash to get to Omar.

"New or old," Omar said, "this dog's on crack.

"Last chance," Harvey said. "What are you and Miller doing with my money? Tell me now or your poodle meets my piranha."

"There goes the train, Harvey," Greenburg said. "Wave good-bye."

"Omar, take the dog," Harvey said.

In spite of the growling and snarling and pulling and straining, Chachi was still a little poodle, and Omar was a giant who with one hand could lift and simultaneously crush the poodle's spine. He reached across the driveway and came at Chachi from above, to grab the dog from the top of its back—a sneak attack and smart strategy considering the poodle was focused on Omar's face.

Except at the last second, as if Chachi had planned it all along, as if the dog had rope-a-doped the giant, he snapped up and behind him with surprising speed and power and chomped down on Omar's index finger.

"Jesus...fuck," Omar said, trying to shake the dog off. "Fuck this dog..."

"Chachi," Greenburg said, too stunned to say anything else. He pulled on the leash, but the dog pulled back, and the dentist couldn't budge him. "Chachi, no..."

Carol, who'd been standing under the portico the entire time, scanning Escalon Drive for the police, came running up the driveway. "Chachi...Chachi...Donald, do something...do something..."

Omar finally shook the dog off his hand, stood up, and took out his silenced Glock. "I'm going to kill this fucking dog," he said to Harvey.

"No," Greenburg said.

"No," Carol said.

"Be my guest," Harvey said.

But before Omar could pull the trigger, Carol pointed down the street and said, "Here they are."

Harvey narrowed his eyes and looked all the way down Escalon Drive and saw a police car heading up the hill. His jaw was clenched, and his mouth was shut tight, but somehow the words escaped. "Put the gun away, Omar. We'll kill the dog another day."

Omar holstered his gun, and he and Harvey walked to the Range Rover.

Chachi growled like a demon until the SUV was out of sight.

27

the new rock of el cab

THE THOUGHT HAD FIRST OCCURRED to Mike while he was floating on the Hello Kitty lounger. It was an inkling of an idea, looking for traction in the midst of Mike's nutty neural pathways. And then Ahab and Ishmael had shown up and thrown river stones at his head and killed the Kitty floater with gunshots and tried to electrocute him with his own Bose in his own pool. The Bose had been ruined—same as Mike's day.

The thought had returned while he and the black woman with the Civil War sword, Ramona Clifton, debated whether or not the Chinese served frozen dog TV dinners. They had been standing by the side of Dr. Greenburg's pool, waiting for Jenny to breathe on Greenburg's dead dog and bring it back to life, which, to Mike's astonishment and abject terror, Jenny actually did, and his mind went to chaos and the thought, again, could find no footing and flew the coop.

It wasn't until this morning, when he'd woken up missing his wife and daughters so badly that his heart hurt, that the thought became fully formed.

It was a long thought that began with the fact that his life had spiraled wildly downward and hopelessly out of control since the moment he had been fired from the firm—every negative and nasty thing that had happened to him had happened because he wasn't working.

Some people are born to the fast lane of life—parties and engagements and galas and high-profile appearances, calendars filled with social and professional affairs. Some people thrive on that frenetic pace. They are risk takers and gamblers. They are hip and happening and *in the know*. They are thin and have outstanding hair. It does not automatically make them successful or happy to be in the fast lane. It is just who they are and how they have to be. It is how they live, their way to survive the weight of the world.

And some people are grinders, born to the work lane. They wake up and drive their aging Acura to the office and do their job. They coach rec-league soccer after hours and then cut their own grass and eat dinner with their wife and kids and play Scrabble and watch TV and eat a bowl of ice cream and pass out in the recliner until their wife gets them up so they can go to bed and do it again tomorrow. They are overweight and balding. It does not automatically make them unsuccessful or unhappy to be in the work lane. It is just who they are and how they have to be. It is how they live, their way to survive the weight of the world.

"We can't all be chiefs," Saint Linda had often said to Mike. "Some of us have to be Indians. There can't be chiefs without Indians."

He was an Indian, Mike was. A grinder. Without work, he'd figured out fast, his family had emigrated to New Jersey and all manner of aberrant, preternatural, and psycho-bad shit had befallen him. If he could just find a job manipulating numbers, if he could just get a line on an open position allocating, tabulating, or correlating numbers, if he could just get that one damn numbers job, he could turn things around, get his life back on track, and fly his family home to Woodland Hills.

Money was an ancillary issue. Greenburg had paid seventy-five thousand to bring his dead dog to life. Danny's commission was twenty percent, and Mike was due half of that: seven thousand five hundred (which he hadn't been paid yet). That would get him some of the way through the rest of the month, but he couldn't count on Danny and Jenny to get him any further.

Hell, he didn't want to count on Jenny. What she had done in Greenburg's backyard was unnatural in the sense that it was against the freaking laws of nature, and nothing good could come from that. He didn't want anything to do with raising the dead for money. That was fast lane stuff. High-wire stuff. He just wanted to press on. He wanted to forget it happened, to put it out of his mind, and get back to grinding out his life as an Indian.

If only he could find a place where a financial position had unexpectedly presented itself and there was an immediate need to hire someone straight away so that the numbers didn't pile up to Pasadena. If only there was—

And then the thought finally came to fruition: El Caballero Country Club.

Which is how he came to be sitting in the office of El Cab General Manager Bob Cutting.

"To tell you the truth, I was glad to get your call, Mike," Cutting said. "Happy to hear from you. Your mother ran the books for twenty-three years. In her own way, she was the backbone of The El Cab Lifestyle. It's the nature of things to change, but your mother never did. We called her "The Rock of El Cab." She kept the club on the straight and narrow. I have to admit, we're a little lost without her."

"I know what you mean," Mike said. "It's been the worst two days of my life."

Cutting had been the club GM for six years. Mike had met him several times at El Cab functions he'd attended with his mother. Cutting had come from Ohio, where he had been the GM of a country club in Cleveland, so landing in Southern California was the best thing that had ever happened to him, and he walked around every day with a smile on his face and a spring in his step. He was fifty-five years old and had thinning red-gray hair. He was overweight and had three young sons, whose rec-league teams he coached when he was done at the club. Mike knew the rest of that story by heart—the lawn mower, the bowl of ice cream, the recliner. Cutting was a grinder, like Mike.

Cutting's impressive office was on the first floor of the elegant El Cab Clubhouse. It was large and wood paneled and had green carpeting that made it feel like an extension of the eighteen-hole Robert Trent Jones Sr. golf course that was right outside Cutting's double French doors, which opened onto a brick paver patio that led to the driving range and putting green. There were framed paintings of famous golfers on the walls. There were leather couches and dark wooden bookshelves. There was an oak desk covered with Cutting family photographs. Seeing them made Mike's heart hurt again.

"The funeral's tomorrow?" Cutting said.

"George Edwards Mortuary in Mission Hills," Mike said, nodding.

"I know a lot of people from the club are going," Cutting said. "She was loved and respected, Mike. I'm sure you'll have a big turnout."

Cutting wore a navy blue blazer, beige slacks, and a blue golf shirt. He looked relaxed and professional, like the GM of the finest country club in the Valley. Mike wondered how Cutting perceived him. He had worn a blue pinstriped suit with a white shirt and no tie. If he looked relaxed and professional, it was only because he was trying to. It certainly wasn't how he felt. His skin was still patchy from where Mrs. Alemi had ripped off the duct tape, and he had sunburn from baking on the Hello Kitty lounger before Ishmael had shot it to shit. His nipples, in particular, were raw and on fire.

"Thank you, Bob," Mike said. "Listen, have you hired someone to replace my mother?"

"We were waiting until after the funeral to think about that," Cutting said sadly.

Mike knew the GM was forlorn for the right reasons—because his friend and colleague, "The Rock of El Cab," had died—but he also knew Cutting was dreading the royal pain in the ass it would be to replace her. Accuracy, honesty, and proficiency don't grow on trees.

"I'd like to take my mother's place," Mike said.

"Excuse me," Cutting said.

"I'd like to be the bookkeeper for the club."

"But you're a senior accountant at a firm, aren't you?"

Should have been a partner, Mike thought. "I left two days ago, after my mother died."

"Why did you do that?"

"I realized, after she was gone, that life was short and doing taxes for real estate developers was unfulfilling. My mother loved El Cab. For twenty-three years, her life was about world-class golf and lasting fellowship. To honor her, and to keep continuity in our lives and at the club, and to be an accurate, honest, and proficient part of that fellowship, of that great golf, would be a higher calling for me. I could start right away, Bob. For my mother, for the club, and for you."

Mike hoped it didn't sound like the utter bullshit it was.

"I don't know what to say, Mike. I wasn't expecting this at all. I mean, of course we'll consider you. I feel like we'll probably hire you, if you're serious about this. I mean, we won't be able to pay you what you made at your firm. Have you considered that aspect of your decision?"

"My wife's going back to work for the same reason I want to come here, fulfillment. Yes, we've considered the financial ramifications."

"What does she do?"

"She's a florist." It was a blazing lie. Marcy had the Thumb of Death when it came to gardening. Mike didn't care. He was going for it. He was all in. "We're at the stage of life where money is secondary. Family, fellowship, fulfillment—that's what we're going for now. Between the two of us, we'll have enough money. We just want to do good work."

The men looked at each other for a long moment and then Cutting nodded, stood up, and came around his desk. Mike stood up too, and they shook hands.

"We'd be lucky to have you, Mike. We really would. I'll get you an application, there's a committee, of course—after the government, there's nothing more bureaucratic than a country club—but like I said, we'd be lucky to have you."

"Thanks, Bob. It means a lot to me."

"Great. Wait here."

The men nodded at each other and then Cutting left the room. Mike sat back down in the leather chair across from the GM's desk, took his first easy breath in two days, and looked out the French doors toward the driving range and putting green. *This will be my world*, he thought, *and life will be good.*

But as he conjured up a vision of himself as "The *New* Rock of El Cab"—the casual clothes, the country club cocktails, the easy eighteen-hole pace, the tidy office, the numbers in straight rows in orderly books—he was interrupted by Judd Martin, who opened the French doors and filled the doorway, holding a handgun like Wyatt Earp.

"No," Mike said. "Not you. Not now."

"Get up you fat fuck," Judd said.

"I'm not fat," Mike said.

Martin was a mental whack-job, exploding with emotional instability, volatility, and violence. His physical appearance had deteriorated to the point of surreal. He was transforming into an actual zombie. He wore the same filthy jeans, work boots, and hunting vest with no shirt. He was pungent, even with the French doors open. In an enclosed space, Mike imagined, Martin's aroma might knock a man out.

As Mike was thinking about that—and about calling for help —a stray ray of the hellish sun caught something on Martin's camo hunting vest and momentarily glistened—a child's badge made of some cheap Chinese metal. It was a Wild West badge emblazoned with the word: *deputy*, part of a packaged set that probably included a holster and two six-shooters and maybe a kerchief and a cowboy hat.

Saint Linda had bought Mike and Danny matching sheriff get-ups with deputy badges when they were kids, and they'd ridden around the small yellow house in Canoga Park on imaginary horses for hours. Mike's memory mind inexplicably traveled back in time to relive their childhood posse but couldn't stay long because Martin was speaking.

"...vested in me as a deputized officer of the Los Angeles Police Department, I claim you as my fucking hostage. I can't kill you, Miller, but I can hurt you bad."

Mike tried to shout for help or maybe just shout, but Judd took a massive stride into and across the room and stuck the barrel of the handgun into Mike's mouth before any sound escaped. He raised his gun hand, lifted Mike out of Cutting's leather chair, and walked him backwards, face to face, through the French doors and across the patio.

28

that's so funny, i don't care if it's true

DANNY KNEW what to do with the seventy-five grand. He had to pay Jenny eighty percent, sixty thousand, and then split his commission with Mike—seventy-five hundred bucks in cash money each. That is what he knew he had to do. He said it to himself when Greenburg handed him the envelope: *that is what I have to do.*

There was an alternate thought in the shadows of his mind. It was a secondary notion that had occurred to him while Chachi was wagging his tail and jumping on Carol like he hadn't been dead for days. He could explain to Mike and Jenny that in order for him to devote his full-time focus to their new partnership, it might be good business to first pay the thirty-six thousand he owed Harvey, thus erasing Danny's debt and allowing him to move out of Mike's garage, open a new office, and find their next dead Hollywood pet. That is what he wished he could do. He said it to himself when Chachi was running around the pool: *that is what I wish I could do.*

But what he *did* do was take the 134 to the 210 to Baldwin and make a left into Gate 8 at Santa Anita Park so he could bet the money on a horse named *Let There Be Linda* running in the first race at 9-2 odds.

Danny liked Santa Anita Park, with its 1930s art deco elegance, its San Gabriel Mountain vistas, its Hollywood history —Louis B. Mayer owned horses here, Seabiscuit won the Breeder's Cup at Santa Anita in 1940, and this was where the Marx Brothers shot *A Day at the Races*. He liked the festivity and majesty of the place, the magnificent one-mile track, the Buglers in their red and gold uniforms playing "Call to the Post," the Grandstand, with seating for twenty-six thousand (more than the Staples Center), the palm-treed infield that could accommodate fifty thousand (as many as the Stanford football stadium). He liked the Club House for lunch; the fabulous Santa Anita hand-carved corned beef sandwiches were the best in LA. The beer was colder at the track. The air was cleaner.

He liked that it was an inexpensive way to spend an excellent day—unless you made a bad bet. If he was feeling flush, he would buy a ten-dollar Clubhouse admission ticket, otherwise a five-buck general admission ticket was just fine. The races were the same either way—electricity in the air, sun on your face.

He liked the paddock, where the horses gathered twenty minutes before they ran in the next race and where you could see up close and personal how massive and muscular they were, how gorgeous they were, how dignified and regal.

He liked the horses and the jockeys and the trainers and the owners. He liked reading their stories and histories—the bloodlines, the breeding, the training, the racing—all of it documented in journals and magazines, a spectacular archive of information with which to find and follow a horse, to measure its potential, to figure its future, to calculate the odds.

He liked the races, the frenetic prancing and pacing at the starting gate, the firing of the gun, and the excitement of the crowd as the horses pounded and thundered around the track, often sprinting neck and neck down the last stretch, nose to nose.

Most of all, he liked the betting, finding the right horse and the right jockey in the right field at the right time on the right day at the right track, the explosive adrenal rush as his horse came around the last turn, the thrill and power of winning, of being in the money.

He had liked the horses ever since his father had taken him to Santa Anita when he was a little boy. His dad said it was a secret he could never tell his brother or his mother, and he never did. Even back then, the horses blew Danny away.

He had been following this filly for two full years (at first because it had his mother's name and then because he liked the trainer, a crusty Tampa veteran named Carl Gristle). She was three years old, sleek and strong, chestnut brown with a black mane. When she was a two-year-old, she had run in the money in several races when the track was very dry and the air was very hot. Then she ran in wetter and cooler weather and placed poorly for a year. Then Carl Gristle became her trainer, and her times improved, and Carl had just last week been quoted saying she was "almost ready" to break through—Gristle code for: *fastest freaking horse I've ever trained*. Yet she was way under the Santa Anita radar. There were other fillies in the race that were bigger and faster. They were the favorites today. *Let There Be Linda* was an afterthought.

Except the track was very dry, and the air was very hot, and the jockey was Garrett Flores, who also ran well in these conditions, had shown chemistry with the filly in past races, and was hungry for a breakthrough of his own—the right horse and the right jockey in the right field at the right time on the right day at the right track.

It was the perfect bet, the bet he'd been waiting for, the bet of a lifetime. If he'd had a million dollars, he'd have put it all on this filly to win on this day in the first race with these horses and the temperature pegged at one hundred six and the track Death Valley dry and Flores in the saddle and Gristle whispering in her ear, but he only had seventy-five thousand, so that would have to do. At 9-2, she would pay eleven dollars for a two-buck bet. He was about to make four hundred grand.

He parked the Pathfinder, grabbed his briefcase from the

front passenger seat, got out of the Nissan, and started across the lot to the track. It was noon on Friday. The first race was in thirty minutes or so. His skin was burning, and he didn't think it was the heat. He thought it was the anticipation of being rich. He was thinking about what he would do with the money—pay Harvey, pay Jenny, pay Mike, buy a new car, rent an office in Studio City, and rent a house in Laurel Canyon—when a black, two-door, Chevy Impala pulled in front of him and cut him off.

Gary Shuler jumped out of the Impala, his gun drawn and pointed at Danny, who looked at the detective with some confusion and then said, "Hey, wait, Gary, right?"

"That's right, Danny," Gary said. "Now, turn around, put your hands on the Camry, and spread your legs. You're under arrest."

He gestured at a Toyota parked right where Danny had stopped in his tracks, a few spots down from the Pathfinder.

"What? No. No way. I just signed you to a ninety-day deal. I'm your agent. You can't arrest me. What are you arresting me for?"

"Put your hands on the Camry and spread your legs."

"Not until you—"

Before he could finish objecting, Gary had spun him around, bent him over the hood of the car, stuck his right leg between Danny's legs, and pushed them open so that Danny was spread-eagle over the front of the Toyota.

"What the hell is going on?" Danny said.

Gary patted Danny down. "Greenburg called me this morning. Can you guess what he wanted?"

"My dentist?"

"Can you guess?"

"Just tell me."

"Protection."

"From who?"

"Harvey and Omar. Harvey wants his seventy-five thousand back, and Greenburg says he gave it to you because you represent a woman named Jenny who breathed on his dead poodle and brought it back to life. Do you have a client named Jenny who breathes on dead poodles and brings them back to life?"

"Yes."

"That's so funny, I don't care if it's true."

Gary took Danny's soft brown leather briefcase off Danny's shoulder, looked inside, and saw the envelope filled with cash.

"That's my money, Gary. Don't touch my money," Danny said, still on the car but craning his neck all the way around so he could kind of see Gary behind him.

"Greenburg said Harvey was very upset. He feels cheated, Harvey does. He thinks you switched Chachis. Bought a new poodle for a few hundred bucks and took his money to bet at the track."

"That's bullshit."

"You're at the track with the money."

"It's bullshit that I bought Greenburg a new poodle. That's the real Chachi, the one who died. Jenny brought him back."

"I didn't think it was possible."

"Neither did I."

"I mean my act. I thought it was already really funny, but now, are you kidding, the dead poodle comes back to life and the dwarf goes on a rampage of revenge? That's hysterical. I'm going to be huge. Seinfeld huge. And I'm going to make my agent a lot of money. Hey, that's you," Gary said, stepping away from the Toyota.

Danny stood up and turned around. His briefcase was hanging from Gary's shoulder, and the detective still had his gun out. Danny glanced at his watch. He had twenty minutes to get into the park and place his bet.

"They're going to make this a TV series, CBS, I'm guessing, but maybe ABC or NBC, and you'll be the executive producer," Gary said.

"Are you insane?" Danny said.

"I think I am," Gary said, walking backwards to the Impala,

keeping his eye and his gun on Danny, "but I have to be. I'm a comedian."

"You can't do this," Danny said. "Shit, Gary. Why are you taking my money?"

"For your own safety. If you lose it at the track—"

"I'm going to win four hundred grand."

"—Harvey will kill you, and I need you alive to be my agent, so you can sell me big time. If you're dead, you can't do that. Now, you can tell Harvey that I took it for safety's sake, and we'll all keep the story going—dentists and dwarves and dead dogs, oh my. Hilarious."

Gary climbed into the Impala, gunned the engine, and drove away with the seventy-five grand. Danny ran after him, but it was one hundred ten on the tarmac, and he had to stop halfway across the lot so he wouldn't drop dead.

29

there's no gray area when it comes to branding human beings

GARY PARKED the Impala in a visitor spot by the Little Valley Trailer Park office, grabbed his backpack from the front passenger seat, and walked to the rotting Airstream. The Ford pickup was out front, so he knew the zombie was in there. He knocked on the door and waited. It was one hundred eight degrees in Sunland-Tujunga at one o'clock, Friday afternoon. He glanced up at the sun and thought it looked pissed off, burning with anger at Earth for cosmic reasons he would contemplate later and add to his act.

After Santa Anita, he had stopped at a convenience store and purchased two Oreo four-packs and a pint of milk. He was celebrating his great good fortune to have hit the mother lode of comedic gold. All he had to do now was mine it for all it was worth. While blissing out on the chocolate cookie drug, he had a happy daydream that he and Pat Paulsen were dressed as forty-niners and were panning for gold in a rushing stream in the San Francisco hills in 1852. They were knee deep in the water and Pat was slapping him on the back and telling him there was plenty of gold to go around.

He interpreted the daydream as a good omen. It was where he wanted to be, where he was going, where he belonged.

"Nobody home," Martin said from inside the trailer.

"It's Detective Shuler. Open the door," Gary said.

"Can't open the door if nobody's home," Martin said. "That's stupid."

Gary shook his head. He felt a bead of sweat run from the nape of his neck down his back to his gun. He reached around and took it out of the holster. "What's stupid is you telling me nobody's home while you're talking to me."

"Take the hint and take a hike. I have company."

"You have company?"

"I'm entertaining."

"I'll have to see that to believe it."

"You don't believe it?"

"It's not that I don't believe it, well, yes it is, I don't believe it. Now open the door, or I'll de-deputize you, and you'll be a zombie without a badge, just another undead real estate developer running around LA with no authority to cause hardship and pain."

"I like causing hardship and pain."

"Open the door."

The door opened, and Martin filled the trailer doorway, looking more dead than alive, holding an electric branding iron, used for claiming cattle, plugged in somewhere behind him in the Airstream. The iron looked red hot. "You going to shoot me?"

The detective side of his brain thought, *That can't be good—the zombie with a branding iron.* But the comedian side thought, *That's as good as it gets.* "It's possible."

"Fair enough," Martin said. He moved aside, and Gary stepped up into the trailer.

Though Gary couldn't have imagined it, the Airstream was even more of a mess than it was the last time he'd been here, which was yesterday. It looked like someone had blown the place up with a pipe bomb and then infected it with slum disease.

But Gary couldn't concentrate on the putrid filth and trash and chaos, and he couldn't focus on the poster of the accountant, which had gone from one big blade in the forehead to multiple blades all over the accountant's face and body, because the accountant himself was blindfolded, gagged, and hogtied on the couch, naked as a baby.

Gary put on latex gloves and moved across the trailer to Mike. "There's no gray area when it comes to branding human beings. It's the sort of thing that juries don't deliberate. They don't even go to the jury room. They just stay in the box and tell the judge to fry the guy. They volunteer to throw the switch."

He told himself to remember those lines—*fry the guy* and *throw the switch*—and put them in his act. Talk about laugh-a-minute material. This kind of comedy was so outrageous that they would have to give it a new name. Zombie-comedy. *Zomedy*.

"I'm exercising my rights as an agent of the law," Martin said, and he pressed the end of the branding iron into a kitchen cabinet door. The wood sizzled.

"Maybe in Tombstone, Arizona, at the end of the 1800s," Gary said. "But not at the dawn of the twenty-first century in Southern California."

Martin let the cabinet burn for a few seconds and then removed the iron and left a smoking black "M" behind. "McCoy Cattle Ranch in Salinas," he said. "Story is a cowboy got kicked in the mouth while branding a Brahma bull with this very iron, and McCoy said he could sell it for new teeth."

"You bought it from the cowboy?" Gary said.

"I bought it from a dwarf in Pacoima. 'M' for Martin. Had to have it."

Mike was positioned on his right side, bare ass facing into the trailer. He couldn't see a thing or say a word, but he could hear every sound. He squirmed and shouted angrily through his gag, but he couldn't move more than an inch, and his cries were deeply muffled.

While Martin moved across the trailer and extended the hot end of the iron toward Mike's butt, it occurred to Gary that the accountant had heard the sizzling wood as well.

"You can't brand him," Gary said, aiming the gun at the zombie.

"Already did," Martin said, and he flipped Mike onto his left side. In the center of Mike's chest was a blazing red "M" that looked mean and nasty and painful as hell.

Good God, Gary thought. In his wildest dreams, he couldn't make this shit up. *They'll get Ben Stiller to play me in the movie,* he said to himself. He wondered who would play Judd Martin—Alec Baldwin, maybe. Or Gary Busey.

"Give me one good reason why not," Martin said.

"Brand him once, you can say it was an accident," Gary said.

"An accident?"

"'Sorry buddy, my bad, I seem to have branded you by mistake. I hate when that happens, don't you?'" Gary said. "But brand a man twice, and that's no accident."

"What is it?"

"A billboard. Brand him once, and people might not even notice. Brand him again and everyone will be pointing at him: *Man, get a load of this guy. Somebody branded him not one but two times.* He won't be able to travel incognito. He won't blend in. We're in the middle of a case, you and me. Mike Miller is our high-speed Internet. He's in the thick of this thing, gathering information at one hundred megabytes per second. We need him under wraps, undercover, and under the radar. He's no good to us if you brand him again. Now sit him up; I want to talk to him."

Mike was hogtied, so he couldn't sit by himself. Martin put the branding iron down and situated Mike in an upright, sort-of-resting-on-his-knees position and then physically held him in place so he wouldn't topple over.

"He's been blindfolded the whole time?" Gary said.

"Since I picked him up at the country club," Martin said. "He has no idea where he is."

Neither do you, Gary thought. And then he turned to face Mike and knew he had found another nugget in his pan. He could feel Pat Paulsen slapping his back in the middle of the stream. His cop intuition and his comedic instinct were both buzzing with the same message: *there's a lot more gold in the water.*

"Hello, Mike," the detective said. "My name is Gary Shuler. I'm a stand-up comedian. I have now heard from several sources that you and your brother are in the business of bringing dead dogs back to life—for seventy-five grand a pop—with a gypsy named Jenny. I would very much like you to gather up your brother and the gypsy named Jenny and bring another dead dog back to life, and I would like to be invited to that show because I think it will be hilarious. If I removed your blindfold, you would see how sincere I am about being at the next Jenny the Gypsy Show, but I'm not going to remove your blindfold because I think there's some great comic tension to be gained by revealing my true identity to you later as opposed to now.

"Deputy Martin here will be in frequent contact with you—I know you're excited about that—to find out exactly when and where the next Jenny the Gypsy Show is going to happen. You may need to kill somebody's dog, but I think that's fine because you're going to bring it right back to life. If you don't get me a front row seat on, well, let's just pick a day, say Sunday, then I'll allow Mr. Martin to go zombie on your ass. I haven't known him very long, but I feel sure he has more monstrous things in mind than branding you. Do you understand what I'm saying? I'm going to take the gag out of your mouth, and I want you to tell me you understand what I'm saying."

Gary took the gag out of Mike's mouth.

"I'm having the worst fucking week *ever*," Mike said.

Gary put the gag back in Mike's mouth, turned to Martin, and said, "Put him in your truck, cover him with a blanket, take him home, and follow him like a shadow."

The detective still had his gun pointed at the zombie, so Martin lifted Mike up and over his shoulder like he was a bag of feathers instead of a naked accountant, walked to the trailer door, and said, "Monstrous doesn't begin to describe what's in my mind." Then he left the Airstream.

Gary watched them go and nodded to himself. While eating Oreos in his car after leaving Santa Anita, he had felt it was time to get rid of the zombie, and the zombie himself had just confirmed that feeling. He had also been thinking it was time for him, as a comedian, to become proactively involved in writing his new act. Up to now, he had been reactive to the hilarity, but he had responsibilities as a professional funnyman to do more than report the proceedings. It was time to insert himself into the story.

He looked around the Airstream and thought, *How can I zero out the zombie and keep the comedy coming at the same time?* And then he smiled because his comedic engine was firing on all cylinders.

He took the envelope with the seventy-five grand out of his backpack, put it in one of the myriad empty fast food bags strewn across the floor, and buried the bag at the bottom of a pile of other radioactive refuse.

We'll let Harvey handle the zombie, he said to himself.

30
however, there were also no absolutes anywhere

AFTER GEORGANNE DIED, Harvey cancelled the high-stakes poker parlor she ran in the back room (now his office) and started loan sharking. He also considered becoming a bookie and had taken a trip to Santa Anita to explore the possibility of joining forces with a dirtbag named Morton Minder (known by all as Morton Mindy), who knew the trainers and grooms and jockeys and had weaseled his way into the kind of all-access behind-the-scenes permanent pass that, as he told Harvey, *"gave gamblers a boner."*

Morton Mindy took Harvey on a tour of the park, and while they were strolling through a stable, a groom and a bug boy entered from the other end, leading four thoroughbreds back to their stalls.

As Morton Mindy and Harvey and the horses approached each other, one of the fillies could not identify Harvey as a human being—as opposed to a wild boar from the woods—and was spooked silly and reared up like a madwoman. She freaked the other racehorses, and Harvey found himself surrounded by the massive and powerful animals, all of them up on their hind legs, all of them kicking and snorting and screaming and bucking like broncos.

Harvey was terrified and stood frozen like a yard statue until the groom and the bug boy restored order. Morton Mindy told Harvey that he was lucky to be alive, that if one horse had clipped him with one hoof, he'd have been one dead dwarf.

Harvey had hated horses ever since that day. He hated Santa Anita Park too. And right now he hated the idea that Danny Miller was betting *his* seventy-five grand at *this* track after ripping off Greenburg with smoke and mirrors and a PetSmart poodle.

After Harvey and Omar had left Greenburg's house, passing the police as they pulled up Escalon Drive, they had stopped by Mike's house in Woodland Hills and by the small yellow house in Canoga Park and by Danny's old office in the distant northern reaches of the San Fernando Valley. They didn't find him here or there or anywhere.

Since Santa Anita was Danny's regular haunt, his home away from home, Omar had called a Clubhouse bartender that owed Harvey money and told him to call back if Danny showed up. Omar's cell phone rang as Harvey was heading back to Pacoima Pawn and Loan: Danny was in the Clubhouse.

Harvey had driven the Range Rover to Santa Anita and cruised the parking lot until they found Danny's Pathfinder. They had waited an hour for Danny to emerge. When they spotted him coming across the lot, Omar slipped out of the SUV and vanished into the heat distortion rising up off the macadam. Harvey waited until Danny was backing the Pathfinder out of the parking spot and then pulled the SUV directly in the Nissan's path of egress, trapping the Pathfinder in place.

Danny got out of the truck intending to get in the Range Rover's face, so to speak, but stopped on a dime when he saw the dwarf lower the tinted window.

Harvey could tell by the widening of Danny's eyes and by the instantaneous change of expression on Danny's face that the talent agent knew he was in deep horseshit. Danny turned to run for his life and ran right into Omar, who grabbed him with two hands and headbutted him into unconsciousness.

Danny fell like a bowling pin, but Omar caught him, lifted him with ease, carried him to the Range Rover, put him in the back seat, and climbed in after him. Harvey raised the tinted window and drove away, leaving the Pathfinder halfway out of its parking spot and turned at an angle that would just block the car parked next to it from pulling out. *Too bad for that asshole,* Harvey said to himself.

Twenty minutes later, Danny started to come around. His eyes fluttered. He licked his lips. He made a sound that said: *I'm in a shitload of pain right here.*

"Oh, Danny Boy," Harvey sang, "the pipes, the pipes are calling, From glen to glen, and down the mountain side, The summer's gone, and all the flowers are dying, 'Tis you, 'tis you must go and I must bide."

Omar had his left hand clamped down on Danny's shoulder —to keep him in place—and his right hand holding Danny's chin, so he could point Danny's face at the rearview mirror, so Harvey could look at his face while he was singing to him.

"Welcome back, Danny. How was your day at the track?" Harvey said.

Danny's eyes began to focus as if he knew where he was and what was happening. He looked at the dwarf in the mirror and said, "Fuck you, Harvey."

Omar released Danny's chin, made a fist, and rabbit punched Danny in the nose, rocking Danny's head back so that it smash-bounced off the headrest behind him. Danny groaned, and his nose started to bleed. Omar grabbed his chin again and pointed him at the mirror.

"How was your day at the track?" Harvey said again.

"Banner," Danny said.

"Did your horse win?" Harvey said.

"Yes," Danny said in a soft and sad and defeated voice.

"What was that?" Harvey said.

"Yes," Danny said again, louder but no less demoralized.

"Congratulations. Tell me about it," Harvey said.

"*Let There Be Linda* in the first race," Danny said. "Paid 9-2."

"Did you hear that, Omar?" Harvey said. "*Let There Be Linda* paid 9-2 in the first race. How much money do you suppose Danny Boy took to the bank?"

"If he bet the seventy-five he stole from us, sounds like four hundred plus," Omar said.

"Precisely right. Four hundred thousand dollars and change. And what does Danny owe us?" Harvey said.

"Thirty-six over three years, the seventy-five he stole with Greenburg, fifty percent of what's left of his winnings, plus damages, expenses, considerations, and pain and suffering. I'd say four hundred thousand and change."

"That's what I would say," Harvey said. "So where's the money, Danny? You're not carrying that much in cold cash. Did they write you a check?"

"I didn't place the bet," Danny said.

"Omar," Harvey said.

Omar rabbit punched Danny in the nose again. Danny's head bounced hard off the headrest. Blood flowed freely from his nostrils.

"Ow, fuck, shit, Jesus, stop doing that," Danny said.

"Where's my money?" Harvey said.

"Gary took it," Danny said.

"Gary who?" Harvey said.

"Shuler. Detective Gary Shuler," Danny said. "He stopped me before I got inside the park and took my briefcase. Jesus Christ, look at my fucking nose."

"Detective Gary Shuler?" Harvey said, using his voice to put air quotes around the word *Detective*. "Why would he do that?" Harvey said.

"He knew you would kill me if I lost it at the track—" Danny said.

"'There will be killing till the score is paid,'" Omar said. "Homer, *The Odyssey.*"

"—so he took it for safekeeping," Danny said. "He needs me alive, so I can be his agent, and so he can keep the story going."

"The story of you stealing my money?" Harvey said.

"I didn't steal your money," Danny said.

"Of course you did. You had this horse on your radar for weeks, and when your dentist's dog died a tragic death—"

"You threw it out the window of a speeding car," Danny said.

"'The joy of killing! The joy of seeing killing done—these are traits of the human race at large,'" Omar said. "Twain, *Following the Equator.*"

"—you conspired with Greenburg to produce a farce called *Jenny and Her Magic Breath* so Greenburg would take the money from me and give it to you to take to the track, where you would, of course, lose every penny."

"If I make the bet, I win four hundred grand," Danny said, bleeding onto his shirt. "And you're wrong about Jenny. She's no farce. She's the real deal, and I'm her agent, and I'm going to make millions. So fuck you, Harvey. Jesus, look at my nose."

Harvey looked into the rearview mirror and saw Danny and his bloody nose and ran a quick equation in his head. There was no chance that Jenny could breathe life into death. Zero chance. It was absolutely impossible. However, there were also no absolutes anywhere. Miracles did occasionally, improbably, and impossibly happen. So if there was just ever so slightly a one-percent-of-one-percent-of-one-percent chance that Jenny could indeed raise the dead, then she would become a license to print money. And if that became the case, then he and Danny would be partners—or Danny would die.

"I want to see her bring a dead dog back to life," Harvey said. "Make that happen on Sunday or Omar is going to excise your heart with a butter knife."

"'By heaven, I'll make a ghost of him that lets me,'" Omar said. "Shakespeare, *Hamlet.*"

Harvey turned the Range Rover into Mike's horseshoe driveway, pulled to the front of the house, turned in his seat, and serenaded Danny again. "But come ye back when summer's in the meadow, Or when the valley's hushed and white with snow, 'Tis I'll be here in sunshine or in shadow, Oh, Danny boy, oh Danny boy, I love you so."

Omar headbutted Danny again, and Danny's eyes rolled back, and he slumped against the door, semiconscious. Omar got out of the Range Rover, came around to Danny's side, lifted Danny out of the SUV, and dropped him near the front door.

Before Omar had a chance to get back in the SUV, a beat-to-hell Ford pickup turned into the other side of Mike's horseshoe driveway and pulled up until it was face-to-face with the Range Rover. Judd Martin jumped out of the pickup looking otherworldly and wild and worse, lifted Mike, naked and hogtied and blindfolded, out from under a dirty tarp in the truck bed, carried him to the front door, and dumped him on the ground next to Danny.

Harvey, Omar, and Martin looked at each other with astonishment, and then Martin got back in the Ford and Omar got back in the Ranger Rover, and both vehicles backed out and drove away.

31
i'm a time bomb

SINCE DANNY HAD UNTIED him and they'd both staggered into the house, Mike had shaved and showered and now stood naked in front of the full-length mirror that Marcy had purchased at Pottery Barn. His sunburned and duct tape-scarred skin looked raw, his nipples still burned, and there were bags under his eyes, but he seemed to look more or less the same as when he was a senior accountant at Wasserman and Waddell, which was Wednesday, two exceptionally long days ago.

He seemed to look more or less the same, that is, but for the "M" that Judd Martin had branded into his chest. It hurt like hell, the "M" did, but Mike had decided in the shower that he was going to ignore that pain because to acknowledge it was to give Martin power over him, and as weak as Mike was, as emotionally and physically spent and fragile as he was—and Mike knew he could crack open any minute—he refused to be weaker than a zombie real estate madman.

He sat on the bed and called Paramus. It was three thirty in the afternoon in the Valley, so it was six thirty in New Jersey. Marcy's mother, Dianna, answered the phone. She hadn't liked Mike from the beginning, and it had gone downhill fast from there. When he'd asked for Dianna's blessing for her daughter's hand in marriage, Dianna had said no. (Marcy's father, Jim, had said he was on the fence.) And when Mike took the job at Wasserman and Waddell instead of the job he'd been offered at an accounting firm in Hackensack, minutes from Paramus, a job that Jim had helped line up to keep his daughter and future grandchildren on the East Coast, Dianna had declared a sort of silent emotional war that she'd waged up to and including to this very Friday at six thirty, EST.

"Marcy and the girls spent the day visiting schools. Tonight they're looking at rental houses with Jim, just in case," Dianna said.

"In case what?" Mike said.

"You were an accountant until Wednesday. Do the math."

He *had* done the math. That was the problem. His numbers had been bad since Tuesday, and each day since then they'd become worse. He put on basketball shorts and a Lakers T-shirt and walked across the house to the kitchen, where he found Danny leaning against the sink and Jenny sitting at the table. Danny was on his cell phone.

"I'm not a dog whisperer," Danny said. "I have no idea what's wrong with Chachi." Danny's nose was bruised but not broken. His eyes were black and blue enough to make him look vaguely raccoon-ish. He'd called a cab to take him to the track, picked up the Pathfinder, driven it back to Mike's, showered, and changed his clothes as well: black V-neck T-shirt and faded jeans. His hair was behind his ears, still wet.

"What are you doing here?" Mike said to Jenny, grabbing a bowl, a spoon, a quart of milk, and a new box of Frosted Flakes and sitting across from her.

"Collecting my money," Jenny said. "Greenburg paid cash, and my mother wants it now. I don't normally care what she wants, but she's in a bad state of mind."

Mike had thought Jenny was pretty when he'd first met her yesterday at Greenburg's house, but she was there to breathe life into a dead dog—*which she actually freaking did*—so he couldn't concentrate on what she looked like, although he remembered her green eyes and her sexy red sundress because Marcy had one just like it.

Today, Mike thought Jenny looked like somebody else all over again. She wore a denim sleeveless cowboy shirt—embroidered with bucking broncos—open halfway down her chest (he could see her lacy black bra), with denim cut-off shorts (that were so short she might as well not be wearing any shorts at all), blue and white cowboy boots, and a white cowboy hat. She wore turquoise bracelets and rings. *Are her eyes blue now?* Mike asked himself. *Yes, they are. Her eyes are blue and not green.*

Anyway, Marcy's sundress was long ago and far away, before the girls were born, when the newlyweds were young and in love and the door to their lives was wide open. Now, of course, that door was closing fast. He might never get it open again.

It was that thought, that his marriage was in trouble, that made him decide to eat the entire box of Frosted Flakes.

As he filled his bowl, he thought, *I'm a time bomb, and my fuse is lit. The slightest provocation, and I will explode.* There was no point in wondering how his life had come to this, no erasing the last three days. Though he looked familiar, he was not the same man he was on Tuesday, before his mother died and his world went wild. Once upon a time, he was a normal person. Now, he was a time bomb.

"My mother has no state of mind," Mike said to Jenny.

"A deal's a deal, Dr. Greenburg," Danny said. "Your dog is alive as promised. His disposition has nothing to do with it. You don't get your money back. I'm sorry you're upset, but maybe that's why Chachi's growling at you." And he clicked off the call and said, "I'm getting a new dentist."

Mike poured milk in the bowl and shoveled Frosted Flakes into his mouth. Danny grabbed his own bowl and spoon and joined Jenny and his brother at the table. As he reached for the cereal box, Mike pulled it away.

"Going to cost you," Mike said to his brother.

"Fuck you, Mike," Danny said. "I could have left you naked and hogtied in the front yard. But I didn't. Now give me the goddamn Frosted Flakes." He reached across the table, and Mike whacked his arm away with his spoon.

"Seven thousand five hundred," Mike said.

Danny looked at Jenny, and she said, "My Frosted Flakes are sixty thousand. I'll take cash."

Danny sat back, took a breath, and said, "I don't have the money."

Mike stopped eating. He had bills to pay and not enough savings to pay them. He needed his share of the fee. He was a fifty-fifty partner in whatever the hell it was they were doing here. In his mind's eye, he saw the sizzling fuse approaching the explosives, snaking across the room, very close now. "What did you say?"

"I don't have the money," Danny said.

Mike could feel the heat of the fuse, which was maybe just one inch from the case of dynamite that was his life. This was forever the Story of Danny: frustration after disappointment after fuck up after scam. It had never changed for as long as they had been brothers. Mike resented him, distrusted him, disliked him, and probably hated him. He knew Danny felt the same way in reverse. Mike didn't care. He was all out of caring.

"What happened to it?" Jenny said, looking like some kind of stripper cowgirl.

"I went to the track and—"

The sparking fuse arrived and lit the emotional dynamite that was Mike, and in one mad moment of force and energy, he exploded out of his chair and turned the kitchen table over onto Danny, who fell backwards onto the floor while Jenny jumped up out of the way of the flying Frosted Flakes and milk, which went everywhere across the kitchen.

"You lost the money on a fucking horse?" Mike said, screaming while pouncing on Danny, who was flat on his back.

The grown men rolled across the kitchen floor, grabbing each other in headlocks like they were twelve and nine years old.

Danny had length and leverage, but Mike had weight and surprise and experience—he had wrestled in school all the way to tenth grade when his shoulder was dislocated in a brutal pin that had ended his junior varsity career. Danny had run track until cigarettes and pot and beer and girls distracted him. *He's still fucking distracted,* Mike thought as he fought for control and tried to squeeze the life out of his brother.

"I didn't lose it, you crazy asshole," Danny said, fighting back hard. "Gary Shuler took it before I could place my bet."

"The stand-up comedian?" Mike said, and then everything got strange, which is to say stranger still.

32
this is what insanity must feel like

COMPETING with the grief and emptiness he felt for his mother, the befuddlement and rage he felt for being fired, the exasperation and fury he felt for his idiot, irresponsible brother, the apoplexy and terror he felt for the bat-shit crazy Judd Martin, and the confusion and fear and incredulity he felt for Jenny, the Cowgirl Stripper who brought dead dogs to life, competing with all of this was the muscle memory of his high school wrestling moves.

Ankle picks and arm cuts and Piute rolls and cradles. Arm drags and takedowns and half Nelsons and full Nelsons. Mike and Danny rolled across the kitchen, covering themselves with spilled milk and soggy Frosted Flakes.

"How do you know Gary Shuler?" Danny said, leaning a forearm into Mike's throat.

"How do you know him?" Mike said, executing a reverse and shoving Danny's face into the floor.

"I signed him to a ninety-day deal," Danny said, reaching back and digging his fingers into Mike's face, looking for an eyeball to poke. "He's a new client. He followed me to the track."

Mike chomped down on Danny's middle finger, which,

instead of an eyeball, had found Mike's mouth—a super personal fuck you. Danny screamed and pulled his hand away.

"Why did he follow you to the track?" Jenny said. The Frosted Flakes had landed at her feet. She lifted the box and snacked on the dry sugary cereal.

"To keep me alive. He thought I'd lose the money and then Harvey and Omar would kill me," Danny said, punching Mike while shooting his legs around and sitting up in such a way that Mike was behind him, his arms wrapped around Danny's waist

Mike groaned and grunted and strained to control his brother, leaning into him, pulling him one way and then the other, muscling him back down on his stomach. "You would've lost the money. You know why? Because you're a loser. You've always been a loser. When you were six years old, you were a loser. And every year after that you became a bigger loser than you were the year before. It made me sick to my stomach to grow up in the same house as you. All my life, I've wished you were never born."

"I mean this from my heart, Mike. I've wanted to kill you since Dad left," Danny said. "I fantasize about killing you. Killing you would be better than sex. Every night, before I go to bed, I pray to God that one day he lets me kill you."

"Who are Harvey and Omar?" Jenny said.

Danny threw an elbow that caught Mike in the ear. It hurt like hell, but Mike refused to let go. The last time they had fought like this, they were fifteen and twelve and Danny got the upper hand and made Mike cry uncle. There was no goddamn way he was crying uncle this time. They smashed into the overturned table and then crashed into the lower cabinets. *This is what insanity must feel like,* Mike thought, *when a thin slice of your consciousness knows you've lost your grip on reality but can't do a damn thing about it because the rest of you has gone stone-cold crazy.*

"A dwarf and a giant," Danny said. "Sadistic loan shark and his violent sidekick."

"Ahab and Ishmael," Mike said, remembering the Hello

Kitty, the river stones, and the Bose Wave. "We had a pool party."

"What do they have to do with it?" Jenny said.

"They gave Greenburg the seventy-five cash and found out about Chachi," Danny said. "They don't believe it's the same dog. They think I bought a two-hundred-dollar poodle at PetSmart and was going to put the rest on a horse, which I was. And I would've won four hundred grand, except I never made the bet because of Gary Shuler."

Mike was flabby and out of shape and his muscles, such as they were, were getting tired, though not as tired as his brain, which was ready to release the final thin line connecting him to the real world. But that final release, Mike sensed, the letting go of what was once his reality, is where he would find the final animal burst of power he needed to choke the ever-loving shit out of his brother.

"This is your fault," Mike said, cutting the last line and forcing Danny facedown onto the kitchen floor (Danny's arms under his chest). Mike put all his weight on him, pushing Danny down through the ground, crushing his ribcage, making it hard for his brother to breathe. "You sucked me into your fucked up world, and now my world is as fucked up as yours," Mike said. "I've lost my job, my life, my family, my wife. I've lost everything because of you. You know what? You can pay me back by dying."

"You can't kill me, Mike," Danny said, grunting the words out, finding it harder and harder to fill his lungs with air.

"Why not?" Mike said. His body ached, his head hurt, the kitchen was spinning, his nipples were on fire, and the "M" on his chest was throbbing.

"*The Oath*," Danny said, coughing and spitting. The way his arms were pinned, his elbows were being pulverized into bone dust.

"Fuck *The Oath*," Mike said.

"If you kill me, you break *The Oath* you swore on Mom's dying heart," Danny said. "You'll burn in hell with Linda."

"Mom's in heaven," Mike said, and saying those words out loud made tears come to his eyes. For the first time since Saint Linda had died, he allowed himself to see the vision of her having a heart attack at El Caballero Country Club, keeling over her desk, clenching her chest, blinded with pain. He began to cry. But still he would not relent the pressure he was putting on Danny. He was physically forcing his flimflam man brother into and through the floor, where he could then metaphorically bury him forever.

"Not if you break *The Oath*," Danny said. "If you swear an oath to someone and then break it, that person goes to hell too, for making you swear an oath you later broke."

Now Mike saw the paramedics picking his mother up off the floor, strapping her into the gurney, and rolling her out of the club and into the ambulance, oxygen mask in place, IV dripping, Bob Cutting in the background saying, *"So goeth the rock of El Cab."* "That's not true," Mike said, and he heard his own voice and thought, *I sound like a lost fucking soul because I am a lost fucking soul. I am without a soul. I am soulless.*

"Ask Jenny," Danny said.

"Is that true?" Mike said to Jenny.

Jenny placed the box of Frosted Flakes on the counter, grabbed a kitchen chair, and moved it right next to the brothers, who were snorting and grunting and wheezing. She sat beside them and said, "What's true is that if we don't undo *The Oath*, you two will kill each other, and I'll never get my money. So first, we undo *The Oath*."

"How do we do that?" Mike said. He was red in the face and felt like he was having a heart attack like his mother. Cramping pain gripped him from his calves up his thighs through his buttocks and up his back across his chest and down his arms. His head was exploding. Below him, Danny was turning blue.

"I bring your mother back to life," Jenny said, "and we get her to release you."

Mike let go of Danny and fell back on his butt against the lower cabinets, Frosted Flakes plastered to the side of his face and somehow stuck up his ass, pulling at his hair, tears streaming down his face. He had never felt so upside down and inside out. Gravity? No gravity? He could no longer tell. "This is crazy, this is crazy, this is crazy, this is crazy, this is crazy, this is crazy, this is crazy, this is crazy..."

Danny rolled onto his back, soaked with spilled milk, trying to regain feeling in his ribcage and elbows. "The funeral's tomorrow," he said, rasping.

"Then you have to hurry," Jenny said.

33

a whole other can of shit

DANNY DECIDED that doom was on the horizon because the plan included Paul the Pervert. The clown stood beside the Pathfinder, smoking his horrendous cigar, wearing his blood-stained, rat-shit costume, his supinated Docksiders, his creepy makeup, and his rainbow wig, watching Mike and Danny argue about whether the back seat should be up or down.

"We're not going to sit her up like a fucking puppet. We're going to lay her down in the back and cover her with a sheet. Rest in peace, Dan. Ever heard of it?" Mike said, putting his hand on the rear seat to push it in the down position. Both back doors were open, and Mike was leaning into the Nissan on one side, and Danny was leaning into it on the other side, holding the seat in its up position.

"She won't know the difference," Danny said.

Since their Frosted Flakes fight in the kitchen, they had both showered again and stayed on opposite sides of the house until it was time to drive to George Edwards Mortuary in Mission Hills on Chatsworth. Now it was time: eleven o'clock on Friday night. It was one hundred five degrees.

"If we get pulled over and she's sitting up, we can say she's asleep," Danny said. "What do we say if she's lying down in the back under a sheet, Mike? Use your head. Cops don't like corpses in cars in the middle of the night."

"Cops pull us over, I'll put my arm around her, and we'll make out like sloppy drunks," Paul said.

"You know she's dead, right?" Danny said.

"Dead chicks dig me," Paul said.

"I am not sitting in the same car as this clown," Mike said.

Paul the Pervert was part of the plan because the George Edwards Mortuary had a security system that was wired into the electric panel, and the clown, who was working for LA Water and Power, a guy on the line when he got electrocuted on Fairfax, was the only one Danny knew who A: could find and flip the breaker to kill all the power in the building, B: was idiotic enough to come along and steal a dead woman from a funeral home, and C: was so entirely insane that no jury anywhere would believe his testimony should they get arrested and hauled into court.

The back seat stayed up, and the ride to Mission Hills was silent. Danny drove, Mike rode shotgun, and Paul sat behind the driver. Danny used the quiet time to consider the items that were bothering him.

Item number one was that he was driving to a mortuary to steal his dead mother's body so that Jenny could breathe on her and bring her back to life. He knew this was an item he had to reconcile, but the idea of it was so big and bright and hot it was like looking into the sun.

So he turned away and considered item number two, which was the seventy-five thousand dollars in cash money that Gary Shuler had taken from him before he could place what would have been the winning four-hundred-thousand-dollar bet on *Let There Be Linda*. He couldn't begin to understand how or why that had happened, and thinking about it gave him a headache.

So he moved on to item number three, which was the fact that Harvey and Omar were going to kill him if he couldn't resolve issue number two, so scratch contemplating item number three, which was a tad too frightening to consider while he was driving to a freaking mortuary.

Instead, he marched forward to item number four, which is where his brain had wanted to go since he'd decided to consider the items that were bothering him.

Item number four was Jenny.

Four point one was the color of Jenny's eyes. They were brown the first time he'd met her, green later on, and blue today. He had surreptitiously looked and looked and looked at her since she'd arrived in the afternoon to collect her sixty thousand dollars, and he didn't think she was wearing contacts. And if she wasn't wearing colored lenses, then what the hell was happening with her eyes?

Four point two was her clothes. What was with the sexy cowgirl get-up? Where did that come from? Jenny had gone from a Catholic school mouse to a super model in three days. *Normal women don't do that,* Danny thought. Of course, normal women don't raise the dead, so there was that. And her lacy black bra. There was that too.

But it was four point three that rang all the bells and blew all the whistles. *I can't get her out of my mind,* Danny thought. *She's a smoking hot mystery, and I can't get her out of my mind.*

The reason item four point three was a problem was because Danny had a rule about falling for clients, and the rule was: don't do it. Falling for clients was bad for business. Falling for *any* woman, in fact, was bad for business. But Jenny was definitely not just any woman, and now he couldn't get her out of his mind. He would have to make some decisions about that, formulate some kind of plan of attack, but not right now because right now they had arrived at the George Edwards Mortuary.

As the mortuary's accountant, Mike had known what kind of security system George Edwards had installed—and what it cost, and how much of the purchase price could be deducted as a business expense—and Mike had told the clown, and the clown had seen that system all around LA.

Paul had said that killing the main breaker would cut off the security system but that the security company would read that as a power outage and not a break-in, that they would contact LA Water and Power to report the outage and that they would then call the business owner and tell him the same thing. And because they weren't calling with news of a break-in but instead were calling to say that LA Water and Power was going to check on the outage and fix it fast, then probably the business owner wouldn't drive to the mortuary in the middle of the night and might not even contact the police. And even if the police were contacted, it wouldn't be reported as an emergency, so the cops might take their time cruising by.

In the clown's estimation, they would have fifteen minutes to get inside the building, collect the deceased, and drive back to Mike's house in Woodland Hills.

Danny pulled the Pathfinder into the mortuary, drove around to the back of the building, and parked under the wide porte-cochere next to a hearse, no doubt the hearse that would carry Saint Linda to the cemetery tomorrow morning after the service.

Paul found the breaker box on the side of the funeral home and killed the main switch. All the interior and exterior lights went out. Mike shined a flashlight on the back door, Danny kicked it in, and the three of them stood there looking at the open doorway. As expected, no alarm went off. It was coal black inside the building, and it was silent. The time was eleven thirty.

Mike wore a black suit with a black tie and looked like John Belushi in *The Blues Brothers*. Danny wore black jeans, a black T-shirt, and black Nikes. They looked like abject amateurs for the illegal task at hand, but compared to Paul the Pervert, who stood beside them in his rat-shit clown gear, they looked like consummate professionals.

"She's not going to get up and walk over here," Paul said.

"Stop talking," Mike said.

"Let's go," Danny said.

They went through the busted back door into the mortuary.

Pointing his flashlight ahead of them, Mike led the way through the maze of carpeted hallways to the huge viewing room. They stopped in the double doorway, and Mike shined his light from one end of the room to the other.

George had set out more than one hundred folding chairs in the vast open area because Mike had told him to expect a big crowd, which is what El Cab general manager Bob Cutting had told Mike, to expect a big crowd. At the far end of the viewing room, there was an open casket between the plush curtains.

"We're the first funeral tomorrow morning?" Danny said to Mike.

"First funeral," Mike said.

"So she's definitely in the casket?" Danny said.

"Definitely in the casket," Mike said.

"We should do this," Danny said.

"We should," Mike said.

"Walk right over there and do it," Danny said.

"Walk right over there," Mike said.

But they just stood in the dark silence, looking across the sea of seats at their mother's open casket, illuminated by the beam of Mike's flashlight.

What the fuck am I doing? Danny thought. *It's one thing for a person's life to spin wildly out of control, for a person to lose his house and his office and get wrapped up with a cocaine-addicted dentist and a crazy comedian cop and a sadistic dwarf loan shark, but it's another thing altogether for a person to bust into a mortuary and steal his dead mother out of her casket. That's a whole other can of shit.*

To open *that* can of shit, Danny discovered, was to ride a speeding rollercoaster down memory lane, which is where Danny went. There he was with Linda at Little League practice, glowing with pride that his mom could hit ground balls to the infield better than any of the dads. There he was in the kitchen of the small yellow house, scarfing down his mother's enchiladas—the best enchiladas anywhere, ever. There he was in high school, his mother defending him to the asshole assistant principal after

Danny had been caught cutting biology class to sit in on another theater class. There he was, and there he was, and there he was, and there he was...and there *she* was, right now, dead of a heart attack and lying in the open casket across the black windowless room.

Mike turned off his flashlight, and they stood there for what seemed like thirty minutes but was in fact only three. They were surrounded by dark utter silence. No ticking clocks, no whirring HVAC, no phones ringing, no piped-in Muzak, no padded footsteps hurrying down carpeted halls. It was, Danny imagined, like standing deep inside a mountain tunnel—no light, no sound, no air, no world. Except his brother was beside him. And so was Paul the Pervert.

"She's not going to get up and walk over here," the clown said.

"Stop talking," Mike said.

"Let's go," Danny said.

Mike clicked on his flashlight, and they crossed the room to the casket and stood at the open end, where Linda was resting in peace.

Danny didn't know how long he'd been holding his breath. He didn't even know that he *had* been holding his breath. But after a few minutes of looking down at his mother, his lungs and his brain were ready to explode, so he opened his mouth to breathe and words came out. "Nice casket," he said.

"Matte maple finish with a Rosetan interior," Mike said.

"Like a hotel in a box," Paul said.

"Stop talking," Mike said.

"I know that suit," Danny said.

"She liked that one," Mike said.

"I like that one," Paul said.

"Stop talking," Mike said.

"She looks peaceful," Danny said.

"George did a nice job," Mike said.

"She looks good," Danny said.

"She looks *real* good," Paul said.

"Stop talking," Mike said.

"I'm just saying if she wasn't dead, I'd do her," Paul said. "It's a compliment."

Mike grabbed the clown and pulled him to the ground, and the two men wrestled around in the dark on the viewing room floor until Mike had Paul in a nasty headlock.

"Stop it, Mike," Danny said, the beam of the flashlight bouncing helter-skelter around the room.

"Tell him to stop talking," Mike said.

"Stop talking, Paul," Danny said.

"Tapping out," Paul said, and he tapped Mike's leg.

Mike let go of the clown, picked his wallet up off the floor because it had fallen out of his pocket while he was wrestling Paul, and the men stood again at the open casket, Mike and Paul breathing harder than they were breathing a minute ago.

"Are you carrying her?" Danny said to Mike.

"No," Mike said. "Are you?"

"No," Danny said.

Paul raised his hand to speak, but Mike shined the light in his face and said, "Don't even go there." Then he looked at Danny and said, "We'll carry her together."

And the brothers lifted Linda out of the coffin, carried her through the mortuary to the Pathfinder—Paul the Pervert leading them with the flashlight—seat-belted her into the back seat behind Mike, and drove to Mike's house in Woodland Hills, where Jenny was waiting.

34

she'll be a wonderful mother

MIKE SAT in the front seat of the Pathfinder and tried not to lose his mind. For one thing, he had rubbed his nipples raw while wrestling with the pervert clown on the mortuary floor. For another thing, the brand on his chest was throbbing. And for yet another thing, he was nauseous to the nth degree at being so close in such a confined space to a dead body, no matter that the body was Saint Linda—he had nearly passed out carrying her to the car. But if it was *physically* challenging for Mike to make it home in one piece, there were other challenges that made his physical state of being seem like cotton candy.

Mike was not a religious man. His mother didn't have the time, money, or inclination for an organized church, and so he hadn't been raised that way. She had encouraged him to find and forge his own spiritual path, and he had decided that there was an order to the universe and that the best way for him to serve that order was to keep his numbers straight and accurate. He believed that if a person did not serve the order of the universe in the best way that they could, there would be karma to pay. And the way he figured it, the payback he had already received would pale in comparison to what the universe would do to him for stealing his dead mother and bringing her back to life. The fate of his soul was up in the air, and there was no way to know where the hell it would land. But if it was *spiritually* challenging for Mike to maintain his sanity, there was still another challenge that made his spiritual state of being seem like buttered popcorn.

Mike was a married man, yes, but his marriage was in abeyance, meaning his wife had jumped ship for Jersey. And so right now he was a *separated* man, and a separated man had the same sexual needs and desires as a married man but no wife to satisfy them. He was only human, Mike was. Despite everything and all of it, he had to admit that he was attracted to Jenny Stone —her hot cowgirl get-up, her green and then blue eyes, her tight little body. There was something innocent about her, but there was also something naughty, beyond even the whole breathing-the-dead-back-to-life thing she had going on.

After the Frosted Flakes fight, Danny had left the kitchen to shower and change his clothes and gather his wits. Mike had stood the table right side up, grabbed a chair, and commenced eating the entire box of cereal—what was left in it, anyway. Jenny had pulled a chair beside him and put her hand on his arm and said that she would clean the kitchen when they were gone. It was a small moment, but she was close to him, and her voice was soft and kind, and her touch was warm and gentle, and her eyes looked like the tropics, and she smelled like mystery, and her lacy black bra made his groin grow.

As the Pathfinder pulled into his horseshoe driveway and rolled up to the front door, Mike decided that he would have to make some decisions about how to approach Jenny, formulate some kind of plan of attack, but not right now because right now he had to carry his dead mother into the house.

Danny sent Paul packing as soon the Pathfinder was parked. The pervert clown grumbled something about imprinting himself on Danny's mother, like a doe on a faun, but he got in his truck and drove away without incident.

When Paul was on his way to wherever it was Paul went at night, Mike and Danny carried Linda into the house and laid her out on the living room sofa. Jenny adjusted Linda's arms so that it looked like the dead woman was taking a ten-minute nap instead of an eternal sleep.

The three of them stood there looking at her for what seemed to Mike to be a long, long time. Or maybe it seemed like a long, long time because of the size of the thought that hit Mike's head.

He was standing at the bottom of a deep grave that he had dug with his bare hands. He was wearing a blue pinstriped suit, and he was covered with dirt and mud and filth. It was pouring down rain, and he was soaked. He was barefoot. What the hell had happened to his goddamn shoes? He looked up. Rain hit him hard in the face. There was no way out of the grave.

And then he was in his living room, confused and lost and in pain he had never thought possible. He looked at his hands, expecting them to be caked with mud. He couldn't stop looking at his hands.

Someone was standing beside him. Jenny. She held his hands with her hands. He turned to her. Her face was close to his face. She was beautiful. He hadn't had sex with anyone but Marcy in decades. If he could do it with anyone, it would be Jenny.

"Are you okay, Mike?" Jenny said.

"What do you mean?" Mike said.

"You're crying," Jenny said.

Holy fuck, Mike thought. *I really am crying*. He wanted to dry his eyes, but he either wouldn't or couldn't let go of Jenny's hands. He just stood there, looking into her eyes and holding her hands. And she was doing the same thing right back at him.

"Are we doing this?" Danny said.

The mood was broken, and Mike and Jenny let go, and Mike wiped his eyes and looked at Danny and his mother and said, "We should say a few words."

"It's not a funeral," Danny said. "It's the opposite."

"Then we should say the opposite words," Mike said.

"What does that even mean?" Danny said.

Mike had to think about it. That sentence had fallen out of his mouth unexpectedly, and he didn't know what it meant. And then he did.

"She'll be a wonderful mother," Mike said, and he smiled at Jenny.

Jenny smiled back and then looked at Danny as if to say: *your turn.*

Danny looked at Mike and Jenny and then at his mother on the couch and said, "She'll make the best enchiladas in the Valley." Then he looked at Jenny, and *they* shared a smile, which Mike couldn't help but notice.

"She'll be the Rock of El Cab," Mike said.

"She'll hit a hell of a ground ball," Danny said.

"She'll be kind and loving and understanding and a living example of hard work, accuracy, honesty, and proficiency," Mike said. "She'll be the best mom ever."

"Amen and peace out," Danny said.

Mike nodded, and both he and Danny turned to Jenny, who looked at Linda, kneeled beside the sofa, made a sad little sigh, put her face very close to Linda's face, and gently blew on it. Then her lips turned ever so slightly up at the corners, and she stood.

They waited in silence until Jenny said, "This could take a few minutes."

"That's fine," Danny said. "Can I talk to you in the kitchen, Mike?"

"It can't wait?" Mike said, gesturing at Linda and thinking: *Typical Dan. Mr. Distraction. Can't even focus on bringing his dead mother back to life.*

"Jenny said we have a few minutes," Dan said.

The brothers left the living room and walked to the kitchen. As she had promised, Jenny had cleaned the room while they were at the mortuary. Danny shut the door for privacy, turned to his brother, and said, "What the fuck was that? You're hitting on her?"

"No," Mike said, leaning against a counter. "Yes. Probably.

Definitely. So what?"

"So you're married, asshole," Danny said.

"Separated," Mike said.

"One week. Less than a week," Danny said.

"Feels longer," Mike said. In his mind, he couldn't believe how long it felt—years, lifetimes, galaxies ago, when he'd been a different man.

"You have no idea what you're doing," Danny said, taking a step toward Mike.

It was true, and Mike knew it. If you had asked him on Monday—*on Monday!*—if he would be stealing his deceased mother out of a mortuary that Friday and laying her on his living room sofa so that she could be brought back to life, he would have said you were crazy. Now *he* was crazy. He had no idea what he was doing, and he didn't care. "We have chemistry," Mike said. "It's burning down the house."

"That's stupid and ridiculous and stupid," Danny said, moving toward Mike. "Did I mention it was stupid? You don't know her at all, and she doesn't know you."

"Oh, I know her," Mike said. "I looked into her eyes."

"What color were they?" Danny said.

"Which day?" Mike said.

"Okay, bad example," Danny said, and he stopped four feet from Mike. "Just keep your hands off my client."

"*You* keep your hands off your client," Mike said.

"What does that mean?" Danny said.

"I saw you smile at her. You're as attracted to her as I am," Mike said. "If I don't sleep with her, you will."

"I don't sleep with clients. It's bad for my business."

"It's our business, fifty-fifty, and I do sleep with clients because I'm a badass man."

"You're out of control," Danny said, taking one angry step toward his brother.

"*You're* out of control," Mike said, and he took an angrier step toward Danny.

The brothers were face-to-face, maybe one foot between them, and they were both hot under the collar.

"You and Jenny, that's not happening," Danny said, and he grabbed Mike by the lapels of his black suit jacket.

"*You* and Jenny, that's not happening," Mike said, and he grabbed two handfuls of Danny's black T-shirt.

They shook each other and pulled each other, each one battling to keep their balance. Their faces were red with anger.

"I'm very hungry, that's what's happening," Linda said, opening the door and walking into the kitchen. "Is there anything to eat in this house? Stop fighting. You're giving me a headache. Why are you both wearing black? Is it somebody's funeral?"

She crossed the room to the refrigerator and opened the door as if she had not died of a heart attack on Tuesday. Mike looked at Linda and at Danny and then at Linda and everything about his universe that was one second ago in flux now stood stock-still.

saturday

35

moron depot

DANNY DIDN'T SLEEP. It had been one hundred degrees in the garage, and the fan that made a dying animal noise had at long last suffered its inglorious, inevitable death, first whining to an intermittent whir and then hissing to an everlasting stop. The irony of its demise, juxtaposed with Jenny's resuscitation of his mother, had not been lost on Danny, not even at three o'clock Saturday morning.

But if the gasoline-infused heat of Mike's garage had made it hard to sleep, then thinking about Jenny while sweating bullets in his bed had made it harder again by half. Was he obsessed with her? He had never in his life been obsessed with a woman before. Women had been obsessed with him, but he looked like Brad Pitt, so of course Hollywood women were falling all over themselves. But it had never happened the other way around. So what the hell was going on here?

There was only one explanation: Jenny was a voodoo queen, and she had put a spell on him.

That sounded stupid, but it wasn't. Jenny *was* a voodoo queen (for Chrissake, she could raise the dead), and he was mesmerized by her beauty and power—he was under her spell in that sense. *I'm a deer in her headlights*, he thought, *waiting to be mowed down in the middle of the road. Women like Jenny are murder on me.*

Women like Jenny? *Women like Jenny?* There were no women like Jenny. Maybe that was it. Maybe his obsession was due in part to the fact that Jenny was the most special woman he had ever met. Maybe it was that and the further fact that she rocked a lacy black bra.

At four a.m., he got out of bed and went inside to sleep in the air conditioning and found his brother sitting in the living room, on the same sofa where they had put Linda. Mike was staring at the television, watching home movies with the sound turned off. He looked worse than he had looked these last few days, and, Danny thought, Mike had looked progressively shittier as the week went on. He was still wearing the black suit he had worn to carry Linda out of the mortuary. His skin was pale and peeling where his sunburn had been especially nasty. He looked like he hadn't even tried to sleep.

Danny sat on the other end of the sofa. Mike did not acknowledge him. Without saying a word to each other, they watched grainy black and white movies shot thirty years ago at family functions. Mike had paid to transfer the films onto DVDs and then taken the transfer expense as a write-off. He had thought that deducting the old home movies made him cool and had lorded it over Danny—because Danny didn't think of it first. It didn't make Mike cool. Mike was an asshole then and an asshole now, sitting on the same sofa where they had put their mother when their mother was dead.

They must have both dozed off because at six thirty, they both woke up. The home movies had ended two hours ago.

"When you're out of *The Oath*, you're out of my business," Danny said.

"I'm not out of anything until you pay me the seventy-five hundred," Mike said.

"I can't pay you until I get the money back from Gary Shuler," Danny said, and in his mind, he ticked off all the complicating complications of his complicated life—Shuler, of course, and then Harvey and Omar, although why they were in second place he had no idea, Greenburg because he was just so fucking pathetic, and now, like always, his asshole brother. And Jenny. Oh yes, and the fact that his mother was alive again.

"After the zombie hogtied and branded me, Shuler showed up and said he wanted to see Jenny bring a dead dog back to life," Mike said. "He said he wanted to see that on Sunday."

"That's tomorrow," Danny said.

"I know the days of the week," Mike said.

"Shuler has the seventy-five grand," Danny said, mostly to himself, and the gears in his brain groaned back to life after having been blown to bits by the resurrection of his mother. "And Harvey and Omar said the same thing to me. They want to see a dead dog brought back to life on Sunday or they're going to kill me and probably you."

"They can get in line," Mike said. "Shuler said if there's no show on Sunday, he's going to let Judd Martin torture me to death."

There has to be a way to tie it all together, Danny thought, *Shuler, Harvey, Greenburg, there has to be an angle.* He could always find the angle, he was the Crown Prince of Angles—so where was the angle here?

He looked at his brother, who appeared to be a lump of laundry—soiled, wrinkled, lifeless. He was going to tell Mike about tying it all together, not because he cared what his brother had to say, but because he thought talking about it out loud might break his mental logjam and let the angle appear. He opened his mouth to say that they needed to connect the dwarf and the giant to the comedian cop and the dentist, but instead of that sentence, a single word fell out. It wasn't a word Danny was expecting. In fact, it was the last word he ever thought would fall out of his mouth when what was on his mind was the angle. But it *had* fallen out, and now Danny knew why. The word was "Chachi."

"What?" Mike said.

"Greenburg's dog."

"What are you talking about?"

"Tying it together."

"Tying what together?"

"The dog has a bad disposition."

"So what?"

"So we tell Greenburg we're going to give his poodle a cost-free attitude adjustment, then we kill the dog, have Harvey and Omar and Shuler watch Jenny bring it back to life, Shuler gives us the seventy-five grand, I pay you, you move to New Jersey with Marcy and the girls, released from *The Oath*, of course, and Harvey gets your share of the business, which sucks but is better than Harvey murdering me."

"And Mom?"

"What about her?"

"She was dead."

"She woke up. It's a miracle. Hallelujah."

He was so happy with himself, Danny was. As he had done so many times before, he'd found the angle. He could feel his mojo rising. It lifted him off the couch. He paced the living room, the logistics of the weekend coming into focus. *I'm back in the saddle*, he thought. *I'm at the gate and ready to run.*

"That's your plan?" Mike said.

"That's my plan," Danny said.

"Just one problem," Mike said.

"What?" Danny said.

"Everything," Mike said, "except Harvey murdering you. That part is perfect."

"This right here, what you're doing now, this kind of negativity," Danny said, "is why your life sucks and mine doesn't. You're in the failure business, *Failures Are Us*, and I'm in the construction business, *Ladders Unlimited*."

"You're in the moron business," Mike said. "*Moron Depot*."

"We're at the bottom of the hole here, and I'm building the

ladder to get us out, and you're sitting in the dirt saying, 'This ladder won't work, and that ladder won't work, and no ladder will work, and I'll just give up and stay in the hole and cry like a fucking two-year-old so that Jenny will have pity on me because pity is all I have going for me now.' And the whole time you're feeling sorry for yourself, you're missing the fucking point, which is that this is rock bottom. There's nowhere to go but up. Nothing else can happen that could dig this hole any deeper."

Mike's cell phone rang as if it were the period to Danny's sentence. Mike had put his phone on the coffee table. He reached out and hit *answer* and *speaker*.

"Mike Miller."

"Mike, George Edwards. Something terrible has happened. I don't...I'm not sure...I just...your mother is missing."

"You can always dig deeper," Mike said, looking at his brother.

"What was that?" George said.

"What do you mean she's missing?" Mike said.

"I arrived at the mortuary five minutes ago, and I went straight to the viewing room, as I always do, and she was gone."

"She's deceased, George. She couldn't have gotten very far," Mike said.

"I don't know what you mean," George said. "I've called the police."

Whatever logistics Danny had been calculating had to be refigured now that the police had been added to the equation. *No problem*, Danny said to himself, sitting back down on the sofa. *I need a story for the police. A little story for the police is all I need.*

"You have to come right away, Mike," George said, the consternation in his voice reaching the red zone. "Your mother is missing, and there's no time to waste. The police are on the way. I'm very sorry, Mike. This has never happened before...thirty years...never happened. Terrible, just terrible."

And then George clicked off the call, and Linda entered the living room from the bedroom hallway.

"What's never happened before?" Linda said, crossing the room and sitting opposite her sons on one of the club chairs across from the sofa. "Who was that on the phone? What was he so upset about? Why did he call the police? Never mind, I don't care. I want to go home. Daniel, drive me home. I want to take a shower and change my clothes and go to the club. I have work to do. Quarterly reports, inventory, payroll. What day is it? Is it a workday? Why don't I know what day it is? Why am I sleeping here? Where's your family, Michael? Why aren't you at the office? Why is Daniel here? I would like one of you to tell me what's going on."

Danny looked at his mother. *I'm going to need a bigger story*, he said to himself, *a huge freaking story is what I'm going to need, a story the size of Montana.* And his mojo, which had been rising like a rocket ten seconds ago, flamed out and fell from the sky.

"Deeper and deeper," Mike said.

36
the highlight of my routine

ONE OF THE perks of being a police officer who told jokes in clubs, Gary had discovered, was the surprising number of comedian-cop groupies who'd fallen onto the bar stool beside him after his set, then fallen into the front seat of his 1965 Impala at closing time, then fallen into his bed after a nightcap—*fallen* being the operative word, seeing as how, as a rule, not one of the women had met a drink she didn't drink.

Gary was a bourbon guy. Knob Creek. It was above his pay grade, but he enjoyed the smooth buzz he got from the top-shelf brown liquor, so he ordered it the nights he performed—the rest of the time he ordered whatever was in the well. He never drank before his set, but after he left the stage, he would land at the bar, order a double KC rocks, drink it slow, and wait for a comedian-cop groupie to wander along. It had happened more than Gary imagined it would. It had happened last night, Friday night, after his late set at Ha Ha on Lankershim in North Hollywood.

He had not done any of the jokes from the smash-hit routine he was currently writing—the one with the dwarf and the giant and the piranha and the zombie and the dentist and the dentist's dead dog in a bag and the branded brother of his agent and Jenny the Gypsy. That story was still magically unfolding.

Instead, he did his routine about the Asian dry cleaner from Van Nuys who, after a long day of sucking in perchloroethylene (the carcinogenic solvent that causes smog and other bad news), surfactants, and detergents strong enough to dissolve plastic, dressed himself up as Frank Gorshin (or maybe Jim Carrey) playing the Riddler in *Batman* (green unitard decorated with questions marks and a matching mask). When he was in costume and high on fumes, the Asian dry cleaner broke into West Hills houses with a video camera and an Uzi and filmed the folks he was robbing while he robbed them. That one was a crowd pleaser for a certain kind of crowd.

Anyway, San Fernando Valley realtor Suzie Shupe fell onto the stool beside him at two in the morning. Gary thought she was a few years older than he was, maybe fifty-two, maybe fifty-five. He didn't care. He wasn't particular at two in the morning when it came to comedian-cop groupies—and the brown liquor had warmed him up.

Suzie was shorter than him, and everything about her was round, her face, her eyes, her mouth, her boobs and hips and belly, her arms and legs—and yet she was not fat, just very round. She had big blonde hair with dark roots, and like a lot of fifty-something single workingwomen, she knew how to use makeup. She had red lips, eye shadow for days, mascara galore, and round cheeks pink with blush, or possibly it was the wine. She was not as pretty as some of the comedian-cop groupies who'd landed on the stool beside him, but she was prettier than some others, which meant that she was pretty enough for Gary, who'd bought her a merlot. They had talked about nothing and laughed at less, and then Suzie had fallen into the Impala. Several nightcaps had followed.

They had drunken, sloppy sex, which Gary had to admit was worlds better than no sex, and passed out naked at five a.m.

At eight o'clock, Omar muscled the door open, and Harvey walked into Gary's apartment and headed straight for the bedrooms, where someone was just barely moaning.

Gary lived in the Villa Allegro apartments on Magnolia between Radford and Ben in Valley Village. It was a four-story, block-long complex, with Spanish-style architecture, pink-stucco exterior walls, a red tile roof, and little patios with glass sliders on the upper floors. It was a pleasant-looking, middle-income apartment building for elementary school principals, restaurant managers, and LAPD detectives, one of hundreds just like it spread across the Valley.

Gary had a two-bedroom/two-bath unit on the fourth floor that faced the back of the building—the parking lot and fenced garbage and recycle area. His little patio was directly above the dumpsters.

Fancy furniture wasn't important to Gary. He had a flat-screen TV and a sofa and some tables and not much else. His life was comedy and police work. He didn't have the time or energy for IKEA. What he had instead was a waterbed and a sweet collection of lava lamps. He was a toddler when the hippies were happening in the late 1960s, but it was an era that interested him later in life because that's when Pat Paulsen had found fame on *The Smothers Brothers Comedy Hour*.

Harvey opened the door to the first bedroom and found Gary's home office, an unsettling combination of jokes and crimes. He continued down the hall to the second bedroom and pushed that door open and found Gary and Suzie sharing an early morning hangover fuck, Suzie riding Gary, her arms reaching behind her, hands on his legs, back arched, little round mouth emitting a super-soft, high-pitched moan.

While Suzie was fucking him, Gary was holding her tits and thinking that if her moan were any higher pitched or less audible, it would be a dog whistle. And while he was thinking that thought, he was also thinking he should add the dog-whistle-sex bit to his act somehow. And while he was thinking *that* thought, he saw Harvey and Omar enter his bedroom and so was *also* thinking his act would have to be an HBO series, what with the sadistic dwarf and the violent giant busting in on his dog whistle sex.

"Don't let me stop you, well, yes, actually, let me stop you right now. Omar, what do we have here?" Harvey said.

Omar moved to the bed, where Suzie, who might still have been drunk from the night before, was just now realizing that she and Gary were not alone. She opened her mouth to scream when she saw the size of the giant approaching the waterbed, but her voice disappeared entirely into the dog whistle register, and nothing at all came out of her mouth.

"What we have here, Harvey," Omar said, "is a round mound of hound." He towered over the comedian-cop groupie, who was still as stone with shock and fear and incredulity, buck naked and frozen solid, Gary's dick still inside her, for Pete's sake. "Good night, hound," Omar said, and he hit her on the top of the head with his fist, as if his fist were a mallet (which it kind of was), and her skull was a fence post (which it might as well have been), and he was driving the fence post deep into hard earth. He knocked her out cold, and she fell forward in slow motion and landed face down on the pillow beside Gary.

"I couldn't write it better if I tried," Gary said. "One minute I'm getting laid, and the next minute you pound the round mound of hound into the ground without a sound. I say it all the time because it's true. It's a laugh a minute out there."

Harvey and Omar cracked up, and Harvey climbed onto the bed by Gary's feet. He looked resplendent this Saturday morning, wearing a seersucker suit with a pink shirt and sky-blue bowtie. On his little dwarf feet he wore leather dress sandals.

"Oh, Detective," Harvey said, putting *Detective* in air quotes, "if you enjoyed that, you're going to love this. Omar, escort Detective Shuler to his patio, please."

"Wife says to her husband, 'Honey, whisper dirty things in my ear,'" Omar said, lifting Gary off the bed, holding him under the armpits, facing him out, and carrying him so that Gary's feet didn't touch the floor. "Have you heard this one?"

"Not that I remember," Gary said. He was completely naked and considerably hung over, though not so hung over that he couldn't recognize comic gold when he saw it. No one would believe this part of the story, the part where the dwarf and the giant broke down his door, interrupted his sexual intercourse—by bonking his groupie on the top of her head—and carried him nude to his patio. They wouldn't believe it, but they would roar with laughter. *Thank you, Jesus,* Gary thought. *This is hilarious shit!*

The cop on Gary's shoulder said, *Snap out of it, Gary, you're a LAPD detective. Act like one—offer some resistance, threaten to arrest them, call for backup.* But the comic on his other shoulder said, *Ignore the idiot detective. You've been digging for comic gold all your life, and now you've hit the mother lode. Stake your claim and mine this vein for all it's worth. HBO awaits you—violence, nudity, foul language, and sex!*

When he wasn't listening to the voices in his head, Gary was wondering, *Why are we going to the patio?* And then Omar crossed the living room, and Harvey slid the slider, and Omar stepped outside and turned Gary upside down and suspended him in midair over the patio railing by holding onto one ankle

"What does the husband say?" Gary said to Omar, who appeared upside down to him. Gary's head was spinning, and his arms and free leg were dangling in space four stories up. *I'll die if I fall from this height,* he thought, *and I'll die naked* because just then he remembered he had no clothes on.

"Husband says, 'Kitchen, living room, dining room, patio,'" Omar said.

"Hilarious," Gary said, but he didn't laugh because he thought he might puke.

"We went to Dr. Greenburg and asked him to return my seventy-five thousand dollars, and the dentist said he handed it to your agent," Harvey said.

"I don't like heights very much," Gary said, underplaying the fact that he didn't like heights at all, especially when he was hanging upside down by an ankle. He hadn't liked heights since he was a kid in Chula Vista, California, and had climbed a tall tree and then was too afraid to do anything but hold on for dear life. *Just climb back down, Gary Shuler Vista,* the crowd had called up at him. But he was frozen with fear and wanted an Oreo. The firemen had to get him with a hook and ladder—as if he were a cat.

"And so we went to Danny Miller, who we followed to Santa Anita, and he said that you had found him first and taken my seventy-five thousand dollars from him before he could place his bet. Is that accurate?" Harvey said.

"True fact," Gary said.

"So do you have my money?" Harvey said.

If I don't pass out, Gary thought, *this will be the highlight of my routine.* "No," he said. "I gave it to a zombie named Judd Martin. You can find him at the Little Valley Trailer Park in Sunland-Tujunga, on Sherman Grove near Foothill, trailer seventeen. It's in a paper bag on the floor. He's got a gun, a knife, and a branding iron."

"You gave my money to a trailer park zombie?" Harvey said.

"It's a laugh a minute out there," Gary said, trying to be comical. But instead of humor, he heard in his voice the sound of fear, which was an emotion he would have to explore at a later date because now his head was exploding and his heart was pounding like a motherfucker. He wished he could be there when the dwarf and the giant confronted the zombie, but mostly he wished Omar would put him back on his patio. *I need an Oreo right now,* he said to himself.

"Is it me," Harvey said, "or is he not as funny as he used to be?"

"It's not you," Omar said, and he let go of Gary's ankle and dropped him headfirst four stories.

37

somebody somewhere going to pay something to someone

DR. DONALD GREENBURG never scheduled office hours on Saturday, but today he made an exception for Ramona Clifton, who had become his closest friend, trusted confidante, and personal bodyguard since Thursday, when she saved his life with her Civil War sword at Pacoima Pawn and Loan. He was paying for her friendship, wisdom, and protection—whitewalls and gasoline for her Eldorado, cost-free dental work—but so what? Ramona was all he had going for him, and if he had to buy these things for her to get these things from her, then he would open his wallet. *For God's sake*, Greenburg thought, *at this point I'd open a freaking vein.*

He had finished filling her cavities and was washing his hands. She was sitting in the dental chair, holding a mirror in front of her face, admiring his handiwork. It was just the two of them in the office at eight thirty in the morning.

It had been hard for him to concentrate on what was happening in her mouth because of what was happening with her breasts, which were in the same vicinity as his hands. She was wearing a blouse that was pulled tight across the front—buttons holding on for dear life, by a thread, as it were—and with every breath, her breasts would rise and fall, ebb and flow —a magnificent rolling tide of tits.

He'd had sexual stirrings over the years—for various hygienists and dental assistants—but he'd been numb for a long while now. Carol had broken his manhood, and the gin and cocaine had anesthetized him to the pain. The lust he felt for Ramona had awoken his libido. He couldn't get enough of her, and he wasn't sure how long he could control himself.

But it was more than her curves that turned him on. She was a strong woman who spoke her mind and told the truth, whether or not you wanted to hear it. It was exhilarating to be with her. She might do or say any honest thing. She was the first honest person he'd met in ages. There was no subtext with Ramona. It was thrilling.

She viewed the world through refracted lenses that bent the light at outrageous angles, allowing her to see straight through what appeared opaque to him. She judged everyone, including him, but didn't hold her judgments against anyone, also including him. She had told him that the world *"was what it was because that's what it was, so you have to deal with what it is because that's what it is."* She was a breath of fresh air in his suffocating life.

On top of all that, she was his private ninja. Indeed, her Civil War sword was leaning against his exam room wall. She had inherited it from her uncle as it fell from her family tree, branch to branch, over the generations. The story was that a distant Clifton had been gifted the sword by his commanding officer after the Battle of Jonesborough in 1864, a Union victory that led to the fall of Atlanta, where the Cliftons hailed from before they moved west one hundred years later. It was either that story or the one where her uncle had stolen it from a collector in Fullerton and given it to Ramona's mother before heading to jail, which is how it came to be in the back hall closet, where Ramona had discovered it at age fourteen. No matter, Ramona had dropped out of high school to work as a hair stylist and had spent some of her money on fencing lessons. She was a natural. There was talk of an Olympic tryout. It never happened.

"Dan Miller called as I was leaving the house," Greenburg said.

"He the hair dude think he a movie star?" Ramona said.

Of course she would remember Danny's hair. She'd grown up in Anaheim, in the Hispanic slums of Disneyland. Maybe she'd seen her father five times in her entire life. Her mother owned a small salon, which is how and why Ramona became a hair stylist after she dropped out of school in the ninth grade. She was between jobs right now.

"Yes," Greenburg said. "The talent agent."

"What he want?" Ramona said, angling the mirror and smiling so her gold tooth caught the overhead light.

"He said he'd thought about Chachi and had reconsidered his position and offered to do a free attitude adjustment."

"Ain't no such thing as free, DG," Ramona said. "Somebody somewhere going to pay something to someone."

"You're right about that, RC," Greenburg said, leaning against the sink, drying his hands, and drinking her in. Her skin was smooth dark chocolate and soft as silk. Her nose was wide, and her lips were full. Her eyes were mahogany brown. She was thirty-eight years old but seemed younger, except when she seemed older.

"He was a damn dead dog," she said.

"Yes, he was."

"Now he mean as a mule."

"We have him leashed to a pipe by the pool. He's growling and snapping at us."

"You got to deal with the dog, DG, before he get worse."

"I don't see how he can get worse. I'm hoping he gets better from here. I thought about it, and it can't be an easy transition going from dead to alive. Maybe it takes him a few days to get re-acclimated. I'm giving Chachi the benefit of the doubt."

He moved beside the dental chair and looked down at her.

She'd worn a mini-skirt to the office, and her legs were thick and muscular. *These are the thighs of Athena,* Greenburg said to himself. If he could slide that skirt up just a few more inches, then he'd be on his way to Mount Olympus. "The way he stared at me, after I leashed his collar to the stake, that was worse than the growling and the snapping," he said. "Just drilling me with his eyes, like he wanted a piece of me something bad.

"Like the way you staring at me?" she said.

"I...uh...well...I..." he said. He was embarrassed, but he also wasn't embarrassed. From their very first meeting at the pawnshop, he'd thought this was their destiny.

She put the mirror down and reached her hand out and felt the woody in his pants. His eyes rolled back in his head. "You hard as a hammer, DG," she said.

"That's what you do to me, RC," he said.

"You like my ladies?" she said, moving her other hand to her top blouse button.

Sweet mother of Jesus, it's happening, Greenburg thought. "I definitely do."

She undid the first button, which fled to freedom upon its release, exposing the tops of two great mountains of brown flesh. "I'm thinking you want to get all up in here and rub around."

"Good God, yes," he said.

She undid the second button, and her blouse went wide open. She wore a leopard-print bra with a flimsy front clasp that couldn't quite contain the treasures with which they'd been entrusted.

"You wearing a ring, DG," she said.

"Bad habit."

"I don't want to hear nothing about no guilt."

"Apart from removing the noose from her neck three days ago, I haven't touched my wife in twenty years. I have no guilt."

"You still love her?"

"Not for a long time. We don't even like each other. What we have is a chemical codependence that will never go away but will never amount to anything either."

She pulled him a little closer by his cock and said, "I don't want no husband. I want a man can buy me nice things. You that man?"

"I think I am," he said, moaning his way through the sentence.

"Then you *my* man," she said, "my skinny white man."

"Skinny white man, yes, that's me."

She pulled him all the way beside her, and with her other hand, she put his hand on her chest. He undid the clasp and her tits fell out all over the place. He made a soft sound and then bent over and put his mouth on them.

"You best call the hair dude think he a movie star because your damn dead dog need a new point of view," she said, running her fingers through his thinning hair, "just like his daddy."

38
an intellectual chuckle that would make pat paulsen proud

THE LAST THING in the world Mike wanted to do was stand beside George Edwards in the viewing room of the mortuary in front of his mother's empty casket and talk about the tragedy of her missing corpse, yet here he was.

As he'd turned off Chatsworth into the mortuary driveway, he had wished the place didn't just look like an Olive Garden restaurant, he'd wished it really was one and that it was open at nine thirty Saturday morning. *I could eat a million fucking bread-sticks*, he had thought as he parked under the carport—next to the hearse that would have carried his mother to the cemetery had she not been drinking coffee in his kitchen instead of being dead.

"It's a hell of a circumstance, Mike," George said. "I've turned it over in my mind a thousand times since six thirty, and I can't imagine who would do such a thing."

It was the first time in fifteen years of doing his taxes that Mike had ever heard George use profanity. By all outward appearances, the mortician seemed as kind and courtly and formal as ever. He stood ramrod straight. His gray suit was impeccable. His black shoes were polished to a military patina. But Linda's unexplained absence had him rattled. Some of his ceremonious air had been let out of the bag. The voice that had calmed countless grieving families now needed calming.

"The question I can't stop asking myself is: *Why?*" George said. "What is the motivation? What purpose could there be for taking a deceased woman from her casket?"

"Matte maple finish with a Rosetan interior," Mike said, nodding at his mother's casket. What had the pervert clown called it? Oh, yes, a hotel in a box.

George had said on the phone that he'd called the police, so Mike wore the same suit he'd planned to wear to the funeral— navy blue Brooks Brothers—so it would seem he'd been unprepared for the news of his missing mother, that he was fully expecting an emotional morning at the mortuary until George called to say stop the presses.

"What is there to do with a dead body?" George said, answering his own question with a question. "It's terribly concerning."

Mike imagined George had multiple concerns: Mike's and Dan's emotional well-being, the complicated algebra of the police investigation multiplied by the wave of negative publicity that would consume the mortuary in the ensuing days, weeks, and months, and, of course, the mortician's potential liability— legally, financially, and morally.

"As you know, I'm fully insured, Mike, and the mortuary won't contest your claim, should you make one. My assistant will give you the contact information for my insurance carrier and my attorney. We were victimized as well, as a result of this tragic crime, and so I suspect there will be some back and forth before a settlement can be reached, but, again, the safekeeping of your mother was my responsibility, and I accept..."

Mike didn't hear a thing George said. He tuned the mortician out as if turning the volume down on his Bose Wave, which was still at the bottom of his pool along with the Hello Kitty lounger.

Instead, he looked at the empty coffin and remembered pulling Mrs. Peterson from her casket and dumping her on the floor and climbing into it and Judd Martin holding a knife to his throat. So much had happened to him since that day—Wednesday—that he thought of that now as the good old days, before he'd been duct taped to a chair or hogtied and branded like a steer.

"...There's simply no explaining why someone would break into a mortuary in the middle of the night and steal a corpse."

"Necrophilia," Mike said.

"I don't understand," George said.

"Erotic attraction to the dead," Mike said. "To a necrophile, this place is Match.com."

"I meant, why you would say something so disturbing?" George said.

"I'm under a lot of pressure, George. It's possible I'm cracking," Mike said, knowing full well he'd already cracked.

At that moment, a voice came from behind Mike and George. Both men turned to face it. "They cut the main power to the building. That's why the alarm company didn't read it as a break in. Whoever did this thought it through."

"Mike Miller, Detective Shuler," George said. "Detective, Mike Miller, the deceased's eldest son."

"Gary Shuler, Mike. Nice to meet you," Gary said, shaking Mike's hand. "I'm sorry about your mother. Just when you think something like this could never happen anywhere, it happens in the Valley."

Mike was aware that he was shaking Gary's hand, but his mind was imploding and exploding at the same time, making his jaw clench and his heart stop and his eyes go wide and his blood go cold. "Shuler," he said softly. He couldn't blink. *My eyelids are stuck*, he thought.

"Detective Shuler specializes in unusual cases," George said. "Your mother's disappearance meets his criteria."

"George, would you mind if I asked Mike a few questions in private?" Gary said. His left arm was in a makeshift sling, and the left side of his face was bruised. He had a fat lip.

"Not at all," George said. "Mike, again, I'm so very sorry this happened."

And then the mortician crossed the viewing room, lined with chairs that were supposed to be filled with mourners, and exited into the whisper-quiet hallways.

"Stand-up comedian," Mike said.

"Your face is priceless right now," Gary said. "This moment is why I left your blindfold on."

"You're a cop? And you deputized that insane zombie? Are you fucking crazy?" Mike said, his thoughts smashing together like electrons in a particle accelerator.

"It's a small moment, of course, not a belly laugh or even a guffaw," Gary said, "more of a thoughtful snicker."

"He said he had monstrous things in his mind, and you told him to *stalk* me."

"The audience will forget the bit about the blindfold as the story moves on."

"What part of *To Protect and to Serve* do you not understand?"

"And then, when I get to this moment, where you see me for the first time in the funeral home and I describe the look in your eyes when you realize who I am, they'll recognize that I set them up all along, and they'll have an intellectual chuckle that would make Pat Paulsen proud."

"What the hell are you talking about?"

"This—you, your brother, the dead dog, my act. What are you talking about?"

"You let Judd Martin brand me," Mike said, his hand moving to his chest.

"Actually, I stopped him from branding you a second time. I thought that might be one step too far for that particular joke."

Mike's eyes were blinking now—about a thousand times a minute. He couldn't process the idea that a LAPD detective considered his being branded a joke. "If you thought it was funny enough, you would have let him brand me twice?"

"If I thought it was funny enough, I would have let him brand you three times. In comedy, third time's the charm."

"Also, strike three, you're out," Mike said, pulling his phone from his suit coat. This was his chance to get rid of the zombie and comedian cop all in one bold strategic move. Finally, *finally*, the moment had arrived that could turn his life around. Here, in front of his mother's empty casket, his fortunes would change and his fate would float to the surface. "It's time to tell people who and what you are. I was a respected accountant. Someone's going to believe me. You're history, Shuler. I'm turning you in. I'm calling the police."

"I am the police," Gary said.

"No," Mike said. "You're a runaway squad car whose screws are so loose that your wheels have fallen off, and you're crashing through the guardrail into the aqueduct."

"That's hilarious," Gary said, taking out his pocket pad. "Can you say it again? I want to get it word for word."

Mike dialed 9-1-1.

As it was ringing, Gary wrote down Mike's funny quote and said, "You can call them if you want to. But when they get here, I'll have them arrest you for breaking and entering and stealing you dead mother. I know you did it." He took Mike's driver's license out of his pocket and held it up for Mike to see.

"9-1-1," a voice said on the other end of the phone.

Mike held the phone against his chest, which hurt a little because the brand still stung. He looked at the license, at his name and photograph, and said, "That's not mine."

"9-1-1," the voice said again.

"You should check," Gary said. "You don't want to make a mistake here. I'll tell you why in a minute. That's called comedic tension, by the way."

"I know what comedic tension is," Mike said, removing his wallet. "People think accountants have no sense of humor, but they do. Accountants are very funny, in fact." He opened his wallet, and his license was missing. He was surprised, and then he was surprised that he was surprised. Hadn't he just this morning told his brother that you could always dig deeper? Yes, yes he had. He just hadn't expected to dig this deep this fast.

"9-1-1," the voice said.

Mike clicked off the call.

"I found it under the casket in the shadows," Gary said. "George was so upset, he didn't see it."

It must have fallen out of my wallet when my wallet fell out of my pocket when I was choking the pervert clown, Mike thought, and he said, "I don't like where this is going."

"You're going to like it less if we get there," Gary said, "because I'll dust for prints and find yours and probably your brother's all over of the mortuary. The DA will press charges and put your face on the front page of the *LA Times*. You'll be the freak accountant who stole his dead mother—the necrophile son. You know what that means?"

"Erotic attraction to the dead," Mike said with a voice so glum he didn't recognize it as his own.

"It means here's why you don't want to make a mistake: your friends and family and colleagues and associates and complete strangers will see your face and read your story and know who and what *you* are," Gary said. "You have daughters, right? You want them to read about you having sexual relations with your mother's corpse?"

Mike lost feeling in his extremities.

"That would be hilarious," Gary said. "But there's something even funnier waiting in the wings."

"What?"

"I think you think you can bring your mother back to life— that's why you broke down the door and carried her away—and bringing your mother back to life would be the funniest thing that's happened in two thousand years. If you let me include it in my act, I'll return your license. Double or nothing, Mike— bring back a dead dog, the money's yours; bring back your dead mother, the mortuary's a mystery; ruin my act, you lose the money, you face the zombie, you go to freak prison. What do you think?"

What Mike thought was that he had mutated from Partner Accountant to Freak Accountant in less than a week. He could feel his heart skipping beats in his chest. He could feel the blood pulsing in his ears. How could he agree to those terms? How could he not agree? He noticed for the first time that the detective looked beat-up and decided to change the subject.

"What happened to you?" Mike said.

"Two guys dropped me four stories into a dumpster. I landed on my left arm and shoulder. I'd be dead, except for someone had thrown out an old mattress. I don't really need the sling. I'm trying it out as a prop. Maybe when I reach this part of the story, I'll put it on for effect."

"Why didn't you arrest them?"

"They have hilarious roles in my act. One's a dwarf; the other's a giant."

"Ahab and Ishmael."

"You know them?"

"They tried to electrocute me in my pool."

"That's hysterical," Gary said, pocketing Mike's license and walking away. "You can tell me about it tomorrow when you raise the dead."

39
he'll be dead when we kill him

DANNY PARKED the Pathfinder in front of the sky-blue craftsman cottage and went up the walk, where, two days ago, Jenny's mother, Maggie, had nearly decapitated him with her serrated grass whip. He climbed the skewed steps, crossed the slanted porch, and knocked on the crooked, carnival funhouse door. While he waited for Jenny to answer, he looked through the three warped windows that made up the door's uppermost panel. The Northridge Quake had done a number on the inside of the house as well—cockeyed walls, tilted ceilings, drunken floors. *If you drop a marble in this place*, Danny thought, *it will never stop rolling.*

He stepped away from the windows and looked back at his old and weary SUV. He could see the dent in the door where Maggie had kicked it in with her Croc before whipping her whip at his neck. He remembered she'd said, *"Make us some money, Pretty Boy, or you'll be solly, Cholly"* as she went cackling into the house.

Yeah? Danny thought, *Pretty Boy made you sixty grand so far, so shove your grass whip up your solly, Cholly ass.* Then he made a little face because, okay, it wasn't quite *exactly so far*. It was more like he had *almost so far* made them sixty grand. He had to get the cash from Shuler before he could say it was *exactly so far*. And that's why he'd come to the flatlands of Northridge—to get the money back.

"This is a surprise," Jenny said, coming through the front door onto the porch. She was wearing white, skin-tight, see-through yoga pants with a thong underneath and a white bikini yoga top that left even less to the imagination than the see-through pants, which showed every curve, every line, every everything. Her hair was pulled back in a loose ponytail. Her lips were painted devil red. She was barefoot, and her toes and fingernails were painted to match her lips. She was smooth and toned and sexy as hell.

She's so freaking hot, Danny said to himself, though he couldn't help but notice her eyes were now midnight black. "I went to Ralphs. They said you don't work there anymore."

She laid her mat on the porch and began to stretch and pose and bend her body into positions that made him think of sex—specifically, sex with her.

"On Thursday, I made sixty thousand dollars in less than five minutes. I'd have to work three years to make that make much checking groceries."

"That's why I had to see you."

"Because I quit working at Ralphs?"

"Because I have to ask you a question. Remember Gary Shuler?"

She spread her legs, and he made a noise of pleasure he hoped she didn't hear.

"Is that the question?" she said.

"No."

"He's the stand-up comedian who took the money from you at the track to protect you from the dwarf and the giant."

"Yes. Except he's a police detective who specializes in unusual cases."

"Not a comic?"

"*And* a comic. His cases are his routines."

She closed her legs and rolled onto her stomach and lifted her ass in the air. Danny held his breath and counted silently to five to stay focused. Then he swallowed hard and exhaled.

"He's writing a routine about us," he said.

"Who's us?"

"Mike, me, you, him, Harvey, Omar, the dog, the dentist, all of us. We're his new comedy routine, and he wants to keep it going."

"Keep it going where?"

"He'll return the money if he can watch you bring a dead dog back to life tomorrow night." Then Danny had an hour-long debate that took a fraction of a second inside his head about whether or not to mention Mike and the zombie because he didn't want Jenny caring about what happened to Mike. In the end, he decided the first order of business was to get her on board. Plus, even if she did care about his idiot asshole brother, Mike was no romantic threat to him. For Chrissakes, he looked like freaking Brad Pitt, didn't he? What did Mike look like, Paul Giamatti? "Plus, he won't let the zombie kill Mike."

"There's a zombie trying to kill Mike?"

Shit, Danny thought, *I should never have said anything.* "Hey, someone wants to kill me too?"

"Yes. The dwarf. That's why the comedian cop took the money, to protect you from Harvey. Why does he want to kill you?"

"I owe him money, and if he sees this business is real, if he can watch you bring a dead dog back to life tomorrow night, then he'll be my partner, and he won't kill me."

Jenny slowly lowered her ass in such a way that made Danny swoon. Then she rolled over again and arched her back so that it appeared she was in the throes of a mind-bending orgasm. Danny wished he was in the throes of it with her and went woozy. For a moment, he thought it might be the heat. Today was forecast to be the hottest day yet—one hundred fourteen in the shade—and it was already one hundred nine at ten thirty in the morning. But then he licked the salty perspiration off his upper lip and admitted that even if it were thirty degrees and snowing, he would still be sweating bullets watching Jenny run through *The Kama Sutra* on her catawampus porch in what might as well have been her birthday suit.

"Do you have a dog in mind?" Jenny said.

"Chachi."

"Chachi's not dead."

"He'll be dead when we kill him. That's my question. Can you bring something back to life more than once?" *Jesus,* he thought, *how long can a yoga orgasm last?*

"The dentist is going to let you kill his dog again?"

"He won't know. He called me asking for his money back because the dog had a bad disposition—"

"In the kitchen. I remember."

"—and I told him Shuler had the money. Then I called him this morning and said we'd do a free attitude adjustment, and *he* said no. And then he called me back and said he changed his mind, and I drove to Ralphs to find you, and they said you'd quit."

Finally, the yoga orgasm ended, and she lowered her back and rolled over again, and Danny relaxed, except she arched her back once more, supporting herself on her hands, thrusting her chest in Danny's face. Through her yoga bikini top, he could see that her nipples were hard, and the words *Oh my God* slipped out of his mouth, or maybe he just thought they did.

"The free attitude adjustment is killing the dog and bringing it back to life again in front of the comedian cop, the dwarf, and the giant?" Jenny said.

He couldn't take his eyes off her tits. He didn't know how long he was looking at them, but she caught him staring and smiled, and he thought her eyes changed color there for a moment, but then they were black again and she was speaking to him.

"We get the money if we kill Chachi and then bring him back while those guys watch?"

"That's the angle, yes. What do you think?"

"How they hanging, Pretty Boy?" Maggie said, pushing through the front door and joining them on the porch. She wore a colorful summer kaftan with a royal blue turban on her head. In one hand she carried a pitcher of something cold, and in the other hand, she held two glasses. She was barefoot.

Danny had the feeling she was naked under the kaftan but expelled that thought from his mind in the time it took to blink his eyes. "Good to go, Maggie. How are you?"

Jenny switched poses, sitting up, facing Danny, her legs spread eagle. Was it possible the temperature could get this hot this fast? Was the weather that fucked up? He could hardly think.

"She shaves that sweet thang, Pretty Boy," Maggie said, handing Danny one of the glasses. "Does that make your dingle tingle?"

"Mother," Jenny said.

"I'm playing with him," Maggie said, filling Danny's glass with a cold drink.

Danny held the glass to his face. It was like molding a melting ice cube to his cheek. It felt so good. "Lemonade?" he said.

"Squeezed the lemons with my bare hands," Maggie said, filling the second glass for Jenny and placing it on the floor beside the yoga mat. "Imagined they were your nuts, so, believe me, I got every drop of juice."

"That's disgusting, Mother," Jenny said.

"Anyway, drink up, Pretty Boy. It's hot as a twat out here." And she cackled her way inside the house.

Danny watched her go and held the glass to his lips.

"Don't drink that," Jenny said. "It's poisoned. She tries to poison me every day."

She lifted her glass and shot the lemonade out onto the lawn. It burned the scrubby grass brown on contact.

Danny didn't know what the hell to think except that he wanted to get under those yoga pants in the worst damn way. Instead, he smiled at Jenny and nodded thanks.

She twisted her torso and stretched her arms above her head. Her right breast was within his arm's reach. More than anything he wanted to hold it in his hand.

"I think you're asking me to do a second job for free before you've paid me for the first one?" she said. "I think there must be other agents who would never ask a client to do that. Is that really what you're asking me to do, Danny?"

"No, of course not. I'm throwing in my commission." *Screw my brother*, Danny thought. *He'll go along to get along or he'll face the zombie.*

"So I'm doing the dog again for fifteen thousand? That's a thirty-seven five average."

Jesus Christ, she was a sharp little sex machine. She'd planned the whole thing—the see-through pants, the hard nipples, the freaking thong. He hated being out-maneuvered by a client, but he was soft clay in her hot wet hands, and she wasn't just a client, she was the *Golden Girl*. Not to mention that he was a desperate man in desperate times. "Thirty-seven five average," Danny said. "Are you in?"

She twisted her torso the other way. Her left breast was every inch as fine as her right one. "How are you going to kill the dog?" she said.

40

do you remember anything about this third world slum?

OMAR TURNED Carol Greenburg's Mercedes into the cracked concrete shithole on Sherman Grove near Foothill and said to Harvey, "Do you remember anything about this Third World slum?"

Harvey remembered more about the Little Valley Trailer Park in Sunland-Tujunga than he cared to admit.

He remembered being on the lam from the law in London and arriving in LA with Georganne when he was eight years old —when he was Young Harvey. At LAX, she had grabbed their one solitary suitcase—filled with nothing but cash money—and hailed a cab. He remembered that the driver was an old black man named Stuckee.

"Where can we go that no one will find us?" Georganne had said to Stuckee.

"One time met a man moved to the valley in the Valley," Stuckee said. "Nobody never saw him again."

"Brilliant," Georganne said.

And so Stuckee drove to Sunland-Tujunga and deposited Young Harvey and his mother in front of the decaying Little Valley Trailer Park office.

It was decades ago, but if Harvey closed his eyes, which he

did while Omar turned the Mercedes into the cesspool, he could see himself as Young Harvey, hear his mother's voice, smell the old black man, who chain-smoked Tiparillos and was saturated with their sweet cigar aroma.

"I remember Coca Cola bottles," Harvey said to Omar. "Park by the office. Let's see what the manager has to say about zombies."

In fact, Harvey remembered that when he was eight, the office manager, a blurry alcoholic named Tom Collins, of all things, told Georganne that trailer number six was vacant. She paid a month's rent with cash up front, and she and Young Harvey moved in.

Georganne hired Stuckee to be her driver, and the old black man picked her up the next morning and every morning after that and drove her all around the Valley looking for a business to buy. It was summer, and Georganne told Young Harvey to play outside with the trailer park boys, of which there was an existing gang of four.

The leader of the gang was a hulking twelve-year-old bully named Hal who called himself Rocky because he thought himself a boxer and would hit the smaller boys with his fists if they called him Hal. The other three boys were nine and ten years old, and they took their marching orders from Hal and called him Rocky—so he wouldn't hit them with his fists. As a gang, they were Little Valley Trailer Park trash.

The arrival of an eight-year-old dwarf was just the kind of entertainment Rocky had been hoping for, and after a week of watching Georganne drive off with Stuckee, he knocked on the door of trailer number six and told Young Harvey to come outside.

"Come outside," Omar said to the wheezing asthmatic trailer park manager, a pale ghost named Marvin who wore an oxygen mask connected to a tank on wheels that followed him like a puppy on a leash, "and tell us about the zombie."

"Don't know nothing about no zombie," Marvin said

through the screen door. "And if I did, I ain't telling no dwarf and no giant." Then he wheezed and was gone.

It was one hundred twelve degrees at eleven thirty on Saturday morning. There was no breeze, no shade, no relief. There was only the heat hanging in the air, wrapping itself around Harvey's neck and squeezing the memories out of him.

He remembered that Young Harvey did not want to go outside with the trailer park boys. He had not played with them as his mother had said. He had stayed inside and watched the small, malfunctioning TV left behind by the last tenants of trailer number six, who'd either made it back to Mexico or were murdered by drug dealers *en route*, Tom Collins wasn't sure which. But for reasons Young Harvey (or Old Harvey) couldn't fathom, he opened the door and went out to meet the gang.

Rocky led them to a ratty picnic table in a far corner of the trailer park, hidden from view behind a ramshackle storage shed. All the boys had bottles of Coca Cola.

As he had done with each member of his gang, Rocky tried to bend Young Harvey to his will. He started by demanding that Young Harvey call him Rocky, and then he put a fistful of worms on the picnic table and demanded that Young Harvey eat one as a form of gang initiation. The other boys, Rocky said, had eaten worms when Rocky told them too. Now it was the boy dwarf's turn.

Young Harvey refused to eat a worm, and Rocky made the gang hold the boy dwarf's arms and then threw worms at his face. With dirt and worms on his cheeks and in his hair and up his nose and down his shirt, Young Harvey still said no. Rocky said he didn't understand why the boy dwarf wouldn't eat a worm. He said that if the boy dwarf didn't eat a worm, then he would shove one down his throat. He said that given those choices, he didn't understand why the boy dwarf wouldn't eat one on his own. "I don't understand," the bully said to Young Harvey and to his gang. "I don't understand."

As he and Omar walked past trailer number six on their way

to trailer number seventeen, Harvey remembered that even as an eight-year-old boy he had learned from his mother that violence was something everyone understood.

"If the zombie does not understand that the money is mine," Harvey said to Omar, "then he will have to be educated with violence."

"Do you have a lesson plan in mind?" Omar said. He was armed, as always—silenced Glock, massive Bowie knife, brass knuckles.

"I would like you to break every bone in his body, one at time, until he cooperates or dies," Harvey said. "And to honor my memory of the Little Valley Trailer Park, I would like you to start with his eye sockets."

"Who says you can't have fun in hot weather?" Omar said.

Harvey nodded, remembering it was hot behind the ramshackle storage shed too. Baking back there in the summer trailer park heat, Young Harvey said he would eat a worm if the gang let go of his arms. Rocky ordered his gang to release the boy dwarf, leaned all the way across the picnic table, and said, "Do it."

But before Rocky could put the period on that two-word sentence, Young Harvey smashed him in the eye with the coke bottle. Rocky went down on the ground, bleeding from his broken eye socket, his world now screaming pain.

Instead of running for his life to trailer number six, Young Harvey hit Rocky again and again with the coke bottle, breaking Rocky's nose, smashing his teeth, opening a deep nasty gash in the gang leader's skull.

When the bully was gurgling his own blood, Young Harvey stood over him and said, "If you ever threaten me again, *Hal,* I'll kill you." Then he looked at the other boys, who were frozen in stunned silence, and he swung the bloody coke bottle in a wide arc. The gang ran for their lives.

Young Harvey looked down at Rocky and considered going to the office so Tom Collins could call an ambulance. Instead, he hit the bully one last time, a direct shot to the boy's other eye, breaking that socket and knocking Hal unconscious. Then Harvey walked back to trailer number six. He took the bloody coke bottle with him, knowing even then it would be evidence against him when the bully came to and help arrived.

As soon as Georganne returned with Stuckee, Young Harvey told her what had happened, and she knew it was a matter of minutes before the bully's parents got home from work and saw their son and called the police. That meant their time in the trailer park had come to an abrupt end—abrupt meaning immediate, meaning right then at that moment Georganne had Stuckee drive them to the failing pawnshop in Pacoima she had purchased that very afternoon. As they pulled out of the decrepit rat's nest, Georganne told Young Harvey how proud she was of what he'd done. "If only I could have been there to see it happen," she'd said. "If only."

"Oh zombie, where art thou?" Omar said to Harvey.

The dwarf and the giant stood in front of the empty trailer pad looking at thin air. Trailer number sixteen was on one side, and trailer number eighteen was on the other side, but there was no seventeen between them. Trailer number seventeen was gone as were the zombie's pickup and the zombie—and gone with them was Harvey's money.

"I will guard the office door while you ask Marvin the manager that very question," Harvey said, starting back to the trailer park office.

"If only you could watch me break his eye sockets," Omar said, slipping on his brass knuckles.

If only, Harvey thought.

41
comeback of the year

MIKE LEFT the mortuary and drove straight to the Denny's in Woodland Hills on Burbank Boulevard. He needed time to think things through and a cup of coffee to keep him company—maybe a little breakfast.

He had a back booth to himself, and he ordered a Belgian Waffle Slam—two eggs over easy, two strips of bacon, two links of sausage, and a golden waffle smothered with butter and syrup.

While he scarfed down the Denny's, he pondered his predicament, and the more he thought about what he thought, the more he felt the feeling he was feeling was *grief*. And because he had so many truly troubling players on the field at the same time, he believed he was experiencing all five stages of grief at once, an emotional concurrence and coalescence he was sure would land him in a psychological textbook, were he sharing the booth with a psychologist or a textbook writer.

He thought about Gary Shuler, who in his own way was even crazier than his zombie deputy, who was himself violently insane. He thought about Ahab and Ishmael, who had terrorized him on his home turf. He thought about Greenburg the Dentist and his dead poodle, which was no longer dead but would be dead again tomorrow and then would be alive again after that.

He thought about his life being inextricably intertwined with these lunatics and their lunacy and ordered the The Grand Slamwich—two scrambled eggs, crumbled sausage, shaved ham, and American cheese on potato bread, grilled with a maple spice spread and served with crispy hash browns.

While he slammed the Slamwich, he thought about his flim-flam man brother, who had taken advantage of *The Oath* Mike had sworn on their mother's dying heart and moved into his garage and involved him with Jenny Stone, who could breathe life into death and with whom he wanted to have sex—despite her eyes changing color like he changed socks (when he was an accountant and used to change his socks, that is...or was).

He thought about Marcy and the girls. They had left for a Jersey summer vacation one week ago and were now measuring for curtains in their new house and enrolling in Paramus private schools. He missed his daughters terribly. He wanted to see them so badly he could have tasted it were it not for the maple spice spread on the Slamwich, which dominated the flavor profile despite the American cheese and shaved ham.

He thought about his mother. But those thoughts were so convoluted and complex and complicated—and they had so many tentacles wrapped around bizarre and disturbing and perverse and corrupt and deviant and sinister side thoughts—that he couldn't do it without another cup of coffee (maybe cup seven or eight or nine; he'd lost count after five). And then he was so wired on caffeine that he ordered the Lumberjack Slam—two buttermilk pancakes, a slice of grilled ham, two bacon strips, two links of sausage, and two eggs sunny-side up served with hash browns and whole wheat toast.

As he completed the triple play of Grand Slams, he realized he was ultimately grieving the loss of his honesty, his purity, his privacy, his virility, his family, and his sanity. He staggered out of Denny's into the horrible heat of the day and, despite the caffeine, fell asleep in his car. *Perfect practice,* he thought as he drifted off, *for that time on the horizon when I'm homeless and penniless and pathetic and alone.*

He arrived home in the early afternoon, put his wallet and cell phone and car keys on the kitchen table, grabbed a glass from the cabinet, and filled it at the kitchen sink while looking out at the backyard, where Saint Linda sat on the edge of the pool, her feet in the water. She still wore the navy blue business suit Mike had chosen for her funeral—the same suit she'd been wearing in her casket only yesterday. There was no way to reason her being alive. She simply was.

Acceptance, Mike thought, *the fifth stage of grief. I've come through to the other side and discovered that over here I'm as insane as I am back there.*

And then his cell phone rang. He took a last look at his mother, sat at the kitchen table, and hit the speaker button because he was too weary to hold the thing to his ear.

"Mike Miller."

"Mike, hi. Bob Cutting. El Cab Country Club."

Oh great, Mike thought, *the general manager calling to bust my balls about bailing on him.*

It was only yesterday that Mike had been sitting in Bob's office, waiting to fill out the application for Linda's job—since it was only yesterday that Linda was still dead. Judd Martin had slipped into the office, kidnapped Mike at gunpoint, taken him to the end of the Earth somewhere, and branded him like a steer. Now Cutting was calling to find out what kind of asshole leaves a meeting without an explanation.

"What can I do for you, Bob?"

"Well, for one thing, Mike, we got word that Linda's funeral was postponed, and I wanted to make sure everything was okay, see if there was anything we could do on our end."

"Nothing you can do. We're working it out over here."

"You sure?"

"Pretty sure. We'll let you know about the funeral."

"All right then. Just so long as you know we're here for you."

"Appreciate that."

"Listen, Mike, you left my office yesterday before I got you the application."

Here it comes, Mike thought. "I'm sorry about that, Bob. Couldn't be helped."

"Don't apologize. I'm the one who's sorry. You shouldn't have to fill out an application. You are, or were, a senior accountant at a successful firm, which means you're more than qualified. And you're family. That counts for a lot at El Cab. I've spoken with the board. We'd like to offer you Linda's job. Same salary and benefits as Linda. Assuming you're still interested, the only question I have is: When can you start?"

Mike was blown away. Somehow, he had forgotten he'd even asked for that job. So many thoughts flooded his mind, but the first thought was: *I'm saved*. He opened his mouth to say, *Monday morning*, but another voice, a voice behind him, came out instead.

"Why is Bob Cutting offering you my job?" Linda said.

Mike turned to his mother, who was standing at the stove, and clicked off the call. How could she be in his kitchen? Five seconds ago she was sitting poolside, soaking her feet. *There's no way a woman her age can move that fast and be so silent*, Mike thought, *especially a deceased woman*.

"Because they think you're dead," Mike said.

Linda lifted a cast iron frying pan off the stove and walked slowly toward the table in a way that woke Mike up. He pushed his chair back and stood.

"Why do they think I'm dead?" Linda said, making her way around the table.

Mike backed away from her. It looked like his mother, and it sounded like his mother, and it walked like his mother, but there was something about her that wasn't his mother at all, something askew in her general vibe, something cockeyed about her karma. "Because you died, Mom."

She tilted her head to the side as if Mike were speaking Swahili. "What do you mean I died?" She held the iron pan against her chest, one hand on the handle, the other holding the top edge. She was slow and deliberate as she crossed the kitchen. He realized she was boxing him into a corner, and he couldn't stop her from doing it.

"You had a heart attack, and you were dying, and then it seemed like you died."

"*Seemed* like I died?"

"You woke up, and now you're alive, but people thought you were dead, so we're working it out."

"By stealing my job?"

Mike was trapped between the fridge and sink. His only escape was straight through Linda. But she was holding the frying pan like a sledgehammer and drilling him with eyes he didn't recognize. Christ almighty, she was looking right through him.

"I didn't want El Cab's numbers to fall out of line while you were dead, uh, gone, so I'm a placeholder until you get back."

"You're lying to me, Michael."

Her voice was soft and sharp and cut him like a knife. He couldn't ever remember her sounding like this. He thought he might be afraid of her.

"What? No, I'm not lying to you."

"What about *your* job?"

"I took an unlimited leave of absence after you died...after I thought you died."

"Marcy had no problem with that, you quitting your job because you thought your mommy died, you little pussy?"

His eyes shot open. She had never called him a name like that in his entire life. "Marcy's in New Jersey with the girls for the summer." It wasn't the whole truth, but it also wasn't a lie. "I'm not a little pussy, Mom. Don't call me that."

"You're a fat fairy, and you've been one since the day you were born. Now take me home. I hate this house."

"You can't go home yet. You have to stay here a little while longer. And stop calling me names. I don't—"

She swung the iron pan at him, not actually trying to hit him, but definitely trying to scare him, and he flinched like a second-grader.

"How long do I have to stay here?"

"Until people understand that you're alive and not dead."

She swung the pan again, and he flinched again, and she laughed, a disturbing sound he had never heard her make when she was alive before she was dead.

"Then get the word out. Tell everyone I'm making the come-back of the year."

She put the pan on the stove, opened the fridge, found a bottle of beer, unscrewed the cap, and took a swig. He couldn't recall her *ever* drinking beer before.

"Mom," he said, "when you were dying you made me swear an oath."

She drank again, maybe half the bottle, and then belched. Michael was in shock.

"What kind of oath?" she said.

"You made me swear to watch over and take care of Danny, whatever that means, whatever is necessary, no matter what very bad thing happened to him or to me or to us."

"So what?"

"So Danny doesn't want me to take care of him, and I don't want to take care of Danny, and so I want you release me from *The Oath.*"

She walked across the kitchen to where he was still trapped in the corner and patted his face, though not before he flinched.

"Take me home, and I'll consider it," she said. "Make me stay here one more day, and you and Daniel will have many, many years of living hell together."

Then she shot the rest of her beer, put the empty bottle in his hand, and left the room.

"I'm not fat," he said softly to no one.

42

i don't have another leash

DONALD GREENBURG HAD sex three times with Ramona Clifton—twice in the dental chair and once on the maple desk in his office. In order to screw her on his desk, he had to move his computer, his lamp, his phone, and his fish bowl.

While he was moving the fish bowl to the credenza behind the desk, he'd noticed that one of the goldfish was dead—the pale gold one—though not floating upside-down dead on the surface, more like torn-to-shreds dead all over the bowl. The killer was the reddish gold one that Jenny Stone had murdered on this very same desk—upon which he was about to fuck Ramona for the third time since filling her cavities. *Come to think of it,* the dentist had said to himself at the time, *I'm just filling a different cavity.* Anyway, then Jenny had breathed on the reddish gold one, and it had come back to life, and she had dropped it in the bowl.

But the thing about the reddish gold one was that it had kept banging its head against the glass while it stared at the dentist— while Greenburg fucked Ramona—as if trying to get at him somehow. She was lying on the desk, and he was standing so that he was facing the credenza, and he could see the damn fish bang-bang-banging its head against the glass. Or maybe he had imagined the whole goldfish thing since his blood at the time had been in his dick and not in his brain.

After the sex, he had taken Ramona for lunch at Marmalade Café on Ventura Boulevard in Sherman Oaks, and then they had gone to the Galleria shopping mall, a short drive down Ventura, and he had bought her two blouses, a pair of shoes, fancy sunglasses, and a new watch.

Then he'd gone home, slipped into his office, poured himself three fingers of Tanqueray, cut himself three lines of cocaine, and considered Carol, who was doing yoga by the pool when he'd arrived.

His wife had been wearing a fantastical green leotard with a matching green headband. In the headband, Carol had placed a single plume of a tall green feather to make her look—and so to make her feel—like Gertrude McFuzz, one of her favorite Dr. Seuss characters. She had plugged her iPod into the Apple player and turned it up loud so that the soundtrack to her yoga session was *Seussical the Musical*.

Upon seeing his wife, Greenburg had expected—was even secretly hoping—to feel guilt or shame or regret or sadness but instead had felt...*manly*. Yes, for the first time in years, Greenburg felt like a man, granted, a skinny white man, but still a man—Ramona's man. And then, as the gin and coke relaxed him, he felt guilty for not feeling guilty, which made him feel relieved that at least he had guilt-once-removed if not guilt-in-the-first-degree.

Greenburg had seen Chachi too, when he'd stood in the living room and looked out through the French doors. The dog was still leashed to a pipe at the far end of the pool and was chewing something, maybe a bone, to death, its eyes glued on Carol. The dentist and his wife did not say hello, and Greenburg had gone to his office and sucked down two of the three lines and finished two of the three fingers of Tanqueray when his cell phone rang.

It was Carol calling from the pool.

"Yes," Greenburg said.

"He's biting through the leash," Carol said.

"I thought it was a bone."

"Come out here, Donald. He's almost through it."

She clicked off the call. Greenburg snorted the last line, swallowed the rest of the gin, licked his gums, and went out to the pool.

He stood beside his wife, and together they watched Chachi rip and tear at the leash, growling like a demon, foaming at the mouth, staring at them the entire time. The upbeat "Biggest Blame Fool," a full-cast, *Seussical the Musical* production number, blasted across the backyard through the sound system.

"Jesus, he's almost through it," Greenburg said.

"That's what I told you," Carol said.

"How long has he been doing this?"

"All night, all day, how should I know? Get another leash. He'll bite that one in half any minute."

"I don't have another leash."

"Then do something else. Pick him up. Put him in the garage. He's just a poodle. Be a man for once in your life."

I was a man this morning, he said to himself. *Not once, not twice, but three times.*

"I am doing something else," he said to her.

"What?"

"I'm having his attitude adjusted for free."

"There's no such thing as free."

"That's what Ramona said."

"Who's Ramona?"

He opened his mouth to explain, but Chachi chomped completely through the leash and, free of the pipe, ran across the yard at incredible speed and jumped through the air like a heat-seeking missile and hit Carol's chest, knocking her to the ground. In a violent frenzy fueled by hyper-strength and hellish power, the little white poodle bit and clawed at her face.

"Get him off me, get him off..." Carol said, shouting and shocked and already cut and bleeding.

Greenburg froze and blinked and froze and blinked for what was only a few seconds but seemed longer and then moved to his wife, reached down, grabbed Chachi, and pulled him off, holding the dog at arm's length with both hands.

The dog growled and barked and roared and shook like a madman, snapping at the dentist with rage and fury.

"Stop it, Chachi, stop it," Greenburg said.

He remembered that Carol had told him to put the poodle in the garage, and so he started to backpedal his way across the patio, never taking his eyes off the dog, which was three feet from his face, but his foot caught the leg of a lawn chair, and he went down hard, the poodle on top of him.

Chachi scratched and bit Greenburg's face and hands and arms and chest as the dentist struggled to hold him at bay. *Jesus Christ*, Greenburg thought as he fought for his life, *how could a poodle be so strong, so fast, so vicious?*

Each bite, each scratch was impossibly painful, and the bleeding dentist had a moment where he thought that Chachi was trying to kill him—not just trying to bite him but trying, intentionally, to kill him.

Fifteen feet away, Carol was on her hands and knees, looking down at her blood dripping onto the flagstone, the top of her head facing her husband, who was fighting the dog—and losing the fight. The pool was right behind her. "Here on Who" blasted from the speakers. Her single green plume was broken at a cock-eyed angle.

Beneath the animalistic survival instinct that had kicked in to keep him alive, beneath the bark and growl of his bloodthirsty dog, beneath the *Seussical the Musical* soundtrack to the savage attack, beneath the peripheral glimpses of his wife bleeding by the pool, beneath all of that was the thought in the back of Greenburg's mind that there was something wrong with his heart.

It was pounding, of course, Greenburg's heart, but more than that, his entire chest cavity was screaming with pressure, and his left arm was going numb even as he struggled to hold Chachi away from his face, and he couldn't catch his breath, he couldn't breathe. *Oh my God, I'm having a heart attack*, Greenburg thought.

The dentist knew he had to get the dog off his chest or he'd die right here on the patio. He rolled hard to his left and in the same movement threw the poodle with his right hand with all the power he could muster.

The dog flew through the air and smashed into a table, shook its head for two seconds, and then shot like a bullet toward Carol, who at that exact moment was lifting herself up off her arms so that she was upright on her knees.

The poodle hit Carol in the neck and bit down hard, opening her carotid artery and sending a pumping pulse of blood into the air. Carol's eyes went wide with shock. She opened her mouth but couldn't make a sound. She fell on her back, head and neck hanging over the edge of the pool, her blood turning the water red.

Greenburg saw it happen, saw his wife ferociously murdered by his dog, and felt the adrenaline surge through him. Twenty-five years of empty, painful coexistence went out the window. All he could think of was their college romance, their dental school love affair, their early years in the Valley when he was building his practice, before the vodka and Percocet and cocaine and gin took hold of them.

He got to his feet, ran across the patio, grabbed the dog, and crashed them both into the shallow end of the pool.

He held the dog under the water, shouting at the top of his lungs. "Die, you fuck, die."

But the poodle would not die. It fought like the devil, and then Greenburg lost his footing and slipped underwater as well, the two of them face-to-face, eye-to-eye, the dog snapping and scratching and trying to shake free, not to save his own life but to kill the dentist.

And then Greenburg was up again, sucking in oxygen, holding Chachi beneath the surface. The dentist couldn't believe how long it took the dog to die, minutes and minutes of thrashing and splashing, but finally the fight was over, and the poodle was drowned.

Greenburg let go of Chachi and the poodle floated to the surface—lungs filled with water, eyes open, mouth frozen in a fiendish snarl.

And then Greenburg saw his dead wife, and his chest cavity exploded as if he'd swallowed a grenade. Every muscle in his body burned with agony. His vision blurred. The world began to spin and go dark. He pulled himself to the edge of the pool, collapsed on the stairs, half in the water and half out, and stopped breathing.

sunday

43

somebody cross a line can't be crossed

GREENBURG WASN'T DEAD. His heart didn't explode. It was true he had stopped breathing, but only for a minute, and then his breath was dangerously shallow and weak, though enough oxygen had reached his brain so that he didn't stroke out or hemorrhage or expire while he was lying unconscious on the pool steps.

When he'd opened his eyes and came to, it was ten o'clock and quiet on the patio. Pool lights below the surface gave the water a dreamy red-amber glow. He was weak and in shock and entirely disoriented. He had a nightmarish memory of what had happened and knew he needed help. He'd crawled across the flagstone on his hands and knees, trying not to look at his wife, who had bled out and was whiter than white, eyes open but seeing nothing—the *Seussical* corpse of Carol Greenburg. He reached the outdoor furniture and called Ramona on the poolside extension.

She'd arrived before eleven and found him draped over a chaise lounge, his legs akimbo on the ground, too weak to lift himself up. She'd helped him into the house and guided him to the bedroom, where she laid him on the bed, stripped him down, and cleaned his wounds. She'd dressed him in a gray Garth Brooks T-shirt and khaki shorts and left the room to get him a glass of water. When she'd returned, he was asleep.

He awoke again at seven thirty Sunday morning. She was lying beside him, watching the TV at the end of the bed, a Jesus talk show discussing the promise of everlasting life in heaven. He hoped Carol had made it there, but he doubted she did.

"That your dead wife by the pool?" Ramona said.

"Yes," Greenburg said.

"You kill her?"

He shook his head. "Chachi."

"The poodle killed her?"

Tears came to his eyes as he relived the attack in his mind. He saw his wife go down, her artery open, her blood spout into the pool as if from a stone cherub fountain. He heard her trying to scream but unable to make a sound beyond an inhuman gurgling noise that was both terrifying and pathetic. "He chewed through the leash and assaulted us."

"The white poodle?"

"It was a horror movie."

"The little white puppy poodle with the bad attitude?"

"Blood and death."

"Where he at?"

"I drowned him in the pool."

"Say what?"

"I held him under the water until he drowned. I killed Chachi. I murdered my own dog."

Ramona turned off the TV, got up off the bed, and crossed to her Civil War sword, which leaned against the dresser. Despite his state of drowsy shock, he knew she was onto something.

"What's wrong?" he said.

"You take your damn dead dog out of your pool?"

"He floated to the surface, and I left him there."

"Then we got a problem, DG."

She stood at the end of the bed, holding her sword with her right hand and tapping the broadside of the blade into her left palm.

"Don't leave me hanging, RC," Greenburg said.

"Ain't no damn dead poodle in the pool."

Greenburg sat up on his elbows. "What?"

"You sure he dead?"

"Drowned dead. I'm sure."

"Voodoo girl breathe on his drowned dead poodle ass?"

"No."

"Then he didn't do no damn dead doggy paddle, did he?"

"No way."

"Somebody come get him, DG."

Greenburg sat all the way up, his back against the headboard. He was still woozy, but her focus, her energy, her charisma, her brute sexuality was waking him up in a hurry. "Who?"

"You tell me."

The dentist thought about it for a moment, and then his eyes opened and narrowed at the same time—simultaneous suspicion and conviction. "Dan Miller."

"Hair dude think he a movie star?"

Greenburg nodded. "I called and told him I'd changed my mind about the free attitude adjustment. I told him Chachi was getting worse, not better. He said he'd be here at nine to pick him up and would bring him back first thing Monday morning."

"It always the hair dude."

"I was in and out of consciousness. I remember I heard—or dreamed I heard—someone slapping the water. I had an out-of-body experience and could see myself on the steps, half in the water and half out. I could see blood on my arms and legs and hands. I could see Carol on her back, dead as dust. And some-one...someone was skimming Chachi out of the pool. Yes, yes, I remember it now; they were catching him in the net, slapping the water to get him closer. I remember."

"Was it Miller?"

"Yes—and a horrible, disgusting clown. I thought it was part of the same dark, terrible dream because there could never be a clown that grotesque in reality, so I let it go and must have passed out again, but now I remember. It wasn't a dream. It was Miller and a clown. They took Chachi."

Ramona nodded and said, "Somebody cross a line can't be crossed."

"Not somebody," Greenburg said. "Dan Miller."

"He got your dog *and* your money?"

"He told me Shuler had the money."

"So hair dude got your dog, cop got your money, dwarf got your Lexus, and you got nothing. That about right?"

The reality of it depressed him. He felt his chin fall to his chest.

She walked to his side of the bed, reached out with her sword, put the tip under his chin, and lifted it up. "You know what that mean, DG?"

No," he said. Having his woman put her cold blade on his hot skin excited him in a way he didn't expect.

"It mean we getting your dog, your cash, and your car. It mean we at war. You hear what I'm saying? It mean we on a mission."

Greenburg knew that a war and a mission would take guts and courage, and he didn't have either one of those things at the moment—if he'd ever had them. But Ramona had guts and courage by the boatload. She was the most spectacular woman he'd ever met. She was strong and fearless, and through her he could feel his strength and courage coming back, his adrenaline flowing, his heart pounding like a jackhammer.

"What about Miller?" he said.

"He a fly on the wall. We going to slap *his* ass."

He loved the sound of that, *loved it*. He'd never liked Miller and couldn't wait to *slap his ass*. But first he would have to dispose of Carol's body—*Poor Dead Carol* is how he would think of her now—and then he would have to clean the blood from the pool, and then he would have to get rid of the leash, and then he would have to handle the Seuss Club women, who would come looking for his wife and demand answers.

There would be lying, he knew, phenomenal lying. But he was nothing if not a phenomenal liar. *Look at the lies I've been telling myself for thirty years*, he thought.

"And Shuler?" he said.

"He a dirty cop. We going to clean *his* ass."

She was talking about revenge, and it sounded sweet and fired him up. He couldn't stand Shuler from the first phone call, and now that he knew the detective had his seventy-five grand, he wanted to *clean his ass* but good. He felt the muscles in his legs fire like pistons and stood up, ready for battle.

"What about Harvey?" he said.

"He a damn dwarf. We going to kick *his* ass."

"He has a giant."

"Bigger they are, harder they fall."

He was totally turned on by her confidence and power, which confused him because how could he feel so alive after what had happened to him and his wife and his dog just yesterday afternoon? But that was the confusion of a weakling, the confusion of a man who no longer lived in this house, the confusion of his past.

This was the *new* Don Greenburg and his sword-swinging woman. This was the *new* Don Greenburg, who named names and took numbers. This was the *new* Don Greenburg, who, after watching his wife bleed out and then drowning his dog the day before, had a hard-on like a Harley Davidson at seven thirty the next morning.

He walked to the end of the bed and stood beside her, a flag-pole in his khakis. "You're not scared of them?"

"Ain't nobody mess with my man."

He put his arms around her and kissed her on the mouth.

She looked down at his shorts and said, "Keep that rocket in your pocket, DG, and tell me something."

"Anything, RC," he said.

"You got a gun?" she said.

"I've got Sally," he said.

44

a runaway train on a track to destination unknown

MIKE WOKE up at eight a.m. Sunday in a hot stinking sweat, staggered out of bed, and stood before the full-length mirror beside Marcy's makeup table, the one she'd bought at Pottery Barn, to look at his naked body. He did not like what he saw.

His hair was thinner than he remembered, and there were dark circles under his eyes that made him look like a balding raccoon—no surprise there; he'd hardly slept since Linda died, and when exhaustion had roped him in at four in the morning, his head swirled with nightmares nearly as extreme as the waking life he was actually living.

He was pale and flabby—even when he sucked his gut in. He flexed his muscles, hoping to see some sign of the young buck who used to cut down trees with a chain saw, but that kid was nowhere in sight. He was soft all around.

The "M" Judd Martin had branded into his chest was scabbed over and still sensitive to the touch. His sunburn had peeled and left pink patches behind. On the outside, he was a mess. On the inside, he was a runaway train on a track to destination unknown.

He had called Marcy last night to tell her he'd been offered the bookkeeping job at El Cab, hoping that splinter of good news might loosen her up little, but he never got to that part of the conversation because he'd said he had something to tell her, and she'd said she had something to tell him too, and she wanted to go first, and then she did, and that was that.

What Marcy had said was that she'd met a man. Her mother knew a handsome, successful, athletic pediatrician with two sons whose wife had died three years ago. The pediatrician was just now getting back into social circulation, and Marcy's mother had introduced them, and they'd gone for coffee without any kids. Marcy had told Mike about their date, but his brain became a Chinese garbage scow, and he was sifting through the foreign rubbish on a misty Chinese river and didn't understand a word she'd said because she was inexplicably speaking Chinese.

When she'd hung up, he had fallen face first on the bed, hoping he would suffocate in his pillow, but instead he'd had nightmares about zombies and dwarves and giants and dead poodles and pediatricians and Marcy and his mother, and he woke up at eight o'clock in a hot stinking sweat.

He knew that beneath the layers and layers and layers of bizarre emotional upheaval he'd experienced since last Monday —*last Monday*—was an all-encompassing sadness and sense of loss. And he knew that the only way through the sadness was to face it down and fight back.

He put on a bathing suit and went out to the pool, thinking an early swim might just be his first step toward normality, but he heard reggae coming from the garage, and instead of jumping in the water, he followed the music.

Danny and Paul the Pervert were drinking piña coladas at the Tiki bar. The clown wore his full, rat-shit regalia and was the designated bartender. Danny wore hip surfer shorts and no shirt and sat on a barstool. There were umbrellas in their drinks. It was ninety-five degrees in the garage.

Reggae blasted out of Danny's iPod player. It was either Bob Marley or Ziggy Marley or Stephen Marley or The Wailers or somebody who sounded like one or all of them. Mike wasn't really a reggae guy and couldn't tell the difference.

"Turn it down," Mike said from the doorway, shouting over the chorus of "I Shot the Sheriff."

"We're celebrating," Danny said, also shouting. "Make my brother a piña colada, Paul. He looks like he could use one."

The clown made Mike a drink in Danny's blender, which added to the uproar.

Mike took five steps to the Tiki bar and ripped the iPod out of the player. "What could you possibly be celebrating when the whole goddamn world is falling apart?"

Danny pointed at a pink, plastic beach pail ten feet away. Chachi was in the pail, vicious snarl on his dead poodle face.

"We don't have to kill the dog," Danny said. "Hip, hip, hooray. Greenburg did it for us. Drowned him in the pool."

"Not before the beast killed his wife," Paul the Pervert said, handing Mike the drink. "Ripped her throat wide open."

"Greenburg's dead too," Danny said. "Chachi tore him up. He looked dead anyway."

"Backyard was a blood bath," the clown said.

"We get the poodle already dead; we don't owe the Green-burgs shit because they're dead, and somebody else finds the bodies, so we're out clean, and, oh yes, not dead," Danny said. "It's a trifecta. I always drink piña coladas when I hit a trifecta."

Mike swallowed the entire piña colada in one shot. The rum bit through the cream of coconut and the sweet tang of the pineapple juice. As the drink went down, Mike knew he should feel some kind of compassion for the late dentist and his wife, knew he should worry that Danny and the clown had left clues at the murder scene that would lead the police to his house, knew nothing good could come of a dead poodle in a pail in his garage. He knew all this and said, "So we're on for tonight?"

"Showtime," Danny said. "Midnight."

"We have to get the word out," Mike said, handing his glass to Paul and gesturing for another round.

"I think Harvey and Omar may kill me," Danny said, "so I'll tell Shuler."

"I may kill Shuler, so I'll tell Ahab and Ishmael," Mike said.

"I'll tell Jenny," Danny said.

"*I'll* tell Jenny," Mike said.

Paul poured rum in the blender, filled it with ice from a small cooler, and clicked on the motor.

"She's my client," Danny said.

"She's my client too," Mike said.

"Till midnight," Danny said. "Then you go to New Jersey forever."

"Not until you pay me seventy-five hundred dollars," Mike said.

"There's no money for us," Danny said.

The clown killed the blender, poured the piña colada in the glass, put an umbrella on top, and gave the drink to Mike.

The news that Danny did not have their money did not surprise Mike. It pissed him off but did not surprise him. "What do you mean there's no money for us?" he said.

"I had to pay Jenny our commission to do tonight's show," Danny said. "She gets the whole seventy-five grand from Shuler or she doesn't bring the dog back. If she doesn't bring the dog back, then Harvey has Omar crush my skull. I had no choice. Those were her terms. I had to make the deal so at least we'd be free of each other."

Mike glared at his brother, let the rage and disappointment rise through him, and swallowed the second piña colada in one shot. As the frozen Hawaiian cocktail went down, Mike knew that without the seventy-five hundred he would miss a mortgage payment, a car payment, a credit card payment, and a life insurance payment, knew that missing those payments would drag his credit scores into the toilet, knew that not even Bob Cutting would hire a bookkeeper who missed multiple payments and had credit scores in the toilet. He knew all this and said, "The money doesn't matter."

"What?"

"Shuler's got evidence it was us at the mortuary. His deal is double or nothing. We bring the dog back; Shuler gives us the money, except now we don't get any of it, oh well, another Dan Miller fuck up. We bring Mom back; Shuler doesn't arrest us, except we already brought her back, so the money doesn't matter because we're going to jail." Then he handed his glass to Paul and said, "Put some rum in it this time, clown."

Paul made him another drink, heavy on the rum. And made one for himself too.

"It's all right, not a problem, we can make that work," Danny said. "Shuler knows Mom died. He confirmed it with your mortuary guy. So we make a big show of the dog, like nothing could be bigger than bringing the poodle back from the dead, and when the poodle is barking, Mom walks into the room out of nowhere, I mean we throw open the door, she's backlit, music's playing, and we introduce her and blow his mind. His mind would have to be blown. It *will* be blown. He gets his comedy cornerstone. We get the money *and* the get-out-jail card, *and* you go to New Jersey."

The blender roared, chopping the ice, chilling the rum, creaming the cream of coconut. Mike shook his head, disapproving of the plan while knowing there was no other option, and said, "Or we don't pass go; we don't collect two hundred dollars."

"Why not?" Danny said.

"Because Mom won't release me from *The Oath* because we won't let her leave the house."

"So *you* don't pass go," Danny said.

"If I don't, you don't," Mike said.

"Because?" Danny said.

Paul put the drinks on the bar. Mike picked his up and took three steps to Danny so that they were face to face.

"Because I'll hound you every day for the rest of your life," Mike said. "I'll be your moral conscience, the ever-present angel on your shoulder whispering in your ear. I'll watch over you every minute of every day of every week of every month of every year, just like Mom made me swear on her dying heart. My oath is your oath."

Mike watched the reality of *The Oath* hit Danny in the head like a two-by-four, clinked glasses with Paul, and he and the clown swallowed their third piña coladas in one shot. As the rum-heavy frozen concoction went down, Mike knew there was something fundamentally wrong with his mother—separate and apart from the fact that she was alive after she was dead— who had called him a fat fairy and a pussy and swung an iron pan at his head, knew there was something fundamentally wrong with his brother, who insisted on digging the hole deeper and deeper without being aware that he was the one holding the damn shovel, knew there was something fundamentally wrong with himself for shooting piña coladas with the pervert clown on Sunday morning instead of calling the whole thing off before everything went in the shitter. He knew all this and said, "She's going to ask what the hell's happening here tonight."

"What the hell *is* happening here tonight?" Linda said, entering the garage from the laundry room off the kitchen.

She still wore her blue business suit, but she had one of Marcy's aprons on over it and was holding a mixing bowl and a whisk. Mike looked at her like she was from another dimension because, well, she *was* from another dimension.

"We're having a party for you, Mom," Mike said, "to introduce you to some people and get them used to the idea that you didn't really die, so you can go home. How does that sound?"

"About time, fairy boy," Linda said. Then she turned her attention to Paul, who was already blending piña colada number four for Mike, and said in a voice dripping with sexual overtones and undertones and tones not yet defined, "Hey there, clown man? Where you been all my life and death?"

"What's happening, pretty mama?" Paul said.

"You and me in the kitchen," Linda said. "I'm baking us a sardine-jalapeño pie."

"Katy bar the door," Paul said.

"It's a date," Linda said, and she started back to the kitchen.

Danny looked at Mike with a touch of panic and followed after her. "Mom, you have to let Mike out of *The Oath* so we're not tied to each other for the rest of our lives."

"The only thing I *have* to do, flimflam man, is get down with the clown. And then she rapped a hip-hop melody as she left the garage, Danny in her wake. "We're going to party tonight, uh huh, that's right, get down, get tight, get outta sight, c'mon clown man, I don't bark, I bite."

Paul looked at Mike and said, "Hubba, hubba."

Mike put his empty glass on the Tiki bar, got close to the clown, and said, "If you touch my mother, I'll kill you."

Paul stopped the blender, poured number four in Mike's glass, and said, "There's three things in the world you can't stop: a natural disaster, a human apocalypse, and a clown with a boner for an old broad. I'm all three rolled into one." Then he followed Linda and Danny into the house.

Mike lifted the glass and swallowed the drink in one shot.

45

pleasant is as pleasant does

AS HE PULLED the Pathfinder onto Vanalden from Parthenia, it made perfect sense to Danny that the police department would expel Gary Shuler like a stone in a shoe, not to one of their distant community stations (no, that would not be far enough away for his special brand of bizarre) but instead would banish him to one of the LAPD towing garages, where he would be out of sight, out of mind, out of touch, and out of luck.

Ross Baker Towing in Northridge had been the landing place for the comedian cop. It had been a service center for fleet rentals before tow trucks took over the car yard. Now it was a jail for disobedient automobiles—and also Detective Shuler's Office of the Absurd.

Danny made a right into Ross Baker and drove to the back of the lot, past additional outbuildings small and large, past a hundred delinquent vehicles, (whose owners would pay big bucks to bail them out), past the trucks that brought them here.

He'd been towed before, Danny had, though never to this obscure auto outpost. Still, he had a ping of compassion for the drivers of these vehicles, meaning he knew what a pain in the ass it was to first find the damn car and second write the damn check to get it back.

If he'd recognized that ping as compassion, it would have taken him by surprise since that was an emotion foreign to his nature. As such, he'd missed it entirely—it blew by him like a thoroughbred—because he was thinking about his brother, his mother, and *The Oath*, which had started in the hospital as a yoke around Mike's neck but had somehow become a burden that would bind them together for a lifetime.

While Linda and Paul the Pervert shared sardine-jalapeño pie and flirted without normal human inhibition, Danny had tried to convince her to release Mike from bondage. If she wouldn't do that, Danny's argument had been, then Mike would be Danny's cross to bear, which, in effect, would be the opposite of what *The Oath* was intended to prevent in the first place. It would, in fact, Danny had said to Linda, be the terrible bad thing she had meant to protect him from when she made Mike swear it on her dying heart.

"Kiss off, Daniel," Linda had said. "I'm getting busy with the clown."

His mother had made it clear that the only way out of *The Oath* was to get her back into her life after death—living in Mrs. Alemi's small yellow house, keeping the books at El Cab—and Danny knew that the only way to do that was to clear the decks, meaning get the money from Shuler, get Jenny paid, get Harvey on board so Omar wouldn't crush Danny's skull, and get Mike on a jet to Jersey.

He parked the Nissan in front of Shuler's official abode, an abandoned cinderblock warehouse at the far corner of the complex (a former tire storage facility emptied of everything but the smell of vulcanized rubber), and walked to the front door.

It was only a fifteen-second walk from the truck to the building, but that was plenty of time for Danny to think about the moon and stars and Jenny Stone.

She's a drug I can't quit, Danny thought. *My heart's pounding, my hands are sweating; it's like I'm having withdrawals, like I haven't seen her in weeks.* And then he remembered it was yesterday he'd sat on the crooked porch while she did porn yoga in her see-through porn yoga clothes and her mother had given him a glass of poisoned lemonade. Yesterday.

I'm going to Northridge as soon I leave here, he said to himself. *I have to see her.*

And then he arrived at Shuler's rusted metal door, where a LAPD sticker, worn and torn and adhered to the mottled coating of oxide, was the only evidence of police presence on the car jail lot. It was ten a.m., one hundred eight degrees.

The door was unlocked because the handle was busted. Danny pushed it open, went inside, and was confronted by a wall of heavy-duty cardboard boxes. Not your everyday garden-variety wall, more like the Great Wall of China. There were thousands of boxes on metal shelves that reached fourteen feet in the air and stretched from the front of the warehouse to the back, from one side to the other. The boxes were labeled with color-coded dates and names: *January-March 1982, Bellamy-Benjamin; July-September 1974, Greenhouse-Gregory.*

'82? Danny thought. *'74? This place is deep storage for shit the police would rather forget—the perfect place for Shuler.*

Though they filled the warehouse corner to corner, the shelves were not organized in straight rows. They were haphazardly placed at odd angles so that they created a crazy maze—like a Midwestern cornfield carved by aliens. Because of the height of the shelving and because the shelves were abutted one against the other, end to end, to form the twisting and turning aisles, and because they were so densely packed with boxes that Danny doubted he could slide an envelope in there anywhere, there was no way to see across the warehouse.

But he heard voices. And he recognized them too.

He started through the maze and found himself dead-ended several times, but finally followed the voices to a clearing in the center of the warehouse, an open area surrounded by shelves, probably thirty feet by thirty feet. On one side of the clearing, there were file cabinets positioned along the edges near the shelves. On the other side was a makeshift stage, half a foot high and ten feet wide by five feet deep. A large sheet of plywood covered with brick wallpaper was the backdrop for the stage. A sign nailed to the "brick wall" read: *Joke House.*

In the middle of the clearing was a LAPD desk circa somewhere in the '60s. Harvey stood on the desk, pointing a handgun at Shuler, who was seated in his desk chair. The dwarf wore a seersucker suit and a pink shirt with a matching pink tie and quintessential white bucks. Omar stood beside Shuler and had a hold of the detective's right wrist so that Gary's right arm was extended straight out in front of him, elbow hyperextended enough for the pain to keep the cop in place (in case Harvey aiming a gun at him wasn't enough motivation) and his right hand was palm down on the desk, fingers spread. With the hand that wasn't holding Gary's wrist, Omar held his Bowie knife. The bare bulbs hanging down from the ceiling reflected off the blade, sending beams of light around the clearing.

Danny hid behind a metal shelf and peered around the boxes into the clearing.

"I'm a patient person to a point," Harvey said to Shuler. "But beyond that, I can be abrupt, even unpleasant. And I'm afraid, *Detective,* that you have stretched me past my outer limits."

"Hard to imagine you as unpleasant, Harvey," Shuler said. His face was contorted because Omar was stretching the ligaments in his elbow past their outer limits. "But Omar is another story."

"I'm offended," Omar said. "I could have dropped you into the dumpster that didn't have the mattress. That was a pleasant decision on my part, you have to admit."

"I meant to thank you," Shuler said.

"Pleasant is as pleasant does," Omar said.

"Shall we try again?" Harvey said. "This time, for each incorrect answer, Omar will remove one of your fingers. Which one first, Omar?"

"I'm thinking thumb," Omar said.

"The opposable thumb," Shuler said. "Hilarious."

"My thought exactly," Harvey said.

Danny watched wide-eyed because he had never before seen a real-life, actual torture session. On TV he had. Everyone had seen one on TV. All you had to do was tune in to 24. Kiefer Sutherland had become rich and famous by torturing bad guys on that show. Which was a funny thought to occur to Danny because every now and then someone would tell him he kind of looked like Kiefer Sutherland, when they weren't telling him he looked like Brad Pitt. *That's exactly what I look like*, Danny thought, *a combination of Sutherland and Pitt. Leading man material, that's what I look like.*

"Where is the zombie with the trailer with my money?" Harvey said.

"That's three questions," Shuler said.

"One question with a double preposition," Omar said.

"Regardless, *Detective*, it is one answer," Harvey said.

"Sunland-Tujunga, pad seventeen," Shuler said.

"That is not the case, so where are they?" Harvey said.

"Somewhere else?" Shuler said.

"When people ask you where your thumb is, you can tell them the same thing," Harvey said. "Omar."

"No more hitchhiking, gardening, or umpiring," Omar said as he lowered his blade toward the tissue where Shuler's thumb was connected to his hand.

"I'm outta there," Shuler said like an umpire.

What's my angle? Danny thought. *I need an angle.*

There were two possibilities. First was that Gary knew where the zombie and the trailer and the money were and was lying because he thought losing a thumb would be good for his act. He was letting Omar slice his thumb off for laughs because he was planning to spend the seventy-five thousand on thumb reconstruction surgery. It wasn't likely, but it wasn't impossible. Shuler was that crazy.

Second was that Gary wasn't lying and didn't know where the zombie and the trailer and the money were.

The first scenario sucked.

If Gary *was* lying, then he would spend the money attaching some kind of prosthetic digit to his opposable thumbless hand, and the money would be gone, and Danny would be stuck in Mike's garage with his brother and his mother—*Jesus Christ, his mother*—because he would lose Jenny as a client because he wouldn't be able to pay her fee for breathing life into Chachi the first time, and if he lost Jenny as a client, then she wouldn't breathe life into Chachi the second time and Harvey wouldn't believe him about Jenny breathing life into anything at any time and then Harvey wouldn't be a partner in Danny's *Bringing Dead Hollywood Pets Back To Life* business, and Danny wouldn't be able to pay Harvey back the money he'd borrowed and lost at the track, and Omar would kill him with Gary's severed thumb, shoving it down Danny's throat until he choked to death, which is why the first scenario sucked.

In the second scenario, Gary *wasn't* lying and didn't know where the zombie, the trailer, and the money were, which meant the money was as gone as it was in the first scenario, which meant the second scenario also ended with Danny choking to death on Gary's bloody thumb, which is why the second scenario sucked as bad as the first one.

Either way, lying or not lying, if Shuler showed up at Jenny's show without a thumb or without both thumbs or without any or all of his fucking fingers, then Jenny would suspect something was awry, and she would demand her money up front, and Danny wouldn't have it, and Jenny wouldn't breathe life into Chachi the second time, and Danny would choke to death on Gary's goddamn thumb.

On top of all *that*, Shuler was everybody's best bet to find the missing money in the first place. Without his thumbs, maybe Gary would give up and move back to San Diego, and the whereabouts of the money would remain a mystery. Harvey needed Shuler too.

That's the angle, Danny thought. *The show must go on with Shuler all thumbs.*

All of that thinking happened in half a blink, the time it took for his eyelids to go up. In the second half of the blink, as his eyelids came down, Danny stepped into the clearing, into the light, walked toward the desk, and said, "Hey, Harvey, whoa, what's going on here? Omar, buddy, come on, man, what are you doing? How's he going to hold a microphone and give the crowd a thumbs-up at the same time if he's only got one thumb?"

Harvey pointed the gun at Danny, sang, "Oh, Danny Boy, the pipes, the pipes are calling," and fired two shots.

46

zombies don't like marvin gaye

WHEN HARVEY and Omar busted in his office door at Ross Baker Towing and entered unexpected and uninvited, Gary did not yet know Judd Martin had moved the trailer off pad seventeen and out of the Little Valley Trailer Park. So he wasn't lying when he told the dwarf the zombie was "somewhere else." That's all he knew at the time.

It wasn't until after they'd left that he'd called Judd Martin's cell phone, a phone owned by Buddy Morris, the plumber who'd owed Martin a favor and paid it off by letting the zombie live in his empty Airstream...and by lending him one of his plumbing company cell phones.

Gary could punch the buttons with one hand—left or right— because Omar had not removed either of his thumbs. He had used his right hand to call the zombie.

Martin had answered and said, "Nobody here."

"That's stupid," Gary had said. "You answered the phone."

"No, I didn't."

"Yes, you did."

They arranged to meet near the Shoin Building in The Japanese Garden in Woodley Park on Victory Boulevard and Woodley Avenue in Van Nuys at noon.

Gary arrived first. He had not been to Woodley Park since he'd attended a classic car show several months ago. In addition to classic cars, the park was also home to the best cricket games in LA. There were five cricket grounds, and Woodley weekends featured expats of England and India and Australia and other British-influenced countries that played the gentleman's game, which was rocket science to Los Angelenos.

The gleaming glass Tillman Water Reclamation Plant was in Woodley as well, and six and a half acres of Tillman was dedicated to The Japanese Garden.

Gary knew the Woodley Park Japanese Garden was rated the tenth greatest Japanese Garden in the world by magazines that rate such things, but he had no idea what magazines those were or how they went about rating them. Despite that, he found it hard to believe there were nine Japanese Gardens on Earth greater than this one.

He had often stopped at the garden before comedy gigs, when he needed to feel the harmony between universe and soul, when he needed to reestablish the balance between his Yin and Yang, when he needed ultimate tranquility to remember he was born to be a stand-up comic.

Amidst the stone lanterns and lakes and waterfalls near the Shoin Building that housed the tea garden, teahouse, and tatami, was a bench tucked into an alcove that looked out over the serenity. Gary chose this bench for his rendezvous with Judd Martin.

On most Sundays, Gary knew, there were people in The Japanese Garden seeking solace—not unlike Gary did from time to time. But he suspected that today the garden would be empty. He had checked the weather, and at high noon, the temperature was forecast to be one fourteen, the hottest June Sunday on record.

After he'd called Judd Martin and set their meeting, Gary drove straight to a grocery store and bought a box of Oreos and quart of milk. He ate more than a dozen of the drug cookies and downed almost all the milk. As he was gorging and blissing, he wondered if he was celebrating his fabulous comedic luck—he had nearly lost his fingers to the dwarf and the giant (*hilarious!*) —or if he needed deep emotional relief from the trauma he had experienced as Omar's knife pushed closer and closer to his hand.

In the end, it didn't matter. He had Oreos and milk and his thumbs and a great new bit for his act. *I'm sorry it went down the way it did,* the detective thought, *but thank you, Danny Miller.*

Gary arrived first and patted himself on the back for being right about the heat: Woodley was empty, and there was no one in The Japanese Garden. He thought a moment of meditation might be called for and began to free his mind of all debris, but his Yin and Yang were thrown way out of whack as Judd Martin arrived at the bench.

Gary had seen him two days ago, on Friday, when Martin had branded Mike Miller, and the zombie had been too close to the line that separates living from dead.

It seemed to Gary that Martin had now crossed that line and was straddling a new line: the divide between the dead and undead. He was a walking nightmare, and Gary wondered why the police didn't arrest him for terrifying normal human people. He took out his gun and pointed it at the zombie, who sat on the other end of the bench looking like hell on Earth.

"You going to shoot me?" Martin said.

"I think so," Gary said.

"Fair enough," Martin said.

"I heard you and the Airstream no longer reside at the Little Valley Trailer Park," Gary said.

"Where'd you hear that?" Martin said.

"Through the grapevine."

"So there really is a grapevine? I thought that was something people said."

"It is something people say. I just said it."

"You and Marvin Gaye. I used to like that song, once upon a time."

"Once upon a time?"

"When I was human. Before Miller murdered me and I became a zombie."

"Right."

"Zombies don't like Marvin Gaye—or any music. It hurts our brains. Except for Meat Loaf. Zombies like Meat Loaf. Meat Loaf is zombie music."

Meat Loaf is zombie music, Gary thought, *I have to write that down.* But he couldn't get to his pocket pad because he didn't want to lower his gun because he thought he might have to shoot Judd Martin any minute because there was steam or smoke or some kind of inhuman vapor wafting off the zombie, who appeared ready to explode somehow. His teeth were crusted yellow with thick gunk. His eyes were red-red-red. His hair was a matted hornet's nest. His camo vest, jeans, and boots were vile. He had not changed clothes in a week. He smelled like death.

"Where's the Airstream, Judd?" Gary said.

"I had to move it."

"Why?"

"The wrong kind of people moved into sixteen, and the neighborhood went south."

"Who could possibly be the wrong kind of people for you?"

"Frat boys. Kryptonite for zombies."

Kryptonite for zombies! Gary thought. *Funny stuff!* "So where did you move it?"

"Somewhere else."

Gary recognized the irony of the answer, of course, and thinking about irony made him wonder if Judd Martin was putting him on, if his zombie act was just that—an act. If it was possible that Martin had been an extra on the Warner Brothers lot in an apocalypse project, walked home in costume, stayed in character, and lost himself in the role. He decided it was impossible. *Even Robert Downey Jr. couldn't pull this off,* he thought, *although he could play me in the feature.*

"I have a job for you, Deputy," Gary said, looking at the toy store badge pinned to Martin's putrid camo vest. He would deal with the location of the Airstream later. There was pressing business at hand. "I got a phone call from Dr. Greenburg. Remember him? Mike Miller's brother called, and you answered because Miller was duct taped to a chair."

"Dead goldfish swimming in the bowl," Martin said.

"He called me today, Greenburg did, about the seventy-five thousand dollars."

"Hard cash for something about his wife's dog and a woman named Jenny."

"He thinks I have the money, and tomorrow morning he's going to have his attorney sue me and send the police department to get it back."

"Do you have it?"

"No. But Jenny the Gypsy goes down at midnight, and I'll find out who does."

"I want that money."

"If you convince Greenburg to change his mind about his attorney, I'll tell you where it is. If you don't convince him, I'll have to close the case and take back your badge, you'll lose the money, and you'll have to stop stalking Mike Miller."

Martin stood up and filth fell off him. Gary kept his gun pointed at the zombie, who either didn't notice or didn't mind. The sun was inconceivably hot.

"Given the opportunity, I can be painfully persuasive," Martin said.

"Escalon Drive in Encino," Gary said. "I'll give you his address."

47

i'm a swinger

MIKE MILLER SAT on the settee in Jenny Stone's cockeyed parlor. It was noon on Sunday. The air was one hundred fourteen degrees. He'd climbed her crooked steps, crossed her slanted porch, stood at her lopsided door, and rang her doorbell, which had chirped like a wounded bird. That was amusing to Mike because lately he'd been thinking of himself as having a busted wing. But the time for self-pity was over. He was fit to fly.

Jenny had answered the bell with red hair—*Auburn! His favorite!*—and green eyes, wearing a multicolored, psychedelic, neon bright, flower-power, micro mini dress and white go-go boots, looking like Nancy Sinatra or Goldie Hawn from *Laugh In*, a 1970s dancing queen. He'd told her he was on his way to see Ahab and Ishmael and that Chachi was secured and dead—or re-dead—that the show was on for midnight and that he had something he wanted to ask her. She'd invited him in, led him through her house of many angles to the parlor, and sat next to him on the settee. He'd opened his mouth to make a date, the doorbell had chimed, Jenny had gone after it, and he'd had this thought: *Mike Miller has balls.*

After Marcy had told him about the handsome jock pediatrician she'd blind dated, most of which he'd missed because she'd been speaking Chinese on a garbage scow on the Yangtze River, Mike had tried to suffocate himself in his pillow. Of course, he hadn't suffocated himself. Instead, he'd decided to ask Jenny Stone out on the town. *Two can play this game,* he'd said in his head. If Marcy could have sex with a pediatrician (he had no idea if Marcy was having sex with him or not, but his imagination sure thought so), then he could have sex with Jenny Stone (his imagination felt strongly about that too). *Tits for tats,* he had thought at the time. And yet he still didn't have the courage to make his move.

He had hoped an early morning swim would snap him out of it, but he'd been distracted by reggae music and had ended up getting drunk on piña coladas in his garage instead of doing laps in his pool.

What happened after that had turned out to be the straw that broke the camel's back: Paul the Pervert and his mother hooked up in a way that defied all rules of romance.

While Linda and the clown ate sardine-jalapeno pie in the kitchen, holding hands, making eyes, and flirting in ways both nauseating and terrifying, Mike went to his bedroom, passed out, and had a terrifying dream about Marcy having wild sex with the pediatrician while her parents cheered them on—especially Marcy's mother, who kept yelling *Mike Miller has no balls, Mike Miller has no balls* throughout the dream.

He'd shot up like a rocket at eleven a.m. with this realization: if the clown could hook up with a woman—even if that woman was his recently deceased mother—then by God, he could hook up too. He'd found the bottom of the barrel of humanity and discovered it wasn't him; it was Paul the Pervert. The clown was Mike's measuring stick. If Paul had balls, even half an electrocuted nut, then Mike had more than that. It was the first good news he'd heard all week.

He'd showered and shaved and put on clean jeans and loafers with no socks and his favorite black and blue, short-sleeved, mafia-style silk shirt (the kind Tony and his mobsters wore on *The Sopranos*), and driven to Northridge, where he now sat on Jenny's settee and thought, *Mike Miller has balls.*

"What the hell are you doing here?" Danny said to Mike as he followed Jenny into the parlor.

Mike looked at his brother in shock. Not so much because Danny had arrived in Jenny's parlor at this particular moment, although that was certainly bad timing and, yes, shocking—Mike hadn't even considered adding *Danny-showing-up-out-of-the-blue* to his *things-that-could-go-wrong-with-asking-Jenny-out list.* No, the really shocking part of this equation to Mike was the way Danny looked.

For the entirety of their lives, in every instance Mike could recall, Danny had looked like a movie star or a rock star or a movie star playing a rock star. Even when they were boys at the small yellow house, Danny had looked like a Calvin Klein model, and Mike had looked like an accountant—*only grade-school bookkeeper in the Valley* is what his flimflam father had said.

But Danny was a mess today, and Mike was a *Sopranos* goombah. The tables had turned. Danny's nose was still a little swollen and his eyes a bit black and blue from when Omar had rabbit punched him in the back seat of the Range Rover after Harvey had picked him up at Santa Anita on Friday. And there was a gash-like bruise on his forehead that hadn't been there this morning. The bruise was turning black and blue and was crusted with dried blood. His brother's clothes were wet and ragged, as if he'd been dragged across a mopped warehouse floor. There was also dried blood on Danny's black T-shirt. He looked like a beat-up junkie.

The shock wore off in a microsecond, and Mike stood up and said, "What the hell are *you* doing here?"

"I went to Shuler's office to tell him about the midnight show, that we were all in."

"*And?*" Mike said.

"And Harvey and Omar were there to cut off Shuler's thumbs," Danny said, "and Harvey took two shots at me, and I fainted and smashed my head, and Omar dragged me across the floor and laid me out on Shuler's stage and threw a bucket of water on me, and I came to and told them about the midnight show and the dead dog."

"Who killed him this time?" Jenny said to Danny. She stood by the coffee table in front of the settee. Danny stood by the door. Mike stood at the opposite end of the coffee table from Jenny so that the three of them made an isosceles triangle.

"He was dead when we got to Greenburg's," Danny said with a shrug. "Drowned in the pool."

"I meant: *and what the hell are you doing here?*" Mike said, glaring at Danny. His brother glared back at him, and they both glanced over at Jenny, and their isosceles vibe went from bad to worse to weird.

"I can't get you out my mind," Danny said to Jenny. "Thinking about you makes me crazy. I can't wait one more minute. Will you go out with me?"

"I call *bullshit*," Mike said. "You can't ask her out. I'm asking her out."

"I asked her first," Danny said.

"I was here first," Mike said. "And if she didn't answer the door, I would've asked her first too."

"Woulda, coulda, shoulda," Danny said.

"Screw you," Mike said, and he looked at Jenny. "My brother's never had a relationship with a woman that's meant anything to him. He's shallow and hollow and superficial. Did I mention he's a whorehound?"

Danny looked at Jenny and said, "My brother's had one relationship his whole life, and it's been miserable and loveless and empty. Did I mention he's married?"

"Separated," Mike said.

"One week," Danny said.

"The amount of time is irrelevant," Mike said. "It's the separated part that counts. I'm a free agent, that's the point. I'm available."

"Available loser," Danny said, and he took a step toward Mike.

"Whorehound douchebag," Mike said, and he took a step toward Danny.

"I'm taking her out," Danny said, and he took another step.

"*I'm* taking her out," Mike said, and *he* took another step.

"Not if I kick your ass first," Danny said, and he stopped in the middle of the parlor.

And then the idea that he looked like a mobster somehow took over Mike's brain, and he took a step to the middle of the parlor and said, "*Fuhgeddaboudit.*"

They stood toe to toe. Danny grabbed Mike by his *Sopranos* shirt, and Mike grabbed Danny by his bloody black T-shirt, and they drilled each other's eyes.

"Loser," Mike said.

"Deadbeat," Danny said.

"Con man," Mike said.

"Fat man," Danny said.

"I'm not fat," Mike said.

"When we were in school," Danny said to Jenny without letting go of Mike's mobster shirt, "the kids had a song."

"Don't do it," Mike said, eyes wide with bad memories.

"Everybody knew the words," Danny said.

"Not everybody," Mike said.

"All the teachers," Danny said.

"Two teachers, maybe three, okay five," Mike said.

"It goes like this," Danny said.

"I hate this song," Mike said.

"Big fat Mike needs a hunger strike," Danny sang in a mean-spirited, third-grade voice, "big fat Mike will break your bike, big fat Mike go take a hike."

The brothers started to wrestle, but Jenny stopped them before it got hot. "I choose Mike."

The men stopped, still gripping each other.

"What? Him? I don't believe it," Danny said.

"One condition," Jenny said to Mike.

"What is it?" Mike said.

"Ménage a trois," Jenny said in a voice laced with sexual innuendo.

The brothers let go of each other's shirts and faced Jenny, blinking like idiots.

Somewhere in the darkened rubble of Mike's marriage, when his daughters were young and the sexual spark between him and his wife had already been extinguished by car pools and play dates, Mike had asked Marcy about having a threesome. There had been a single young mother at school who'd flirted with Mike *and* Marcy at a third grade choir performance, making it clear she went both ways. That night, after the girls were bathed and read to, Mike had suggested an evening of red wine and low lights and hot sex with the single young mom, who also happened to be Jamaican. Marcy had squashed the idea (and Mike's libido) like a bug, and Mike hadn't thought of it again in years.

Flashing forward into the moment, he imagined the kind of wicked women Jenny liked to play with. Asians. Africans. Europeans. Norwegians. Latinos. Long legs. Soft skin. Big breasts. He felt his groin swelling. It made perfect sense that Jenny was a swinger. How could he not have considered it already? And in this brave new world of zombies and dead dogs and resurrections, Mike wondered why he couldn't be reborn too—as the swinger he once wanted to be.

"No problem," Mike said. "I'm a swinger."

"I can't believe you chose Mike," Danny said somewhere beyond incredulous.

"You and me and who makes three?" Mike said to Jenny, gloating at Danny, already picturing Jenny and some Mexican *mamacita* making him feel like a man.

"Him," Jenny said, pointing at Danny, "and you and me makes three."

Mike looked at his brother and made a horrified face like vomit was on its way up.

"You look like you screwed the pooch, fat man," Maggie said to Mike as she entered the parlor. "What's the problem? You never crossed swords with your brother before? Don't worry about it. You and Pretty Boy are closet fairies anyway." She wore denim overalls and nothing beneath them. Her eyes and hair were wild, feral. She carried a tray with three glasses and pitcher of something pink. "I made punch," she said. "Who's thirsty?"

48

the most fucked up thing
i heard since yesterday

SAWED-OFF Sally was the name of Greenburg's twelve-gauge, double barrel, sawed-off shotgun. He kept it under the bed because Poor Dead Carol was—*had been*—in a constant state of delirium imagining one day some creep would see her at yoga and follow her home to ravage her in her own bedroom while Donald was building crowns and bridges, and so she would have to shoot the son of a bitch. Or maybe Donald would be home and then *he* would have to shoot the son of a bitch. *"Either way,"* Poor Dead Carol had said, *"we need a shotgun."*

The whole thing was absurd on so many levels that the dentist had never known where to start when she'd brought it up. Usually he'd started with two fat lines and four fingers of Tanqueray. But then he'd bought a sawed-off shotgun.

Poor Dead Carol had insisted they name the gun so the son of a bitch who had followed her home after yoga to ravage her wouldn't be suspicious when she called out: *"Donald, get Sally, and get her now!"*

He had never fired the shotgun because no one had ever followed Poor Dead Carol home to ravage her. Surprise! And so Sally lived under the bed, where Greenburg had forgotten about her until Ramona had asked him if he'd had a gun.

The plan was to clean up the bloody mess Chachi had made —before Greenburg drowned him in the pool—and then take back the Lexus, the Mercedes, the money and the dog from Harvey and Omar and Shuler and Miller. That was all they had so far.

It was three o'clock in the afternoon. The weather service had missed its mark by two degrees: it was one sixteen. Greenburg couldn't believe how hot it was and wanted more than anything to be in his office sipping cold gin, but instead he was sweating bullets scrubbing the flagstone patio with bleached soapy water and a wire-bristle broom. He wore a wide-brimmed straw hat to keep the sun off his face, a white, wife-beater T-shirt, powder-blue board shorts with a white floral pattern, and flip-flops. He had already changed the replacement cartridge filters twice and had destroyed the bloody ones, bagged them, and driven them to a Sylmar dump on the far side of the Valley. He'd dropped the leather leash down a Van Nuys sewer. The good news was that the filter had done its job. The pool was clear and clean. Greenburg had checked and doubled-checked the disinfectant level of the water, and there was no sign of foul play in the pool. When he finished bleaching the patio, there would be no evidence of Poor Dead Carol's death at all.

Except for the body. And Ramona had taken charge of that. She'd carried Poor Dead Carol's corpse to the garage, the body thrown over her shoulder like a sack of potatoes. She'd steadied it there with one hand while holding her sword with the other and said, "Don't ask me no questions, DG. I won't tell you no lies."

"I won't tell you no lies either, RC," Greenburg had said.

She'd been in there a hell of a long time.

He *had* lied, however, to Emily Portobello, one of the more obnoxious Seuss reading group women—maybe the most obnoxious. Portobello had surgically lifted her breasts so many times that her nipples—*Good God*, Greenburg had often asked himself, *how many different nipples have they put on those things?*—now pointed due north.

Emily had called asking for Carol, and Greenburg had said his wife had gone to visit her Canadian cousin somewhere in the northern Nunavut Territory—a stunning lie. Emily had said she didn't know anything about Carol taking a trip to Canada and had never heard about Carol's cousin in the northern Nunavut Territory or the southern Nunavut Territory or anywhere in the Nunavut Territory and then said there had been a Seuss reading group medical emergency (a last-minute rhinoplasty) and that she had to find Carol right away. *"Right away means now, Donald,"* she'd said.

Greenburg told her to follow her nipples until she got to Canada and then to keep on going, and then he'd hung up, feeling better about everything.

Indeed, except for wilting in the heat, he was feeling better by the minute. Ramona had told him he looked like he'd been in a street fight with a hooker high on crack cocaine, and he'd looked at himself in the mirror and thought she was right. He liked the thought of himself in a street fight with hooker high on crack.

I could take her, he thought while dumping a puddle of bleach on the patio, near the edge of the pool, where his wife had fallen, bled out, and died. And then he said it to the imaginary hooker junkie out loud, "I can take you."

"Seventy-five grand says you can't," Judd Martin said, moving across the patio toward the dentist.

Greenburg turned to the voice, saw the hellish figure striding toward him holding a hunting knife, and froze, eyes wide. Greenburg wasn't a fan of zombie films, though he had seen previews and posters from time to time and had even watched an episode or two of *The Walking Dead*, so he knew, like most everyone else, what a zombie looked like. But the zombie concept had always struck him as scientifically improbable if not impossible, which is why he wasn't a fan of the genre. Anyway, this was no Hollywood production, this was flesh and blood *or something* coming toward in him real time—a true-life (true-death?) zombie in Greenburg's very own backyard. The smell of the thing alone was horrifying. In his head, Greenburg screamed for help, but his throat was constricted with confusion and shock and fear, and so he made no noise at all.

Martin knocked the wire-bristle broom out of Greenburg's hand and the straw hat off his head and gripped him by the throat. By instinct, Greenburg put his hands on the zombie's thick and filthy arm.

"I'm an undead deputy of the LAPD," Martin said. "It has come to my attention through back-channel communications that you're calling your lawyer tomorrow to sue a certain detective who you think has your seventy-five thousand cash dollars. Is that correct?"

Greenburg couldn't make a sound because the zombie was choking off his airway. He thought he might die of strangulation in the next minute or two.

"I told said certain detective that I would persuade you otherwise regarding your lawsuit, but I've changed my mind. Turns out I'm overcome with the desire to open your chest, remove your heart, cook it on your gas grill, and eat it for lunch with a cold beer—fast food for zombies. I didn't catch your answer about the lawsuit. Yes or no? I don't hear anything."

And then the unmistakable racking sound of a shotgun loading a shell into the chamber filled the patio.

"I bet you heard that, motherfucker," Ramona said.

The zombie turned to her. "You I wasn't expecting."

"Let go of my man, or I'll blow your damn zombie head off your damn zombie body," Ramona said, racking the second shell into the chamber.

Martin released Greenburg and said, "That's the only way to kill a zombie."

"No shit, Sherlock. I watch TV. Now drop the damn knife and

get down on your damn knees or I'll blow your damn dick off. Pretty sure that ain't no damn fun for a zombie neither," Ramona said, aiming the gun at his groin.

Martin dropped the knife and got down on his knees, facing Ramona and Greenburg, who moved away from the zombie and stood beside his woman, ten feet in front of Martin. Greenburg's throat hurt, but Ramona pointing Sawed-Off Sally at the undead deputy's face helped him forget about the pain.

"Shuler sent him to keep us from going after the money," Greenburg said. "He made up a story about me calling a lawyer and sent the zombie to do his dirty work."

"We way past lawyers now, DG," Ramona said.

"I know it, RC," Greenburg said.

"You're not calling your lawyer?" Martin said.

"We going to war," Ramona said. "Get my man's money, his cars, and his dog."

"Shuler doesn't have the money," Martin said.

"Yes he does," Greenburg said. "I pawned my wife's Mercedes for seventy-five thousand and paid Miller so his paranormal partner, a woman named Jenny, would breathe on my dead dog and bring him back to life, which she did, except it turned out badly, so I told Miller I wanted my money back. Miller told me Shuler took it from him. Shuler has the cash. He lied to you about the lawyer *and* the money."

"He lied to me?" Martin said.

"You lost your damn zombie mind?" Ramona said. "He a cop and a comedian."

"Of course he lied to you," Greenburg said. "Twice."

"Fool me once, shame on you," Martin said.

"Shame on Shuler," Greenburg said, and a plan took shape in his gin-soaked head.

"Fool me twice, shame on me," Martin said.

"Shame on the motherfucking zombie," Ramona said. "I say we kill his ass right now."

"I just cleaned the pool," Greenburg said with something else in mind.

Ramona glanced at him out of the sides of her eyes. "What you thinking, DG?"

"I'm thinking this is about my dog, RC," Greenburg said. "I'm thinking he knows what it is?"

"What you know about DG's dead dog, zombie?" Ramona said.

"It's a jigsaw puzzle with a million pieces," Martin said.

"You best put them together or your face going to be a damn jigsaw puzzle," Ramona said.

Martin told them about Mike Miller turning him into a zombie, about Shuler deputizing him after someone murdered Greenburg's dog, about stalking Mike Miller, about Miller's brother, Danny, telling him (thinking he was Mike) about the seventy-five grand and the dead goldfish swimming in the bowl, about branding Miller with a cattle iron, about Shuler telling Miller he wanted to be part of the Sunday night, Jenny the Gypsy Show, featuring the dead dog resurrection, about the meeting with Shuler in The Japanese Garden, where the detective sent him to get Greenburg out of the game or else lose the money and his badge, not to mention he'd have to stop stalking Mike Miller.

"That the most fucked up thing I heard since yesterday," Ramona said.

"What time's the show?" Greenburg said.

"Midnight," Martin said.

"We got to crash that party," Ramona said.

"We've got to find it first," Greenburg said.

"Hair dude took your dog. Wherever he at, your cars and your cash going to be there too," Ramona said.

"I don't know where Dan Miller is," Greenburg said.

"I do," Martin said, taking off his badge and tossing it to the dentist. "When I was branding his brother, I asked him how it felt. He said it was almost as bad as Dan moving into his garage.

I've been to the house. If you don't blow my dick off and you give me five minutes alone with Mike Miller, I'll take you there and get your money and shove your dog down Shuler's throat."

"How do we know we can trust you?" Greenburg said, looking at the tin toy badge.

"I'm a zombie," Martin said. "You can't trust me."

49

the business of life and
death is about to change

"LOOK AT MOBY DICK," Omar said to Harvey, "wearing his funeral suit to the circus."

"If I don't get my money back, he'll go straight in the casket," Harvey said. "We won't even have to straighten his tie."

"Don't call me Moby Dick," Mike said. He had chosen a black suit with a navy blue shirt and a black and blue paisley tie. It was the suit he'd planned to wear to the Wasserman and Waddell New Partner Party in his last lifetime one week ago.

Harvey and Omar were standing at Mike's front door. It was five minutes to midnight. The temperature was one ten. The Weather Channel had said Los Angeles was now *Hell on Earth*. They'd done a half-hour special segment by that name to demonstrate how dangerous the LA heat had become, to emphasize the fact folks and their pets should stay in their houses to be safe. *Not my house*, Mike thought as he stepped aside and let the dwarf and the giant into his foyer.

After leaving Jenny's crooked cottage, he'd spent the afternoon wrestling with a feeling he'd been unable to pin to the mat: *lust*—an irreconcilable thumping in his chest. He wanted to have sex with the voodoo queen; he couldn't deny it. But he also missed Marcy and his daughters and longed for them to come home. *Longing* was the feeling under the feeling he was feeling.

But the feeling under the feeling he was feeling wasn't stopping him from spending the night with Jenny Stone. No, the feeling he was feeling under the feeling he was feeling under the feeling he was feeling that was stopping him was *horror*.

He was horrified at the picture now and forever engrained on the inside of his eyeballs—the image of crossing swords with his brother. It made him physically ill—weak and nauseous, though not so sick he couldn't also feel hunger.

To think things through before the midnight show, he'd stopped at Cupid's on Lindley Avenue in Northridge, not far from Jenny's house, for a quick hot dog. Instead, he had eaten two with mustard, onions, and chili (Everything), two with mustard, onions, and relish (Triangle), five small bags of chips, and three large sodas. He had just said, "Large soda," so he didn't even know what he'd drunk, just that they were large.

As he'd pulled into his driveway, the Cupid's sugar and fat bliss wore off entirely, replaced by a single thought: *Linda*.

To Mike's knowledge, no other dead human being had ever been brought back to life with the same consequences as Linda. Jesus didn't walk around Palestine hoping to get his book-keeping job back after *he'd* been risen. Some people said they saw him, and so he was risen, and so Christianity started, and so...*big deal*, Mike thought. His mother was burning like the Cuyahoga River—baking sardine-jalapeno pies and threatening him with frying pans and busting his balls to get out of his house and get on with it.

Palestine had Jesus and Paul the Apostle. *So what?* Mike thought. He had Linda and Paul the Pervert.

He found Linda locked in Bethany's bedroom. She wouldn't open the door. "I'm getting pretty for my party, fairy boy," she'd said. "Don't talk to me till midnight."

Danny had left a note on the kitchen table: *at the track—back later*.

So Mike took a shower and watched TV and wondered if anyone else in America was having a week like he was having.

And then it was five minutes to midnight, and he shut and locked his front door and followed the dwarf and the giant to the living room.

Located directly behind the foyer, the large living room stretched across the back of the California ranch. A wide hallway bisected the house, separating the living room from the foyer so that you had to cross the hallway to enter the living room, even though the whole house was basically an open floor plan. Turn left and the hallway led to the bedrooms. Turn right and it led to the kitchen at the back of the house, which was connected to the dining room at the front of the house.

Once in the living room, the far right wall was a double doorway into the kitchen; the far left wall was a stone fireplace. Leather sofas and maple coffee tables and upholstered armchairs and a flat-screen TV and various lamps and bookshelves and framed family photographs were arranged to look like a Pottery Barn showroom.

During one of the renovations, Marcy and Mike had replaced the entire back wall of the living room with French doors that opened to the patio and the pool so that guests—Harvey and Omar, for instance—could stand in the foyer and look straight through the house to the backyard.

Chachi's body was laid out on the coffee table in the middle of the room. Shuler was seated on the sofa that faced the foyer, at the cushion closest to the kitchen. Harvey and Omar took the sofa facing the French doors, opposite Shuler, so that the coffee table with the dead dog was between them.

Danny stood in front of the fireplace. He wore a black T-shirt, black jeans, and black Nike cross trainers. His hair was behind his ears. The gash on his forehead had been cleaned. He'd put a bandage on it. Spots of blood had leaked through the bandage.

Mike followed the dwarf and the giant into the room and stood opposite Danny, in front of the armchairs closer to the kitchen, so that everyone formed a square around the poodle on the table.

"Thank you for coming tonight. What you're about to see will make you the hottest comedian in the business," Danny said, looking at Shuler first and then at Harvey, "and will make you one of the richest men in America."

"I don't want to say your life depends on it," Harvey said to Danny, "but your life depends on it."

Shuler smiled and wrote the exchange in his pocket pad.

"Then without further ado, please welcome Jenny Stone," Danny said, dimming the lights and gesturing at the double doors to the kitchen.

Jenny came through the darkened doorway into the light of the living room and stopped so everyone could see her. Her hair was even more auburn and her eyes were greener still, and she had changed into a full-length, sequined red gown slit high on her hip and cut low around her tits, which were spectacular in any light.

Harvey, Omar, and Shuler fell silent—an occurrence as rare, Mike imagined, as the alignment of Mercury, Saturn, and Venus over the Pyramids of Giza, a once every twenty-eight centuries or so event he'd learned about while helping Julia study her astronomy, before she and her mother and her sister fled to Paramus...oh, how he missed them. The point being whatever the dwarf and the giant and the comedian cop were expecting Jenny Stone to be, they weren't expecting her to be anything like this.

And neither was he. *Holy Mother of God*, Mike thought, his jaw dropped open. *She's not a voodoo queen. She's Jessica Rabbit.*

The gown glittered as she walked like a runway model around Shuler's couch, in front of the French doors to the fireplace, where she stood beside Danny.

"What you're about to see now," Danny said, "is nothing short of a miracle. The dog is dead; there can be no doubt of that. Mike..."

Mike picked up the iron fireplace poker he had earlier in the evening leaned against the armchair beside him, took a step forward, and poked Chachi with it—once, twice, three times. The poodle was deceased. Mike stepped back and leaned the poker back against the armchair. He hated dead bodies, even dead dog bodies, so this part of the show was torture for him. But Danny was directing, so he had to do it.

"I hate this fucking dog," Omar said.

"Be that as it may," Danny said to Omar and to the group, "it is time to forgive old grievances, wipe clean the slate, and blaze a new trail. The angles are infinite. The upside is without limit. The business of life and death is about to change in our financial favor."

He nodded at Jenny, and she moved to the coffee table. As she bent down to the dog, Mike looked at her tits spilling out of her dress and momentarily forgot what the hell was happening here in his living room. And then he remembered, and the chaos coalesced, and he found himself even more confused, astounded, and afraid than he'd been before he'd looked at Jenny's tits spilling out of her dress.

Jenny looked into the poodle's face, frozen in the ferocious snarl with which he'd drowned. She made a sad little sigh and gently blew on the snarl. Then her lips turned ever so slightly up at the corners, and she stood, looked at Shuler and Harvey and Omar, and walked out of the living room and into the darkness of the kitchen.

"Now what?" Shuler said.

"Now we wait in wonder," Danny said.

"I'm wondering where my money is," Harvey said.

"I'm wondering how deep I can shove that poker up Danny's ass," Omar said.

"I'm wondering how long will it take," Shuler said.

"I'm wondering why you don't see the comedic tension," Mike said to Shuler, remembering their meeting in the funeral home. "What kind of crap comedian are you?"

"White whale spouting," Harvey said to Omar.

"And me without my harpoon," Omar said.

"Don't call me a white whale," Mike said to Harvey.

"Be quiet, be patient, and ponder your fabulous futures," Danny said.

Harvey and Omar and Shuler all took an impatient breath and looked at the dog on the coffee table. One minute went by, and then another minute. A clock on the mantel clicked off one hundred twenty seconds of silence. *Tick, tick, tick, tick, tick...*

And then Harvey sang softly, "Oh Danny Boy, the pipes, the pipes are calling, From glen to glen, and down the mountain side..."

Omar reached out, grabbed the poker, and stood as if he'd had enough and was ready to hurt someone—or everyone.

"The summer's gone," Harvey sang, "and all the flowers are dying..."

Shuler stood, pulled his gun, and pointed it at Omar.

Harvey pulled his gun, pointed it at Shuler, and kept singing, "'Tis you, 'tis you must go and I must..."

Bark, bark. Bark, bark.

The room was instantly suspended in space and time—except for Chachi, who stood on the table, wagging his tail like the happiest poodle in the pound.

"Oh my God," Harvey said, astounded and horrified in the same breath. And then he stood on his couch cushion and said it again. "Oh my God..."

"Hilarious," Shuler said, but his voice was void of all hilarity and instead was filled with amazement and terror.

"I hate this fucking dog," Omar said with a touch of fear in his voice, and he took a step away from Chachi and held the poker out to defend himself.

Mike had seen it before, with his mother and with this very same dog, but breathing life into death had the same effect on him all over again: a sense of deep and debilitating dread, as if something was very wrong with universe.

"And now, gentlemen," Danny said, "I'm pleased to present my mother, the late Linda Miller. Mom..."

Danny gestured behind Harvey and Omar toward the hallway, and Linda appeared, looking, Mike thought, like Elsa Lanchester in Boris Karloff's *Bride of Frankenstein*, hair frozen in a frightening black beehive with white streaks highlighting the sides, dark lips, wild eyes, wearing a white, toga-like gown, a woman of the netherworld. Mike had seen her alive again since Friday, and he was stunned and terrified as if for the first time.

Harvey spun around on the couch to see her, Omar turned too, and Shuler looked up and away from the poodle. All of them gasped out loud.

Bark, bark. Bark, bark.

And then the French doors exploded into the living room, a smashing, crashing tidal wave of wood and glass and Greenburg and Ramona and Judd Martin.

50

you owe me one, fairy boy

THE DENTIST, his woman, and the zombie were armed to the teeth. Greenburg was packing Sawed-Off Sally, Ramona had her Civil War sword, and Martin held his snubnose in one hand and his nine-inch hunting knife in the other. Before the dust settled and all in the same blazing-blinding moment...

Greenburg pointed the shotgun at Danny, his nearest target, and said, "I want my dog, my cash, and my car."

"You're kidding," Danny said.

Harvey pointed his gun at Greenburg, and said, "If anyone kills the agent, it's me—immediately after I shoot the dentist."

Ramona bounded over the sofa and around the dog on the coffee table—*bark, bark*—put the point of her sword against Harvey's neck so that the dwarf's skin was dangerously indented, and said, "Do we look like we kidding, hair dude?"

Omar pointed his gun at Ramona's head and said, "Not *we, we're*. Do we look like *we're* kidding? *We* is the first-person plural pronoun used in the subjective as a contraction with *are*, the present-tense conjugation of the basic verb *to be*, used here in the plural because there are three of you. Jesus. Grammar anyone?"

Bark, bark. Bark, bark.

Judd Martin moved to Mike, pointed his snubnose at Mike's

face, and said, "I've waited all my life and death for this moment, Miller."

Shuler put his gun on the back of Martin's head and said, "This is how you kill a zombie, Judd."

"Fucking TV," Martin said without turning around or lowering his snubnose. "Now every asshole's a zombie killer. You going to shoot me in the head, Detective?"

"Ninety-three percent chance," Shuler said.

"Fair enough," Martin said.

Bark, bark. Bark, bark.

And then Saint Linda the Undead moved to the middle of the room, surveyed the scene—everyone stalemated with guns and knives and swords pointed every which way at everyone else—and said, "This is my soiree, and you're having all the fun."

Mike looked past Martin's gun at his recently dead mother. He wanted to put his thoughts together into some kind of cohesive whole, but he couldn't do it. For the first time in memory, he couldn't account for his life. His ledgers were no longer balanced. He had carried the weight of the week with him, and now his back was broken. He didn't know what to do. He didn't know what to think. He didn't know what to feel. He didn't know what to say. A dead dog was barking in his living room. The Bride of Frankenstein was addressing the band of lunatics. His brain was chaos. His heartstrings were pulled asunder. He refused to cry out loud, but his eyes filled with tears.

"Chin up, fairy boy," Linda said to him as he wiped his eyes. "Let's get this party started." She walked past Danny to the light switch and said, "Here's a parlor game called 'Run for your Life.'"

And then she flipped the switch, and the room went black.

Mike ducked. He didn't know why. He just did. Maybe it was his knees buckling more than any kind of conscious ducking motion. Anyway, it was a good thing he did because Martin's gun went off right where his face had just been.

Mike took off for the double doorway behind him and ran

into his kitchen. In the living room, he heard pandemonium—
guns going off, people shouting, Chachi barking.

The kitchen was dark as well, but his eyes were adjusting to
the LEDs on the coffee maker and microwave, and he had a
moment where he wondered where Jenny had gone—why
wasn't she in the kitchen? But the moment didn't last because
the zombie was in the kitchen as well—Mike could smell him,
even if he couldn't see him yet—and Martin's eyes, Mike
figured, were adjusting to the darkness too.

And then the hulking shape of the zombie appeared out of
the shadows, and the blue-green lights of the LEDs glinted off
his Bowie blade, and Mike knew there was only one way out.

He ran though the mudroom into the garage, where his
brother had been living and working without permission since
Wednesday. There was a box of who-the-hell-knows-what
blocking the door to the backyard and pool, so Mike ran to the
Tiki bar in the center of the garage. The light was on, and he
frantically tried to locate the remote garage door opener. He
couldn't find it.

"The more you run, the more I enjoy it," Martin said,
entering the garage and walking toward the Tiki bar. "Zombies
feed on fear. And I'm having a fucking feast with you."

Mike wanted to be brave. He told himself be brave, but he
couldn't find any courage inside him. He faced Martin and
backed away until he hit the garage door.

"You don't have to do this," Mike said.

"It's the *only* thing I have to do," Martin said. "After you're
dead, I'll retire south of the border, where zombies wear serapes
and sip sangria."

Inside the house, an engine was roaring. It sounded as if
Harvey had driven his Range Rover through the front door.
Mike's head hurt, his ears burned, his heart pounded.

And then Martin was right in front of him. The zombie held
the knife up and turned it this way and that. "I'm going to stick

it in your stomach, Miller, and twist it back and forth like a screw until you're dead."

Mike couldn't speak, couldn't find his voice. But the thought in his head was, *I'm going to die with my eyes open*. And then somehow his voice appeared, and he said it out loud. "I'm going to die with my eyes open, you zombie fuck."

"Suit yourself," Martin said, and he moved the knife back behind him (like it was a softball he was going pitch very fast) to shove in Mike's gut at full force and then froze. His eyes opened wide and then wider, and then he started to shake, and his jaw dropped open, and he was shaking out of control, and blood was coming out of his mouth and his nose and his eye sockets, and he was shaking violently, his head going up and down like a hideous zombie bobble doll, and there was blood covering his face and neck, and the engine was roaring and roaring, and then the motor-driven blade of Mike's Makita chainsaw tore though Martin's chest and shot blood all over everywhere, and still the zombie shook like the devil.

And then the chainsaw stopped, and the garage went quiet, and Martin fell dead to the floor, chainsaw jammed in his back, jutting out through his chest, blood pooling all around him.

Mike looked down at the zombie in silent shock and then looked up and saw his mother standing in front of him, Martin's blood speckled on her white toga-gown.

"You owe me one, fairy boy," she said, and she took the remote from the folds of her gown and hit the button. The garage door went up. She went into the zombie's pocket, pulled out his keys, ran to his beat-to-hell Ford pickup, got behind the wheel, and backed across the lawn to the street, where she stopped, pointed the remote at the garage, at shell-shocked Mike, and hit the button.

The door went down as she drove away.

Mike stepped over the zombie and walked back through the mudroom and through the kitchen and into the living room, now lit by a single table lamp on the fireplace end of the sofa facing what used to be the French doors.

He'd expected to see bodies strewn about but instead saw Danny sitting on the sofa beside the table lamp. The room was trashed. He walked to the sofa across from Danny and sat down. The brothers looked at each other and said nothing for one hundred twenty seconds.

"Where's Martin?" Danny said.

"Mom cut him in half with my chainsaw," Mike said. "Where's the dog?"

"Shuler grabbed him." Danny said. "Where's Mom?"

"Drove away in Martin's truck," Mike said. "Where's Greenburg?"

"Harvey and Omar took him hostage," Danny said. "Where's Jenny?"

"Left the building," Mike said. "Where's Ramona?"

"Went after Greenburg," Danny said.

The sound of sirens began to emerge in the distance.

"One of my neighbors called the police," Mike said.

"We're going to need an angle," Danny said.

monday

51

all hell will happen

"DEAD IN THE GARAGE," Mike said, "chainsaw sticking out of his chest."

"Bullet holes in the living room," Danny said.

"Furniture overturned, lamps on the floor, picture frames broken; it looked like a gang war," Mike said. "Except there was no gang. Just me and Dan."

"Then the cops came," Mike said.

"And I didn't have an angle," Danny said.

"We were screwed," Mike said.

"And then Shuler showed up," Danny said.

They were in Jenny's crooked kitchen, which was pitched so severely that Danny wondered how cans and canisters and bags and boxes didn't fall off the shelves. Mike and Jenny were seated at the table. Danny stood by the sink. They'd been here ten minutes. It was Monday morning, seven thirty, one hundred five degrees, cloudless sky, burning sun. Projected high for the day: one fifteen.

Jenny's hair was Marilyn Monroe blonde. Her eyes were icy blue. Danny and Mike had woken her up when they rang the wounded-bird doorbell, so she was wearing white, micro-mini silk pajamas that hardly covered her ass or anything else. She was barefoot. Her fingernails and toenails were painted icy blue to match her eyes.

"I thought Shuler grabbed the dog and left the house," Jenny said.

Danny poured a glass of tap water and caught a glimpse of himself in the window above the kitchen sink. His eyes were bloodshot from lack of sleep. He hadn't showered or shaved. The bleeding had stopped, but his forehead bandage was stained a deep, dark red. His nose was less swollen, and his eyes less black and blue, but he still looked like he'd been boxing without gloves. He wore black board shorts, a red V-neck T-shirt, and flip-flops. His hair was back behind his ears, and his sunglasses were up on top of his head. He thought he looked like Brad Pitt in *Fight Club* and wanted to savor that moment, but he was still shaken from the night before, so he let the thought go.

"He did. He took Chachi and followed my mother," Danny said, turning to face Jenny and Mike, leaning against the counter and sipping the water.

"That's how we know she's in the small yellow house," Mike said.

"Then he put the poodle in his office and drove back to Mike's," Danny said.

"There were two cops," Mike said. "One old, one young. The old one grilled us while the young one looked around the house."

"I stalled for time," Danny said, "told him it happened so fast, the lights went out, there was chaos and confusion, giving him nothing really, then the young one said, 'I'm going to check the garage,' and I thought, 'Game over,' and then Shuler came in —*from the garage*—and said he'd gotten a call about a zombie home invasion, that the garage was clean. Then the old one rolled his eyes and looked at the young one and said, 'Doughnuts and coffee; you're buying,' and they left."

"What about the zombie?" Jenny said.

"He's still in there," Mike said. "And unless you breathe on him, he's not going anywhere."

"Where did *you* go?" Danny said to Jenny.

"Home," Jenny said. "Harvey and Omar and Shuler weird me out. They're not everyday people."

Says the woman who breathes life into death, Danny thought.

"The point is Linda's out there in the world," Mike said. "And she's supposed to be dead, and if they find her alive, if Mrs. Alemi rents her house to someone else and my mother is in there, then all hell will happen. The point is what do we do now?"

"You have more experience with living dead things than we do," Danny said.

"Lookee here," Maggie said, coming into the kitchen before Jenny could speak. She wore a cow-print muumuu as eye-catching as it was frightening. She wore bunny rabbit slippers. Her hair stood out and up at as many angles as the house itself.

"Mother, go to your room," Jenny said.

"Not so fast," Maggie said, crossing to Danny at the counter. "Pretty Boy blew up my beauty sleep, and I want to know why."

She was in Danny's face before he could move away. Her breath smelled hideous, *just like...just like...wait, yes, the horse, that's it*, Danny thought, *the racehorse with the jockey and the carrot.*

He'd once tried to sign a washed-out jockey who fancied himself a Vegas magician, though the only thing he could make disappear was a carrot—and he needed a horse to help him do that. The jockey took Danny to the stables one day to film his audition—a thrill for Danny until the jockey stuck a carrot in his own mouth and fed a horse—like Neidermeyer in *Animal House*. But though it was funny in the film, watching someone French kiss a horse in the flesh was sexually grotesque.

And then the jockey demanded Danny do it. To get the guy's money, Danny had forced a smile, put the carrot in his mouth, and turned to the horse. The smell of its breath as it closed in on Danny's end of the carrot was an olfactory nightmare Danny couldn't expunge from his memory to this day. He'd buried it deep, it was true, but now Maggie had brought it back.

"Get out of my face, Maggie," Danny said. She'd tried to cut his head off with a serrated grass whip and poison him with lemonade and now she was trying to suffocate him with her horse breath, and he'd had enough.

"Make me, Pretty Boy," Maggie said in a threatening tone.

"Mother," Jenny said.

Danny put his arms up to push her out of his way—not knock her down, just move her aside so he could sit at the table —and she opened the drawer beside him and pulled out a carving knife and held it against Danny's throat.

"Mother," Jenny said again. "Put the knife down and go to your room."

Maggie cackled. "Not this time, Blondie. This is the end of road for Pretty Boy."

Danny could feel the sharp blade of the knife pressing across the full width of his neck. He tried not to move, not to breathe. He looked into Maggie's eyes and saw soulless black pools of death. Then he looked past Maggie and saw Jenny stand. She was as close to naked as a person could be and still have clothes on. *Dear God, if you let me live through this and have sex with her, no matter what color her hair is, I'll teach Sunday school for the rest of my days*, Danny thought.

"Stand up, Mike," Jenny said, her eyes on Maggie.

"What?" Mike said. He was frozen at the table, one eye on Maggie and his brother and the knife, the other on Jenny's tits, which were spilling out of her thin silk top.

"Stand up," Jenny said.

Mike did as he was told.

He had not slept all night, but he'd showered and shaved at six a.m. and changed out of his Wasserman and Waddell New Partner Party suit and into blue and red plaid golf shorts, a blue Ralph Lauren polo, and blue, slip-on sneakers.

"Stand still," Jenny said, and she unclasped his belt and slid it off his shorts. Mike's mouth fell open. "Last chance, Mother," she said while removing Mike's belt.

"For Pretty Boy, maybe," Maggie said. "Not for me."

And then the muscles tensed in Maggie's arm as the message arrived from her brain to slice Danny's throat wide open. But before she could move the blade, Jenny crossed the kitchen, slid Mike's belt over Maggie's head and around her neck, looped the notched end through the buckle, and pulled it tight, strangling her mother while moving her away from Danny.

"What the hell are you doing?" Danny said to Jenny, and he thought he might have been shouting.

Maggie dropped the carving knife, which clattered to the kitchen floor, and put her hands on the belt around her neck, struggling to get it off, battling to breathe. But Jenny pulled tight and tighter, and Maggie's eyes bulged out.

"Murdering my mother," Jenny said.

Maggie made terrible sounds and thrashed around the room, crashing into the kitchen table and whacking it into a chair, which then smashed hard into Mike's balls. Mike screamed, grabbed his nuts, fell back against the wall, and slid down to his butt.

"What?" Danny said to Jenny. Of all the things that had happened in the past week, Jenny Murdering Her Mother With Mike's Belt was in the top tier of terrifying—and yet was still oddly arousing.

"I'm murdering my mother," Jenny said.

"You can't do that," Danny said.

"I've done it dozens of times," Jenny said. "But then I feel guilty, and I can't leave her dead. She's my mother. Know what I mean?"

"I have no idea what you mean," Danny said. "You've killed her dozens of times? Why have you killed your mother dozens of times?" Then he looked over at Mike and said, "Are you hearing this?"

Mike couldn't make a sound, couldn't even nod. He was

watching Jenny strangle Maggie with a powerfully painful look on his face that was half about the violent death scene playing out in the kitchen and half about his balls, which he held with both hands, and also half about his dick, which was somehow getting hard.

Maggie thrashed back and forth and then fell to her knees, her face turning blue, still fighting like the devil.

"She gets to a point where I can't control her, and then I kill her and then bring her back and then kill her and then bring her back and then kill her and then bring her back and then kill her and then bring her back," Jenny said. "I probably shouldn't be breathing life into things in the first place."

You think?!! Danny said to himself.

Maggie was running out of steam. She leaned sideways and went from her knees to her ass. Her gurgling-gagging-wheezing noises became softer. Her hands fell away from the belt and jiggled at her sides. Jenny kept tightening and tightening.

"Your mother will get to this point too," Jenny said.

"Where we can't control her?" Danny said.

"It happens," Jenny said. "Sometimes faster than other times."

And then Maggie's legs began their final-throes-of-death kick. Once, twice, three times.

"So what do we do then?" Danny said.

Maggie made a final gasp and died, blue in the face, eyes popping out of their sockets, tongue hanging out of her mouth, cow-print muumuu up around her thighs.

Jenny held the belt a bit longer, just to make sure Maggie was dead, and then let her go. Maggie's face fell to the kitchen floor.

"It's up to you," Jenny said, moving to Mike and handing him his belt. "She's your mother."

52

and i shall move the
world

ON THE DAY Harvey Mineral turned sixteen, his mother came into possession of a tractor-trailer filled top to bottom with the newest Nike basketball shoes. Georganne had called in a few favors—one of which included breaking a man's legs—to acquire the contents of the cross-country truck, and she'd done it for one reason only: to teach her son a life lesson on his special, coming-of-age birthday.

Using the identification of a man who'd died in the 1960s, Georganne had years before purchased a small warehouse for cash in Panorama City in which she ran a back channel, international wholesale outlet.

"Harvey," she'd said as they stood before the mountain of shoeboxes, "these shoes are worth tens of thousands of dollars to wherever it is they came from and to wherever it was they were going, but I know a man in Bulgaria who's built a black market highway into Nigeria, and the Bulgarian has bid one hundred thousand dollars for the shoes—and he'll cover shipping. And he'll pay cash."

Harvey remembered wanting a pair of the shoes, which Georganne had given him, of course—Happy Birthday—but more importantly, he remembered the lesson his mother had taught him that day: *if a product can make X-amount-of-money in the free market, then it can make many times X-amount-of-money in the black market.*

That's why he'd had Omar grab Donald Greenburg instead of Danny Miller when Miller's mother killed the lights and the guns went off after the Penthouse Pet brought the poodle back to life—Harvey needed Danny Boy.

He no longer needed the dentist.

While driving to the white whale's house in the middle of the night, Harvey had decided that someone would suffer for the annoyance and inconvenience and wasted time, effort, and energy he'd had to exert to recover his money. He equally despised both the sniveling dentist and Danny Boy and thought: *one of those two morons will pay the interest on the default with spilled blood and broken bone.*

And then the Penthouse Pet breathed on Chachi and Harvey knew he needed Miller. Not to sell the product—Danny Boy couldn't sell a cold drink in the Sahara. No, he needed Miller and his Mickey Mouse talent agency as a front for the business *he* had in mind.

Danny Boy and the dentist and the Penthouse Pet had demonstrated that someone would pay seventy-five thousand in cash money to bring their beloved dead dog back to life. That was now a fact of the free market and was the business plan Miller had offered him before the show began. "Fifty-fifty," Danny Boy had said. "All you have to do is let me live, and I'll do all the work and give you half of everything."

But if Hollywood celebrities and professionals would pay that much to bring back lost loved animals, what would North Korea pay to bring back Kim Jong-il? One billion? Five billion? What about other despotic nations and dictatorships? What was the black market price to bring back their late *los presidentes*? And drug cartels and mafia families and corporate kingpins? The possibilities were endless. The upside was infinite.

So Harvey grabbed Greenburg instead.

They had taken the dentist to the pawnshop, gagged him, and tied him by the wrists to a ceiling beam in Harvey's private office so that the dentist was held upright in the middle of the room, arms above his head—close to the point of dislocation, of course.

And now it was nine forty-five, Monday morning, and Harvey was giddy with anticipation. He'd hardly slept, barely touched his toast and tea. How could he? His entire universe had changed with a single breath. The dog had been dead. There was no doubt about it. He was sitting not three feet from its carcass when it stood up and started barking. *He'd seen it with his own eyes!* He was going to make a global fortune *and* torture the dentist to death.

Be still my heart, he said to himself as Omar pulled Greenburg's Lexus into the Pacoima Pawn and Loan parking lot.

The Mexican clerk, an older man named Umberto, was behind the counter, and Harvey told him he didn't want to be interrupted unless it was an emergency. Umberto, who walked with a limp and knew everything there was to know about guns and ammo, said, "Si, senor," and did not ask a single question, a lesson he'd learned the hard way—and the reason he walked with a limp.

Harvey shut the double doors to his soundproofed office, turned to Greenburg, who was pale and thin and pathetic, and said, "Good morning, Donald. Let's begin with pain you're familiar with."

Omar walked to the dentist and showed him slip-joint pliers, large and angry looking. "I'm going to remove your teeth with these," the giant said. "It's going to hurt."

"I'll take your gag out," Harvey said, pulling a step stool to where the dentist was suspended from the rafters, "so you can scream as loud as possible. No one will hear you except me and Omar, and we'll enjoy it." And then, standing on the stool, face to face with Greenburg, Harvey removed the gag from the dentist's mouth.

"Fuck you, you insignificant dwarf," Greenburg said, shooting out the words with hatred and fear. "You think you're a tough-guy big-shot, but you're a small-time small-fry. You're nothing. You hear me, Harvey? You're a lightweight. You're..."

And then Omar moved in with the pliers, grabbed Greenburg's right central incisor, and began to yank it out. Greenburg screamed horrible, terrible, bloody murder.

"You're misinformed, Donald," Harvey said. "At the stroke of midnight, I became a Maker of Kings."

Just the sound of it in his own mind—*Maker of Kings*—made Harvey delirious. The vast sums of money awaiting him were secondary; he had mountains of cash in his safe. What he didn't have locked away, what he'd never had, what he'd wanted more than anything was to be *consequential*. He wanted to be larger than life, global in a way that transcended space and time. He wanted history to remember him as *momentous*.

Before bedtime, as a young boy, Georganne would turn out the lights and recite the same quote for Harvey to dream upon. The man she was quoting was Archimedes. *Give me a lever long enough and a fulcrum on which to place it, and I shall move the world.*

Jenny Stone was his lever. Danny Boy's talent agency was his fulcrum. He would alter the course of history for the rest of time. He would move the world.

Omar stopped pulling on Greenburg's front tooth, turned to Harvey, and said, "I could pull it faster, but getting there is half the fun."

Greenburg's screams became panting moans of agony. Blood and sweat and tears and spittle spewed from his mouth as he continued to harangue Harvey. "You're meager and meaningless...

Omar inserted the pliers, pulled on the tooth. Greenburg resumed screaming like a man on fire.

"I'll be acclaimed and lionized," Harvey said.

Omar removed the pliers.

Greenburg was crazed with crackling pain, sweating

profusely, crying and spitting and sputtering. "Trivial and trifling..."

"Powerful and influential," Harvey said.

"Pointless and forgettable," Greenburg said.

"Esteemed and exceptional," Harvey said.

"Irrelevant and—" Greenburg said, interrupted by Omar, who put the pliers back into the dentist's mouth and gripped the tooth.

Greenburg shouted and shrieked and shook like a live wire, practically pulling his arms out of their shoulder sockets. Omar removed the pliers, and Greenburg, crying now, puking, running out of steam, spit blood and invectives at the dwarf.

"Nothing...you're nothing...nothing..." And then he was gagging and crying and choking on his own vomit and lost his voice and his power.

"The good news, for me," Harvey said, "is that we're going to pull *all* your teeth."

Omar grabbed the incisor again and Greenburg screamed and screamed, and then the giant ripped the tooth from the bone and held it up for Harvey and the dentist to see.

"No doubt they've been saying this since dentistry day one," Omar said, "but that was like pulling teeth."

Greenburg sagged, lifeless, without even the strength to cry, held up only by the ropes attached to the ceiling beam.

Harvey loved this image of Greenburg and wanted to remember it forever. *This is,* he thought, *the official beginning of my rule as Maker of Kings.* He climbed down off the stool, moved it closer to and beside the dentist, then climbed onto the top step, lifted Greenburg's face, and shaped it into a smile to display the bloody gap-tooth opening smack dab in the middle of the dentist's mouth, took out his cell phone, and clicked off a selfie of the two of them together.

Before he could click off another one, the double doors to Harvey's office burst open, and Umberto stood in the opening with a look of abject terror in his eyes. Both the dwarf and the giant turned to him.

"You must like limping," Omar said.

"This, Umberto, does not look like an emergency," Harvey said.

And then Ramona leaned around the Mexican, her Civil War sword in his back, and said, "Look like one to me, damn dwarf motherfucker."

53

this is the defining moment of my life

THE SOUND of Ramona's voice, strong and fearless, gave Greenburg goose bumps—and the beginnings of a hard-on. He managed a small smile, opened his eyes, and looked up to see Ramona charging toward him and Harvey and Omar, using Umberto as a shield.

Harvey reached for his gun but realized it was on his desk. "Omar..." he said.

He didn't have to say it because Omar had already dropped the pliers and pulled his silenced Glock from his shoulder holster. He aimed and fired three shots, all of which hit Umberto in the chest, killing him instantly.

As the third bullet thudded into the Mexican, Ramona reached the men and pushed-shoved-threw the dead body into and onto Omar, who tripped and fell backwards over an end table, dropped his gun, which bounced across the room and under a sofa, and tumbled to the ground with Umberto on top of him.

At the same moment, like some kind of Bruce Lee ninja, Ramona kicked the step stool out from under Harvey, who crashed hard to the floor.

Then she looked at Greenburg and said, "You got to get your shit together right now, DG."

What a woman! Greenburg thought. *My woman!* He felt his heart pounding again. He felt anger and violence rising up inside him, negating the pain in his mouth and his head and his arms. "Cut me down, RC," he said.

She whipped her razor-sharp sword through the air and sliced the ropes that had held him in place. He fell forward, legs like rubber, and she caught him.

In that same five seconds, Omar tossed Umberto across the room, stood up, pulled his badass Bowie knife, held it like a gang banger looking to excise someone's heart, and said to Ramona, "Let's dance, bitch."

And Harvey shook off the hard fall, lifted himself to his hands and knees, and began to crawl toward his desk, toward his gun.

"You fuck up the dwarf," Ramona said, "I dance with the giant."

And she pointed Greenburg at Harvey, who was crawling away from them, and pushed him hard enough in that direction so that the dentist flew through the air and landed on top of the dwarf.

Greenburg wasn't accustomed to fucking anybody up— except himself, and he did that with cocaine and gin. He hadn't fought anybody in, well, ever. He'd avoided all physical confrontation since his ninety-eight-pound-weakling childhood in Albany.

And so he was slow on the draw, and Harvey was immediately on top of him, pounding him with his little dwarf fists. Harvey had hit the dentist before, and Greenburg hadn't liked it then either. He put his hands up to defend himself and rolled his head to the side to avoid getting whacked in the mouth, which was bleeding badly and hurt like all hell again, and saw Ramona and Omar squaring off. It was a vision, Greenburg knew, he would never forget for the rest of his life—even if that were only ten minutes more.

Omar circled Ramona, hunting blade glistening in the overhead lights, sadistic smile on his face. "I'm going to cut you into bite-size pieces, cook you over a fire, and feed you to my dogs. I'll roast you rare, because they like the blood."

Ramona did not flinch. She held her sword in front of her, kept her balance the way she'd been taught when she'd trained for the Olympics, and said, "You want to dance with me, Scarface, you going to have to do more than talk. You going to have to bust a move."

And then the dwarf put his little hands around Greenburg's neck and started to choke him to death. Harvey's hands weren't large enough to actually wrap themselves all around the dentist's throat, but he had a good enough grip that Greenburg was struggling to breathe and would eventually suffocate. Greenburg knew he had to fight back, but his muscles—such as they were—felt like bags of wet sand. And his mouth was killing him. And he couldn't take his eyes off Ramona.

Who in their right mind would stand their ground against Omar Creech? The man was a sadistic freak of nature—unnaturally huge, inhumanly strong, unreasonably agile, reared by Harvey to inflict pain and suffering on men twice Ramona's size, raised to enjoy it.

Omar swung his knife at her throat, and she ducked and danced away. He came at her again, swinging the blade, missing her by inches. She moved so she was facing Greenburg, so that the giant's back was to the dentist and the dwarf.

Somewhere in the center of Greenburg's gin-soaked heart, the dentist thought he might love Ramona. Or maybe it was all some hazy dream. Maybe it was just time to sleep forever. He was so very tired. He felt himself giving up and fading away, and he didn't mind because his last vision was of the woman who'd saved his soul when he'd thought it was lost forever. He felt himself turning blue and blacking out. "Good-bye, Ramona," he said, calling out to her.

"Fuck that, DG," Ramona said, shouting. "Your big-breasted woman is telling you to get your pasty white butt in gear and kick some damn dwarf motherfucking ass."

And then everything happened at once...

Harvey leaned in and bit down hard on Greenburg's nose, choking and chomping the dentist with every ounce of hatred in his dwarf body.

The combination of pain and sexual exhortation roused the dentist. He found a reserve of strength he never knew he had and smacked Harvey in the side of the head, knocking the dwarf off his neck and nose so that Harvey's legs were on his chest.

Omar slashed forward with the Bowie, a brutal sweep that would have removed Ramona's head from her shoulders had he found flesh.

But Ramona slipped under Omar's arm, slid behind him, spun like Jackie Chan, and whipped her Civil War sword across the back of Omar's knees, slicing deep through pants and skin and blood and bone and severing both of the giant's ACLs in one shot.

Omar dropped his hunting knife and fell to his knees. The pain was so severe, so excruciating, so unlike anything he had ever experienced, that he was frozen in a dual state of paralysis and shock. He couldn't move his legs, of course, but he also couldn't move his arms, couldn't make a sound, couldn't blink, couldn't breathe.

Greenburg saw the giant on his knees and was energized. He grabbed Harvey's ankles and lifted the dwarf upside down. Harvey's keys and wallet and a roll of bills fell out of his pockets, and Greenburg carried him across the office, the dwarf screaming. "Put me down. Put me down, or I'll have Omar—"

As they passed the giant, Greenburg and Harvey saw Omar helpless and silent and gasping, and then saw Ramona whip her sword across Omar's stomach, opening a gash so deep and wide that his gut flopped open, and his organs spilled out onto the floor in a rush of blood. Omar's eyes opened wide, and he fell forward like a redwood.

"Oooommmaaarrrr..." Harvey said. "Oooommmaaarrr..."

Greenburg looked at Omar dead on the ground, blood pooling all around him, looked at Ramona holding her bloody sword, and knew what he had to do, knew all at once he had reached the mountaintop at long, long last. The thought in his head slipped out as spoken words. "This is the defining moment of my life."

"Do it, DG," Ramona said.

"Done, RC," Greenburg said, and he carried the dwarf to the massive fish tank and tossed Harvey up and over the side and into the water with a splash.

"Can't swim," Harvey said, slapping the water, trying to get to the side of the tank. "Can't swim..."

Ramona moved beside Greenburg, and together they watched the dwarf gasp and pant and sink. The piranha swam to the far corners of the tank for safety, and then they circled the dwarf, and then they attacked him.

"He doesn't feed them very often," Greenburg said.

"He feeding them now," Ramona said.

The carnage was spectacular.

The dentist and his woman watched the piranha shred the dwarf and then used Harvey's keys to open the safe. They took all the cash, which filled two large duffel bags, found the remote to Poor Dead Carol's car in Omar's pants pocket, and drove to Encino, Ramona in the white-walled Cadillac, Greenburg in the Mercedes, top down, despite the heat, blood leaking from the hole in his mouth where his tooth used to be.

54

on the road to famous

SHULER HAD SEEN the mortuary photograph of Linda in her casket—meaning he knew what she looked like and also knew she was dead. So to see her walk into Mike Miller's living room dressed like the Bride of Frankenstein was simultaneously shocking, impossible, outrageous, and hilarious. In fact, Gary had thought at the time he might piss his pants. And if *he* had almost pissed his pants, then a comedy club crowd would almost piss *their* pants—some of them might *actually* piss their pants. And that meant he'd reached the climax of his routine.

And then the lights went out, gunshots were fired, furniture was overturned, and the detective went to his knees. He'd kept his eyes on the white toga and had followed Linda to the garage, where he'd watched her cut through Judd Martin's chest with the chainsaw, grab the zombie's keys, and run for the Ford pickup.

At that point, he had sprinted back through the house, grabbed Chachi on a dead run, jumped in the Impala, and followed the Ford to the small yellow house in Canoga Park. Linda had driven like a bat out of hell, and Shuler had wondered why there was never a cop around when you needed one. A fragmented section of his brain knew *he* was a cop, and he'd even said it out loud to the poodle—*I'm a cop*—but they were empty words because the comedian part of him was on cruise control.

He'd left the small yellow house, driven to Ross Baker Towing in Northridge, arrived at one in the morning, and tied the poodle to a tall metal shelving unit directly across from his desk in the open area in the middle of the converted tire warehouse that was Shuler's LAPD Office of the Bizarre, UnGodly, and Otherworldly. He'd put out a bowl of water and a plate of treats and said to the poodle, "If that was the climax, then what's left is the *denouement*." And then he'd said, "*Chao*, Chachi," and left the dog alone, laughing out loud while writing the joke in his pocket pad as he went out the door.

He'd driven to Mike Miller's house, seen the LAPD squad car in the driveway, slipped around the back and into the garage, where Judd Martin was on the floor with the chainsaw sticking through his back and out his chest, took a picture of the dead zombie with his cell phone—a visual reference for when he was writing the scene later—and then went through the mud room, into the kitchen, and into the living room.

He'd told the uniformed cops that he'd received a 9-1-1 about a zombie home invasion and that he'd checked the garage— since it was a known fact the undead congregated near automotive parts—and was pleased to say it was a zombie-free zone. The older officer had rolled his eyes and looked at the younger one and said, 'Doughnuts and coffee; you're buying,' and they'd exited stage right—or maybe stage left. (Gary hadn't yet decided how their departure would best play in his act.)

Then he'd left the Miller brothers alone, not even bothering to tell them to keep quiet—*What in the world would they say?*—and he'd driven home to catch a few hours of sleep because he'd sensed today, Monday, was the first day of his reign as the King Cop of Comedy, and he wanted to be sharp for his coronation later tonight.

He'd returned to his office at eight thirty and spent the next three hours finishing and finalizing his act, going from his desk to his stage and back and forth for three straight hours. In all that time, the poodle had stood facing him, staring at him, growling low, almost inaudibly low—*three hours* of inaudibly low growling and laser beam staring—and it had not once touched the water or the treats. Not a sniff.

At eleven forty-five, Shuler hung up the phone, looked at Chachi, and said, "You don't know it, Chachi, but you are about to become the greatest comedic prop in the history of stand up. Pat Paulsen would have loved you."

The poodle growled.

"Cheer up," he said to the dog, taking an Oreo four-pack from his top desk drawer. "It's a good day to be alive, especially considering what you were yesterday, which was dead. Plus, I just booked the eight thirty slot at Ha Ha—the Monday night Next Comic Standing show—and confirmed three top late-night agents: one for Kimmel, one for Conan, one for Fallon. By nine o'clock, we'll be on the road to famous."

The poodle growled.

Shuler popped an Oreo in his mouth, crossed to a small fridge, removed and drank directly from a carton of milk, then carried the milk to his personal comedy club stage, stepped into the spotlight of his mind's eye, ate the second Oreo, followed it with a swig of milk, and imagined himself in front of the Ha Ha audience.

They loved him. Oh, how they loved him. They had never heard a story like his before. Dwarves, giants, zombies, killer poodles, cokehead dentists, voodoo queens, and con man agents! They pounded the tables, roared with laughter, begged him to stop and then begged for more. He felt goose bumps on his arms. *I'm a supernova,* he thought.

And then he ate the third Oreo and thought it was possible he'd lost his mind. He'd seen an undead woman murder a real estate developer with a chainsaw and considered it a comedic event, a joke to add to his routine, the *super* part of his *supernova.*

For a comic, that could be crossing the line between sanity and insanity. For a detective, it could be something more than that.

He decided he'd gone crazy and gotten funnier at the same time and was pleased with that outcome, and then his ex-wife, Maryanne McCarthy, appeared in a vision before him, wearing a stylish tennis outfit, the same one she'd been wearing when she left him. "You used to be weirder than the crimes you solved, Gary Shuler Vista. Now you're a danger to the community you're sworn to protect."

"I'm also sworn to make them laugh," he said aloud, as though she were really standing there. "Sometimes it's hard to know which way's which."

"When you come to a fork in the road," she said, "take it."

"Yes, yes, Yogi Berra," Shuler said, laughing. "One of the great catchers and comedians of all time. The relational subtext is why the joke works—I'm one of the great cops and comedians of all time."

And then the vision of his ex-wife faded, and he thought there might be some wisdom in their exchange, but he let it go, ate the final Oreo, and walked to the poodle.

"So I'll take you on stage with me, and you'll sit there through my act, building comedic tension, dramatic tension, story tension, all kinds of tension," he said, drinking from the carton. "You're the first character they meet, and then you die a horrible death, and then you come back to life, and then you die a horrible death, and then, well, I don't have to tell you; you were there. So at the climax, the part where I see you raised from the dead with my own eyes, after they've been hearing about you and looking at you all night...forget it, homerun, thank you, Yogi, for the baseball tie-in."

The poodle growled.

Gary kneeled before the dog and patted its head. He wasn't sure he believed it was possible, but he thought he saw the poodle narrow its eyes.

55

the world's not ready
for you

"WHO MURDERS their mother in the middle of the day?" Danny said.

"We do," Mike said. His eyes were heavy with exhaustion because he'd been unable to sleep after Shuler left the house because he couldn't erase the vision of his chainsaw ripping through Judd Martin's chest a few feet in front of his face. If anyone had asked him a week ago what would be the most unlikely thing he could imagine happening one week later, Judd Martin being cut in half by his Makita-wielding, undead mother in his own garage would be near the top of his list. It might have been the very top of the list except for what was happening right now: he and his brother about to storm the house where they'd been raised to kill the mother who'd raised them.

They were in the Pathfinder across the street and two doors down from the small yellow house in Canoga Park. Judd Martin's beat-to-hell Ford pickup was in the driveway. Linda had looked out the window and seen the Pathfinder and drawn all the shades. There was no way to know what she was doing in there. *Waiting for us,* Mike thought, *that's what she's doing in there.*

It was noon on Monday. Twelve hours since Linda had escaped. Four and a half hours since Jenny had murdered

Maggie again, this time with Mike's belt in the crooked North-ridge kitchen. It was one hundred thirteen degrees. A breeze like a blast furnace was blowing across the San Fernando Valley—an unseasonal Santa Ana from hell.

"I don't think there's an angle for something like this," Danny said.

"I have Mom's front door key and back door key," Mike said. "I forgot to give them to Mrs. Alemi."

"She sucks," Danny said.

"Mom or Mrs. Alemi?" Mike said.

"Both," Danny said.

"Mom doesn't suck," Mike said. "Mom's dead."

"Not dead enough," Danny said.

Mike handed one of the keys to his brother. "I take the front, you take the back, we meet in the middle."

They got out of the car and walked to the small yellow house. Mike still wore the blue and red plaid golf shorts, the blue Ralph Lauren polo, and the blue, slip-on sneakers he'd worn at Jenny's. Danny still wore his black board shorts, red V-neck T-shirt, and flip-flops. His hair was back behind his ears as always, but his sunglasses were in place to protect his eyes from the burning glare.

"Why do I get the back?" Danny said.

"She has to defend both doors," Mike said. "It's fifty-fifty she's waiting for you either way."

"Did you bring weapons?" Danny said as they reached the driveway.

"No. Did you?" Mike said.

"No," Danny said.

And then Danny went down the driveway, past the Ford, and around the house, and Mike went to the front door.

As he slid the key in the lock, Mike remembered Saint Linda giving him his own key to the house when he was ten years old, after his flimflam father had left for New Orleans and she'd registered for bookkeeping classes. "This means you're the man of the house, Michael," she'd said. "I don't like asking you to grow up at the age of ten, but I don't have a choice. This is your life right now."

If I've learned anything in the last thirty years, Mom, Mike said in his head, *I've learned it's always your life right now.*

"Mom," Mike said, stepping into the house and shutting the door behind him. There was no entry hall per se. He was in the living room. "It's Mike. Your son."

"I know who you are," Linda said. "And I know what you're doing here."

Mike had forgotten the house was empty, that all of Linda's possessions had been trucked to Mrs. Alemi's self-storage facility in Chatsworth. He had vague memories of the house being empty like this the day they'd moved in, but it had not seemed nearly so small as it did today. Back then, he'd thought the vacant rooms were expansive, and he and Danny had run through them like wild animals. Now, he thought they were shoeboxes buried underground—because the lights were off and the shades were drawn—and that he might suffocate from lack of oxygen.

"What's that?" Mike said. He figured the lights were off because Mrs. Alemi had cancelled the power until a new tenant could be found. That's why the house was so hot, because the air conditioning was turned off too. If it was one thirteen outside, then it was a hundred thirty-five in the house. *The House From Hell,* Mike thought.

There were no clothes in the closets, so Linda was still dressed as the Bride of Frankenstein. Fortunately, she did not have a weapon either.

"You're taking me back," Linda said.

"The world's not ready for you," Mike said. "You're not supposed to be alive. You're going to scare people."

"I'm going to do more than scare them," Linda said, taking a few steps into the room.

"That's what I'm afraid of," Mike said, moving away.

"You're afraid of everything. You always were," Linda said. "A little fat fairy boy afraid of his own shadow."

It was true. He'd been afraid of everything his whole life.

"Do I scare you?" Linda said. She was cornering him, like she'd done in his kitchen when she'd whipped the cast iron pan past his head.

"Yes," Mike said, backpedaling.

"Good," Linda said. "The one who's scared is the one who dies. It's me or you, Michael, so that means it's you."

She was on him in the next instant, so fast he didn't have time to blink. Her hands were around his neck. She was incredibly strong, much stronger than him. He gripped her arms and tried to pull her off his throat. His eyes darted behind her, to the doorway.

"Danny's not coming," Linda said, reading his eyes. "He never comes through when you need him. He's probably driving to New Orleans as I choke you to death. He's a flimflam man and a coward like his father."

Mike thought about fighting back but couldn't get himself to do it. Somewhere under the beehive hair and the toga splattered with zombie blood and the dead, black-pit eyes was his mother —who'd had a heart attack and died in Northridge Hospital. She was in there. She had to be. And he couldn't hit her. He was the good son. He couldn't do it.

He fell to his knees, and she squeezed his throat. He looked up at her face. She wasn't an undead demon; she was Saint Linda rubbing Vicks VapoRub on his chest and neck when he was seven and had a bad bronchial infection. *If that's my last memory*, he said to himself, *so be it*.

And then Danny came screaming into the room and jumped onto Linda's back, which knocked her hands off Mike's neck. Mike fell backwards on his ass and watched in wonder as Linda, his recently deceased, seventy-two-year-old mother, carried his thirty-seven-year-old brother like a bronco throwing a rider or, because it was Danny, a thoroughbred trying to toss her jockey.

Danny had his arms wrapped around Linda's neck and was holding on for dear life. Linda couldn't shake him loose. She bucked back and forth and then ran from the living room into the kitchen.

Mike heard a crash that sounded like someone bashing into the cabinets followed by Danny screaming in pain. Then he heard another crash like someone smashing into the refrigerator followed by Danny screaming in even more pain, and then he heard struggling, fighting, gasping.

"Move, legs," Mike said out loud, and his legs moved, and he stood and went to the kitchen.

Danny was on his back. Linda was sitting on him, straddling his chest, choking him to death. Danny's feet were pointed at the open fridge, and Mike realized that Linda had whacked him hard into the cabinets, loosening Danny's grip, and then cracked his back into the refrigerator, knocking him off her and onto the floor, where he'd bounced hard and twisted so that his feet were in front of the open fridge door.

Linda's hands were around Danny's throat. He was kicking and fighting and trying to get her off, but she was inhumanly strong, and he was loosing steam.

Mike walked to the fridge and stood behind his mother and knew he had to kill her, but he couldn't do it. He ran every other possibility up and down the flagpole in his mind. The scenario he liked best was the one where he took her captive and kept her chained in his garage until she died peacefully of natural causes. Or tied her to his four-post bed and poisoned her slowly over time so she could die peacefully in her sleep.

It was the dying peacefully part that appealed to him. He didn't want his mother to suffer any more than she already had. *For God's sake,* Mike thought, *the woman was resting in peace before she was jarred back to life. And now look at her...she's the Bride of Frankenstein killing my brother.*

And then he looked at Danny dying on the kitchen floor of the small yellow house in Canoga Park, where their imaginations had run wild inside and out, where they had been cowboys and astronauts and firemen and magicians and monsters and soldiers and ballplayers and neighborhood hooligans, and he remembered shooting baskets and riding bikes and climbing trees and jumping fences, growing up side by side celebrating birthdays and holidays and other fun family festivities, and doing homework and going to Little League games and movies and parties and backyard barbecues and remembering all of that made Danny's fades and failures and fuck ups fall away until all that was left was his little brother turning blue and dying on their childhood kitchen floor.

"Leave him alone," Mike said, and he stepped in and grabbed Linda's beehive and ripped her off Danny with the strength of a young parent lifting an automobile off a trapped child. In the same motion, Mike whipped her backwards so that she spun around and fell face forward into the open refrigerator. And then he slammed the fridge door closed on her neck.

And then he slammed it again. And then again.

Linda howled like a wild, wounded animal.

Mike slammed the fridge door one more time and held it there, pushing it as hard as he could against Linda's neck. She made terrible noises, horrible, frightening sounds—roars and groans and screams from some parallel, paranormal plain.

"Release me from *The Oath*," Mike said to her.

"Burn in hell, fairy boy," Linda said, growling like the devil.

Danny sat up, rubbing his neck, and said, "She's a beast."

And Mike said, "*Lord of the Flies*." They had read it together when they were about the same age as the boys in the book, and they had both been empowered by it.

And Danny stood and moved to Mike and helped him push on the refrigerator door.

The brothers looked at each other as they leaned hard and heavy on the door and, as if by telepathy, began to chant. *Kill the beast! Cut his throat! Spill his blood! Kill the beast! Cut his throat! Spill his blood! Kill the beast! Cut his throat! Spill his blood! Kill the beast! Cut his throat! Spill his blood! Kill the beast! Cut his throat! Spill his blood! Kill the beast! Cut his throat! Spill his blood!*

"Release me from *The Oath*," Mike said. "Release me from *The Oath*. Release me. Release me. Release me..."

"I release you from *The Oath*," Linda said.

And then there was the sound of her neck breaking, and she stopped moving and was silent, and she died again—one week after she had died the first time.

56

surreal on top of surreal

"I'VE BEEN THINKING about the porn party plan," Paul the Pervert said, turning his truck onto Chatsworth. "What we need to get us going is a movie of me doing my sex thing, so they know I'm one of them."

"A movie of you doing your sex thing is the last thing we need," Danny said, staring out the open passenger window. The truck had no air conditioning, but Paul had hung a thermometer from the rear view mirror so anyone riding with him (as if *anyone* would ride with him) could know exactly how freaking hot they were. And right now the mercury was pegged at one fifteen. Danny looked at his watch. Coincidentally, that was the time too: one fifteen. "Maybe the last thing anybody needs."

"I'm not talking full-length feature film, just a highlight reel of me getting it on with your mother. Porn party people see that shit," the clown said, "your phone will light up like Christmas."

"My mother's dead in the back of your truck," Danny said. "She has a broken neck."

"Yeah, I don't usually get naked with broken neck dead chicks," Paul said. "But I'd make an exception for your mother."

"If you talk again, I'll grab the wheel and crash us headfirst into a brick building," Danny said, turning to the clown. "Pull over here."

Paul stopped the truck in front of a bus stop across the street from the George Edwards Mortuary. Danny got out, walked around to the driver's side, and spoke to the clown through the open window. "You know what to do?"

"Drive to Vegas and marry your mother," Paul said.

"You're a sick person," Danny said.

"I'm a deep-fried clown," Paul said.

"Mike said George leaves for lunch every day between one and two," Danny said. "The staff does the same. There's just one woman in the office. You should be clear."

"Not a living soul in sight," the clown said. "Hey, maybe I'll tell funeral jokes at the porn parties. Porn people love that shit."

The internal visualization of Paul the Pervert having sex with his broken neck dead mother, who the clown had married in Vegas between telling funeral jokes at porn parties, made Danny's eyes roll back in his head—the secondary image of Paul as his stepfather made his knees buckle. "In and out, understand? No fucking around."

Paul pulled the truck away from the bus stop, turned into the mortuary, and stopped under the carport, next to the hearse.

Surreal on top of surreal, Danny thought, watching Paul get out of the truck. The pervert was adorned in his full rat-shit regalia, and Danny wondered why men with big butterfly nets had not yet hauled the clown to a padded room somewhere psychiatric.

Paul walked to the hearse, looked inside, and then strolled around it—as if a horror house clown perusing a mortuary hearse in the middle of broad burning daylight was not an unusual sight, as if there were horror house clowns across the San Fernando Valley peering into various funeral home vehicles at this very moment.

Paul clicked the handle on the rear hearse door and pulled it open. Then he walked to his truck, opened its back hatch, removed Danny's dead mother, carried her to the hearse, and slid her inside.

She tried to choke me to death, Danny thought as his mother went into the hearse. *If it wasn't for Mike, I'd be dead, and then Jenny would have to bring me back to life, and then I'd get like Maggie and Mom, and they'd have to kill me again and slide me into the back of a fucking hearse.*

And that thought sparked two other thoughts that took him by surprise.

The first thought was that he and Mike had saved each other's lives, something they hadn't done since they were nine and six years old and fighting outer space aliens in the small yellow house backyard. In those days, there was never any question that he would save Mike and Mike would save him. They were brothers and were bound by blood to save each other when bad shit hit the fan. And after all the years of animosity and disrespect and estrangement, it turned out that was still true.

The second thought was that as Linda squeezed his throat and cut off his air and he prepared himself to suffocate and die, right before Mike jumped in and saved his life, the person who appeared in his head was Jenny Stone.

Danny didn't know if he was in love with her or not. How was he supposed to know something like that? He'd never loved any woman. Love was a foreign land for him. He didn't speak the language. He didn't recognize the architecture. His money was meaningless. But his heart was feeling something new, something special, and he wanted to follow that feeling forward, even if the woman he was feeling it for was a supernatural freak of the universe.

As Paul shut the hearse back door, the one woman left in the mortuary office stepped out of the building and into the carport, crossed to the clown, and confronted him between the back of the hearse and the back of the truck.

Danny watched from the bus stop across Chatsworth. He couldn't see the woman's face, but her body language was one part incredulous, one part terrified, one part nauseated, and one part adamant that this disgusting human being dressed as a sewer clown leave the premises immediately if not sooner.

And then the woman slapped Paul across the face and marched back inside the mortuary.

The clown climbed into his truck, rolled out of the George Edwards Mortuary, picked Danny up at the bus stop, and drove off into the Valley.

"What happened with the woman?" Danny said after a while.

"She asked me who I was and what I was doing," Paul said. "I told her I was a pervert clown in the market for a new car and saw the hearse and pulled in to check it out. I said I could see myself in a hearse. Dead or alive, I told her, it was a good ride for me."

"What did she say?"

"She said it was private property, and she was going to call the police."

"Why'd she slap you?"

"I told her the hearse was automatic and that I like a stick and that I had one in my pants, and she could give it a go after she called the cops."

"What are the odds an average Joe on the line could be electrocuted into a coma one day and wake up two days later like you?"

"I said if she shifted my stick, I'd let her play with my ball bearings."

"About the hearse being a good ride for you, the dead or alive part?" Danny said, "I vote dead."

"You're not the only one," Paul said.

57

massive internal combustible confusion

MIKE HAD last seen Mrs. Alemi on Thursday, at her Valley Storage facility, when she'd opened the doublewide unit in which she'd graciously stored the contents of the small yellow house after Linda had died—the first time.

Actually, that was the second to last time Mike had seen her. The very last time he'd seen Mrs. Alemi was an hour or so after that, when she'd found him in his boxers, duct taped to a dining room chair, in pounding pain from where Judd Martin had whacked him upside the head with a snubnose.

Mrs. Alemi did not mention the incident—a kindness, Mike promised himself, he would repay some fine day when the temperature wasn't one hundred sixteen degrees.

As she searched for the key on her ring of keys (because somewhere in the chaos of the week he'd lost the key she'd given him), Mike marveled at how easily he stood here in the heat of the concrete storage yard after breaking his mother's neck with the refrigerator door an hour and a half ago. His knees were not knocking. His pulse was not racing. *If I'd murdered my mother two weeks ago*, he said to himself, *I would have turned myself into the police by now. Or jumped in front of a bus from the guilt. Now*

I'm looking for a new burial outfit—preferably something with a high neck.

He smiled at his macabre joke, and then smiled at his smiling, and then he stopped smiling because there was nothing funny about murdering his mother, and then he practically cried. It was sad and terrible and absurd. His head and his heart were spinning in opposite directions, and the result was massive internal combustible confusion: some things were tragically settled while others were wildly up in the air.

On the settled side of the ledger, Danny had called and said, *"The clown has delivered the package."* Which meant that Paul the Pervert had returned their mother to the mortuary as per the plan. And Mike had said, *"The accountant will collect the clothes."* Which meant Mike would go to Mrs. Alemi's and choose a new funeral suit for Linda. Danny had said they sounded like secret agents, and Mike had said they sounded like World War II spies —both of which they'd been as boys—and they had both laughed out loud. It was the first time they'd shared a laugh in several decades.

What a relief not to have to deal with Linda anymore. His mother reborn as an Undead Tasmanian Devil Woman aside, the whole point of grief, Mike had reasoned, was to bring the sad and sorry episode of a loved one's death to an end. *To end that life for those still living so those still living can go on still living,* Mike thought as Mrs. Alemi found the key and slid it into the padlock.

Grief had a role to play, he'd learned. It served a specific human purpose—to propel people forward through death and loss. It was part of the panoply of emotions human beings were born with and required so they could face the rest of their lives as those close to them passed on. Short sheet a man's grief, Mike had found out the hard way, and all his other emotional gears get thrown out of whack. Now that Linda was dead again, he could commence gluing his unglued world back together and start the healing process, which he'd done on his way to Mrs.

Alemi's, stopping at Earl's on Devonshire to consume a dozen donuts and two large iced coffees.

Also settled—and related to his mother's funeral home return—was the fact that Linda had released Mike from *The Oath* just before he and Danny crushed her neck in the fridge. He'd expected to feel elation at being freed from a lifetime of big brothering his brother, a hopeless task of frustration, annoyance, anger, and regret, and he did feel that way—elation, jubilation, liberation. And yet he had a tinge of an iota of a wisp of sadness too. He'd seen Danny more in the last seven days than he'd seen him in the last seven years, and the result of all the violence and blood and chaos they'd shared was a laugh and a story they would remember and tell each other for the rest of their lives. *If we ever see each other again, that is*, Mike thought as Mrs. Alemi jiggled the key in the stubborn lock.

Also accounted for was Judd Martin, who was dead—*still dead*—on the floor of Mike's garage, the Makita sticking out of his chest. The fear of being kidnapped and tortured and finally killed by the phantasmagorically insane real estate zombie had been a heavy cross to carry around the Valley for a week. Yes, there was some cleaning up to do and a body to dispose of, but Mike felt lighter on his feet, even after the donuts.

Wildly up in the air was the ménage a trois with Jenny and his brother. Creating a visual image on the inside of his eyeballs of that upcoming event gave him goose bumps and simultaneous nausea—concurrent titillation and turmoil. He couldn't deny his sexual attraction to Jenny (though watching her strangle her own mother with his belt had muted the hard-on that had occurred when she'd removed his belt), but the idea of being naked with her and Danny at the same time was unsettling to say the least. *Up in the air is too casual a phrase for the ménage*, Mike thought as Mrs. Alemi pulled the key from the open lock.

And what about Marcy? What about his girls? His family? His marriage? What about the pissant Paramus pediatrician?

Mike wanted to break that fucker's neck in a fridge door. *I could do it*, Mike said to himself. *I've done it before.* Wildly up in the air? Hell yes.

And he was unemployed. So much of his self-esteem, self-image, and self-confidence had come from the fact that he'd been senior accountant at a well-respected company and had lived his life accordingly—in a sweet ranch house with a backyard built-in pool. That was his identity, who he was when he woke up, how he faced the world day after day. He'd had no time during the week to face the sobering fact that he was now a missing person.

Tethered to his unemployment was his empty bank account: he was broke, and the bills were rolling in. He'd been blown off the financial tightrope upon which he'd precariously balanced his life, and he was spinning into bankruptcy. Maybe money wasn't everything, but Mike the Accountant knew it was the linchpin to saving face, the light that would lead him back to his family, the glue that would allow him to rebuild his life. And he had none. No income. No cash on hand. No savings. He realized he was as sad as he'd ever been. *I'm going to lose everything material, everything personal, and everything important*, Mike thought as Mrs. Alemi turned to him.

She saw the sadness on Mike's face and touched his arm. Then she smiled sympathetically and walked away.

Mike watched her go, took a heavy breath, and lifted the extra-tall, doublewide, roll-up garage door. It was pitch black in the unit. He stepped inside, clicked on the lights, lowered the door, and turned to see a decrepit 1980s Airstream, rusted and beaten and giving up the ghost.

"What the hell?" Mike said.

He wondered why Mrs. Alemi hadn't told him she'd stored someone's mobile home in the unit where she had graciously moved the contents of the small yellow house. The stuff of Linda's life was scattered helter-skelter around the Airstream— the sofas, the chairs, the tables and lamps and dressers and bookshelves, the boxes of books and clothes and kitchen accouterment. Mrs. Alemi's seven sons had handled Linda's possessions with care. It seemed unlikely to Mike they would return with a dying Airstream and toss those very same things around without regard for, well, anything.

He decided to ignore the Airstream, find new funeral attire for his mother, and head home to clean up the mess in his garage, but when he moved deeper into the unit, he had a sensation that made his skin crawl. He'd never seen this trailer before, yet it was uncomfortably familiar.

I know this Airstream, he said to himself. *And it knows me.*

He felt himself drawn to the trailer, and with a growing sense of dread, he climbed the Airstream steps, opened the door, went inside, and felt his heart stop beating.

There was a poster of him on the wall—his Wasserman and Waddell photograph blown up to poster size—with knives and screwdrivers and ice picks stuck into it and horrible swear words written all over it. "What the hell?" Mike said in a whisper.

He moved into the filthy, disease infested Airstream, trash and waste everywhere all around him, and then he realized what it was that seemed so terribly, horribly familiar: the smell. It was the smell of the undead, the smell of a zombie, the smell of Judd Martin.

But not just the smell, it was also the sound of the place, the creaking of the floor and the walls and the cabinet doors. Mike knew these sounds. This was where Martin had taken him. This is where Gary Shuler had spoken to him that first time. It was here. Inside this Airstream.

Of course, of course, Mike thought. *I didn't lose Mrs. Alemi's key; Martin stole it from me; it was labeled and numbered with the name and address of the storage facility and the doublewide unit. Then he moved the mobile home here later in the week, after he'd tortured me in it.*

He looked at the couch upon which he'd been naked and hogtied and gagged. He remembered the humiliation and the pain, remembered the sense of helplessness and hopelessness, the feeling of weakness and vulnerability, and he lost his mind.

Then he saw the branding iron on the kitchen counter.

He exploded with rage, ripping through the Airstream like a madman, tearing the place to shreds, pulling cabinets off the walls, smashing windows, throwing shit everywhere, kicking the hell out of the mountain of garbage and refuse that covered the floor, screaming and shrieking and swearing at the top of his lungs.

When he was spent and breathless, he dropped to his knees, tears streaming down his face, and saw that one of the bags was not filled with garbage but was instead filled with...money.

58

when they make the movie of my life

SO MUCH OF Gary Shuler's life had been serendipitous that, by comparison, his ascension to the King Cop of Comedy throne seemed architecturally engineered.

From his first-grade knighting as Gary Shuler Vista through his marriage to Maryanne McCarthy through his unlikely landing at Ross Baker Towing, everything that had happened to him had been coincidental, accidental, incidental, inadvertent, unforeseen, unexpected, unintended, and hilariously random.

And then he'd been gifted Chachi, dead as a hammer, and the disparate plot threads of both his cop and comedic lives had become entangled, and he'd recognized the entanglement as greatness and grabbed hold of it and guided it along the path that had led him to this moment: two minutes from taking the stage at Ha Ha Café Comedy Club on Lankershim Boulevard in North Hollywood.

He'd seen the house, Gary had, and it was everything he'd hoped for. The place was packed. He'd called his cop friends (meaning detectives and uniforms that owed him favors for taking their cases that had come from Mars) and collected his debts. He'd counted two dozen officers. None of them were friends, but all of them wanted to pay off their IOUs, and so here they were, eating wings and nachos and drinking beers and waiting for Shuler to take the stage so they could head home and owe him nothing.

Gary had also seen the booking agents for Kimmel, Conan, and Fallon. They each owed the detective for services rendered as well—a speeding ticket that mysteriously disappeared off the docket, a DUI that went AWOL, a lewd public behavior citation that had vanished in the chaotic fog of the Los Angeles legal system.

Joining them was the Monday night comedy club crowd, here for a few drinks, a few laughs, and few hours away from their everyday lives, which—even by Monday night—had become humdrum enough for a hike to Ha Ha.

The host of Next Comic Standing was a plain vanilla Minnesotan stage named Bland Blaine Blumenthal, who had told Gary he was getting out of the stand-up grind and refocusing his efforts on becoming a game show host. Because his eyes were set unusually close to his nose and because his face was narrow and came to a mousy point and because his coloring was dark for a Minnesotan but about right for a rat, Bland Blaine looked like a rodent, which, Gary thought, did not bode well for his game show host future.

While Bland Blaine warmed the room, Gary looked down at Chachi, who was leashed and standing backstage beside him, glaring upwards, growling imperceptibly low, occasionally flashing a snarl. "When they make the movie of my life, no one's going to believe the last twenty-four hours," he said.

After he'd cashed his chips with the cops and the talk show agents, he got a call from an incredulous sergeant who told him there had been some kind of ludicrous, freak-show, triple homicide at Pacoima Pawn and Loan and since Shuler was the Pawn Palace specialist, he should drive his ass over there and figure out what the fuck had happened.

Has to be Greenburg and Ramona and one of the Millers, Gary had thought, *or maybe both Millers and Greenburg, or anyway, some set of three from that quartet*. But when he'd arrived, he discovered it was Harvey and Omar and Umberto the limping counterman, an unexpected triptych. Forgetting Umberto, who was in the wrong place at the wrong time—as he'd been every morning when he came to work—Gary had focused on Harvey, who'd been fished from the tank with very little flesh on his very little bones, and on Omar, whose guts had been emptied from the flap in his abdomen.

Playing a hunch it was the Civil War sword that had opened Omar's stomach, Shuler drove from the pawnshop to Escalon Drive in Encino and rang Greenburg's front doorbell. The dentist had appeared. Ramona stood beside him.

Gary told them he'd been to Pacoima Pawn and Loan and had seen the bones and the bodies and the ropes hanging from the rafters.

"Not my ropes," Greenburg had said. "Not my problem. And as for being eaten by carnivorous, blood-thirsty fish, well, couldn't have happened to a nicer dwarf."

Gary had held up an evidence bag that contained Omar's slip joint pliers and said, "Found these on the scene. Whose blood do you suppose is on them?"

"I stick them in your neck, it be your blood," Ramona had said.

"Doesn't matter," Greenburg had said. "You don't have compelling evidence to make me submit to a DNA test."

And then Gary had put his hand in his pocket and removed a wad of tissues. He'd opened the tissues and presented the dentist with a right central incisor. "I bet this slides right into the hole in your mouth where your tooth used to be. I bet the judge will think so too. Compelling enough?"

They'd invited him into the air conditioning, and Gary had made a deal for the *denouement*: no evidence and no suspects in exchange for the rest of the story, every detail from the moment Chachi came back to life the first time all the way through everything that happened after the Bride of Frankenstein turned out the lights. They told him the tale, and he'd given them the tooth and the pliers and driven to Miller's house.

After checking the garage and discovering Judd Martin and the chainsaw were gone and the blood had been bleached away, he'd found his agent, his agent's brother, and a disgusting clown lying on lounge chairs and drinking cans of Coors Light by the pool. He'd pulled up a chair and came right to the point: he needed to know what had happened to Linda after she'd escaped to the small yellow house in Canoga Park. And if someone could fill him in on the missing zombie, that would be good too.

"What's in it for us?" Danny had said.

"All of us," Mike had said, "except him. The clown is expendable."

"He means expandable," Paul said. "Since I got electrocuted, my wiener keeps growing. That's why I got a future in porn."

Gary had thought the clown was an excellent, late-story addition and took notes in his pocket pad while he horse-traded the end of his act.

In exchange for the return of Mike's drivers license, which Mike had lost wrestling Paul the Pervert in the mortuary, and Gary deleting the photo he took of Judd Martin, murdered by Makita on Mike's garage floor, they told him everything that had happened, from breaking their mother's neck in the fridge door to returning her body to the mortuary hearse.

Paul had been tasked with disposing of the zombie, and he'd said that was an erotic part of the story unsuitable for human beings of any age.

That was good enough for Gary, who had long thought great comedic stories should have three loose ends. For his epic act, loose end number three was the missing seventy-five grand Greenburg had pawned from Harvey to pay Danny to pay Jenny to bring Chachi back to life, which she'd done on the dentist's flagstone deck.

Gary had the sense that Mike was holding back on the

money, that the accountant knew something about the Airstream he wasn't sharing, but the detective was willing to let it go to settle his loose end logic.

Loose end number two was Judd Martin, the real estate zombie who had met a bloody chainsaw death at the hands of a woman who a few days earlier had died of a coronary and a few days later had died of a broken neck. What had happened to the zombie's body? Zombies with chainsaws sticking out of their chests don't disappear into thin air, not even in the San Fernando Valley. That loose end came with the benefit of introducing Paul the Pervert to the story—*and it will bring down the house*, Gary thought.

Loose end number one, of course, was Jenny Stone. Of all the loose ends of all the stories in all the world, this one was a stunner. The woman could raise the dead with a single breath! Gary imagined the audience laughing out loud while wondering: *What the hell happened to her? Where is she? How do I find her? How do I get her to breathe life into my dead dog?*

"Nothing worse than a story tied up in a perfect bow," Gary said to the poodle.

And then Bland Blaine said, "Ladies and gentlemen, give it up for *Detective* Gary Shuler."

59

i'm the kurosawa of comedy

"IT STARTS WITH A LITTLE WHITE DOG," Gary said to the crowd. "This dog, in fact. I'm not kidding, crime fans. This is the real-life actual poodle that you'll soon see is the star of the story. His name is Chachi, and he's had a rough road this week, so let's give him a big Ha Ha hello and make him feel like a Westminster winner."

He lived for this, Gary did—live and in color on the small, raised comedy club stage, the brick wall behind him, the spotlight in his eyes, the crowd calling out in unison as commanded, "Hello, Chachi." He had them in the palm of his hand after only one minute. *If only Pat Paulsen could see me now,* he thought.

A cute little poodle on a leash looped around the mic stand beside him. He wondered why had it taken him so long to incorporate something like this into his act? The women in the club— the men too but especially the women—*loved* the poodle. Gary had their full and willing attention. They were ready to laugh, ready to like him and his dog, ready to go for a ride in his comedy car. All he had to do was start the engine.

"I get a call one day from a woman who sees this very poodle get tossed out the back window of a Lexus doing seventy-five on

357

the freeway—the sedan, not the poodle, although Chachi might have been doing seventy-five when he went out the window, only your physicist knows for sure. I know, right. It's a laugh a minute out there. Anyway, you're probably thinking: poodle puddle. Nope, not this time. This time the poodle was punted to the side of the road, dead as a dime, and the dog's ID tags directed me to a broken-hearted dentist addicted to cocaine and gin..."

They're laughing, Gary said to himself. *They like the story. They like me.*

He knew, of course, the cops in the house did *not* like him—he didn't like them either. But they were laughing too, although not like the Monday night comedy club crowd, which was laughing because the story was wild and insane and funny as hell and because Gary's stand-up style was killer good tonight and because Chachi was on the stage beside him, growling just loud enough for Gary to hear.

No, the cops were nodding and laughing and rolling their eyes as if to say, *Boy Howdy, that's a Shuler shitstorm of a case. We dodged a bullet on this one because even if it isn't true, some kind of crazy crap definitely went down if for no other reason than that it's a Shuler shitstorm of a case.*

Talk show booking agents never laughed. They sat on their hands, stone-faced, just to make the point that you were not now and not ever going to get three minutes with Jimmy Kimmel or Jimmy Fallon or even Jimmy Crack Corn. They were gatekeepers, and their job was to keep the gate closed. To the talk show booking agents, finding the Next Comic Standing was no laughing matter. *Don't ever laugh at a comedian in a comedy club* was their unspoken credo. And especially don't ever laugh at *Detective* Gary Shuler's crime capers.

But the talk show booking agents *were* laughing, and Gary knew that their laughter was the comedic divining rod of his future—he was going to be a star.

"...And then the dwarf tells the giant to feed the fish. 'Feed the fish,' he says. He means me. I'm the fish food. And the giant says, 'Deep breath, Detective.' And he shoves my face into the tank, which, as I said, was the size of a lagoon, complete with vegetation and currents and tides and a shoal of two hundred red-bellied piranha with razor blades for teeth."

He told them about Harvey and Omar and Greenburg and Carol and Ramona. He told them about Judd Martin and Jenny Stone and Mike and Dan Miller and Paul the Pervert. He did not name names. Instead, he immortalized his characters with epithets: the dwarf and the giant; the dentist, his Dr. Seuss wife, and his sword-swinging girlfriend; the zombie and the accountant; the agent and the gypsy. The clown.

The exception was Chachi, whose name he named as needed.

The Pawn Palace in Pacoima was a comedy club crowd favorite. Gary's description of the Airstream earned laughter and applause. The small yellow house, his office at the LAPD tow yard, the accountant's house...even the locations were funny.

His future was happening in the present, and time became fluid. He could feel his brain splitting and splintering. He was out of body, out of mind, seated at the bar, drinking Knob Creek while watching himself deliver *the funniest story ever told* to a Ha Ha audience—including three talk show booking agents—that loved him like Lassie.

His comedic life passed before his eyes.

He was nine years old and eating Oreos with his parents in their Shula Vista kitchen, telling a funny story about some unlucky kid in chemistry class who accidentally spilled acid on his pants and had to take them off in front of everyone because the pants were disintegrating while he wore them.

He was thirteen years old and playing the role of Albert Peterson in the middle school production of *Bye Bye Birdie*. They were rehearsing in the cafeteria and his line was: "Here's our luggage." At the moment of delivery, the principal and vice principal walked into the room. Without missing a beat, he gestured at the administrators and deadpanned his line.

He was on his honeymoon with Maryanne, at his police academy graduation, home for the holidays after his divorce, in the courtroom under oath, in the heat of intercourse with a woman he hardly knew.

As he bounced through time and mind and memory and comedy, he never lost his grip on the story—the chronology of events, the character arcs, his Machiavellian manipulation of the plot points, the rhythms and cadence of the dialogue, and especially the jokes.

When he arrived at the dentist poolside part of the story—*dentist poolside part one*, he called it (not to be confused with the *accountant poolside story*, in which the dwarf and the giant shoot the Hello Kitty lounger and drown the Bose)—when he arrived at the dentist's pool, where Jenny brings Chachi back to life, the poodle barked on cue, as if he and the dog had trained for weeks to speak at that particular moment.

Because everyone was busy laughing and applauding, Gary imagined it was likely no one in the club had noticed the underlying bite in Chachi's bark, likely no one had seen the accompanying flash of teeth. *He* had noticed it, but he'd let it go because the laughs were rolling in like the San Diego surf. Greenburg, Ramona, Danny, and Mike had each told him about the poodle in the garbage bag, the dogsicle jokes, and the colorful arrival of the Seuss Search and Save posse, and so Gary told the crowd, unfolding the story from each of those characters' point of view. *I'm the Kurosawa of Comedy*, he thought as the club went wild.

And then on with the story he went: back to the Airstream and the branding of the accountant, out to Santa Anita and the confiscating of the seventy-five grand, over to the funeral home and the stealing of Linda (who Gary had labeled the Bride of Frankenstein), until finally he came to *dentist poolside part two*, in which Chachi kills the Dr. Seuss wife and the dentist drowns the dog.

There was, Gary had always thought, a bloodthirsty element to a comedy club crowd. If you weren't funny, they wanted you to bleed to death on stage. And if you were funny, they wanted someone else to bleed to death—literally or figuratively—in your jokes. One way or another, the audience wanted blood.

And so it was with great flourish that Gary told them about Chachi chewing through the leash that was tied to the pipe at the end of the pool. The audience roared with laughter as the poodle attacked the Dr. Seuss wife and the dentist. They howled as the dog opened her carotid artery and it spurted like a cherub fountain.

And then Gary got to the part where the dentist grabbed the poodle and plunged into the pool and drowned it in the bloody water, and Chachi, who had been barking and growling and snarling throughout *dentist poolside part two*, jumped like he'd been fired from a cannon, and chomped the detective in the nutsack.

A million flashbulbs went off in Gary's head, and the world went blinding white. He had never in his life experienced pain like this. Every nerve ending in his body screamed in agony. He could barely breathe. His eyes opened wider than they had ever been, and all he could see was the dog sinking its teeth into his crotch.

Time, which moments ago had been fluid, became a block of ice, and Gary was frozen in the moment for what felt like hours but was really five seconds. And then time exploded forward like a burning train on a one-way track to Ha Ha hell.

"Get him off me, get him off," the detective said, yelling for someone in the house to help him. While he was screaming, one lone lobe somehow bypassed the blazing neurons in his brain, and he realized the laughing crowd thought the dog biting him in the balls was part of the act, as if he had written "poodle punctures comedian's nutsack" in his script.

Gary fell to the floor, and the lone lobe succumbed to the

mind-imploding pain, and he knew he had to act or lose his balls forever.

He dropped the microphone, reached around his back, grabbed his gun, and—*bang, bang, bang*—shot the dog three times in the head at point-blank range.

Brain matter and blood spewed across the stage and up onto Gary and out into the first row of comedy clubbers—as if Shamu had sprayed them with saltwater at a sold-out SeaWorld show— and Chachi died for the third time in a week, his jaw locked solid on Gary's groin.

The attack took thirty seconds from start to finish, and in that time, Gary's world went completely out of focus while it concurrently zoomed in sharp and clear. He had been out of body and out of mind, watching himself in the past, present, and future from the Ha Ha bar, where he'd planned to later drink a double KC rocks and wait for a cop comedian groupie to fall onto the stool beside him. But when Chachi chewed his nutsack, all that went hazy and fuzzy and blurry, and he was sucked back into his body and into his mind, and everything in the world was the dog at his dick.

Now that it was over, gun in hand, he reached down, unhinged Chachi's jaw, and removed it from his crotch. The pain was inconceivable, though it was now the echo of pain more than the pain of the moment. As he breathed in and out and the comedy club again became part of his reality, he looked up and saw half a dozen LAPD detectives storming the stage, guns drawn and pointed at him.

And then they were on him, snatching his gun, forcefully flipping him onto his stomach, cuffing his wrists behind his back. Sergeant Adam Austin, a hardcore career cop who probably detested Gary more than anyone in the LAPD, did the honors.

"Detective Gary Shuler, finally at long goddamn last, you're under arrest. You have the right to remain silent, though we all know that's not fucking possible. And you can bet your goddamn ass that anything you say can and will be used against you in a court of law or in a back alley in the middle of the fucking night, if you catch my drift."

As they dragged him out of the club, Gary thought if he hadn't been in so much pain and if his hands hadn't been cuffed, he would have written it all down in his pocket pad.

60

if a week can change a man's nature

IT WAS five minutes to nine on Monday, and Mike was screwing up the courage to FaceTime Marcy at her parents' house in Paramus, where it was five minutes to midnight. Earlier in the day, she'd agreed by text to accept his call at exactly twelve a.m. her time. He paced in front of the built-in desk in the home-office nook in the corner of their master bedroom. The iMac was ready. The iMike was not. Because though today he'd done plenty to win back his wife and daughters, he didn't know if it would be enough.

He had cried like a child after finding seventy-five grand in a ratty paper bag on the floor of the vile Airstream—itself inexplicably stashed in Mrs. Alemi's doublewide unit. And while he wept, on his knees in prayer position, he'd looked up at the poster of his Wasserman and Waddell headshot, stuck with knives and covered with curses and condemnations and expletives and execrations, and he'd had an epiphany titled: *if a week can change a man's nature.*

With the money locked in the trunk of his car, hidden at the bottom of his golf bag, which hadn't seen a course in many moons, he drove straight to Santa Monica. On the way, he'd

364

called an insane and insanely expensive attorney named Bob Bogatz and put him on retainer.

Stan Wasserman and Ira Waddell were waiting for Mike in the conference room when he'd arrived. Though much had changed in the week since he'd been fired, the room was precisely the same: credenza at one end, flat screen monitor at the other, cherry table, red leather chairs. Stan and Ira had not changed either. Stan was still marathon runner thin, and Ira was a muscle man chiseled from stone. They did not look pleased.

"You hired Bob Bogatz to sue the firm," Stan said.

"Wrongful termination," Ira said.

"He called us," Stan said.

"You can't do that," Ira said.

"He was happy to take the case. What did he call it? Oh yes, unfinished business," Mike said.

A dozen years ago, Ira's personal assistant had been let go for insubordination, poor work performance, tardiness, illegible handwriting, brewing bad coffee, breaking team spirit, and being a bad apple, but she was really fired for refusing Waddell's sexual advances—known in certain circles as attempted rape. Unbeknownst by (and unfortunately for) Wasserman and Waddell, the secretary was Bogatz's kid sister.

Known as The Jackhammer, Bogatz had shoved a wrongful termination lawsuit so far up Stan and Ira's company asshole that the partners were still shitting money they owed Bogatz's sister more than a decade later.

"He sued us before and won, Mike," Stan said. "Almost ruined us. You were here. You saw it happen. We barely survived."

"I think your survival is the unfinished business," Mike said.

"You can't do that," Ira said, pointing a muscular finger in a threatening way.

"What happened to hard work, accuracy, honesty, and proficiency? You were here fifteen years. What happened to loyalty?"

Stan said, standing as if he meant to emotionally stop Mike from hiring Bogatz to sue them.

"You can't do that," Ira said, red in the face, rising beside his partner as if he meant to physically stop Mike from hiring Bogatz to sue them.

Throughout his days at Wasserman and Waddell, Mike had been intimidated by Stan and Ira or, rather, had allowed himself to be intimidated. But sitting here in the conference room, he knew those days were gone forever—he'd survived the zombie, re-killed his own mother, and seen the dead brought back to life. There was no one who could bully him now. *If a week can change a man's nature,* Mike thought, *then I am minnow reborn as shark, roadkill reborn as big rig, accountant reborn as extortionist.*

"Lifting weights doesn't make you smart, Ira. It makes you slow," Mike said. "Now sit down. You're five-six, not six-five. You look ridiculous with those muscles."

Ira blinked with confusion. No one had spoken to him like that in, well, ever. He looked at Stan, they communicated without words, as they had done since sleep away camp, and they both took their seats.

Mike slid a folded piece of paper across the conference table and said, "That's my settlement number, bank routing number, and checking account number. I would have been a partner for twenty years. Lost income opportunity is where my number comes from, in case you were wondering. You'll hear from Bogatz at nine a.m. tomorrow if the money's not wired into my account by the close of business today. Written under my number is his number. You can tell the difference between them by the extra zero at the end of his number."

Ira looked like he was going to explode; he was crimson, muscles bulging. "You have nothing, you fat piece of shit," he said. "No proof, no case."

"For most of the week, you'd have been right about that," Mike said. "I had a lot on my mind, and I'd forgotten about recording the meeting where you were supposed to make me a partner."

"You recorded the meeting?" Stan said, swallowing his voice.

"On my iPhone," Mike said. "My wife was so excited about the partnership thing, you know, after fifteen years, the big raise, the profit participation, the benefit package, and I was going to play her the moment it happened. I thought it would help us rekindle our marriage. Anyway, all the stuff about you pointing Judd Martin's anger and aggression in my direction instead of the firm's and you lying to the lawyers and to the banks and attaching the word embezzlement to my name, I think in court they call that stuff *the truth*. Bogatz has the recording. You probably know that. And Ira, I'm not going to be fat forever, but you, you're going to be a dick the rest of your life."

As he left the office, Mike thought, *Numbers are my nature, and if a week can change a man's nature, then my Numbers of Life have become my Numbers of Ruin have become my Numbers of Chaos have become my Numbers of Vengeance.*

While Mike was meeting with Stan and Ira, George Edwards called and left a voicemail saying he had, uh, happened upon Linda's corpse in the hearse parked beneath the portico and could Mike come by to, uh, arrange anew his mother's end-of-life affairs.

Mike drove to the Mission Hills mortuary, and the men had stood in the display center, looking at Linda's original casket.

"Hotel in a box," Mike said, thinking of the pervert clown.

"Pardon me?" George said.

"Soft rounded edges, matte maple finish, Rosetan interior...all that's missing is room service," Mike said. "I trust you'll make her look as pretty as her casket."

"Her appearance changed dramatically over the weekend," George had said, his voice conveying concern. "At this point, all I can do is my best."

On the one hand, Mike had always liked George Edwards and wasn't intending to squeeze the mortician for money—

George had not misplaced his mother; Mike had stolen her. On the other hand, Mike had had the sense from the beginning that George *wanted* to be squeezed, had more or less asked Mike to squeeze him, had given Mike his permission for some squeezing, had made Mike feel that squeezing would somehow help George assuage his mortician guilt. For that reason, Mike was happy to gently oblige.

"Maybe you should show her to me so I can see exactly what happened to her *after* she went missing from your mortuary," Mike said. "You make it sound like she reappeared as the Bride of Frankenstein. Is that what you're saying? My mother's a monster? I'm asking because at this point my insurance company is chomping at the bit for me to file a claim, which I haven't done yet and don't really want to do on account of my being your friend for fifteen years. We were friends, George. Weren't we?"

Mike left the mortuary with a cost-free funeral, with the thirty-three-hundred-dollar Rosetan casket compliments of the house, and with the mortician's assurances that Linda would look lovely at her service and burial on Friday. George had been relieved and grateful to offer Mike this arrangement, and Mike had been pleased for him.

From Mission Hills, Mike had driven to his bank and then to Mrs. Alemi's office and then to Bob Cutting's office and then to Target and then to Best Buy and then home, where he'd inflated the Hello Kitty lounger he'd bought at Target, plugged in the Bose he'd bought at Best Buy, and floated in his pool while listening to loud music.

After a while, Danny had come out of the garage and jumped in the pool. The brothers swam around and tossed a tennis ball back and forth and didn't say a word until Mike said, "Now what do we do?"

"Now we regroup," Danny said. "We find jobs. We pull ourselves together. We run the next race. Families do that all the time."

"I meant what do we do right now?" Mike said. "Do we order a pizza, rent a movie? What do we do right now?"

They had both smiled, recalling that same conversation in reverse after Linda had died the first time. In the hospital, their words been laced with enduring enmity. In Mike's pool, with the temperature stuck on one twelve, after all they'd been through, including saving each other's lives on Sunday, the words had become less pointed, said with humor and not hatred, meant to bust balls not hurt feelings. It was the tone of voice they'd used everyday when they were boys in the small yellow house, when they were simply brothers, before they grew into estranged adulthood.

They'd played catch in the pool for a minute more and then Mike had said, "Call the clown. Tell him to bring his truck. I need you to move out before nine o'clock."

"Mike, come on," Danny had said, "I have nowhere to go."

"Yes, you do. I made a deal with Mrs. Alemi. You're going to live in the yellow house. It's a two-year lease with an option to buy. I paid the first six months. I put the lease in your name, Dan. It's your house."

Danny had stood still in the water, holding the tennis ball in his hand. Finally, he'd said, "Two questions. First, why would you do that for me?"

"Because you're my brother. I mean you're an incredible asshole, and I know, I know, I am too, but no matter what, you're my brother. That's why. Of course, you're a bigger asshole than I am."

"Not even on my bad days."

"You only have bad days."

They'd laughed and tossed the ball back and forth across the pool and Mike had said, "What's the second question?"

"Where did you get the money?"

"I found Greenburg's seventy-five grand."

"You what?"

"Greenburg's money was in the zombie's trailer."

"Greenburg's money?"

"In a bag on the floor of the Airstream, where he tortured me. He stashed it in Mrs. Alemi's storage unit. I found it when I went to get Mom's funeral suit after we killed her in the yellow house and put her back in the hearse."

Mike took a moment to marvel at that sentence. One week ago, saying those words would have been inconceivable without his voice quivering, his knees shaking, his palms sweating, his heart pounding.

Now, he'd heard his own voice and thought he sounded like Bryan Cranston in *Breaking Bad*, a show he had never really believed but was now about to live.

"What was it doing there, the money I mean?" Danny said.

"My guess is Shuler was hiding it in the Airstream, and Martin went rogue," Mike said.

"Why would he do that?"

"Shuler or Martin?"

"Shuler."

"He's a crazy fucking cop."

Danny nodded. They both knew Shuler was the craziest fucking LA cop in film, television, or real life. The brothers threw the tennis ball back and forth for a bit, and then Danny had said, "Where's the money now?"

"There are three envelopes on the Tiki bar in the garage," Mike had said, "one for me, one for you, one for Jenny. There's seventy-five hundred dollars cash in each one. The rest I spent on the yellow house so you could have a house that wasn't my house. You can live in the master bedroom, put your talent agency in the second bedroom, and put our business in the third bedroom."

"Our business?"

"Miller, Miller, and Stone. Equal partners—a third, a third, a third. I run the business. You run sales and marketing. Jenny breathes on dead things."

"She may not like that deal."

"She doesn't have a choice. She's needs us as much as we need her."

"I owed her all of Greenburg's money, including our commissions."

"She used her share to buy in as a partner. You can give her the money and pitch her the deal. And you can tell her there's no ménage. I don't fuck my partners—literally or figuratively."

"I do. Literally, not figuratively."

"I know. It's okay. I can't change a racehorse into a farm horse. Took me forty years to figure that out. But every thoroughbred needs a jockey. I'm your jockey, Dan. That's the angle. If we're going to make money, you run as fast as you fucking can, but I'm the jockey."

"I like this angle, Mike. It's a good angle. It's an angle with potential."

And then Danny moved to the side of the pool and pulled himself up and out of the water.

"Where are you going?"

"Call the clown."

Mike got out of the pool too. He put on his jogging shorts and running shoes and did two laps around the block in the brutal heat. Then he took his clippers and buzzed his head so his hair was spiky and shaved everything on his face but his new goatee and took a shower and put on his Tommy Bahama blue shirt (Marcy's favorite) and white board shorts.

And then it was five minutes to midnight in New Jersey.

61
welcome to the era of infamy

MARCY WAS way across the Rocky Mountains and the Great Plains and the Mississippi River, three time zones removed from the San Fernando Valley, where Mike contemplated his iMac, and her face appeared, and they said hello, and they talked about the weather. In Paramus, she said, the air was thick and sticky, like walking through maple syrup. In Los Angeles, he said, the air was on fire, like breathing burning coal.

She looked wonderful (even on his computer screen), and Mike told her that. "You look *muy* beautiful today, *Meess Marceeah*," he said, imitating the Mexican maître d' who'd greeted her with those very words spoken in that very voice every morning on their Acapulco honeymoon. She smiled when Mike said it and might even have blushed a bit, though it was hard to tell from so far away.

She said she liked Mike's new style, the short spiky hair and goatee. He could tell by the look on her face that she was surprised at how hip and handsome he'd become since she'd been in New Jersey. It had been a long time since he'd seen that shine in her eyes, since he had surprised her this way—or any way.

And yet he could also tell she was not planning to come home. His new style by itself would not be enough to convince her to return to the Valley. He'd opened the door but would need more than spiky hair and a goatee to bring her back through it.

They talked about the girls. Marcy said Bethany had liked Paramus High School, but Julia had reservations about the middle school she would be attending.

The old Mike would have choked up during this discussion. The old Mike would have been blubbering about how much he missed them and needed them and loved them.

The new Mike felt all those feelings for sure but had anticipated this part of the conversation and was waiting for the right moment to react. And his reaction would not involve weeping, which was not part of the new Mike's repertoire. *The new me holds his cards close to the vest*, Mike thought. *The old me didn't own a vest.*

They talked about Marcy's parents, Dianna and Jim. Marcy said her mother was pushing her to cut the cord, come home, and move on. Mike knew that by *cut the cord* Dianna meant file for divorce, by *come home* she meant move permanently to Paramus, and by *move on* she meant get busy with the pediatrician.

Dianna walked into the room at that moment, in her bathrobe, hair in curlers, without makeup and stood behind Marcy so that Mike could see her and she could see him.

"It's very late in Paramus, Mike," Dianna said, filling her voice with impatience, disgust, indignation, and condescension. "It's after midnight."

Much like Stan and Ira, Dianna had intimidated Mike throughout his courtship and marriage to Marcy. Also like Stan and Ira, Mike's days of being browbeaten by her were over and done.

"Dawn of a new day, Dianna," Mike said. "Welcome to the Era of Infamy."

"What is that supposed to mean?" Dianna said.

"Fasten your seatbelts," Mike said. "It's going to be a bumpy night."

"I don't know what you're talking about," Dianna said, flustered by the confidence in the new Mike's tone of voice.

"Turns out, that's never been my fault," Mike said, waving good-bye and giving her the finger. "Good night, Dianna. I'm going to win back my wife now."

Dianna made a shocked and discomforted face and looked to Marcy for support, but Marcy was smiling and didn't glance up at her mother, and so Dianna glared at Mike and left the room. Mike wished he could have done it in person, but doing it through FaceTime was better than he thought it would be.

"You can't win me back," Marcy said.

"I have to," Mike said. "I need you in my life."

"Your life is unsettled. It's not safe for me or the girls."

"The zombie is dead."

"What?"

"The zombie is dead."

"The zombie is dead?"

"The coast is clear."

Marcy nodded, and Mike had the feeling the nod was involuntary, as if she was unconsciously checking the stalker off her list of reasons not to fly home.

"You don't have a job," she said.

"I'm the new chief financial officer for El Caballero Country Club," he said.

"What?"

"They offered me Mom's job, but because of my qualifications, they gave me a bigger title, more responsibility, and more money."

"As much as Stan and Ira paid you?"

"No. But Wasserman and Waddell gave me a severance check."

"They did? How much?"

"Five hundred thousand."

Her eyes shot wide open. "Jesus, Mike," she said.

"I paid off the credit cards, knocked down some of the mortgage, and bought a bunch of tax-free revenue bonds. We'll have about the same income with fewer financial obligations. Our books are balanced. All systems go. Mom's funeral is Friday. Pack the girls and come home."

Marcy swallowed hard. He could see her struggling. She'd been in the all-consuming pull of her parents' presence for too long.

"Is it the pediatrician?" Mike said.

"No, I don't know..." she said, and she looked away.

And so it all came down to the future in three, two, now-or-never.

"What do I have to do to prove my love, Marcy?"

"Mike, don't make me—"

"What do I have to do to prove how committed I am to you, to the girls, to our family?"

"It's hard for me to—"

"Do I have to burn an 'M' into my chest?"

"Mike, please—"

"Do I have to burn the letter 'M' for Marcy into my chest so that you'll know for the rest of time how deep and true my love is?

"Mike—"

He sat back from the desk so she could see him from the waist up.

"Is that what I have to do to win you back, burn the letter 'M' into my chest?"

"Please—"

"Because if that's what I have to do, then that's what I'll do."

And he ripped his Tommy Bahama shirt wide open with both hands so the buttons flew everywhere around the room, and the "M" that Judd Martin had branded into his chest glowed a sultry red.

"Oh," Marcy said in a voice that purred with shock and sex and lust and love. "Oh, Mike."

It had been a long time since he'd pushed them, but the new Mike remembered where the buttons were.

Some I'll push now, he said to himself. *Some I'll push later.*

thank you

I hope you had as much fun reading *Let There Be Linda* as I had writing it because I had a blast. If you did, it would be fabulous if you could help other lovers of dark comedy and crime thrillers and, well, dark comic crime thrillers find the book by leaving a review and sharing the laughs.

Honest reviews of my books help introduce them to new readers. I would be deeply grateful if you could find a few minutes to post a positive review about *Let There Be Linda*. It only takes a minute to leave an upbeat word or two. Thank you for doing that.

you have never. met an alien. like this one.

"Leder's *Extraterrestrial Noir* is a blistering sci-fi crime thriller that disintegrates genre boundaries and opens the floodgates for messed up hilarity and weirdly relatable adventure!"

An extraterrestrial crashes into a suburban cul-de-sac Colonial, absorbs every binary bit of information ever chronicled in all of human history, rearranges its molecules to present itself as a couple of late and legendary film noir superstars, then immediately displays an appetite for debauchery, depravity, decadence, and destruction, seducing the family into its psychopathic criminal orbit with irresistible Hollywood panache, alluring sexual charisma, and inconceivable intergalactic powers....all in the name of saving them from their inevitable emotional, marital, and financial ruin.

But super-genius-daughter Mike Devine figures out fast that the extraterrestrial's principal plan is to employ its unfathomable interplanetary muscle and implode the planet. Which leaves the fate of her family, not to mention the world, in her twelve-year-old hands.

"If you like giddy, gruesome, edge-of-your-seat tall tales that cross the line and outer space, then blast into orbit with Rich Leder's unputdownable rocket of a read!"

Get *Extraterrestrial Noir* today and strap in for a wild ride!

here's another hilarious dark comic crime thriller from the delightfully bizarre imagination of writer rich leder!

Fountain of Youth? More like murderous medication!

Carrie Kromer pushes the boundaries of science, not her social life. The brilliant behavioral gerontologist's ideas of a good time is hanging out with her beloved lab rats and taking care of her elderly mother and the other eccentric old folks at the nursing home. So on one is more surprised than Carrie when she steals the lab's top-secret experimental medicine for aging in reverse.

Two-time ex-con Johnny Fairfax dreams of culinary greatness. But when his corrupt parole officer tries to drag him from the nursing home kitchen, the suddenly young-again residents spring to his defense and murder the guy—and then request Johnny cook them an evidence-devouring dinner to satisfy their insatiable side-effect appetite.

As their unexpected mutual attraction gets hot, Carrie and Johnny find themselves caught up with the authorities who arrive to investigate the killing. But even more dangerous than the man-eating not-so-senior citizens could be the arrival of death-dealing pharmaceutical hitmen.

Is there true love in all this bloody madness?

Get Cooking for Cannibals today and discover the book that is at times hysterically funny, at other times thrilling, and sometimes both at once—part zombie fiction, part something you've never read before, a black comedy *and* a fast-paced thriller—setting it apart in the thriller genre.

also by rich leder

ROMANTIC SHADES OF FUNNY

Juggler, Porn Star, Monkey Wrench

DARKER SHADES OF FUNNY

Let There Be Linda

Cooking for Cannibals

Extraterrestrial Noir

KATE MCCALL CRIME CAPERS

Workman's Complication

Swollen Identity

Emboozlement

Gottiguard

acknowledgments

Great thanks to two creative artists who have entertained me many times over the years. Geniuses who, in one way or another, inspired the bloody irreverence that became this book. Monty Python, who have made me laugh since 1969 (that's a long time to make someone laugh), and Quentin Tarantino, whose orchestrally violent and hilarious movies often leave me breathless.

For my children, David, Eric, and Kate, who, when they were young and living at home, were the whirlwind embodiment of a wild ride.

about the author

Rich Leder's screen credits include 19 television films for CBS, Lifetime, and Hallmark and feature films for Lionsgate Entertainment, Paramount Pictures, Tri-Star Pictures, and Left Bank Films. He has published eight novels through Laugh Riot Press.

He has been the lead singer in a Detroit rock band, a restaurateur, a Little League coach, an indie film director, a literacy tutor, a magazine editor, a screenwriting coach, a commercial real estate agent, a wedding guru, and a visiting artist for the University of North Carolina Wilmington Film Studies Department, among other things, all of which, it turns out, was grist for the mill.

Contact Rich through his website: www.richleder.com.

www.ingramcontent.com/pod-product-compliance
Lightning Source LLC
Chambersburg PA
CBHW020642120726
47906CB00001B/80